Grant ████

~ A Will Bryant Thriller ~

SOUTHERN CROSS

Tellwell Talent

www.tellwell.ca

ISBN

978-1-77370-017-5 (Paperback)

978-1-77370-018-2 (eBook)

SOUTHERN CROSS

Prologue

Outside Blumenau, Santa Catarina State, Brazil

The rented Fiat hurtled down the dark country road, past gloomy, isolated farms and sleeping cows. Luc Renner knew his friend Marco Hellmer was driving in anger. Luc was a slight and timid man. He understood this about himself and knew also what a pathetic sight he must make now, clasping the handhold on the ceiling with both hands, his feet pushed up against the firewall as if jamming on a massive brake pedal. Every time Marco threw the little Palio around a corner, Luc's breath sucked in his lower lip in something one his friends called "the São Paulo suck," an involuntary physical response by victims of insane Brazilian driving.

He was doing more sucking than Jenna Jameson right now, Luc thought bleakly. He tried to take his mind off of his imminent death by regarding his friend. Talking to the man certainly wouldn't work; it never did with Brazilians. They always laughed at your silly gringo fears, convinced they were the reincarnated Ayrton Senna. Slow down? *Why?*

Pointing out what had happened to Senna never seemed to resonate.

His friend clasped the wheel with only one hand, saving the other for frequent emphatic gestures; in this the Brazilians were so very Italian, and Luc knew Italians well. The Brazilians from São Paulo were the worst, the ones like Marco. They were always trying to be more Italian than their brothers in the boot.

But this wasn't Italian country. This was the Itajai Valley, the Vale do Europeu, as the Brazilians called it. But everyone knew that *European* meant "German" here. An English TV host had once famously described the land between Pomerode and Blumenau as a "Pomeranian Teleportation," a land of blue-eyed, blond-haired men in short pants driving Volkswagens past rice paddies and palm trees and of gorgeous, long-legged models, produced as if on one of São Paulo's assembly lines.

And this was why they were here, Luc admitted to himself in shame. Lust. Lust and one very powerful German who was making them pay for it. One very powerful German they were on their way to see tonight. And now he was really going to make them pay.

But Marco Hellmer had other ideas. The broad-shouldered former *jogador* had done well in football, until a broken leg had ended his career at Santos FC, the one-time home of the great Pelé. He had bounced back and built a successful line of fitness clubs. And there was no fucking way he was going to let Oscar Stumpf take it all away over a little pussy.

"That fucking *veado* Stumpf wants it all, you know that, Luc?"

They were less than a metre away from each other, but Hellmer was yelling and spraying spittle on his friend. Luc knew Marco had an illegal gun that he sometimes carried, and he prayed Marco hadn't brought it with him. But if he was this pissed, Luc was pretty sure he knew what the bulge was in his jacket pocket.

"Of course I know, Marco. Why do you think I'm here? I can't afford it either ..."

"That's not the point, Luc! It's the principle! It's blackmail. It's robbery!"

Luc closed his eyes for a moment, thinking it was the height of hubris for a man like Marco to be taking the moral high ground, or, for that matter, a man like him.

"Marco, my friend, I meant no offence, but think about what Stumpf will do when he ..." This last line disappeared in another São Paulo suck as his darkly handsome friend let the Fiat's wheels scrape the edge of an irrigation ditch. Luc let the question pass. The immediate threat to his future posed by the maniac at the wheel overshadowed the what-ifs of the future posed by the maniac down the road. Besides, Marco had a point—if not in his own case, then certainly in Luc's.

Principles or no, it was true; he really couldn't afford it, less so than Marco. Certainly, he'd used his reputation as a Paris sommelier of minor note to sell fantastically overpriced vintages to Francophile Brazilians in the rich neighbourhood of Morumbi. But recessions hit all wallets eventually, and even people with 2 million reais in the bank would reconsider spending 1,500 of it on a Burgundy. After all, as his humble father used to say, *"C'est pisse, non?"*

But he was doing fine—that is, until he met Gretchen, or, more accurately, had been steered toward Gretchen by Oscar Stumpf. It was the same story they all had; he knew that now. The unrecognized longing suddenly and magically, it seemed, made real in Blumenau. Marco, he knew, could tell a very similar story, as could at least a dozen other men he knew of. Magic and pleasure beyond imagining, you just had to give yourself over to it. And then Stumpf gave you the bill. *Ce'st pisse*, indeed.

But Marco had no intention of paying; it seemed the flawlessly keen businessman from Curitiba had misread the footballer. If so, it was a rare misstep; Oscar Stumpf had been a darling of the generals when they'd run the country and then had seamlessly merged with the new, democratic establishment. But the rumours about him were dark ones, and even if they weren't, Luc figured he ought to have known better. After all, hadn't his father also told him, *"Il n'y a pas de repas gratuit"*? "There's no such thing as a free lunch." God, he should have listened. Why was he here? What was he going to do? He had no gun. And even if he did, he would never use it. So what then, help Marco bury the body? As if Stumpf wouldn't bring bodyguards?

Merde, his head was swimming. He could really use a nice, ballsy Côtes du Rhône right now to steady his nerves. He closed his eyes, something he'd always done as a boy to wish himself somewhere else. It never worked. Instead he became aware of the car slowing. He stirred as Marco shook his arm. *"Levanta, amigo.* We are here."

Lost in his reverie, Luc had failed to notice his surroundings. He realized immediately that this was a mistake. What would his brother, Gaston, the soldier, say about the tactical situation here? A narrow dirt road surrounded by trees. Dark as a dragon's asshole. And straight in front of him, a yellow sign: *Rua Sem Saida*. No Exit. He swallowed hard. He wanted to scream but couldn't. Was it possible to be too much of a coward to even be properly scared? Luc wondered.

His friend hadn't seemed to notice. "Of course the arrogant shit is late. Keep me fucking waiting, will you? I will fuck him in the ass for this, Luc, I will. It stops, tonight!" He made a karate chop hand gesture, catching Luc's left arm.

"Take it easy, my friend, will you? Let's be careful here."

Marco stared back at him. Even in the darkened car, Luc felt the burning brown eyes on him. The man had a power, for sure. Luc admired it. What did the Americans call this sort of relationship? A bromance?

But the fury seemed to abate. Marco was silent, thinking. Then, without a word, he pulled the Bersa .380 out of his jacket pocket and, with his jaw jutted forward, racked the action. Marco Hellmer opened the car door and stepped into the night.

Luc sat frozen as the headlights from behind lit up the Fiat's interior, casting long tree shadows on the road. Marco's face was suddenly in the window.

"Get out, for fuck's sake; let's be ready," he hissed.

Luc remembered science class as a boy in Toulon. There had been a poster on the wall that had fascinated him. It had showed how much you would weigh on different planets—like if you lived on Jupiter, you would weigh as much as a car, that sort of thing.

Feeling very much like he lived on Jupiter, a very heavy little man named Luc Renner opened his door and stepped into the night.

Twenty minutes later

Luc struggled to stop shivering and keep just his eyes and nostrils above the waterline. He had found a shadowed place against the bank of the canal, under the roots of a big rotting tree. At first the smell had made him want to gag—fertilizer and decay, garbage and dead animals. But gagging would get him killed. He couldn't move. He had to stay right where he was. He had a moment of panic: What if they had a boat?

"I told you we should have brought a boat," Angelo grumbled to his boss.

Oscar Stumpf sighed, leaned over, and cuffed the big, slope-shouldered man on the ear. The much younger and bigger man shifted a bit on his feet as his face went beet red. He opened his mouth, heard a dim voice of warning in his head, and decided to shut up. The two were standing on the roadway on top of the levee, rice paddies to one side and a long, deep canal on the other.

Ten metres below them, Luc Renner could hear every word. A metre and a half below them, Marco Hellmer could hear nothing. His blood had stopped leaking into the dirt now. The death rattle was gone. Only the occasional cry of an *urubu* bird broke the silence.

As his men scoured both sides of the levee with guns and flashlights pointed into the inky black, Oscar Stumpf craned his head back and looked up into the clean night. The Southern Cross, his old friend, blazed away above their heads. As a boy visiting his uncle's farm not five kilometres from here, Stumpf had become fascinated with the constellation. You couldn't see it so well from Curitiba with the city's light pollution. But here, it was glorious and made young Oscar understand why it was on the *bandera nacional*. It was the heart of Brazil. It made the daydreamer a believer. Now, living in São Paulo, Stumpf could never see it through the *ar ruim*, the toxic blanket of smog that covered the city of … how many people? Twenty, thirty million. Well, no stars, but lots of money.

Stumpf became dimly aware that he was standing in something. He shined his flashlight at his feet and saw syrupy blood starting to seep around his wing tips. Oh yeah, the dead guy. He stepped away. Time to wrap this up. Men in his position shouldn't have to be out here getting blood on their shoes.

"Come here, all of you boys," he said. The five men he'd brought out to the dead-end road wordlessly encircled him. "Roberto!" he called. The heavy-set, bald black man nodded. "Take this bigmouth's car back to the highway. Run it off the road in thick bushes. Wipe it down. Call Angelo and Duda when you are done for a pickup. No witnesses, and don't give the Polícia Rodoviária a reason to stop you. Okay, Pedrinho?"

The big man smiled and stepped over Marco's body on his way to the Fiat, carefully sidestepping the blood. He was fat and quiet and black, so a lot of people thought he was stupid. Oscar Stumpf was a better judge of people than that, which was why he trusted the man to do the job alone.

Angelo, not so much. A fucking boat he wanted, for Christ's sake. An outboard motor on these shallow canals would have every slap dancer between here and Pomerode sticking their big noses into his business. He wasn't sure he could buy enough cops to handle that. He had to find something simpler for this one, his half sister's boy, to do. She just had to marry an Italian.

"Angelo, you and Duda strip the body of ID and dump it."

Angelo rolled his eyes. Duda stared straight ahead. He looked so much like the lantern-jawed, flat-topped former coach of the national football team that it was the only possible name for him.

"Maybe you would like to go for a swim with him, *muleke*?"

"No, Uncle," the greasy-haired halfwit replied.

"*Meu Deus*, don't call me that out here. Just do it, okay?"

Duda was already moving. Angelo half-opened his mouth as if to appeal, but Duda's glare got him going.

"Now, you two ... come in close."

Klaus and Erich came in tight. He wanted to whisper this last part, on the off chance that a live Luc Renner was still listening. He gave this task to his two youngest nephews because there were some things he wouldn't trust Brazilians with, only Germans. Germans followed orders. They weren't sentimental, and they kept their mouths shut. Klaus and Erich were twins with the faces of choirboys— straight, firm jaws, serious blue eyes, and mops of straw blonde hair. Special boys. Oscar Stumpf had taught them some of his dirtiest skills. They were excellent students.

"Leave with the others," he whispered and then paused as an annoying *urubu* opened up again. "Wait at the only exit. Stay well hidden. If Renner is still alive, he'll have to come down that road. Chances are, it'll be just you and him. Make sure when it's over, it's just you. *Gute nacht*."

Stumpf stood for a moment on his own, arms akimbo, as the boys walked off to their car with intent. He looked around slowly at the moon-dappled paddy fields. Weak window lights dotted the gloom, marking the isolated farmhouses full of solid Germans, stuck in a time warp, working themselves into the grave without complaining. *That could have been my life*, Oscar Stumpf thought. *But I made sure it wasn't.*

He was short but wiry and powerful, balding but in a dignified way, and into his sixties but aging well. He didn't let anything bother him; that was the secret. See the need, take action, move on. Now it was done. Time to go.

The gravel crunched over Luc Renner's head as Oscar Stumpf walked to his Mercedes. Luc had good hearing, better than Oscar Stumpf knew. As in so many other things, his father was right: keep your eyes on the Germans. He suppressed a shiver, clamped his jaw tight, and resolved to wait it out.

In the distance, the horizon had started to lighten. Luc used the starting car engine to cover the start of a long swim. He needed to make it down the canal before day broke.

1

Penha, São Paulo

"Okay, Edilson, read the next one."

"May I borrao your kenifee?"

"Edilson, man, how many times do I have to say it? You don't pronounce everything in English. Don't say the *ka*, and throw out the *e*."

"Then why are they there, Will?"

Will Bryant sighed and wondered why himself. As he so often found himself these days, he was struggling to give a fuck. He regarded his pupil sitting across the small table in the tiny apartment: the small, wiry man with coffee-coloured eyes imploring, *Teach me*. People like Edilson were the only reason he kept at it. That and the kids, of course. What the hell else was a gringo Canadian ex-cop going to do in São Paulo besides teach English?

But then, when were a cop's prospects ever that starry? Not if you were a lowly *soldado* in the Polícia Militar, like his friend Edilson Lopes. Edilson owned the shoebox apartment in the borderline neighbourhood where they now sat, frustrating each other. He shared it with a massive wife and four kids too. They were out now, a condition of the contract. A 50 percent police discount was also part of the contract. Despite Brazilian cops' reputation for being shakedown artists, the last had been Will's idea. What could he say? He felt bad for the guy. A former canine officer, Edilson was now back on the beat (Will had no idea why and was afraid to ask) and moonlighting as a dog trainer. Edilson had been stabbed once, shot twice, and nearly drowned in the disgustingly polluted Rio Tiete when his partner had lost control of their car in a pursuit. This shoebox and 700 reais a week were his reward. No wonder cops sometimes helped themselves here and there.

Plus, Will figured it was always good to keep a local cop close. Despite the fact he'd been here a year now, it was still alien turf. So when his brother-in-law, Roberto, had introduced the man who had trained his revoltingly slobbery guard dog not to bark at the wind (damn, that dog was stupid) and Edilson had grabbed his hand hard and said *"Eu gosto a fala ingles, ajuda me,"* he could hardly say no.

So on top of night-school classes, his day job, and moonlighting, Edilson was studying English in hopes of moving up to the more prestigious Polícia Civil or, even better, Polícia Federal. Suits, mirrored shades, and twice the money for a tenth the danger. Couldn't blame the guy. God bless ambition. It had been a while since Will Bryant had felt any pangs of it. Now he just wanted to get by. Since he had three mouths to feed and only one marketable skill here, he figured getting by was pretty ambitious anyway.

Will caught a glimpse of himself in the kitchen mirror. His dirty blonde hair was in need of a trim but still there, thank God. He was tall and solid, with an athlete's body only now starting to go soft around the middle (a club membership was so damned expensive). His blue eyes still got a reaction from women, but he had the one he wanted.

Will had been a quarterback in high school in suburban Vancouver, and like some sad wash-up who couldn't forget the bright lights, he still flashed back to it as the most contented period of his life. He'd made the plays. He'd called them. With a devastating long-range spiral, he'd made them happen. People had noticed—girls for sure but also, more importantly, university scouts.

The golden years had played themselves out at UCLA. He'd given cursory attention to the books, with "tutors" to help him pass. His days had been filled with practice in the warm SoCal sun and coeds wherever and whenever he wanted. The NFL, ready and waiting. Game night, the ultimate thrill. For hours he would tune out everything but the game. It had mattered, made him hungry, made him fierce. On the sidelines, the scouts had been salivating.

He could still remember every sensation and detail of the moment it had ended, the way he remembered only one other moment in his life. A run for the end zone, only 15 yards out. The hit, his eyes juggling in his skull, helmet flying clean off. Lying on his back, tears running down his face, he had stared into a spotless blue sky and a pitiless sun. It had hurt physically, for sure. He'd known immediately that his left knee had been blown and his leg had been broken. But the tears had come from instantaneous gestalt: it was over. He had been 21.

But his life wasn't over, of course. He had Silvia, his unexpected gift born of trolling the Internet for women after his first marriage had ended. She was a former model, Italian-German, remarkably beautiful even in a country full of beautiful women. Sure, she was a handful (something Latin women all seemed to know how to hide until after the vows). But he was happy all the same, and he'd quit roaming after she'd read the riot act to him one time. Losing his kids had gotten his attention. So he wasn't in charge in his marriage. So what? After he'd handed in his badge, he hadn't felt the need to be in charge of anything anymore.

And he had Lucas and Gabriella. Good kids, worth everything, even worth becoming a lowly expat freelance English teacher. So Lucas acted out, and Gabriella seemed to catch every bug that came along. Again, so what? They were smart, they were funny, and they were beautiful. If it wasn't for them, he would have eaten his gun last year; that was for sure.

"Will?"

Will came to, staring into the mirror.

"Hey, you so good looking you can't stop to stare, no?"

"Better looking than you, *muleke*. Come on, Deyse will be home in 20 minutes. Let's finish."

"Keenives and keenights again?"

"*Pelo morte Deus, no.* How about numbers?"

Edilson grinned back at him. "Sure, brother, I got to learn how to count all the money I'll be making as a *detectivo!*"

Will Bryant might miss Canada, but Edilson reminded him that the people here made it feel almost like home. As a two-time loser, he could hardly ask for more.

2

Metro Linha Azul to Tucuruvi, São Paulo

Jesus Christ, Will thought, *I am really not made to live in this city.* Crammed into the Metro car at the height of rush hour, hemmed in by jam-packed commuters, he cursed his height and broad shoulders. Steamed windows made a sauna for the passengers, of whom more piled on at each stop. Being Paulistanos, they had long since learned to accept perpetual crowding as a fact of life in the biggest city in the Americas. Will Bryant was still getting used to it. To make matters worse, it seemed the driver was either learning the job or halfway through a bottle of Cinquente Um with the way the train was lurching at every stop. Each time one of his neighbours slammed into him, Will seethed. This was no place for a big Canadense.

It really was no place for anyone, Will believed. Back when he'd still had a job and a choice of where they could live, he'd argued with Silvia about moving to Brazil. She had insisted that you could have everything you wanted in

São Paulo, while Vancouver was so limited. Yes, Will had responded, everything you wanted—and a lot of things you didn't. Crime. Traffic. Smog. Broken-down infrastructure. Then he had enumerated his complaints about the place as his wife had seethed. She had taken it personally, as if he'd been taking a swipe at her own family.

Crime: Everyone who could afford it had high walls topped with electrified wire. In some places, you could see an archaeological evolution; as fear had grown, the wall had grown in layers too. A few times, relying on Silvia's doubtful navigation, he'd almost shit himself when he'd looked around and realized they'd strayed into a favela. Hard faces. Pavement giving way to red dirt. Lopsided houses made of cinder blocks and sheet metal. Open sewers. Gangs of lean, dark men grouped around barrel fires. The sudden realization he wasn't carrying a gun. The squeal of tires as Silvia realized the same thing. Relief as they escaped.

Traffic: São Paulo held the world record for longest traffic jam—200 kilometres. Jams were so bad that the rich had given up on cars altogether and commuted by helicopter. Will had only recently learned how to drive Brazilian style: think *Ben Hur* with four wheels. Jam yourself into any available space, or you'll be waiting for hours. Forget shoulder checks; looking out for you is the other guy's problem. And don't put your arm out the window. A motoboy zipping between the traffic lanes on a 600 cc Honda might just rip it off.

Smog: He, Silvia, and the kids had been coming back from the beach one night, hauling ass on the Ayrton Senna, the uncountable towers of the city luminescent in front of them. The fresh smells of the beach and the Mata

Atlantica forests had been replaced by the smells of burning rubber and untreated sewage from the shocking Rio Tiete. "Honey," he had announced to Silvia, "this city smells like shit." Even she hadn't been able to argue.

Infrastructure: Even in the nicer neighbourhoods, like Tremembé, where they lived, in the Zona Norte, the sidewalks looked as if they'd been carpet-bombed. God help the disabled. It had taken Will a while to notice that the only places that didn't have this problem were Paulista Avenue, where the money worked, and Hiegenopolis, where the money, not to mention an ex-president, lived.

And São Paulo was just so fucking ugly. It was all built right to the limit, so little green space or natural beauty. Rio it was not. For a Vancouver boy, spoiled by the ocean and the mountains, it had been a hard sell to live in a city whose most beautiful feature was its amazing graffiti.

As the train lurched again, Will winced in pain from his trick knee impacting a seat. He reminded himself it wasn't all bad. The people were generally pretty nice. There were some parks. It was pretty easy to get around if you didn't have a car (rush hour excepted). And it did have the best damn pizza in the world, courtesy of 6 million Italians.

And his family was here. So that made it home.

Anyway, all that had been a conversation from when he'd had a choice. Suddenly, last year, he'd become a man with no choices.

"*Proximo estacione, Santana,*" the driver droned. Will elbowed and pushed his way off the train into a winter drizzle. Winter. Will still laughed when he saw Brazilians wearing parkas. Most days, shorts and Chinelo sandals were good enough for him. He found a place on the escalator and descended into the bus loop with another several hundred lemmings.

Santana Station was a concrete island in a sea of more concrete, a massive bus loop surrounded by small bars and cheap fry shops, topped with the concrete arches of the Metro. When the waits for buses were long, some commuters would give up and wait it out rubbing shoulders with shopkeepers and off-duty hookers as they grabbed a beer and some fries. Will was tempted to join them. But he was already late, and his kids wouldn't be up much longer. As he waited for the 1018 bus to Ana Rosa, his mind drifted back to the other moment in his life he would never forget a single detail of, back to the moment that had made him a man with no choices. A man who had to call this insane city home.

3

Vancouver, 15 months ago

If he had known ahead of time that his life was going to change in a Tim Hortons, Will Bryant would have appreciated the irony. How very Canadian. After all, there were kids playing hockey on the five-dollar bill. And hadn't Tim Horton played for the Maple Leafs or some shit like that? For a guy whose great-grandfather had drowned in a shell crater at the Battle of Vimy Ridge, it kind of fit.

But all he was looking for was a coffee and a dutchie. He got a lot more.

When he would think about it after, he would replay the walk in through the doors from the parking lot like some slow-mo Robert Rodriguez we-so-bad entrance. Will, Angie, and Pete. Three gunslingers. What bullshit. Yeah, they had guns, but they'd never really expected they'd have to use them.

They worked for an agency he would no longer speak the name of after this incident, like some ex-wife who had thrown his heart on the floor and stiletto-heeled it into mush. They had been out doing surveillance on some fuck who was moving guns but never did his own dirty business. So it had been eight hours of pissing into water bottles (and, for Angie, just holding it) while the asshole had taken out his trash, walked his Shih Tzu, and watched Mexican wrestling. Finally they had given in to human needs and found themselves here.

It was busy. It was sunny. There were skateboarders in the parking lot, and it smelled like weed. Pete, their team leader, was a Blackberry slave, and he lingered behind in the lot.

"Can I order for you?" Will asked him.

"Nah," he said, between mashing gum, "none of your fatso shit for me. I know how to order it. This'll only take a second."

Will rolled his eyes. Guy was a fucking triathlete who was already down to the paint and metal. Great if you wanted to run for a living, but useless when it came to wrestling with the reluctant guests they sometimes shoved into the back of their Impalas and Crown Vics. That was Will's job. Former athlete gone to beef, he knew his role. Hell, Angie was more useful in a fight, and she was 5 feet 4 inches.

But Pete wasn't a bad boss. At least he showed up. Some of the supervisors were strictly virtual, in the rear with the gear, their guns gathering dust in their lockers until their annual recertification. At least Pete suited up and went out. He was even first through the door sometimes. Maybe a ballerina, but a pussy? No.

Angie hadn't waited. She had already gone through the double doors and taken a hard right for the ladies' room. No surprise, after eight hours on a sit. She was a single mom who had fun when she could, kind of cute in a naughty librarian sort of way. After her divorce from a pussy hound Mountie, she'd put some of her alimony into a couple of bolt-on C cups and gone a little wild. Why not? Every time Will heard people dis her for that, he'd shoot them down. It was okay if a man did it, so let Angie have her fun. Also, he kind of had a crush on her. They spent a lot of time together, and she smelled nice. Plus, she was game for a laugh. And Gavin had told him that she was awesome in bed.

Not that he was looking. He loved Silvia, and with two kids now, he wouldn't chance losing them. She wasn't as easygoing as he was, and he knew the consequences of straying: somebody else got Lucas and Gabriella calling them Daddy. Unacceptable. That reminded him: Lucas had a dentist's appointment at sixteen hundred. He'd need to bust ass from work today.

Will was in through the double doors. He looked around, as he always did when entering a room. Habit. A long line on the right-hand side of the counter. A few customers, whose orders had already been taken, on the left. And one guy, wearing a black overcoat, standing right in the middle.

Black. Overcoat. A very hot June. Thirty degrees outside, the sweat coating Will's chest from the Kevlar hugging him tight ... Something was wrong. Wrong. Wrong. Fucking wrong. Tension in overcoat man's broad shoulders. Long, greasy hair. The man was turning now, like he knew he was lasered.

Like a faulty DVD, Will's sound went off. "Auditory exclusion" they called it in training. That's how Will Bryant knew he was in a gunfight before he even saw the gun. When there is a doubt, their trainers had said, there is no doubt. Will's hand went down for his Beretta. He fumbled the draw. He always did. Panic.

Silvia ... Lucas ... Gabriella. He locked eyes for just a second with the brown kid behind the counter. Eyes wide, mouth open. He knew, but he couldn't move. Neither could Will.

Will's gun finally jerked out of his holster, and he brought it up in a very approximate two-handed grip. No time for sights, this would have to be sloppy ...

The big man was now wheeled around to face him, two hands gripped on a Mossberg Defender and a grimace on his face. Heavy brows over a boxer's nose. Meth spider bites all over his face.

They fired together.

Will was vaguely aware of the plate glass shattering in the entranceway behind him as nine pellets of double-ought buck went ridiculously wide of him. But he was more focused on the way his own shots were doing. It was amazing that it was that slow, he would think in retrospect. But at the time all he heard was a long, low scream in his own head. Mmmmwwaaaaa ... ahhhhhh ... ahhhhh ...

Overcoat man's body began to jerk and spasm. The counter behind him shattered as Will mashed the trigger again and again. The big man slumped back against the counter, dropped the Mossberg, and fell flat on his face.

Will was still registering this when a skinny man in a faded jean jacket, a man he'd never noticed, opened up on him with a Browning 9 from the seats on the left. Will turned, sluggishly slow, as if someone had tapped him on the shoulder on the SkyTrain. It seemed to take forever for him to face his tormentor, during which time a nine-mil hollow point punched through his hip. He almost had his pistol to bear on the little shit when the man jerked upright in a Spandau Ballet.

Angie had heard the shots and come out of the john in a combat crouch, shooting perilously close to Will's right shoulder. Whoosh, whoosh ... *What was that?* he wondered as the rounds passed by his cheek. Pete then sealed the deal, standing in the shot-out entranceway and methodically filling the skinny man from hip to skull until he slumped against the counter, sagging like a flat tire until he toppled over onto his side.

Will stared at the dead man and then saw the blood pumping out of his own left side onto the floor. *Fuck, being shot hurts.* He turned to Angie. She reached out for him as his legs gave way and he hit the floor.

His face was in something sticky and warm. He looked past the body of the overcoat man and stared into the eyes of the other man he had just shot. A young brown man behind the counter, his stupid visor knocked off his head, his breath coming in gasps. Will knew that he had shot the boy. It couldn't have been anyone else. Wordlessly, the two stared at each other as madness erupted all around and they both leaked onto the cool tiles.

After that, he looked up at the blades of the medevac chopper as Angie held his hand, and tears streamed down his face. The sky was bright blue with a solitary cloud. Why only one? The flight felt strange, seeming to last forever.

He'd always wanted to be on a helicopter. Now he'd gotten his wish. Where was the boy? Was he here? Was this also his first flight? Will couldn't move his head. He felt hot, then cold, then hot again. He passed out.

He woke up in a dark room. Then he passed out again, thinking of Silvia. He woke up again, for good this time. Silvia was there for real. Her kisses, seasoned with tears, were the proof of his continuing life. Then the first questions. A stern-looking Director Adams fronting a parade of white shirts. Information he didn't want: The kid, paralyzed from the waist down. Lawsuits, maybe a criminal charge.

Then he made the mistake of reading the news online, seeing the cop-hating trolls chime in, as if they knew all about split seconds and life and death. He started hitting the bottle, hard. The walls were closing in.

Three months later, he placed his badge and ID card on the Director's desk. He walked past desks of "old friends" who suddenly didn't have a word to say to him. A security guard escorted him out, the final humiliation. Even worse, he knew it was going to happen to Pete and Angie too. They were "lucky," his lawyer had said, no criminal charges. "Lucky." Like the kid he'd shot was "lucky" to be alive with a lifetime's supply of catheters. Lucky.

Holding hands with his kids on the flight to São Paulo, he did feel kind of lucky. *Just let me keep this, and I will be okay.*

4

Tremembé, São Paulo

The Ana Rosa bus let Will Bryant off in front of a stationery store. He elbowed and shoved his way to the exit, something he always perversely enjoyed. Maybe it reminded him of football. He pulled his hood up over his head against the drizzle and looked at the storefront. Wide-eyed dolls stared back, reminding him of Gabriella's birthday in two weeks. Once things had died down in Canada, he would go back and stock up; toys were ridiculously expensive here. Thank God beer was cheap. This last thought set him trudging for home, knowing he still had a half-dozen Skol left in the fridge, also knowing his relentlessly polite brother-in-law would never poach them.

He walked past the tiny police station on Maria Amalia, with its resident stray dogs and pathetic potted plants. The cops there never seemed to have anything to do, just hanging out all day and chatting up the locals. Maybe that was all their bosses trusted them to do. Still, it didn't seem very effective policing to Will. *Nobody asked you,* he reminded himself. *You aren't a cop anymore. Just a half-assed professor, and a gringo one at that.* One of the cops nodded at him as he walked by, and he responded, *"Oi, boa noite."*

Then, dodging dog shit, he humped up the hill to his "home," if he could call another man's home that. Locals zipped in their Fiats and Nissans down the slope of Rua Francisco Narcizo in the typical Brazilian manner; that is to say, way too fucking fast.

Looking at it from the street, the house was a blank facade and a heavy wooden garage door. The tall walls were topped with sharp metal teeth. Will proceeded with caution over the dark, uneven pavement, a local dog who habitually shit in front of Roberto's door on his mind. Opening the heavy wooden door, the first of two, he almost stepped on a turtle lurking in the open-air entranceway under a bush. "What the fuck?"

He heard his kids stomping down the stairs. *"Papai!"* He opened the inner door, and Gabriella jumped off the stairs into his arms. Ooof, she was getting bigger, and his back was getting worse.

"Daddy, guess what?" She brushed her blonde bangs away from her big blue eyes.

"You got a turtle?"

"How did you know, Daddy?"

"I almost tripped over him. What's his name?"

"Godzilla. Enzo picked that name. Do you like it? He eats lettuce and carrots!" She blew a bang out of her mouth with determination.

"And he eats bugs!" Lucas interjected. He stood behind them on the stairs but reached an arm out to his father's shoulder. Will had noticed he'd only started doing this since the shooting, as if to reassure himself that his father was, in fact, there.

Gabriella shot back, "He does not eat bugs! You eat bugs!" Feisty, only four, but feisty.

Wonder where she got that from? Will thought as the person she got that from came into view at the top of the stairs. Silvia was wearing a translucent top, one she knew drove him crazy, her long copper-coloured hair braided over her left shoulder. She was tall and graceful, olive skinned, every bit the woman he did not deserve but still had, despite every effort to lose her.

"Gabriella, you will be eating bugs if you are not nice to your brother," Silvia said. Lucas smirked and stuck out his tongue.

"Oi, honey, tudo bem?" She smiled at Will. He loved the way she said *hoooney*, all drawn out like that, that and her smile. He wished they had more time alone.

"Muito bom. Muito." Very good. Will Bryant meant it.

Will carried his giggling and squirming daughter up two flights of stairs as she breathlessly related the day's events. His brother-in-law had made a pretty nice life for them all here. The house was a take on traditional Brazilian architecture, open, rustic woodwork spaced by white plaster. Roberto's means allowed for a pretty liberal use of space in a city where space was at a premium. A pool they almost never used and a massive, drool-sprinkling Cane Corso patrolling in a caged enclosure dominated the outside. Will shooed Gabi away and stripped down for a quick shower. With São Paulo's draconian water rationing, it was an exercise in frustration. A trickle of water tapered off to a drip after three minutes, leaving him dabbing away soap and cursing Brazilian inefficiency.

Later, he sat at the table with rest of the adults: Silvia; Roberto, a moderately successful merchant who nevertheless worked himself stupid six days a week; and Tais, Silvia's younger sister and another former model like his wife. Roberto was fit and restrained, looking younger than his 50-plus years, which was amazing when you considered the heavy lifting he did. He was usually pretty quiet, but every so often he would wink at Will as if to say, *Can you fucking believe how lucky we are?* Will looked at Tais, who preferred to go blonde instead of brunette but was otherwise very similar to her sister, and had to agree. Sometimes he even caught himself staring. There was a warmth in her lopsided smile that distinguished her from Silvia. Silvia could be warm too, but her sharp elbows were always there. However much he might wish for an easier ride, Will Bryant knew enough about himself to admit that he liked sharp elbows in a woman.

Roberto and Tais's son, Enzo, was eight. He had grown from a hyperactive pest into a jock with a mild wild streak. He was skinny and Italian dark. Will figured the kid would be in girls up to his eyeballs by the time he was 16. He ate with Gabi and Lucas in front of the TV. Will's second Skol was going down very good when Silvia said, "Thiago called for you."

He raised an eyebrow. "Oh?"

Thiago Waldemar de Costa Gomes, his wife's and now, by extension, his lawyer. Short, round, bespectacled. Lots of angles. He had friends among the police and friends among the narcos. Probably lots of enemies too. Lately Will had been talking to Thiago about protecting his money in Brazil from a lawsuit the kid he'd shot had filed. It forced him to spend a lot more time with the guy than he'd wanted to. Will found Thiago hard to pin down, one of those guys who liked to be all coy about who and how much he knew. He had a big mouth and, Will was pretty certain, a serious hard-on for Silvia.

But who could blame any guy for that. A lawyer, though? Will Bryant figured he'd feel better if she fucked a Mendingo. Still, the guy had his uses. And lately, Will had grown increasingly fond of Thiago. Was he that desperate for friends? He wondered what Thiago wanted and why he hadn't called the mobile. Probably taking any chance to chat up Silvia. But Will was intrigued. And if it could make him some money, he needed some of that.

But there was one more pressing need. He drained his Skol. "Honey? Have you got a second?" His eyes met Silvia's.

She smiled back. "Of course"

Two minutes later, he was opening Silvia's blouse and pulling her beautiful breasts out of her bra. "We have to be quick," she whispered urgently. "Did you lock the door?"

"Both of them," Will said as he stripped her down and bent her over the bathroom sink. They did have to be quick, because soon the kids would come knocking. But, to tell the truth, they both sort of liked it. There was a nasty, stranger-danger sort of feel to it that turned them both on. Will grasped Silvia's breasts from behind as he thrust into her insistently. He pulled her long hair and tilted her head back. She had a pleasured grimace on her face.

A timid knocking on the door. *"Mamae? Papai?"*

Ah, shit. Once, Will Bryant would never have thought he could maintain an erection while hearing a child's voice, but that was before he understood the challenges of being married with kids; if you wanted to have any sort of a life as lovers, you had to steal pleasure in small increments, wherever you could find it. Silvia understood it too. She looked back at him over her shoulder and hissed, "Finish!" She started to shake her ass.

That did it. The two paused together, like dogs unable to unhook. Then Silvia pushed him back gently. She spoke softly to the little voice outside the door as Will collapsed on the toilet seat, panting. *"Gabi, calma. Una momento, por favor."*

That was as good as it got these days. Still, Will stepped into the shower with a smile on his face.

5

Guarulhos

A cargo truck was hot on Will's ass as he got off the *rodovia* and entered Guarulhos. Will put his free hand to his forehead, feeling the thin sheen of flop sweat that was always there whenever he had to drive in São Paulo.

Still, he was lucky to get the Toyota today. Guarulhos was a pain in the ass to get to by bus, and Thiago hadn't wanted to talk on the phone. So Will had to make the journey here, something he'd rescheduled a morning lesson for. Senhora Bottari was a hopeless student, but she was rich and very persistent, never blaming Will for her failure to get beyond the "See Dick run" stage of English mastery. God knew why she cared to learn. She was 72 and afraid of flying, so it wasn't like she was going anywhere. But old people had their own reasons for spending their money, and Will was happy to take it, even if the old bag occasionally groped him. Maybe that was the real reason?

Guarulhos. Long stretches of junkyards and cargo warehouses, rusted hulks on red earth. Empty plastic bags drifting across the roadways, getting stuck in trees. Mangy dogs patrolling. Here and there, a forlorn garden patch, with a proud monument to the Rotarians who had put it there. Will thought of it as São Paulo's toolshed: strictly utilitarian, no frills.

Guarulhos. Shit, he hated the place. Its only real claim to fame was the Aeroporto Internacional and the massive associated cargo lots surrounding it. That and a shitload of love motels, a peculiar Brazilian institution where couples could drive into their own discreet fuckpads and hear and see nobody else while making the beast with two backs on their lunch hour. Yes, lots of bosses fucked secretaries, and hookers turned tricks, but decent folk used them too. Hell, even Silvia and Will had checked in a couple of times.

But take the wrong turn, and it was straight into Crackolandia. Thiago, curiously invincible, had shown Will around one time. Well, maybe not so curiously. Thiago had kept a lot of the local *ladraos*, that is to say, shithead criminals, out of the *penitenciaria*.

Will drove down a few bumpy, narrow streets to a cul-de-sac and came to Thiago's place. Not an awful setting but hardly what you'd expect of a successful lawyer. Looking at it, Will felt sad and worried as well, as if this was what would happen to him if he didn't tread carefully. Brazilian women would put a lot of effort into a marriage, but when you pushed them too far, it was final. Thiago's house used to be loud. Wife and three kids loud. But now it was tomb-quiet. Jacquelina had had enough of late-night calls from gangsters and the dalliances that so often came with that territory. So she had taken the kids and gone to her mother's in Jundiai. So Thiago now occupied the narrow house at the end of the moon-cratered road by himself. Now it was just the fat little lawyer, his cats (Jacquie hated them, so they stayed), and his giant stacks of paper. Thiago swore he used computers, but he could never actually produce one whenever Will came to visit. Buried under the papers, perhaps. The man was useful and even fun sometimes. But lately, the whole scene gave Will the creeps.

Will parked the Toyota and walked up to Thiago's gate. Open. He was getting careless for a man with so many enemies. Maybe he just didn't give a shit anymore? Will padded in cautiously, stepping over a large tabby in the carport who eyed him with disinterest. He squeezed past an ancient Fiat crammed into the microscopic space and walked through another open door into the house. "Thiago? You left your gate open, man ... Are you okay?"

The little man stepped around a corner, causing Will to fart nervously.

"Shit, Thiago, you want a date with the *microondas*? You know what happened to Usman. What the fuck is the matter with you?"

The lawyer peered at him from behind small glasses and scrunched up his nose. He was wearing a bathrobe, clutching a *Folha de São Paulo* newspaper in one hand and a Johnnie Walker Red in the other. "Amigo, if I have a date with the *microondas*, the last person I will invite is you. One of your farts and the whole place will explode."

Will laughed out loud. "Okay, you fucking ambulance chaser, it's good to see you." The two men hugged. "Heard from Jacquie?" Will looked at Thiago hard. The dull stare back was his answer. He let the man go.

"*Café, Willao?*"

"*Sim, por favor.*"

As Thiago put the kettle on, Will considered if the *microondas* jokes had been wise. It was a fresh scab. *Microondas.* The microwave. A funeral pyre for the living, made of old tires doused in gasoline. Locked inside, one unfortunate who had displeased the narcos in some way, like a police informant or a nosy reporter, like in Rio a few years back. Or a lawyer who hadn't gotten the right people off, like Usman Al-Khattib. Usman, Thiago's law-school friend, had failed to get the brother of a big shot in the Primeiro Comando da Capital off on a murder charge last year. The big shot may have been behind bars, but all it had taken was him reaching out with a contraband cellphone, and soon enough, Usman had been in the trunk of a car on the way to his big exit. The PCC wasn't afraid to reach out from inside the prisons and whack cops. What was one lawyer?

Will had thought about that a lot. Had Usman known, in that trunk, all alone? He had represented enough of these assholes that he'd known their ways. He had to have known.

The cop in Will was ready to say, "Tough shit," but the human fact was it was a horrible way to go. Looking over the table at Thiago, he knew his lawyer hadn't shared 10 percent of the gory details. But the PCC had made sure Thiago knew the facts. Video, pictures, everything. They'd even sent a burned and chopped-up doll. Message: we know you have kids. Right about then, his marriage had started to slip.

33

Maybe he'd wanted his family to get a little distance. Will would've done the same. And he probably would've killed a few of the motherfuckers. Thiago had their addresses, and it wasn't like Will didn't know how. He'd had recent practice, after all.

Brazil. Will thought about the paradox of the place for the millionth time since he'd first left the airport and walked into the open-oven heat. So much beauty. Such laid-back, seemingly happy people. Underneath it, violence that would make you puke out your nose, violence that made you want to pick up a gun and do something.

But Thiago had always held him back. Now, Thiago sat behind the stacks of paper and regarded the gringo. "Will, do you ever want to do another kind of work? One that is more suited to your talents?"

Here we go ... Will was surprised it had taken Thiago this long to ask. He stared into his coffee before answering, "Stop speaking lawyer, amigo. If it's a wet job, count me out." His early, visceral reaction to Usman's horrific demise had been replaced with a much more sensible fear of doing 20 years in a Brazilian prison controlled by the PCC.

"What is a 'wet job'? Something at the *praia*, perhaps?"

Will laughed out loud. "No, dipshit, it means killing people. No hits, you got me?"

Thiago looked genuinely offended. "Amigo, of course I would not ask you that. What kind of man do you think I am?"

"A lawyer," Will shot back automatically.

Thiago sighed. "Everybody hates lawyers, until they need us."

"Cops can relate. Okay, so if it's not a hit, what is it? A PI job?"

Thiago stared straight at him. "Yes, if by this you mean *detectivo privada*. That is what I need."

Will knew what Silvia would say. But what about him? Teaching was fine for paying the bills and easy to boot. But he had to admit that he had missed actually using his brain for the last year. "What kind of job? Divorce, fraud, something like that?"

"Will, you know what kind of cases I take. Do you think it would be that simple?" Thiago smiled and shrugged his shoulders like a chef who'd just burned the main course.

Complicated. Will hated that word. But he couldn't contain his curiosity.

Thiago paused and sipped his whisky before asking, "Have you heard of a man named Oscar Stumpf?"

"Nope, should I have?"

"He is the sort of man whose feet never touch the ground."

"Meaning he's a 1 percenter who takes a helicopter to work. Okay ..."

"Have you been to the Litoral Norte lately?" The lands along the coastline between São Paulo and Rio de Janeiro were Paulistas' favourite refuge from their impossible home.

"A few months ago, sure."

"Oscar Stumpf is developing a major real estate project there called Southern Cross. It's aimed at '1 percenters,' as you say, who want to live far away from São Paulo, enjoy a high standard of living and security, and have an easy commute when they need to go to Cidade Louca."

Now he remembered. "Shit, yeah, I saw the construction site in the countryside. Huge. That's Oscar Stumpf?" The plot was massive but was remarkable only for its scale. In recent trips through the countryside Will had seen many planned communities like it, mostly embryonic, catering to a moneyed class desperate to escape the chaotic, ever-growing megacity they had created. The age of heli-commuting had made the concept viable. The only problem was most of the plots seemed be stillborn. Will had noticed very little movement on the ones he saw most often, on the road to the Litoral Norte beaches. Killed by the spike in oil prices, perhaps?

"Yes, that is Oscar Stumpf."

"So what? So he's stuck with a huge plot of land and a dead idea? Sucks to be him."

"Actually, Will, it doesn't suck to be him. How closely did you look at Southern Cross? Did you notice that there was actually something going on there?"

He had to admit he hadn't. "So why is Stumpf's project moving ahead, when everybody else is stuck in first gear?"

"Blackmail."

"Come again?"

"I don't want to tell you any more until you meet my client. I need you to form your own impressions, without influence."

"Okay, is he here?"

"No, he hates Guarulhos."

"How strange."

"I got him to agree to meet you in a place you know well. Bar Canada. Ken will call you when he arrives."

While it was reassuring that Will's favourite watering hole and his fellow Canadian Ken Scribbins featured in this meet, he wasn't sure how much good could come of it. Ken was a good time, for sure, but he was pretty damned reticent on his own backstory. How did Thiago know enough to trust him?

"Oh, and Will, you need to avoid alarming him. He's very nervous."

"Why?"

"Oscar Stumpf tried to kill him."

Will took that in and then looked at the bottles of cachaça behind Thiago. Well, he had wanted some excitement, hadn't he?

"Got anything stronger?" he asked.

6

Bar Canada, Zona Leste

Will held up his end of the bar with lessening enthusiasm. This client he was meeting was already a half hour late. Although why Will expected punctuality in this country anymore was beyond him. Sometimes he was sure that nobody really knew how to use the flashy watches he saw everywhere. But this guy was supposed to be French. Maybe he'd gone bamboo.

Will looked around the too-familiar environs of Bar Canada and took it all in for the hundredth time. The first time fellow English teacher Myron had brought him here, he had found it all kind of pathetic.

"Look, Will, they have a moose head on the wall!" Myron, an American who secretly wanted to be Canadian so people in other countries wouldn't hate him, had been breathless.

"Yes," Will had replied lethargically, "just like home."

But now, over a year later, away from a country he wasn't sure he could go back to, he looked around with affection. Team Canada '72 was always celebrating Henderson's goal behind the pool table. Bob and Doug Mckenzie were always hoisting stubbies behind the bar. Trudeau was always daring people to "just watch me" by the big flat screen with the NHL games on pay-per-view. BTO, Bryan Adams, and Sloan were always on the jukebox. And most importantly, Sleeman's, Molson Canadian, and Granville Island were always on tap. And yeah, they still had that fucking moose head.

He downed the last of a pint of Rickard's Red. Instinctively hovering in the manner of barkeepers the world over, Ken Scribbins was in front of him. "Another one, Willy?"

He winced inside. Nobody had called him Willy since his growth spurt in Grade 9, when he'd begun hurting people for it. But given Ken's easygoing attitude to his bar tab, he overlooked it. Scribbins was short, wiry, and best described as scraggly. He had intense, fishy brown eyes that looked in two different directions. He had some single-ink tattoos on his hands and wrists that made Will think he might be an ex-con. He could be 40, 35, or even 50. He seemed to have an Ontario accent, but like everything else that might reveal background, he was vague about where exactly he was from. He didn't like Celine Dion, the Detroit Red Wings, or immigrants. Beyond that, Will knew very little. Even when there was a hockey game on, his cheering was noncommittal—except when the Red Wings were playing. Then he would throw things and curse.

"Sure, Ken, why not?" He hadn't planned on drinking much, but then again, how often had he sat at this bar and ordered a Coke? Never point never times, that was how often.

"That frog stand you up, eh?"

"Well, he is living in Brazil like the rest of us. Is anybody ever on time here?"

"No, they gonna be late for the 'lympics too. Hahaha." Ken laughed through nicotine-stained teeth.

Will needed to look away for a moment; the fish eyes and teeth were always an unsettling combo with Ken. At that moment, he saw a slight, Gallic-looking man backing out of the doorway, having obvious second thoughts. Will bolted after him, and the man turned and ran.

Will bullheaded through the beaded curtains and past the iron-grilled entryway onto the narrow street outside. The Frenchman's shoe soles were already pelting frantically down the uneven pavement. The Frenchman looked back at him and then caught his left foot in a pothole and face-planted. *"Merde!"* the man shouted. As the Frenchman tried to pull himself up, Will strode up behind him. The Frenchman rolled over onto his back with his hands up. Will became aware of Ken Scribbins walking up behind him.

"Everything okay, Willy?"

Will didn't take his gaze off of the Frenchman's black eyes. "Sure, Ken. Somebody just needs to work on his escape and evasion, that's all." He held a hand out, and the Frenchman took it.

Back in the bar, as the Hip sang "Fifty Mission Cap," Will and the Frenchman stared at each other through the gloom. Will's pint of Rickard's was frosty and tempting, but he hadn't touched it, fearing he'd miss something. He had often used this strategy on the job, staring at recalcitrant arrestees until they felt compelled to break the silence.

In front of the Frenchman sat a glass of Pernod, similarly untouched. Pernod. Jesus H. Christ. But Will's technique worked on the would-be escapee.

"You say I need escape-and-evasion training, but wait until you have heard my story."

"Okay, you have my attention; tell me your story."

"You see, I have done well in business here, but not so well. But maybe, I didn't want everyone to know that," Luc Renner began. "So when my friend brought a business venture to me, I could not say no." He looked around the bar and licked his lips.

"Southern Cross."

"Yes, Southern Cross."

"What was the buy-in?"

"Qu'est-ce que c'est?"

"How much money did they want?"

"One hundred thousand reais in the front, later one hundred thousand more. This I could do, but only just."

"Who got you in? Do you mind saying?"

"Why not, he is dead. Marco Hellmer." His shoulders slumped a little.

"Wait, I've heard of him. He used to play football, right? Santos FC?" If he was dead, why had nobody heard? Will started to get creeped out.

"Yes, that was him. He was a good friend." Renner looked down at the bar glumly.

"And Oscar Stumpf had him killed?"

Renner nodded.

"Why? Thiago mentioned blackmail, but he wouldn't elaborate."

Renner seemed to deflate a little more before speaking. "The project stalled. Gas prices made the commuting aspect unprofitable. Cars can run on alcohol, but not helicopters. So Oscar needed more money."

Renner held up his Pernod for a refill. Why the fuck did Ken even have Pernod? Will wondered.

"Stumpf went after you for more, tried to squeeze it, right?"

Renner nodded again.

"And you gave him a hook, didn't you?"

"Yes." This last came out in a hoarse whisper. They paused as Ken brought over a refill and then disappeared.

"What was the hook, Frenchman?" Will searched out Renner's eyes without success. He felt his frustration building. Pretty soon he was going to be bouncing this prick around the *banheiro* if he didn't get an answer. "Stop fucking around, and tell me! If I read this situation right, your chances of survival are exactly zero on your own, and I ain't going in blind. Now cough it up!"

"You Americans, always so vulgar and threatening."

"I'm a Canadian, asshole, and this is a Canadian bar. Notice the moose? Now tell me, before I really get vulgar and threatening. What ... was ... the hook?"

Renner was silent. And then, "Oscar put on parties, just before he asked us for more money. There were girls."

"And?" He wasn't settling for half answers.

"And they photographed us, all of us. They used it against us, told us we needed to double our money, or it would all come out."

"In this day and age, who gives a shit? This is Brazil, not Saudi Arabia. Nobody cares if you fuck a hooker. Unless you're married. Are you married, Frenchman?"

"No."

Will was getting that feeling again, that fucked-up, creepy feeling. "Then what were you worried about? You are French, after all."

"There were ... complications."

"There you go again, as Reagan said. Evasion is not a good play with me. Cough it up, or the genie forecasts major dental bills in your future." Renner began to speak again, but Will shut him down with a glare. "Especially if you call me an American again. Maybe the hookers were a little too young?"

Now Renner got heated, shoving his chair away from the table. "They were not hookers; they were models! And they were old enough!"

The whole bar had caught the outburst before Corey Hart saved them with "Sunglasses at Night." Maybe Will had pushed too far. "Okay, okay, I didn't mean anything. But there had to be something to embarrass a man of the world like you, am I right?"

Renner sat down reluctantly. "Yes, there were photos. Photos of some very kinky things. And Stumpf had my client list. Very conservative Paulistas, people who wouldn't understand. For everyone I talked to, it was something like that. Some men were married, some were in politics, the military, the police. There was even an archbishop. Everybody had lots to lose."

Will exhaled. Now it was making sense. "But I bet most of these guys paid, right? Otherwise there would be lots of dead bodies or lots of sex scandals, am I right?"

"Yes, most paid."

"What about you? And Marco Hellmer?"

"I couldn't pay, period. And Marco was too proud."

"So how come you are here, and he isn't?"

"Well, Canadian, let me tell you my story of escape and evasion."

Will ordered another round and let Luc Renner tell his story.

7

Mercado Municipal, Centro

Will elbowed his way through the crowds all the way from Metro São Bento, late for his rendezvous. The steep and narrow street was lined with jewellery shops, bums, and hawkers all selling the same brand of chocolate bar. Ragtag street urchins roamed, shoeless, in packs, looking for larcenous opportunities. Vehicles shared the roadway with hordes of pedestrians forced off the too-narrow sidewalks.

São Paulo in winter had two temperatures: mildly chilly and almost-summer hot. Today, edging into late morning, the sun was already burning white in a cloudless sky. Sweat beads ran down his forehead as he forced his way out of the crowded streets and caught a glimpse of the art deco pile in front of him. The Mercado Municipal was a gem of São Paulo life in a pile of garbage. Mendingos towed wheeled carts piled high with recycling while half-naked men with twisted limbs sat on the pavement outside, begging wordlessly. If you wanted the real São Paulo, the kind the helicopter set never saw, Will figured this was as close as you got.

The thought of a *sanduiche mortadella* and a beer drew him closer. Edilson had laughed on the phone last night when he'd suggested the meeting place. "Hungry again, Willao?" What the hell. And he could write it off on expenses this time. Should've met at Figueroa Rubiyat, come to think of it. The glass-enclosed forest in Oscar Freire served exquisite beef and fish dishes to people like Luc Renner's clients. Next time he was expensing that one. Only damned way he'd ever be able to have a steak there again.

So now he worked for Luc Renner, although he preferred to think of himself as Thiago's subcontractor. The scared little Frenchman had disappeared last night after giving Will the details of his near-death experience. He could only be contacted by Thiago, and Will was left with little to go on.

What did he know? Will liked to organize his thoughts in lists. As he walked past tight little shops bulging with prosciutto and salami, wine and beer, olives and tomatoes, he decided to make one. Luckily, Edilson was adhering to Brazilian standards of punctuality and was nowhere to be seen when Will grabbed the only open table at Bar Hocca. He pulled out his notepad and began:

> What I know:
>
> Oscar Stumpf: powerful, blackmails, killer
>
> Luc Renner: blackmailed, broke, scared
>
> Marco Hellmer: 99% positive dead

Southern Cross: going ahead, blackmail money helps

"Models" = sex

What I don't know:

Stumpf: Calling the shots alone, or has help? How ruthless?

Renner: Why blackmailed? ("Kinky" = bullshit)

Hellmer: Why hasn't anybody noticed?

Southern Cross: Is that all? Is there something else?

"Models": Where from, how, who runs them?

Me: What the fuck do I do next?

A vociferous argument between two delivery drivers forced him to look up from his list and got him considering the fact that what he didn't know had his facts outnumbered. And the most important question was the last one: What was he prepared to do? He'd gone over to Thiago's expecting a divorce gig and wound up in the middle of murder and blackmail. Was he prepared to endanger his family for some rich perverts who'd gotten in over their heads? Was he ready to risk going to jail for playing cop in a foreign country? Ordinarily, the answer would be no fucking way.

But the fee for getting Renner's money back was 20 percent after Thiago took his cut. The 20,000 reais was a badly needed financial incentive. Nobody was going to just give it to him. So there was the cash motive, although he still hadn't figured out how the hell he'd explain that to Silvia. But the practical question loomed too: Where to start? How did he go from having an interesting story to prying 100,000 reais out of the pocket of a man like Oscar Stumpf and giving it to a man like Luc Renner? One man would kill without reservation, so it seemed. The other wasn't even supposed to be alive. Maybe just go ask nicely?

As Will snorted to himself, he felt a hand on his shoulder. He started just as Edilson pushed him back down in his seat. Will did a double take as Edilson sat down across from him. "You're in uniform. You think that's wise?"

"Oh, *bom dia* to you also, my friend." Edilson's boyish face looked slightly wounded. Will regarded him wearing the light grey uniform of the Polícia Militar. "Will, you are the guy who wanted to meet in the Mercado, remember? Not very low-key, amigo. Besides, I am on duty, and you need your *sanduíche*. So what is this all about?"

Will looked up at the skylights and paused for a moment. Back home, the Hells Angels had a saying: "Three can keep a secret if two are dead." Will knew that Luc Renner's story was nitroglycerine in the wrong hands, but he was never going to get a handle on it without some knowledgeable local help. Will had already decided that if Edilson warned him off, he was walking away. It was either that, or he had a new partner.

"Let's eat first, amigo. This might take a while."

Over a massive *pastel de bacalhau* for Edilson and a sweaty, salty, messy *sanduiche de mortadella* for him, he laid it all out. Edilson downed his Coke and sat in silence for a minute.

"So there is one famous *jogador* dead, yes?"

"Yeah, probably. He never saw the body."

"But we know who did it?"

"Yes. A rich guy with friends, Edilson."

"But we can solve the murder, right?"

Oh shit, Will thought. *I should've seen this coming.* "Edilson, that's not really the mission here. He asked me to get his money back in return for a promise not to talk. He's scared ..."

"Merda, Will, your head is full of shit!"

The people at the next table over had noticed. A fat man with mustard-stained napkins stuffed into his shirtfront stared at Edilson. Edilson glared back, and suddenly fatso remembered his *sanduiche*.

"Calma se, buddy. You don't seriously propose we solve this case on our own? Don't you think that's a little overambitious?"

Edilson retorted with impatience. "Will, you are a smart guy, and you were probably a good cop in Canada. But you don't know the *ladraos* here, trust me. This fucker Stumpf is not going to let you or this *veado* Renner walk away with his money. Does he seem like he would let you do that?"

Will paused. Of course he was right. Stupid fucking plan. He was out of touch. "No, Edilson, he would kill us both."

"Maybe not just you." He let that last point sink in. "So, two choices you can make."

"Sounds like only one."

"Sure, walk away. Probably smart. But you are my friend, and I can't do this alone."

"Do what alone?"

"Arrest Stumpf for murder."

Ah, shit. Edilson wanted to make Polícia Civil so bad he was going to go up against Oscar Stumpf, his killers, and some very likely equally vicious lawyers. Will had always figured Edilson's brains-to-balls ratio was a little out of whack.

Edilson sensed the unspoken objection. "What else can we do? Ignore him? Marco Hellmer had friends too, Will."

Will couldn't let that one go. "And we both have families! Sometimes I think you are the one who needs a refresher on Brazilian crime. Cops aren't untouchable here, you know!"

Edilson fixed him with a steady gaze. He pointed to a ragged scar on his neck. "You know how I got this? In 2006, the PCC shot up my car while my partner and I were sitting inside. My partner died, choking on his own blood. As soon as I got out of the hospital, I went to the house of the guy who owned the motorcycle the *assassinos* used, with a couple of guys from my battalion. They were having a fucking party, Will. A party to celebrate. We closed the party, you hear me, brother?"

Will knew the stats. In June 2006, the Primeiro Comando da Capital had declared war on the police and prison services, assassinating 46 officers in the first three days of urban warfare. The next three days, it had been 70 members of the PCC who had gone to their graves. The killings had stopped.

"I am not afraid, Will. Maybe I should be, but I am not. But I need your help." He put out his hand. "Your kids live here now. Don't you want them to have a better country? One where somebody like Stumpf pays for his crimes, like the PCC paid for theirs?"

Without thinking, Will Bryant reached across the table and shook his pugnacious friend's hand. Three would keep a secret if two were dead, after all.

Walking out of the Mercado, Will pondered his next move. Edilson took his thought out of the air. He was scary good at that, Will thought. Edilson had cop intuition down to a science. Now if only he could develop a survival instinct, Will might feel better about the partnership.

"Santos, amigo. We need to find out more about Marco."

"I thought you were the Santos FC fan?" Edilson was fanatical about the club in the way only Brazilians could be. His apartment was a shrine.

"*Sim, sim*. But I don't know the man. It's close, and I have tomorrow off. Are you free?"

"I guess I can reschedule Bartolomeu again."

Edilson winced. "The strange kid?"

"Yes, that one." Bartolomeu was the only child of an old-money family. He was 12, overweight, sexually ambiguous, and going through a Goth phase. Will had a hard time not imagining him as a Japanese Manga character during the lessons, always having to remind himself that his money was just as good as anybody else's. Still, the sessions were long and awkward. What if his kids turned out like that?

As they emerged into the over-bright street, now oven-hot, high-pitched screams filled the air. Across the street, two tall and broad-shouldered *travestis* were engaged in a screaming match. *Travestis*. For some reason, Brazil seemed to be the world capital of large, well-muscled transsexuals. Every cop's worst nightmare in a fight. The attitude of a premenstrual woman combined with the strength of a *stevedore*.

"Merda! Those fucking bitches!" Edilson tried to shrink back into the Mercado, but it was too late.

"Ajuda! Ajuda me, Polícia!" Senhora Goncalves had seen him, and it was too late. Resignedly, Edilson got in his rover and called it in. Senhora Goncalves was a nice old lady whose store had a police discount, and service was required.

"Will?"

"Ah, no fuckin' way, buddy. I've dealt with enough dragons, and they are nasty! Where's your dipshit partner?"

"Probably pulling up his pants now." Felipe had a girlfriend in República who didn't mind it quick.

"Well, come on, it isn't physical yet. Just wait for backup!" Just then, the tranny in the pink tube skirt nailed the one in the blue come-fuck-mes in the forehead with a stiletto heel.

"It's physical now, Will!" He pulled out his PR-24 baton and began jogging across the street.

"Ah, fuck you, Edilson!" But he went anyway.

They dodged traffic and made it across the street just in time to see the big black *travesti* in the come-fuck-mes bury one of them in her opponent's crotch. The pink-skirted blonde dropped to her knees in agony. The black *travesti* was winding up for a head shot when Edilson brought his PR-24 across her knee, hard.

It sounded like a phone book being dropped on wet concrete. The gathered bystanders gasped as the *travesti* toppled facedown onto her opponent. Edilson was giving Will a "Was that too much?" look over his shoulder when a scream of *"Puta!"* came from the crowd. Edilson turned to place the source, just in time to catch a metal garbage can square on the bridge of his nose. Edilson staggered back from the dog pile, still holding his baton, blood streaming from his face.

Will just had time to think, *Oh, fuck, I'm up,* when the thrower emerged from the bystanders. Tall and skinny; tight jeans; scraggly, dyed-blonde hair; gold teeth; bulging white eyes in a whiter face, showing a two-day crack jag. He went straight for Edilson, but Will got to him first. Will wrapped a big palm around the man's skinny neck fast and hard, delivering a brachial stun. The crackhead staggered as Will grabbed his shoulders and pulled him forward. He lined up his knee to strike the man's ribcage, inadvertently kicking Pink Skirt in the head in the process. The crackhead tried to look up, and his arms feebly scrabbled up Will's shoulders, but it was no use. *You are getting your dose, asshole,* Will thought grimly. He felt hot death breath in his face as he jackhammered his knee into the zombie's ribcage.

Three strikes and he was out, collapsing onto Pink Skirt. Will heard a squished watermelon sound behind him and looked back to see Sargento Andreatta rearing up to baton him as his last victim dropped to the ground. Andreatta let the baton drop with a flash of recognition. "Gringo, what the hell are you doing here?"

"Just backing up Soldado Lopes."

The thick-shouldered Sicilian's face narrowed. "Well, you're done 'backing up.' So back up, gringo."

I couldn't agree more, you merciless prick, Will thought. He stepped over the moaning ball of dragons and walked over to Edilson, who was sitting on the corner, Senhora Goncalves holding an ice pack to his nose.

"Ahhhh, Will, that was fun, huh?"

"Sure, you fucking psycho. You gonna be okay for tomorrow?"

"Sem problema, gringo, vamos a praia!"

Felipe walked up and surveyed the scene, smiling sheepishly as the members of his *batalhao* quickly restored order.

Will got up and slapped him on the shoulder as he walked past. "Thanks for showing up, you useless douchebag!"

Felipe smiled uncomprehendingly.

On the Metro, Will grinned all the way home. God, he hadn't realized how much he missed it.

Silvia was the recipient of his unused adrenaline that afternoon. They took advantage of a rare kidless moment and afterwards lay side by side, gazing at each other. Her silky copper hair fell over her shoulder. Will closed his eyes for a moment, wondering why he would risk this. He opened his eyes again as she drew closer.

"Will, what is happening with you?"

Ah, here it is. Silvia was the most intuitive person he knew. He was by now pretty much convinced she was psychic. "What do you mean, baby?"

"Don't give me some bullshits, man."

He laughed. She always got that one wrong. "What bullshits, Wife?"

"Your students are calling the house, looking for you. Where are you really going? Another woman? Don't lie!"

54

Ah shit, Bartolomeu was today! "No, no, it's not that!" Better get something out quick, before she cut his balls off. "It's a job, for Thiago."

"You give your lessons for Thiago in his house, no?"

Cornered as he was, he couldn't help but play with her right breast. "This is different."

She looked down at his hand but didn't stop him. "What are you doing, Husband?"

He looked at her brown eyes. "Some investigating, a real estate case. Thiago just needs somebody to collect some facts for him. Edilson is helping me. It's very safe."

"Hmm." She considered. "How much money can you make?"

That ought to do it. There was an element of Lady Macbeth to his bride that he knew well. "Three thousand reais." No sense telling her the whole amount.

"Three thousand?"

He nodded.

"Be careful, Will."

They lay there until footsteps sounded on the stairs.

8

Rodovia dos Imigrantes, Destination Santos

Will dozed intermittently as Edilson manoeuvred between trucks on the Imigrantes. The road was spectacular—high-arched overpasses wound through verdant hills interspersed with vast lakes, tunnels punching through the harder parts. Overall, it was proof that a country so in love with driving could build roads when it got its shit together. Edilson's old Gol was a convertible, and it was top-down weather, so Will tried to stay awake and enjoy the scenery.

It was hard, though. Gabriella had been sick last night, so he and Silvia had taken turns looking after the little one. Gabriella had thrown up on herself and, being a girl, had been mortified and embarrassed. Finally, some children's Gravol combined with princess stories had gotten her to sleep just as the rooster across the street had sounded the neighbourhood wake-up call. So Will hadn't exactly gotten up funky fresh this morning.

Edilson's battle with the dragons had not left him in any better shape. Both eyes were swollen, and his sunglasses were held up by a thick bandage.

"These are not coming off today, even if we see a movie!" Edilson had announced.

"Good, 'cause you are fucking ugly, dude."

"Obrigado, idiota."

Will snickered as they passed his favourite billboards. One was for a brand of wheels called FAG. The other was for Baby Piss diapers. Awesome.

"What are you laughing at, amigo?"

"Remember how every time we go past Drogaria Farto, I laugh?"

"Sim, Drogaria Pum, nao?"

"Ha, ha, *sim.*"

"Your wife was right; you are a child."

"Thanks. So, boss, what do we do first?"

"Go there and ask around. See if anybody's seen him."

"You know his haunts?"

"Haunts?"

"Where he hangs out?"

"No, but I know the team, and I know Santos. We will find out something."

"We gotta be careful. Nobody knows he's dead."

"So we don't either, brother."

"Hope you have a good poker face, especially if we wind up talking to his mom."

"Poker face?"

"Sem expressao."

"You leave that to me, Will."

They passed through a low set of hills and then saw Santos looming in the distance, the Atlantic Ocean shimmering in the distance. Limestone cliffs, topped with fearsome green, punched through by violating roadways. Light blossomed, then died, as they entered tunnels again and again. Will nodded off again.

When he came to, it was to the rutted backstreets of Santos. They crisscrossed canals as they made their way to the Santos FC practice grounds. Santos FC. The little beach-city club that had once boasted the best player in the game—Edison Nascimento, later known, as so many Brazilian players were, by just one nickname: Pelé. He had grown up playing in his bare feet and had come through this town, these fields, to be the most famous Brazilian who ever lived.

If Will Bryant knew one thing about Edilson Lopes, it was that you never, ever, ever, insulted Pelé in his presence. The guy hadn't spoken to him for a month one time after he'd mocked Pelé for selling everything from cars to tampons. "Hey, Edilson, look at Pelé on that Poupa Farma ad. Guy probably has trouble making *poupa* at his age. Hey, where are you going?"

So now, Will just sat in silence as Edilson parked the car next to the training camp fence. Edilson sat and stared awhile. Will could imagine him doing this a lot, reliving boyhood fantasies, envying kids who got the chance to be this close.

On the field, kids he guessed were 10 to 12 years old were being put through their paces, squaring off against other kids as they practiced ball handling. Across the field, another, younger group was doing sprints.

Will was now in his own reverie, thinking about Lucas out there. Lucas was already skilled with the ball, and he might be somewhere like this in a few years. Or his dad might be dead.

He pushed the guilt away. He couldn't have told Silvia. No way could she handle the whole story. But the guilt lingered. Maybe it was the way he'd made it about money instead of what it was really about: ego. The scrap with the *travestis* yesterday had fuelled his desire to get back into the game, to feel alive again, instead of feeling like a half-assed librarian.

Was this why they were here? So he could play cop again?

"Will?"

"Yes?"

"You haven't asked me why we're here."

"I trust you. I am guessing Marco Hellmer was still involved with the club somehow."

"*Muito bom*, Will. Yes, he was. He coached here part time, when his schedule allowed. You know, I talked to him a few times?"

"No shit?"

"Yes, shit. He took the time to talk to fans. He was tough on the kids, though."

"How so? Did he hit them?"

"Never that I saw. But he would yell at them, say some pretty bad stuff, man."

"Product of his generation?"

"More like a *mal humour*."

Mal humour. Bad attitude. Will considered what Luc Renner had told him about Marco, how pissed off he'd been at Stumpf, how Renner had tried to reign him in. He could sense a little more clearly how things had gotten violent. But he also wondered for a moment why he was only finding out now that Edilson knew, at least in passing, their victim. Put that away for now.

"Let's see if anybody here knows anything." Edilson was climbing out of the Gol. "Let me talk, please."

"Why?" Will thought his Portuguese was pretty good.

"Because you speak Portuguese like Mick Jagger."

"Okay, fuckface, you speak English like Joel Santana!" Edilson snorted. The Brazilian coach of the South African team in the 2010 World Cup had English so garbled it was a national joke, one the genial coach was happy to make money off of. Will moped behind Edilson as he called out to a loitering man near the entrance, "*Oi, gente!* Is Marco here, man?"

The stoop-shouldered man in the Santos FC tracksuit squinted suspiciously. "Who is asking, *mane*?"

Mane meant a lazy bum looking for handouts. Most people who talked to Edilson like that quickly regretted it. But different turf, different rules.

"You must have seen me here before. Marco and I are old friends."

The goon started to walk over to them and stopped halfway. "Everybody's an old friend. Now fuck off, and stop hanging around here like a *pedofilo*, watching the kids." Satisfied with that, the goon folded his arms.

Uh-oh.

Edilson smiled and cleared his throat. "How about I come over there, rip off your arms, and fuck you in your own ass with them, you sisterfucking trash?"

The goon went red from neck to scalp and was about to stride over when a voice called out from the sidelines. "Stop, Laerte, please. What do you two want? I am trying to have a practice here!"

Edilson stared the now-stationary goon down while Will answered, "We were just wondering where Marco Hellmer was, Coach. We needed to talk to him about a business matter. It's quite urgent."

The coach gave an exasperated slump. "Reynaldo!" he yelled to an assistant. A tall black man ran over to the coach, and they conferred in whispers. Edilson was still staring down the goon when the whistle blew. The kids on the field broke up and headed for the benches, laughing and backslapping.

The coach walked up behind the goon and whispered in his ear. He came over to them as the goon walked away unused. The coach was impressive. Tall, flat stomach, wiry muscles, fiery eyes. Arms crossed, he regarded them warily. "Marco and his business. What next?"

Edilson forgot about the goon and turned to the coach. "Deninho. I watched you play in the eighties and nineties. You knew how to move the ball. You played with Marco Hellmer."

Deninho was unimpressed. "You read a book. Good for you. Now why are you interrupting my practice?"

Fuck this, Will thought. *Aren't people in this country supposed to be laid-back?* Then why the hell were they getting the ice bucket here?

Edilson wasn't put off. "I apologize. We are private investigators working for a client who invested in a real estate scheme Marco also invested in. A project called ..."

"Southern Cross," Deninho finished for him.

"You've heard Marco speak of it?" Will asked.

"Only every day for the last six months. You see, Marco and I went into business together after our playing days ended. We also stayed active with the talent-development program here. I spent more time with him than I did my wife. We were fifty-fifty partners in the clubs. That was why I couldn't understand why Oscar Stumpf didn't also ask me to invest. I have the money."

"When did you last see Marco? We really need to talk to him. We think this whole thing is a scam, and if we can get more investors together, it will be easier to recoup the investments ..." Will fell silent as Deninho walked up and stood toe to toe with him.

"Bullshit! Don't act like you don't know!"

Will squirmed. This guy was pretty switched on. "Know what?"

"That Marco Hellmer is dead."

Edilson spoke up. "How do you know that?"

He answered Edilson but kept his eyes on Will. "Because this is the first week in 30 years he hasn't called me."

Will stepped back and asked the question that needed asking. "So why haven't you called the police? And why don't you seem to give a shit?"

"Because he deserves to be dead."

The three stood in silence for a moment. Then Edilson asked, "Care to tell us why?"

Deninho looked around. The kids were pouring back onto the field. "I will tell you. But not now, not here. And only if you keep your mouths shut. I help you with your investigation, you try not to destroy my business?"

Edilson asked, "Your business?"

Deninho clenched his jaw. Will interjected, "We get it. Help us, and it's a deal. Where do you want to meet?"

"My house. Avenida Siquero Campos. By the double canal." He wrote the digits out for Edilson and dismissed them. "Be there at seven."

Avenida Vincente de Carvalho, Santos

Will and Edilson walked off the caipirinhas and *isca de peixe* on the beachfront. Santos was a sort of miniature Rio, right down to the swirling pavement tiles. The warm evening had brought out the crowds. Skaters and shirtless cyclists roared past them. Parents tried to pry their kids off the playground equipment along the beach as dark set in. Everyone else was just getting started. Out in the massive harbour, low-slung transports manoeuvred for position. The landward side was dominated by narrow tower blocks, built crowded together to maximize beachfront real estate. Some of the towers had a pronounced lean, but in true Brazilian style, they stayed occupied. Maybe people wanted to roll out of bed into the bathroom?

It was sweltering, wet, loud. Shouting youths hovered in groups, without a hint of menace. Oily food smells and ambient alcohol filled the air. Police cars rushed around with red lights on, going nowhere important. Rollerbladers, suicide-fast, never losing it. The beach sounds of surging waves. Brazil incarnate. Will stood still for a moment and relished the place. Edilson grabbed his arm and broke the moment.

Edilson was confused. "I don't understand this guy. They played together in Os Peixes for 10 years. Then they go into business together and get really rich. Now, he doesn't give a shit if his brother is alive or dead? It's crazy." He shook his head and looked down, narrowly missing a hit from a skateboarder.

Will sighed. "Edilson, I know these guys are your idols, but don't let that make you forget that they are people. People fall out. They fuck each other over for money, sex, ego, whatever. Who knows what happened? Hopefully we find out, tonight."

Edilson peered out of his sunglasses. "I can't see a fucking thing, brother."

Avenida Siquero Campos, Santos

The two men arrived outside Deninho's house at the appointed hour. They stepped through the portico into the entranceway. Like all homes of the Brazilian rich, it was walled, the interior a guarded mystery from the street. Inside, it became apparent where much of the *jogador's* money had gone. Hardwood floors. Teak trim. African antiques. Art, most likely original, but what did Will know? Servants, two that he could see, probably a couple more.

They rounded a corner to find a tense-looking host wearing chinos and a yellow button-down, working on a double Scotch rocks. Behind him, a lit dining room through glass doors showed a family dinner still in progress. Will was pretty certain there would be no introductions. Guess Deninho wanted to keep this quarantined. Who could blame him?

Deninho had the servant take drink orders and ushered them out to the patio. It was a thing of wonder. Will had always marvelled at how Brazilians, forced to live behind walls due to their paralyzing fear of crime, managed to construct oases of peace in the space available. In his case, Deninho's means allowed for quite an oasis. Two circular pools, one large, one small, almost intersected on the sepia-tiled surface. A low wall of irregular stones with a waterfall running its whole length was partially obscured by fronds. Benches and statuary were highlighted by blue pot lamps.

Edilson whistled. "Nice."

"Thanks. Let's get this over with." Their obviously impatient host ushered them over to a long bench by the water wall, obviously hoping the noise would mask conversation. They sat on a gentle curve, Deninho keeping his distance. The water flow covered the uncomfortable silence. Will looked up and thought he could make out a few stars of the real Southern Cross.

Ordem e Progresso was the motto emblazoned over the Cross on the *bandera nacional*. Will was seeing a lot of progress in his time here. Deninho and, until recently, Marco Hellmer had been living embodiments. But the order seemed more elusive. It kept Brazil interesting.

"What kind of man wears sunglasses at night?" Deninho broke the silence. "Cruising faggots, junkie singers, and gangsters. I can't figure out which one you are."

Edilson exhaled through his teeth. Will watched carefully. Usually someone got punched in the throat next, but Edilson was on his best behaviour. Slowly, he reached up and removed his glasses, revealing two black eyes.

Deninho was nonplussed. "I guess gangster it is. Good, I hate singers and faggots."

Will tried to get things on track. "Marco Hellmer and you fell out; that's obvious. Our question is why."

Deninho swirled his Scotch and crossed his legs. "Why do I get the feeling you two aren't businessmen? You seem more like cops. And since you are about as Brazilian as a McDonald's hamburger, that is really strange. Marco was a bad guy but not bad enough for the CIA to care, I think."

Will smiled. "I'm not Brazilian, true. But I'm not a cop, and I'm definitely not CIA. And this is a private investigation." Mostly true, he was just leaving out Edilson. That was probably a good idea. Feelings about the Polícia Militar were often mixed.

Edilson sat silently. A torch shadow played on his face.

Deninho considered for a long moment and then spoke. "I thought I knew the guy. Years of road trips, shared girls, tough spots, on and off the pitch. Well, I didn't." He swirled his Scotch again and looked away. "One day last month, he ordered a computer in his office destroyed and replaced."

Edilson asked, "Destroyed? Why?"

"It was his habit. It had been for at least 10 years. I always assumed it was something to do with security."

Will was puzzled. "The whole computer? Why not just the hard drive?"

Deninho laughed. "Honestly, we are two dumb farm kids who got rich playing football. I don't think he knew what a hard drive was. But he did know how to use a computer." He got a sour look on his face and took a swig of Scotch.

Edilson was getting impatient "So the computer was destroyed?"

Deninho was in no hurry. "No, it wasn't. It got mixed up with another one. It was sent for repair instead."

Will knew where this was going now. "And his browser history was pretty interesting, wasn't it?"

Deninho was stone-faced. "*Senhor*, 'interesting' is one way to put it. The IT guy showed me the pictures. Have you ever seen child pornography, Detectives?"

Both men nodded. "In our work, yes," Edilson added, a trifle unnecessarily.

"Well, I never had. It was ... horrible. Dark things, terrible desires ... some boys, but mostly girls. And some ... well, some were very, very young." He drained the Scotch in one go.

"You confronted him?" Will could imagine how that went.

"Yes. At first he acted like it was no big deal, but then, when he saw I did not think it was a joke, when I told him I was going to the police if he was not honest, well ..."

Edilson leaned forward. "Well?"

Will winced. Edilson might be a good street cop, but he needed to learn how to use silence if he was going to be a good investigator. Will had once sat wordlessly in the box with a detainee for 20 minutes before the guy admitted that his rapist cousin was hiding in his basement. Sometimes you just needed to let the wheels turn. Depending on IQ, that could take a while.

Deninho, however, had the IQ to make his choices quickly. "Well, he told me why Oscar Stumpf hadn't asked me to invest in Southern Cross."

That was it. "Because you couldn't be blackmailed for being a pedo."

Deninho nodded silently. "I told him to leave, that we couldn't do business together anymore. He begged me to reconsider, but I wouldn't. That was the last time I saw him."

Edilson had one last point. "You never told us why you figured he was dead, other than he didn't call you. After that last conversation, I don't think I would call you either."

"True, Detective, true. But that was not all."

True to form, Will used the silence. The pools gave off dappled light on the walls.

Deninho gave up. "My staff said he came back two weeks later and got his stuff. He told his secretary he was going south."

"South, as in, Santa Catarina?" Will knew where Marco had gone but couldn't show his hand. This guy would remember.

"Going after Oscar Stumpf with a gun, then disappearing off the face of the earth. What would you conclude, Detectives?" Deninho's tone was final. He swirled the cubes in the empty glass.

Edilson might have needed to work on his questioning but not his memory. "How did you know he had a gun?"

"Because he stole it from me. We still have that deal?"

Will nodded. "Thanks for the drinks."

9

Bar Canada, Zona Leste

Ken Scribbins washed the bar glasses and eyed the clock over the entrance. A couple lingered over their drinks a little too long for his liking, but he was sure they'd clear out when he started dropping hints. Ken was good at dropping hints. He had learned how as a young fish in Millhaven in '85, keeping the cons off his ass (literally) by doing little things like sitting next to the biggest stud at chow and driving his fork right through his would-be boyfriend's hand. While the formerly enthusiastic harvester of young ass had screamed and clawed at his by now useless appendage, Ken had calmly sauntered off to the other end of the hall, smiling at the Quick Response screws as they'd rushed in. "Who, me, Officer?" was a face he'd perfected over 10 years in Canada's worst prisons. He had no regrets. Was he a psychopath, as more than one prison shrink had told him? Probably, but who gave a fuck? In prison, being a psycho was a good thing. He'd seen what happened to nice, normal people in there. They got used as asswipe by the real demons, the people Ken used his powers against.

Ken had been in a riot once, in Archambault. Now there was a shithole. A couple of the real hard cons had wanted to a do a number on a couple of hostage screws, get real medieval on their asses. Ken had talked them down to the point where they'd realized two raped and murdered guards were a very bad thing indeed when their colleagues took back the prison. Ken had had no desire to eat bologna sandwiches with no teeth for two years, so he'd saved their lives.

Ken sometimes did good things for very self-centred reasons. He had a hard time understanding it himself. It probably would have surprised a lot of people, not the least Will Bryant, that Ken's favourite movie was not *Coed Slaughter 4* or *Even More Chicks With Dicks* but *Forrest Gump*. Ken loved to think of himself as that feather, just floating around on the breeze. He had to agree with Forrest's mama, who said that "Life is like a box of chocolates" and all that shit. That kind of explained to him how he wound up down here with a pretty good life, not leaking out his guts in a prison shower stall the way you would figure made sense, given his history. How Ken wished he'd had a momma who said smart things like Forrest's. All his momma had ever said to him was "Go to the store and get me another quart of rum." Fucking bitch.

Still, it had all turned out all right, courtesy of his Newfie pal Seamus Deane, with a little help from that feather. Ken had gotten paroled in '98 with scant prospects. But Seamus had remembered him from Kingston (another shithole) and had gotten him to help on a few hash runs. Ken had liked that work. Sure, it had sucked when the seas were rough, but he'd quickly adapted, as he had in the joint.

When Ken had gotten his GED, he'd quickly understood that the best adjective to describe him was adaptable. He evolved, even if he didn't look very evolved.

Ken knew he was ugly, knock-down, holy-shit ugly, yet he still had success with women. In the manner of the truly adaptable everywhere, he focused on his strengths, which he understood to be (1) his dancing and (2) his huge cock. That was generally sufficient.

But back to Seamus. Seamus had wanted to branch out. He'd had a buddy doing coke runs out of Curacao. Seamus wanted in, and he needed a partner. Coke made Ken a little nervous. Hash was one thing. It was seen as soft and generally didn't carry such hard-core sentences as the hard stuff like coke and smack. Ken had done time with guys rotting away on multi-decade jolts for running the hard shit. But it was in the Caribbean. When the fuck was Ken Macleod ever going to see the Caribbean?

Those were the days. Sun, ganja, rum, tanned brown bodies, and more cash than he would ever see again, which he spent on all of the above. The feather had landed in some really sweet-smelling shit this time. But it couldn't last. It never did. Maybe that was why the Beaners got those drama masks with "Laugh Now, Cry Later" tattooed on them.

In September of 2002, he got caught doing a run. Caught not by the cops but by pirates. Pirates of the Caribbean. No shit. But they weren't those funny, gay Johnny Depp pirates. They were the "force you to crew the boat to the destination until we kill you and take your shit" pirates.

It was 10 days before Ken, half-mad from dehydration, threw himself over the side. He woke up on a sand dune the colour of silver. Around him were lakes of impossible blue. In his fucked-up brain, he thought for a while that he was on another planet. He'd seen a really weird science fiction film once where this scientist keeps surviving the end of the world and wakes up in the end on this beach on another planet or something. Far out. So Ken believed he was on another planet for two whole days, until he met some tourists.

Now Ken realized that the place he'd been in was Ceará. He had read a *National Geographic* about it while in Kingston. This article had also informed him that Ceará was in Brazil, and that was fucking awesome. The feather had made a soft landing, again. Because there was something else Ken, now named Ken "Scribbins" for legal reasons, knew from his readings, limited though they were, on Brazil: if you knocked up a Brazilian chick, they couldn't throw you out of the country. This was no real challenge for a man as adaptable as Ken Scribbins.

So now, after years of adventures up and down the coast and more children than were legally necessary, Ken sat in his own bar, waiting for the last two assholes of the night to leave, so he and his colleagues could conduct a little business.

Weird to call a couple of cops "colleagues," given his history, but one of the many things Ken Scribbins liked about Brazil was that the lines between cop and con were a lot hazier here than they were back home. And money was money. After all, he was adaptable.

His cue to close up was when one of his colleagues walked in the door. It had started raining again, and Will Bryant shook himself off like a big dog in the entrance. Got the jukebox wet when he did that, Ken observed. Still, the dude was big, he spoke English, and for an ex-cop he wasn't a prick. Part of being adaptable was having useful friends.

Something in the way Will glared at the couple that were holding up closing time was enough for the man to seek Ken out and ask, *"A conta, por favor?"* Ken nodded and brought over the bill.

The door opened again, and Edilson Lopes came in behind his partner. Edilson shook off the rain and tossed his coat over the jukebox. That really pissed Ken off, but he said nothing. Cops in Brazil didn't have to be polite or answer complaints like the cops back home. So being quiet was the adaptable way to go. Besides, Will mostly kept his buddy in check, which kept other cops in check, which was good for business. Ken had lots of interesting stories, most of which he couldn't tell his colleagues, as they almost all involved criminal activity of some sort. So he stayed mysterious, which seemed to work out okay. Ken knew Will wasn't stupid. He'd seen Will eyeing his tats, so he knew the guy had to have an idea where he'd come from. But Will didn't ask, so Ken didn't tell. Maybe Will was adaptable too.

The couple departed as Edilson shrank into the shadows by the entrance, awaiting their guest. Will walked up to the bar and asked, "How's business?"

"Shitty, thanks to the rain. How's your business?"

"About to get more interesting."

Ah, shit. Not in my bar, Ken pleaded silently. "Are we expecting that frog?"

"Yes."

"Well ..."

Will guessed his concern. "We're not gonna fuck him up. He's our client. We just need to have a frank discussion, that's all."

Edilson glared menacingly from the shadows. Dude was small, but he could be scary. Ken was glad he wasn't the guest of honour tonight.

Will ordered a glass of Germana and sipped his cachaça slowly while he thought it all out. Edilson had been glum on the ride back from Santos last night, so he hadn't been much of a sounding board. Something about finding out one of your idols had feet of clay, he supposed. That had given Will a chance to work it all out in his head while Edilson drove. That was okay. Will had needed the chance to think, and the Imigrantes at night demanded Edilson's full attention anyway.

So Marco Hellmer was a pedophile, which meant that Luc Renner probably was too. Will's background checks hadn't found any obvious common thread between the two otherwise. But both had been blackmailed into Southern Cross, whereas other rich men with more socially acceptable habits, such as Deninho, had been left out. What about all those other prominent men with deep pockets? Well, if the results of Internet sting operations were any guide, they were all likely short eyes too. Was there something about men who could have anything that left them wanting something nobody was supposed to want?

But why was Oscar Stumpf blackmailing anybody at all? So many people were involved that it couldn't possibly be revenge. Was it politics? Not by Will's reckoning, as there were four *deputados* and two *senadors* involved, from three different parties. Did Stumpf need the money that badly? It didn't look like it, but then the rich were often good at keeping the facade up until it all went over the cliff. Will didn't have access to bank records, so he didn't know. He knew it would have to be a pretty damned urgent need for Stumpf to risk his reputation getting involved in something so seedy. All it took was one leak ... but that had to be why the blackmail was about something so reprehensible the victim's compliance was virtually guaranteed.

And what was Oscar Stumpf's reputation, exactly? He had come out of the army in the 1970s. He had served in military intelligence, so he knew how to get information and, more importantly, how to judge its value. He had used his contacts, first in the junta, then in the democracy of the 1980s, to advance diverse business interests. He was in media (a natural fit), ethanol production (a cash cow, subsidized by the state), and shipping. But Grupo Stumpf's biggest holdings were in construction. There were a hell of a lot of pictures of Oscar Stumpf in a hard hat out there.

But the early 1990s had not been kind to Oscar Stumpf, despite his cozy relationship with the first post-junta governments. The Plano Real, in which Brazil ditched the hyperinflated cruzado in an attempt to stabilize the economy, had been hell on many of Stumpf's moneymakers. He'd stayed afloat but just barely. So maybe he did need the money? That was a long time ago now, and Will was certain a man like Oscar Stumpf would have recovered by now. He would've found a way. And his old patrons were still prominent and powerful. In Brazil, bad things didn't happen to men like Oscar Stumpf.

There was so much they didn't know yet. Will felt an excitement he had missed without realizing it. The opening stages of a file. Gathering the first few leads. Putting the first pieces together. Now they knew why powerful men were being blackmailed. Only Luc Renner could tell them how. Will had called Thiago as soon as he'd gotten back from Santos. A few months ago, he would never have called so late, but with Jacquie and the kids gone, he knew the little lawyer barely slept anymore anyway.

"Hmmm." Thiago had been noncommittal at first. "He said you were pretty rough with him last time, Will."

"Tough shit, Thiago. You knew who you were hiring. And he doesn't get his money if I can't get answers. Which he hasn't given me yet."

"Would you show up for an invitation like this?"

"Relax. I'm not gonna rip out his fingernails. I might even spring for the Pernod."

"Hmmmpf."

Luc Renner was only 15 minutes late, walking in the door with searching eyes and leaden feet. He sat at the table pointed out by Will. He said nothing, not even bothering to remove his sodden overcoat. Edilson stayed in the shadows. Ken knew he ought to make himself scarce, but he had to watch. He stayed at the far end of the bar under a picture of k.d. lang. Ken had been grilled by cops many times but had never gotten to see it from this vantage point before. He felt as if he were standing behind one of those one-way mirrors, waiting for the perp to crack, or whatever the fuck cops said.

Will sat down wordlessly and put a glass and a bottle in front of Renner. Their guest helped himself to one and a half glasses and then wiped his mouth and looked up at the much-larger man in front of him and asked, "So, what news do you have? I didn't come here in this pissing rain just for a drink, you know."

Ah, the French, they always amazed Will. No matter how few cards they held, they just couldn't resist the urge to be arrogant.

Ken had a pretty good idea of what was coming next and smiled to himself.

Will smiled too. Then he kicked Luc Renner's chair out from under him.

Renner squirmed on the floor, stunned, holding his elbow.

"You got a lotta fucking nerve coming on like that, considering what we know about you. Should we tell you what we know about you? Hah? That's right. You wanted a news update, didn't you?"

Will stayed seated. Renner lay on the floor, pondering whether he should even try to get up or if this would simply invite more violence. "You ... you work for me! You can't ..."

"I work for Thiago Waldemar de Costa Gomes, attorney at law. And he approved this message. Now, you did want the facts, right? And we did find the facts. We found the fact that your buddy Marco was—how to put this nicely?— 'interested in youth affairs.' And there is no fucking way you did not know that, because so are you. So if you want your money, you are going to tell us everything this time, or guess what happens next."

"You can't threaten me. I'm not scared anymore! So go ahead and kill me. You get no money!"

He was hot, genuinely so, Will figured. The guy had reached his breaking point long ago. Shoulda probably searched him for weapons ... oh well.

"Why would we kill you? Oscar Stumpf could take care of that. No, what happens is we get your money anyway, but you get nothing. See, this case is very interesting, and we've already found out so much that we're sure Senhor Stumpf will be reasonable and pay us to go away. After all, the only thing more pathetic than a rich pedophile is a poor pedophile ..."

"Then you know nothing, you goddamned oaf!" Renner was in overdrive now, veins bulging, spittle flying. "He'll kill you too. It's nothing to him!"

"Then perhaps we have no alternative but to continue working together. But we cannot have lies, Luc." It pained him to say the man's name. "They do not contribute to trust."

"Fuck you!" Renner scrambled to his feet. "See you in hell!" With that he strode quickly to the exit, right into Edilson's right fist. The punch propelled him backwards. Will stayed in place. He really hadn't planned on this, but he had brought muscle, hadn't he?

He was even more surprised when Ken Scribbins vaulted the bar, came up behind the staggering Frenchman, and snapped his head back with a handful of hair. The bartender frog-marched the suffering Renner to the bar, produced an evil-looking knife, and put it between Renner's legs.

Ken got real close and stage-whispered, "You know what a gelding is, motherfucker?"

Renner cried out wordlessly. Will wondered if they had locked the door.

"A gelding is a horse with no balls. Since you haven't been using yours right, how about we just take care of this gelding right here?"

Whoa, this was getting out of hand. "Talk, and I can call them off," Will said. "Tell us everything, and nobody else needs to know. You don't have a choice. Who are you going to complain to?" Will knew that physical coercion rarely worked. But it might this time because this subject was supposed to be dead anyway. And if he'd done what Will figured he'd done, nobody was going to be throwing him any parades if he came back from the dead.

Renner nodded almost imperceptibly. Ken and Edilson melted away as quickly as they'd barged in. Will handed Renner a bar towel. He almost felt sorry for the guy. He was rat meat, and he knew it. But Will reminded himself he didn't know the other half of the story. He only knew what had been done to Luc Renner. He didn't really know what evils Renner had done to others. The silence was eternal, but Will knew how to wait.

Finally: "You never asked me why I did not go back to France. You were not curious?"

"I assumed you had too much at stake here. Was I wrong?"

"Your guess was right, and so was Oscar's. You see, I am not Luc Renner. I am Jean-Pierre Broussard. Jean-Pierre Broussard is wanted by the Gendarmerie Nationale on 42 counts of sexual interference with minors. It's who I am."

"I see."

"I doubt that you do. You and your friends just showed how you feel about people like me. Of course, you are not the only ones. Very often I feel like this about myself ..."

"Melodrama. Move on."

"I am simply trying to get you to understand why I would risk everything I have built in Brazil to risk discovery again. I had put everything behind me, or so I thought. False documents, plastic surgery, money transfers using a shell company ... my parents' idea. They were the only ones who knew the truth. I thought I had put the desires behind me too. But it's so basic to who we are. We can accept this about gays but not pedos?"

"No speeches. This isn't a NAMBLA meeting." Will had sometimes wondered if trying to cure pedos was as pointless as trying to make gays straight, but he didn't have a problem letting gays be themselves. He couldn't say the same for pedos. "So you were susceptible. We can agree on that now. So tell me how Stumpf got you in."

"I knew Oscar from before. He was one of my best wine clients. He was very discerning. One day, he asked me for my client list. He was looking for investors."

"Were all your clients pedos?"

"Of course not, what an idiotic question!" Renner/ Broussard huffed. Will visualized letting Ken carve him like a turkey.

"So he was just looking for names, then?"

"Yes, he knew nobody shopped at my store who didn't have money. My cheapest bottle is 200 reais."

A lot of money to turn into piss, Will thought. He liked wine, but not that much.

"Then what?" Will asked.

"He asked me to host a very private event, at his expense. He gave me the guest list. No additions, no spouses or guests. No catering. Only me, some *charcuterie avec fromage*, and some hand-picked wines. At an after-hours club in Morumbi he chose."

This was getting interesting. "How many guests?"

"Just 12. When the time came, his security people searched everyone for electronics. There was some animosity about this, but it was Oscar Stumpf, so ..."

"So they knew not to piss him off."

"Yes. He is known as connected. He is also known as ruthless."

"Why?"

"I have heard talk about what he did in the army in the '70s."

Of course, "military intelligence" in 1970s Latin America tended to mean "secret police." Will was beginning to understand a bit better how the man operated. "What happened at this party?"

"At first, just small talk, drinking nice wine, etc. But I could tell some guys were uneasy."

"How?"

"I overheard two of my clients, one of them a Japaneiro in the import-export business, the other a GM executive. I keep track of my clients, and I was sure these guys didn't know each other. But there they were, huddled in the corner, asking each other, 'What the fuck are you doing here, etc.?' I thought that was strange. But it got worse."

"How?"

"After the presentation on Southern Cross, there was a lot of skepticism. These guys weren't fools; they knew this project was risky. Too many units, too dependent on oil prices, too far away, etc., etc. But Oscar didn't blink an eyelid. He told everybody, 'All your questions will be answered by the dossier under your seat.'"

"And were they?"

Renner/Broussard was back on the Pernod. He took a long sip. "Oh yes, they were." He fell silent and then tilted his head back to the ceiling. "Every man, including me, picked up his dossier. The cover page and the first few pages were standard stuff. Then I turned to page four and saw my wanted poster from France. I couldn't breathe. There was more, lots more. Stuff off the Internet, stuff I thought only the NSA could get. I was feeling dizzy. I looked around the room. The other guys were sitting there, pale, shocked. One guy was swilling 1,000-real Burgundy straight from the bottle. Another rushed into a corner and vomited. Now I knew how those two clients knew each other."

"And how did Stumpf look?"

"He looked like he had just eaten a very good meal. He lit a huge cigar and smiled. A couple of guys headed for the door, but security stopped them, of course. Then he announced, 'My friends, now that I have your attention, I wish you to turn to the last page.' I didn't want to, but of course I had to."

"What was on the last page?"

"Just a number in red. Our investment. And a date, time, and GPS coordinates."

Will was impressed. As sales pitches went, it was the ultimate offer you couldn't refuse. And Stumpf had pulled it off like a Bond villain.

"How did it end?"

"With a speech. He could tell what kind of effect he'd had, so he decided to cool things off a bit. 'My friends, now we all know the truth about ourselves. Now we can be free. I am not stealing from you. I am offering you an investment opportunity, one which may well pay off for us all. In the meantime, let me assure you that I know how to entertain my friends, once I understand their tastes. And if my friends can be discreet, then so can I.' I could tell that a lot of guys started to feel better at that point."

"Did you?" Will wanted to punch him again.

"Of course." He smiled.

Restraint was getting hard again for Will. "So he told you how much he was shaking you down for."

"The first instalment, at least."

Yes, that was how Stumpf operated. There was a second, maybe even a third punch. He had that figured right, for everyone but the mercurial Marco Hellmer and the parsimonious "Luc Renner."

"What about the date and GPS coordinates? Was that the entertainment?"

"Oh yes." He closed his eyes. Behind the bar, Will could hear Edilson ushering Ken into the back before he pulled out his knife again.

"Tell me more."

Renner/Broussard closed his eyes as he relived it. "It was like something out of Scheherazade. Six of us arrived at a resort hotel in Blumenau. Marco was there, the first time I knew they also had him. We had been friends for years, and I never knew ... Anyway, we were all introduced to our 'friends' there ... It was like Oscar Stumpf had read my mind, given me what I most wanted."

Will fought his urges to strangle Renner and kept the conversation moving. "Tell me about her."

"You always have a picture in your mind, that woman that you want more than air, the Goddess. You know what I mean, Will?"

His look was intense, full of Gallic passion, and it unnerved Will. Still, he thought of Silvia, the first time they'd made love. Holding her in his arms, not believing his luck. Wanting her more than air. The Goddess.

"That was where I met Gretchen. You can't imagine it, Will, I—"

Will cut him off, fast. "I don't want to. How old was she?"

Renner looked back coldly. He wasn't ashamed of what he was. Why couldn't they be ashamed of what they were? He sure as hell would be.

"I didn't ask for ID."

Will leaned forward, putting his still-considerable forearms on the table.

Renner caught himself. "But 15, I think."

"I bet that's a little old for you, no?" Will was feeling a coat of psychic slime building up on him.

"Perhaps," he said, unperturbed. "But she looked much younger. And her skills ..."

He let that last one hang there. Will got a mental image of this shithead ogling Gabriella and pushed it down, way down. Beating the shit out of his informant was a last resort, however tempting it might be.

"What about the others? Did they also get what they wanted?"

"Oh yes. Stumpf had paid very close attention to our Internet profiles and could tell exactly what each man wanted. We were all surprised that none of the girls were squeamish, that it seemed they had all been ..."

"Trained," Will finished the very sick thought.

"Well, anyway, after a week of this, with the promise of more, we went back to our lives. Then he contacted me again. By now, I was in touch with Marco regularly. I called him as soon as I got off the phone with Stumpf's man."

"They wanted more. And you couldn't pay."

"No, not without selling my business, which I think Stumpf wanted anyway. And Marco ... well, Marco wouldn't pay. He could; he just wouldn't."

"A pedophile with principles." Will smirked.

"Laugh all you want. Marco was a brave man." Renner looked into his glass.

"Marco got himself killed. And you too, almost."

"Maybe they will get me yet. You won't stop them."

"Honestly, I don't give a shit about keeping you alive. I want Stumpf. If that keeps you alive, well, that's just collateral damage."

"So, what can I do to interest you in keeping me alive?" Renner crossed his legs and balanced his chin on a fist. The dark eyes had intelligence and calm charm. Will reminded himself what desires were behind those eyes.

"Get useful, very quickly, and don't fuck me around. And if I find out you are still fucking kids, I will feed you to the piranhas. *Entende?*"

Renner looked at Will evenly. "*Oui.* Now, what do I need to do to be 'useful'?"

"You still have contact information for some of your fellow 'victims'?" Will let the irony in the term hang.

"Yes."

"Call them up. You've been underground for a few weeks now, and some of my information is getting a little stale. I want to know what Stumpf is up to now."

Renner was horrified. "But ... they will know I am alive, and Stumpf will find out! Him thinking I'm dead is the only thing saving me ..."

Will looked back coldly. "I already told you I don't give a shit about keeping you alive."

"Then why should I do this, why?"

Will heard commotion in the kitchen. Ken Scribbins was probably going for the cutlery again.

"You hear that, Luc?"

"What?"

"That is the sound of a very crazy ex-convict who owns this bar and who has probably killed a few of your kind in prison. And I am guessing it wasn't pretty. So how about we just leave you two alone?"

Will stood up to leave. Renner was panicking. How quickly the arrogance could be replaced by grovelling.

"No, no, no, sit down, please. Just tell me we can take steps ... so they don't find me ..."

"Relax, asshole." Will sat down. "I'm not going to give him your home address, and you are going to call from pay phones. Any meetings will be in a public place, and we will be watching. We certainly don't like you, but you are worth more to us alive than dead."

"Unfortunately," Edilson said as he stood behind Will.

"Now take this cellphone." Will slid a prepaid throwaway across the table. "Use it to call and answer myself or Edilson only. Understood?"

Renner nodded.

"And get the fuck out. It's closing time. Ken needs his beauty sleep."

10

Alameda Santos, São Paulo

"Galetos? This buddy of yours can be bribed by a lunch at Galetos? I wish all of my snitches were so easy." Will was standing in front of the ubiquitous São Paulo business-lunch hangout, sweating his nuts off in the one o'clock sun.

They were here at Thiago's insistence. The previous night, a trip to the lawyer's house and a bottle of cachaça shared between the three of them had led to two revelations Thiago had been holding onto: (1) Thiago's old friend Usman had been investigating Stumpf's links to a PCC-run brothel in Blumenau with a *Folha de São Paulo* reporter named Sergio Yamada, who had a thing for Galetos chicken. Hence the meeting. (2) Right before the PCC burned up Usman on a stack of tires, Thiago had talked him into giving up a .357 revolver the lawyer had been carrying for protection. Bad timing.

After Edilson and Will had come off the ceiling over Thiago's secretiveness and after Thiago had stopped blubbering over getting his friend killed, they had made some decisions. They needed to see what Sergio Yamada had on Oscar Stumpf. And they needed to be very, very careful about making sure they didn't burn too.

But all three men had agreed to press on. They accepted the risk that Renner was going to fuck up; lonely and needing validation, he would almost certainly return to his old haunts, until Stumpf caught wind and snuffed him. They just had to hope they got something on Stumpf before that happened.

What the fuck had Will gotten himself into? And was his agenda the same as everybody else's? He figured he needed to watch Edilson closest of all. The man had serious unfinished business with the PCC. Will figured that might be the whole point of his involvement, but he couldn't be sure just yet. Conflicting agendas were a very bad thing, indeed. Even worse was a man with the resources of Oscar Stumpf on their asses.

So they had agreed on what Will thought of as a Crazy Ivan play. Former QBs like Will always thought in terms of plays. In the Cold War, when Russian submarine captains thought they were being followed by a Western sub, they would sometimes do a 180-degree turn on their tormentor. A Crazy Ivan. It was often enough to rattle the other guy, throw him off his game. Will had seen some of the more savvy criminals he'd surveilled do much the same thing. Making the hunter the hunted. They had all agreed that being passive would only result in a slightly later date on their tombstones. So they were going on the offensive. Picking Sergio Yamada's brain was the first step.

Beside him, Thiago was exasperated. "I sense you are more comfortable meeting your 'snitches,' as you call them, in drug dens and strip bars. My friend Sergio is no such beast. And don't call him a snitch. Anyway, what do you have against Galetos? The chicken is nice!" He patted his ample belly, which stretched against the buttons of a guayabera shirt. Will was certain he'd formed his opinion on Galetos chicken based on lots of experience. "Reporters are used to expense-account lunches. He's a creature of habit."

Reporters. Will gritted his teeth. Since his ordeal after the shooting, and in fact long before, hardly his favourite creatures. But the good ones, the ones who didn't simply poach their stories off the AP wire, the ones who knew where the bodies were buried ... well, they had their uses. A pragmatist like Will Bryant might even buy one lunch if it would help him get a few inches closer to Oscar Stumpf. Getting closer to Oscar Stumpf was like going up the river in *Apocalypse Now*. It was his mission, so he was going to make it happen, but he sure as shit wasn't looking forward to it.

Sergio Yamada showed up right on time, by Brazilian standards. Thiago grabbed the slight Japaneiro in an effusive hug. Sergio was still Japanese enough to accept it with mild discomfort. He wore bright colours, with spiky shoes and modish hair. The thick glasses and crow's feet were the only concessions to age. He then held out his hand to Will. "Pleased to meet you, Mr. Bryant," he said in flawless Oxford English.

Okay, maybe this guy wasn't a hack. Could be worth shelling out for the chicken. Still, when Will had heard "Yamada," he had been hoping for a business lunch in

Liberdade, maybe one of the better spots like Tako or Yassu ... but this guy had to like Galetos.

They had taken a table at the far end of the sidewalk glass enclosure. The greenhouse heat of the midday sun had driven the Avenida Paulista business-lunch crowd into the air-conditioned interior. Will didn't mind the heat. And the freedom from curious ears was essential. Outside, the suited and cellphoned elite and the insufferably gorgeous businesswomen in tight tube skirts and stiletto heels drifted by in a rushed cloud. Only the traffic remained stationary.

Thiago had to prompt his friend, who lingered uncertainly over a draft beer. Cops and reporters always sniffed each other out like rattlesnakes in mating season.

"Sergio, I know you have been following Oscar Stumpf for years. Could you give my friend Will a little background?"

Sergio cleared his throat. Will got an unpleasant flash: Sergio in his starched red shirt, trapped in a mound of gas-soaked tires. He pushed it away.

"You probably know Oscar Stumpf as a real estate developer and construction magnate today. He has other interests, but that's his primary business. But do you know how he made his first fortune?" Sergio looked around the room and then his eyes narrowed on a brown-suited man lingering too long outside.

Will was tempted to laugh out loud at the pretence of tradecraft, but he let it go. "No, I don't."

Sergio paused for effect. "Neither do I."

"Pardon me?"

"I have worked financial news for 20 years. Always, when you are investigating someone, the first question is how did they get into the game? How did they make their money? The answer with Stumpf is nobody knows. He isn't from a rich family. His father was a butcher."

The irony, Will thought.

Sergio continued, "So, usually, when that happens, it's drug money. But in all the years I have been watching him, I have never come across a single indication of this." He then sucked all the meat off a drumstick in one go. *Jesus Christ*, Will thought, *this guy has the worst table manners of any Nip I've ever met. Maybe that's why the Yamato race treated their expatriate comrades like shit back in the mother country. Too Brazilian, not Japanese enough.*

Sergio continued, "He doesn't move drugs."

Will wasn't convinced. "Maybe he's just too good to get caught? Or too connected?"

Sergio smiled smugly. "Or maybe the army really made him, like the Americans say, 'all you can be'?"

Thiago leaned forward. "How?"

Sergio looked around again. This time, there was nobody to narrow his eyes at. "All I know is he was in military intelligence in the mid-seventies. And that means only one thing: Operation Condor."

Will was keenly aware that he was a poor study. "What?"

Thiago said, "Operation Condor was a continent-wide effort, coordinated by the CIA, to guarantee cooperation between the militaries and police forces of South America to combat Communism. Brazil was involved, along with Argentina, Chile, Uruguay, and others. Perhaps as many as 30,000 people were 'disappeared,' including two of my classmates at Anhembi Morumbi. Stumpf had to have been involved."

Will leaned back in his chair. He had always defined himself, to the extent that he cared, as politically slightly to the right of Genghis Khan. To him, all this shit was just commies whining about losing the Cold War. He was interested in what Stumpf was into now, not 40 years ago. And he definitely wasn't into signing up for some pinko crusade against the Great Satan.

"So he whacked some reds. How'd he make a fortune out of that?"

Thiago looked offended. "So easy it is for you to say. Okay, Will, so you don't care if some rebel gets shot? Perhaps I don't either; I never agreed with Horacio or Marcella, and I am quite sure they would have put me up against the wall if the party had ordered it. Poetic justice for them to run into Stumpf, I suppose, except ..."

"Except?"

"What happened to their children, Will?"

Sergio interjected, "In Argentina, at least, we know that the children of the disappeared were given to regime supporters. Hundreds have been reunited with their biological parents since the government there began investigating in earnest. But in Brazil, there has been no accounting."

Kids. That was different. "That's shitty to be sure. But how does this relate to Stumpf and his mystery millions?"

Again, Sergio did his theatrical scan of the room. It was clear to Will that nobody in earshot gave a shit. "Last year, I went to Asunción, Paraguay. Back in '92, a survivor of Operation Condor and an investigating judge found an archive there on Condor. I found Stumpf's name in it."

Now Will had dropped the cool act and was leaning forward. "What was he into? What made him that money?"

"The whole point of Condor was that South American countries could do each other favours to sort out their problems. Oscar Stumpf was part of that. In 1978 he was a liaison officer in Buenos Aires. There are fragments of correspondence between him and agents of the Vidalia regime in Argentina. But not enough to prove anything, so I've never been able to publish. But I am sure his fortune comes from this time, and it is blood money, Mr. Bryant. In 2008, my paper published allegations that the military dictatorship killed two former presidents; I was part of that team. I am not afraid. But we need proof before we publish. But how he made the money? Gold teeth?" Sergio Yamada suppressed a ghoulish laugh and drained his beer in one go.

"How did he turn blood into money?" Thiago wondered aloud.

It came to Will absolutely clear. "He killed on consignment. They shipped; he filled orders."

As the office drones headed back to their hives, all three men held up their glasses for another drink.

11

Oscar Freire, São Paulo

Will looked around at the plastic surgery triumphs walking decorative dogs and felt like a Jew at a pig roast. It was probably costing him money just to stand on this street. Oscar Freire was where the rich who rode helicopters from places like Southern Cross actually let their Salvatore Ferragamos touch the pavement. Here, if you felt like you needed a $2,000 fountain pen, it could be had. These were the sort of people Luc Renner had been fleecing for overpriced Bordeaux until he'd made the mistake of doing business with Oscar Stumpf, the man they were meeting today.

Three days prior Sergio had casually asked, "Do you want to meet him?" and Will had felt his courage falter. He had been flabbergasted that Sergio had that sort of access and said so.

"Well, he may be powerful. He may be secretive. And he may hate reporters. But he's a businessman, and businessmen need publicity. And that means he has to deal with me." That smug smile again.

And so, here Will was, as dressed up as he ever got, painfully aware that his court suit didn't fit him anymore. He was also painfully aware that he looked nothing like the stringer for MacLean's he was supposed to be posing as. But he couldn't exactly introduce himself as "Will Bryant, washed-up ex-cop. Gonna try and send you to prison," now could he?

The last couple of days had crawled by. Edilson had called and told him he was working on the PCC angle. But Will had had nothing to do, so he'd returned to his old routine. He'd spent the weekend with his kids, driven out to Atibaia, taught a few lessons. But he'd been moody and distracted, suddenly tuned in to how mundane this routine had become. People talking to him had needed to repeat themselves. He'd been zoned out, thinking about coming face to face with Oscar Stumpf.

Will had dealt with killers before but, if the stories about Stumpf were even partially true, nobody on his scale. How would that feel, shaking that hand? Melodrama. Keep it cool, fool.

Well, he hadn't exactly had nothing to do. Sergio had given him some homework. A collection of his own reporting, the Asunción Arquivos do Terror, and some documents released by the Cardoso government in 2000. The picture was fragmentary at best, and there was no smoking gun, but he now knew much more about Oscar Stumpf than he had a few days before.

Oscar Stumpf had been born in 1948 to a second-generation German father and an Italian-Argentine mother.

He had grown up in Curitiba and earned a place in the Academia de Militar das Agulhas Negras, the Brazilian West Point, in 1966 as part of a new wave of middle-class officers who were transforming the *ejercito*. He had been a star right away and had been sent to intelligence training as soon as he'd been commissioned in 1970. His fluent Spanish would come in handy in the years ahead as the military dictatorships in Latin America banded together with the assistance of the CIA to fight what they saw as a rising tide of Communism. In 1964, the generals had overthrown the regime of the left-leaning President "Jango" Goulart when his proposed economic and social reforms began to smack of Marxism. They'd commenced what was, compared to events elsewhere, a moderate authoritarian regime.

But people had still disappeared. They had still been tortured. They had still been executed. Lieutenant Stumpf had been sent on his first assignment in Uruguay in 1971. Probably not coincidentally, as the Brazilian government was suspected of having helped their compatriots there defeat leftists in a rigged election.

The year 1973 had been a big one for Stumpf. He'd trained under the notorious French general, assassin, and torturer Paul Aussaresses. Aussaresses had learned his trade in the Algerian Civil War, massacring civilians in reprisal raids, staging faked suicides of opposition figures, and generally being a first-class medieval nightmare. Will didn't have a hard time imagining what Stumpf had learned from the one-eyed killer. Just in time too, because September had brought the fall of the Allende regime in Chile and the genesis of Operation Condor.

In 1976, after participating in counter-insurgency operations against the Marxist guerrillas in Araguaia, now Capitano Stumpf had been sent to Buenos Aires as a military attaché. The Asunción Arquivos had little to say on what he'd done there, but the files from the Argentine secret police agency SIDE suggested frequent contacts, as his name came up often. Also mentioned in the Arquivos in the same document as Stumpf was an agent of the Chilean DINA named Enrique Arancibia Clavel. Clavel, the killer of two Chilean generals who had opposed the Allende coup and a central figure in Operation Condor, had recently died after serving 20 years in prison.

Clearly, Stumpf didn't want to wind up like Clavel. Will had a feeling that was the motivation for the murder of Marco Hellmer and maybe everything to do with Southern Cross. After all, nobody knew where the bodies were buried, did they? Presidente Sarney had said publicly that they pretty much didn't even ask. And if Oscar Stumpf had learned from people like Paul Aussaresses and Enrique Clavel, there might be a lot of bodies. Maybe some of them weren't even Brazilians. After all, Operation Condor was all about helping out your neighbours, wasn't it?

Was that it? Was Southern Cross being built over a grave? It would be pretty hard to dig up the backyards of the movers and shakers on a hunch, wouldn't it?

It was a moment of clarity that Will Bryant savoured, standing in the sun in his too-tight suit, devoutly wishing for a caipirinha in his hand. A moment that came all too rarely to a victim of two concussions.

Sergio was suddenly standing beside him. "You're not getting married, you know. It's only a lunch meeting. Brazilians aren't that formal."

Fuck that. "I am not showing up in a golf shirt and chinos for this guy." He took in the fact that Sergio was wearing a golf shirt and chinos. "No offence."

Sergio snorted. "Suits he doesn't care about. But he hates lateness."

"He's in the wrong country then."

"Let's go."

They dodged traffic to get across the street, entering an air-conditioned foyer to be greeted by a man dressed as a gaucho.

"He chose the meeting place?"

"Of course. He chooses everything. He is what you call, a 'control freak.'"

"I guess you can take the boy out of South Brazil, but ..."

"Yes, he likes his meat. If you are a vegetarian, the salad bar is very good."

"Do I look like a vegetarian, Sergio?"

Standing uncomfortably in his too-small suit, Will Bryant looked to Sergio Yamada like someone who ate vegetarians. "Then enjoy your *picanha*."

Will figured in the presence of a wolf like Oscar Stumpf he'd be lucky to get down a salad. Ordinarily he'd clean out the place. The two men were ushered past standing sides of beef propped up next to open flame and massive salad bars flanked by rows of olive oil and balsamic vinegar. Despite himself, he started to salivate a little. They took a booth in the back. "Senhor Stumpf's favourite," the supercilious maître d' dressed like Tom Mix told them.

"Bebidas, senhors?"

"Sim. Caipirinha com Sagatiba por favor." Will could handle his liquor and needed a belt for this one.

"Coca, por favor," Sergio replied. Will was surprised. Like most reporters, he was a lush. Three days ago, they'd had to pour him into a cab. "I don't drink around this man. Maintain control. He counts on you losing it."

"Then he'll have to buy me a lot of drinks."

Sergio rolled his eyes at the Canadense. "He can afford them. Can you?"

Will looked evenly at Sergio. "I know bad men, Sergio. I'm no virgin."

"You don't know any this bad." Yamada ran his fingers through his spiky hair, looking around nervously.

The nerves started rubbing off on Will too. He wished that drink would arrive. Looking around in hopes of spotting the waiter, Will noticed something else.

Will had seen only a few pictures of Stumpf but knew it was him as soon as he walked in. The guy had juice around here and parted the crowd like a rabid skunk. Will had grabbed a seat facing the entrance, an old cop habit. It gave him time to read a subject, time he now savoured. He watched the man in studious slow motion.

Navy golf shirt. Khakis. Over-the-top Rolex and subdued platinum chain, the only admissions of wealth. He didn't need to display. Receding hairline, slicked-back hair, obviously coloured jet black to hold off advancing age. Will would bet on a Viagra prescription and an acrobatic 21-year-old in the background. Short, a slight gut but kept under control. The remnants of a soldier's muscles on sun-spotted arms. Control. As he came closer, navigating smoothly, steel-blue eyes. Cold.

But smiling and polished, he put his hand out.

Sergio was on his feet. "A pleasure as always, Senhor Stumpf. Allow me to introduce my Canadian colleague, William Cousins."

Stumpf regarded him and put a hand on his shoulder. Could you feel power? The squeeze was barely perceptible, but it was there. He smelled clean and subtly sweet.

"Canada. I love Canada. So clean. So cool. So empty. Everything this country is not." His teeth were bright and straight. "And what could possibly interest Canadians about a simple Brazilian businessman, Mr. Cousins?"

Will hesitated a moment, knew he was being probed. "Men with your portfolio are never simple, *senhor*. You always make a good story."

The drilling eyes stayed firm. "And what kind of story are you writing, Mr. Cousins? The kind of left-wing muckraking Senhor Yamada and his friends at *Folha* specialize in?" He grinned over at Sergio. "What crime have I committed now? Perhaps one of my construction trucks ran over a capybara?"

They all shared a forced laugh while they took their seats. "I hope you like meat, Mr. Cousins. Have you been to a *churrascaria* before?"

"I was thinking of skipping the hotel and just sleeping in one."

Stumpf uttered a machine-gun laugh and switched to Portuguese. "I like this guy, Sergio. He is not your average gringo. So I think you have brought him here to knock me out, hmm?"

"*Eu entende, senhor. Eu fala Portuguese.*"

"Just checking, Cousins."

"Actually, I am just writing a story on heli-commuting. It could be the wave of the future in Toronto."

"But of course you are. Toronto. An interesting town. So much more manageable than this chaos."

"But not as exciting. Do you prefer order and boredom over excitement and chaos?" Jesus, he was sounding like a VH1 shill interviewing Justin Bieber. Well, you had to come in soft at first with this guy.

"A tricky question, Mr. Cousins. I am certain Canadians look at us and think, *Why can't we be this exciting? Why can't we be so spontaneous, so musical, so … sexual?*" He was talking with his hands now. Will was beginning to get how persuasive the man could be. Stumpf continued, "But you have to see that this African nature in our country comes at a price. Crime is tolerated. Garbage lies in the street. Taxes aren't collected. Policemen are just another category of criminal. Enjoy your boring country, Mr. Cousins. Good hospitals are more important than samba."

"Oh, I don't know, *senhor*," Will said. "Some of your hospitals are pretty good. Your middle class is expanding. The favelas are being pacified. You are hosting the Copa de Mundo and the Olympics."

Stumpf snorted and waved his hand. "Look at our sidewalks! You must be able to afford a good watch, Mr. Cousins. So why aren't you wearing it?" Stumpf asked, chuckling.

Will had to admit Stumpf had a point. But wasn't a businessman supposed to be a cheerleader? Or was the pessimism part of the sales pitch?

"So why invest in Brazil, then? Surely you don't want my readers to hear nothing but problems?" He made to continue, but Stumpf cut him off. A frequent habit of powerful men.

"The problems are opportunities, as the Chinese like to say. The problems encourage people like me, who want to build a different lifestyle here." The drinks arrived, and Stumpf paused to sip at his Scotch. "This is why I started building for the heli-commuters. These people will build a new Brazil, not the people who pay for tennis shoes in 10 instalments."

Will noticed the thinly veiled contempt of the underclasses and said nothing. From what he'd seen, the people Stumpf catered to couldn't get a lawn mowed without the people in the mortgaged shoes. He sipped his caipirinha. Stumpf was watching him. "Caipirinhas and women. Two things in Brazil that are impossible to compare to anywhere else, no?" He dipped his fingers in his Scotch and licked them. Will had a sudden insight that perhaps Stumpf had hit on blackmailing pedophiles as a reflection of his own proclivities. For the moment, it was just an instinctual conclusion. Maybe he wanted to believe it.

"Certainly, *senhor*." Will held his smile for a moment. "Tell me about Southern Cross."

Stumpf held his arms on the table and leaned back, as if preparing for some physical exertion, warming up for the pitch. "Southern Cross is a little bit of Canada on the outskirts of São Paulo. Consider that one of my competitors has even named his project 'Canada.' That order and predictability that you take for granted is much in demand here. In Southern Cross, there is order. Cleanliness. Privacy.

Security. Neighbours can associate on their lawns, something I am sure is common in Canada, but here, the walls we must live behind make it impossible. In Southern Cross, the walls on the outside free the people on the inside."

"Don't you think there's a danger in further distancing the rulers from the ruled?"

Stumpf looked at him as if he were a lunatic. "That sounds Bolshevist, Mr. Cousins. Are you a Bolshevik?" He tempered it with a phony smile.

I'm asking the fucking questions here, Will thought. Now he was getting under the skin. "Bolsheviks don't tend to have long careers in financial news, Senhor Stumpf. But the question remains. How do the inhabitants of Southern Cross stay engaged with the people who work for them and buy their products?"

"Their money stays engaged. That is all that is required. You make it sound as if my clients are some class of African kleptocrats. But our money stays in Brazil, and so do our children. Your 'engagement,' as you call it, means little to people who are afraid their children will be kidnapped for ransom."

He was sounding political now. "Have you ever thought of running for office?" Will asked, noticing that Sergio was watching intently.

"Too many compromises. I am not a man of compromises." He smiled a tight smile and sipped his Scotch. "I am a soldier." He straightened his back as he said it.

"Tell me about that."

Stumpf narrowed his eyes. Will again noticed the Rolex. Clearly, Stumpf wasn't afraid to wear it. Will then noticed the two lunks taking up a table by the door and drinking water and understood why.

"What do you want to know?"

"What did you do in the army?"

"Military intelligence."

"I gather that must have been pretty boring, since Brazil hasn't had any wars to fight for a long time." Will was goading him now, seeing if he would jump.

"There are always wars to fight."

"Which war was yours?"

Stumpf seemed relaxed. Will knew he was being clumsy. "Surely intelligence officers in Canada don't talk about their work?"

"If they do, they write a book."

Stumpf smiled tightly. "Well, perhaps I will someday. Perhaps you can buy it."

"Perhaps you can autograph it." *The chapter about Operation Condor, perhaps*, Will thought.

"Anyway, who cares about this. It was a long time ago."

"Some people care very much about what Brazilian military intelligence was doing in the 1970s." Dangerous ground was ahead, and Will knew he was being ham-fisted. But he had to push it, had to see what was under the control. He might not get another chance.

"Bolshevists. And reporters." Stumpf sneered. Another sip of Scotch.

"And Bolshevist reporters." Will eased back.

Stumpf laughed. "Exactly!"

Will took the exit. No point in making him mad. "Who are your investors?"

Stumpf looked exasperated. "That is almost as sensitive a subject as intelligence work."

"Shall we discuss the weather?"

"My investors are friends, prior associates in other ventures, and people they have vouched for. I do not need to advertise. I want people who know what they want and aren't afraid of risk."

But who are afraid of prosecution, Will thought. "Can I talk to some of them?" he asked as guilelessly as he could.

"No, you may not."

"It's a real estate project, not a child porn website. Why the secrecy?" Will noticed a reaction at the mention of CP.

"You are a very curious reporter, Mr. Cousins. More like a policeman, I think."

It was Will's turn to hide a reaction. "If by that you mean I am an asshole, thank you. Comes with the territory, I think."

"Why so interested in my investors? Do you think I am laundering money?"

"I write for investors. Like most people, they like to ride the elevator with people like themselves."

"Very good answer. Did you practice that?" Stumpf was goading him now.

"Men like us practice everything, *senhor.*"

"Yes, I think that's true." They were interrupted by a gaucho with a skewer of beef. "Try the *picanha*, Mr. Cousins. Good fuel for combat."

Will grabbed his tongs and pulled a bloody piece onto his plate. "Is that what this is? Combat?"

"All life is combat."

"Spoken like a soldier." Will speared a tender piece of beef and put it in his mouth. The taste was subtle, salty, rich with intoxicating fat.

"Once a soldier, always a soldier. Once a cop, always a cop."

"I wouldn't know."

"Of course." Stumpf tasted his *picanha*. "Delicious, don't you think?"

"Almost as good as the women."

Stumpf laughed around a mouthful of beef. "Almost. Where are you staying, Mr. Cousins?"

Shit. He hadn't thought of that. A lie was only three questions deep, and he wasn't deep enough for the likes of Stumpf. "Golden Tulip." He would have to remember to bribe Vincente on the front desk.

"Acceptable. Have you been out much in São Paulo?"

Ever the gracious host. Was Stumpf going to try to blackmail him too? "I've been pretty busy. But I know what I like." He was daring Stumpf to probe further.

"And what does William Cousins like?"

"Like Martin Luther said, wine, women, and song."

"Certainly São Paulo has the last two in great abundance, but wine? As a proud southerner I would love to sing the praises of Rio Grande do Sul wine, but let's be honest."

"Wine is important to you, *senhor*?"

"I thought this was a business piece."

"It is. But us Norteamericanos like a face on our money. Indulge me. My readers may even learn something about wine, which they love to spend money on but know very little about."

"Like so many rich men, Mr. Cousins, I delegate this responsibility to someone more knowledgeable."

"Anyone you'd recommend?"

"I would, but sadly he appears to have gone out of business."

"It wasn't that Frenchman in Morumbi, was it? He came recommended." Now Will was in his element, pushing the envelope disguised as a guileless fool, trying to get Stumpf to say something about Luc Renner.

Stumpf speared a sausage on his plate and devoured it in one bite. "Lots of Frenchmen sell wine here. Most of them trying to rob us gullible provincials. Why are you so interested in this one?"

Stumpf rested his fist on his chin as he stared at Will, sausage grease trickling between his fingers.

Will tried the cool save. "Because he had a going-out-of-business sale. Thousand-real bottles for only five hundred." He wasn't fooling himself anymore. He felt as if Stumpf had turned the tables on him. Stumpf had to have known the man had simply not shown up one day, and that was that.

"Perhaps you ought to be writing for *Wine Spectator*, Mr. Cousins. As for me, I can always get fleeced somewhere else." Stumpf was now looking at Will as if his shoes were mortgaged. Maybe that was good. He had always relied on the Lieutenant Colombo act with people like Stumpf. If they felt superior, they made mistakes. But Will appeared to be making enough for both of them.

But Stumpf hadn't asked, "What Frenchman in Morumbi?" had he? Stumpf was now looking rather put out and glanced over his shoulder in the direction of the two lunks by the door. Time to go.

"Perhaps we can meet again and talk more. As for me, I have a pressing engagement, and I must leave. But please, stay and enjoy." He stood to leave. Will and Sergio stood and shook his hand.

When he came to Will, Stumpf held the shake a little too long, a little too hard. He smiled, but the look was unmistakable: don't fuck me. Will was suddenly drained. How did it feel? He didn't know the answer. Too much to process.

The two lunks by the door wordlessly followed Stumpf into the street. One of them looked uncannily like Duda.

Will slumped back into his seat. Sergio was watching him intently. "Well, what do you think?"

Will held up his glass for another caipirinha. "He's a killer. And he knows I'm a fake." He took out his cellphone and dialled the Golden Tulip.

"Be careful."

"Being careful is so yesterday."

12

Clinicas, São Paulo

Metro Clinicas was a bit of hike from Oscar Freire, but Will had walked these streets before and liked it. Besides, the Oscar Freire station on the Linha Amarelha was still under construction, so he didn't have much of a choice.

After Oscar Stumpf had left, Will and Sergio had let off steam on Stumpf's considerable dime. Sergio had relaxed in the absence of his nemesis and matched Will shot for shot. Will had poured the Japaneiro into another cab just before sundown, to the obvious relief of the set-upon gauchos.

Will, on the other hand, was a big man with the capacity to absorb the punishment. Still, he was glad for the walk through Clinicas, which he always found a refreshing island of sanity in the middle of São Paulo. After crossing a sketchy and much-graffitied pedestrian overpass, he descended to a wide boulevard with a massive hospital complex on both sides. The hospital zone led to an enforced silence, which distinguished this area from much of the rest of São Paulo.

The people on the street were mostly dressed in surgical scrubs or lab coats. The night was on the cool side, and the air here felt clean. Will's mood was buoyed by this as much as the drink and the knowledge that he hadn't completely fucked up his first meeting with Oscar Stumpf. Well, at least he thought he hadn't.

He called Edilson and, getting the machine, left a message for Edilson to call him tomorrow. He needed time to digest things. He went into iPod mode. Stereolab played discordant and mechanical sounds. He found it strangely appropriate for São Paulo.

> They are one of the same
>
> Two inevitables
>
> We can't avoid dying
>
> Bursting through our barriers
>
> They are one of the same
>
> Two inevitables

He entered the wide underground passage to the Metro. The space was cool, decorated with murals, clean. It felt more like Paris to Will, maybe La Défense? In his old job, he'd had a lot of opportunities to travel; it gave him a wide array of yardsticks for comparison. Maybe he would've been happier in São Paulo if he had less to compare it to, he reflected.

As his mind wandered, it wandered back to Stumpf. All he knew now about the man led him to conclude that Southern Cross was far more than a tawdry blackmail scam. It was a system, a system with a goal. Oscar Stumpf's background in military intelligence had given him ample experience in running such systems.

Will was not unfamiliar with them, either. In his past life, the office he'd worked out of had had large charts on every available wall, detailing the linkages between suspects, businesses, places. Some of them were mind-numbing. The analysts who kept it all straight were a special breed, not the sort you'd want to play chess against if there was any money riding on it. But most of them were wall-flowers, not street types. Oscar Stumpf was definitely no wallflower, but he was keeping one hell of a lot of balls in the air:

His 'legitimate' businesses.

His intelligence network (how else had he known so much about Luc Renner, Marco Hellmer, and their deviant friends?). This meant technical sophistication, maybe people inside government?

The brothel in Santa Catarina, masquerading as a modelling agency. The probable links that required with the PCC.

Southern Cross itself. Controlling the ground. Keeping the secret.

Will wouldn't know for sure until he'd talked to his partners, but he figured his next step was to go south. Find some of those girls. See who would talk. A tall order.

Will boarded the escalator down to the platform. The station was deserted. Rush hour was over, and Clinicas was one of the few stations on the Metro with excess capacity anyway.

People are pressed, liberties crushed

Shouldn't it resound, cry of our soul?

It is so faint I can't hear it, I know it's there

Somewhere, somewhere, somewhere

The music synched with his thoughts as he stared into the track. The answer was somewhere, somewhere, somewhere. And it involved a whole bunch of people whose liberties, and bodies, had been crushed when he'd still been a child. What had he gotten into?

He felt the rush of air signalling an oncoming train. He looked to his left and saw a shadow moving over his shoulder. Instinctively he began to spin around. He caught a handful of jacket as he felt the push.

The hard blow between his shoulder blades knocked the air out of him as he toppled forward into the track bed. But he still had that handful of jacket, and his assailant came with him. Spinning, Will landed on his side across the tracks. His attacker lay next to him in a grotesque parody of a lover's spoon. The lights of the train blinded him as he scrambled for the shelter of the overhang. Will was unthinking, reacting, his mind a blank. A thought forced its way to the surface: Where was the third rail?

He rolled over the side of the tracks. His attacker reached out and grabbed his pant leg, staring in horror and desperation. He looked a lot like Duda, Will thought as he took a mental snapshot. The smell of superheated metal permeated his nostrils. At that moment, he thought he screamed, but he couldn't be sure. As before, in the Tim Hortons, he heard nothing.

The train separated him and his attacker in a blast of hot sparks and wind-tunnel air. Will curled tightly against the wall. The attacker's hand still clutched his pant leg. Everything else was on the other side. He smelled iron now. The end of the hand pumped out its last supply of blood. Will kicked it off in revulsion.

After a minor forever, the train departed. Will's brain began to reawaken from survival mode as he stared at the puddle of gore that had been his attacker. The train driver must have seen the "accident." Otherwise he would have stopped. Now the tracks were clear for the authorities, who were no doubt on the way. There was a police station just around the corner. Being friends with a lowly *soldado* would not carry enough pull to get him out of this mess. He had to get out of there before they showed up. He pulled himself up over the ledge and onto the platform, scrambling to his feet in time to see a tall man in a black leather jacket sprinting up the escalator.

I know you, asshole. I saw you in the restaurant. Will forced himself to scan the body parts of his attacker and spotted it, lying off to the side. He jumped into the track bed again and grabbed "Duda's" Glock. Sitting next to it was an intact spleen. Vaulting up over the side again, he sprinted for the escalator, past an astonished *dona de casa* in a floral hat. As he ran, he ripped off his blood-covered suit jacket and threw it in a trash can at the top of the escalator. No point being the guy with all the blood on him when the cops showed up.

He had just seen the man from the platform duck down a side corridor when three Polícia Militar sprinted toward him. It took a supreme effort of will to slow his pace and breathe normally. The Glock felt heavy in the small of his back.

The three cops didn't slow down as they raced down the escalator into the station. Will took a chance that there wouldn't be any others for a minute and sprinted after his other attacker. He raced down a corridor, the Glock in his hand now. A man in a lab coat gaped at him.

"Polícia!" he shouted. "Did you see a tall man in a black leather jacket?"

The man gaped, staring at the Glock. Civilians took longer to process this kind of shit, even here.

"Tell me where he went!"

The man's eyes never left the Glock as he pointed to a stairwell leading up to the street. Will took the steps two at a time and rounded a corner.

More steps. The barrel of a gun and one eye looking down at him. A flash. He felt the round, close. He dropped to his belly, felt the stairs in his ribs. He brought the Glock up, fired fast and wild. He struggled back up the stairs, firing blind at his opponent's last position to keep his head down. Now he really had to get out of here. He heard sirens getting closer. He came up the stairs in room-clearing mode, scanning with the pistol. His lungs burned. Across the street, the tall man, now without a jacket, was getting into the front seat of a black Renault.

Will started into the street, where an ambulance almost killed him.

When the cavalcade of emergency vehicles had passed, the Renault was gone too.

It dawned on Will that he was an illegally armed foreigner far too close to the scene of a crime. He limped across the street, his bad knee sending shooting pains into his slowly reawakening brain, and dumped the Glock in a trash bin after a hurried wipe-down. He patted his pockets and sighed with relief when he found his cellphone. If it had been left at the scene ... He tried Edilson again and got him on the third ring.

"Come and get me. Oscar Stumpf just tried to kill me."

13

Rua Itaopolis, by Pacaembu Stadium

Edilson drove fast as Will hunched down in the back seat.

"Shit!" Will swore.

"What, man?"

"My fucking iPod. I can't afford another iPod."

"Are you fucking kidding me, gringo? Somebody tries to assassinate you, and you are worried about your iPod? *Meu Deus*, and you call me crazy!"

Will laughed out loud. "Assassinate me? Maybe they were just trying to give me a hand ... get it?"

Edilson groaned. "You call me a fucking psycho? Listen, you need to focus: Did you leave anything behind there that can identify you, besides your iPod and your jacket? Was there anything in the pockets?"

Will tried to remember. "No ... at least I don't think so." He felt drunk now.

Edilson slammed the steering wheel in frustration. "Think harder, man! If there's even a credit card receipt there, you'll have to come up with a story for why your jacket is there. They'll know there was a foreigner there, because of your iPod and your jacket ... I bet they're from Canada, right?"

"Yes." Will was not liking the implications.

"Of course, that's if they do a proper investigation. That doesn't always happen here."

"But somebody died who worked for Oscar Stumpf."

"Somebody who did very illegal things for Oscar Stumpf."

"I see your point."

"Well," Edilson said, looking over his shoulder after bullying a Fiat out of the fast lane, "maybe we're about to find out how much influence Oscar Stumpf really has. This time he could actually be our best friend."

"Until he tries to kill me again."

Edilson laughed. "Oh *verdade*, amigo, until then. But next time, we'll be ready." He tossed a heavy object wrapped in a rag into the back seat. It bounced off Will's trick knee.

"Ow. Jesus fuck, Edilson!"

"*Desculpe*, buddy. And don't say this about Jesus. A little insurance. Take it; it's yours. Untraceable. From the 'accidents will happen' collection, understand?"

"I understand." Will unwrapped a Taurus .40 calibre, a gun he was certain was formerly destined to be found in the hand of a previously unarmed but now very dead *ladrao*. "Why do you think he moved so fast? Have you been watching Renner?"

"Like an owl, buddy. Oh, that's what I forgot to tell you." He tossed the late edition of *Folha* onto Will's lap. Marco's death was on the front page. "They found Marco's body. He's panicking."

Edilson continued, "Stumpf knew about the body before Sergio did. So he must have somebody on the cops down there. We need to be careful. And you mention military intelligence, Southern Cross, and French wine merchant, in the same conversation, on top of that? You're lucky he didn't have you shot for dessert. I told you not to get drunk."

Will bristled at the lecture from Mr. Reckless himself. "I did not get drunk. While he was there."

"Ah, so that's how you think when you're sober? It's a good thing there's not a lot of crime in Canada. I don't know how you guys would cope."

Will saw the smirk and laughed. "Okay, smart guy. Tell me what to say to Silvia, then?"

"Ah."

"I thought so."

They pulled hard down Maria Amalia onto Francisco Narcizo, where Edilson, who couldn't wait to get on, deposited Will. The man wasn't afraid of shootouts with vicious gangsters, but pissed-off wives were another thing entirely, Will observed.

Will tucked the Taurus away as best he could and tried to enter quietly.

She caught him on the second-floor landing. "*Oi, gatinho. Tudo bem?* Trying to sneak past your wife again?"

He turned to face her. Her face was so mobile. Sometimes it could be the most open and warmest he had ever seen. This was not one of those times.

He kept turned so as to hide the Taurus and considered his words before he spoke. "It's this job, love. We need to talk."

Her face opened somewhat; the grimace softened. "Are you in trouble, honey?"

"We all might be."

She gave him some space to clean up. He hid the Taurus in a high cabinet in the office, locked it, and pocketed the key. He relished a hot shower, but the water was a trickle due to rationing again, and he had to content himself with being merely moist. He changed and came downstairs to face the jury.

The jury sat on the sofa, arms wrapped around her knees, peeking out at him from behind long chocolate bangs. What kind of a husband would endanger her?

He sat down and told her more or less the whole story. She listened carefully and then slapped him hard, once, in the mouth. "Listen to me, cop!" she hissed, a contemptuous emphasis on the last word. "You came down here to get away from this life, this violence, and now you bring it to your family? How can I explain this to my sister? To Lucas and Gabi? Where can we go now?" She was crying now.

"I am so sorry, my love. I never wanted this. But it just … crept up on me …"

"Now it has crept up on us."

"I know. But the only thing I can do now is attack."

She was silent and then surprisingly said, "Yes, you are right. You have to kill this man."

He was stunned. This was a woman who felt bad if she let a houseplant die. "Kill him? But I thought …"

"That I was a *pacifista*? Yes, love, I am. Except when my family is threatened. Kill this Oscar Stumpf, or it will never be over. Promise me you will do this, and soon."

The words came out before he could think. "Yes, I promise." He had his wet job after all. From the most unlikely of sources.

He reached out to her. They made love, heedless to discovery, and fell asleep entangled.

14

Tremembé

A few shots of good cachaça had produced a sleep Will Bryant had desperately needed. He woke to the sun, filtered through balcony shades, a light breeze toying with the thin drapes. Gabi drooled on his chest, a tiny snore escaping her lips. He kissed her on the forehead and gently slipped out of her grasp. Staring back at his daughter, he dressed as he came to terms with his new reality.

He was a hunted man. A very powerful person wanted him dead. He was also possibly wanted by the police. The first step was to find out about that.

Edilson was unusually attentive to his phone today. "I haven't been to work yet. But there's nothing on the news."

"Strange."

"I don't think so. That's his guy down there. And if he says it is, then he has to explain why his guy was pushing you in front of a train. How do you gringos say it? 'Awkward'?"

Will breathed a little easier. For reasons all cops would understand, death was less fear-inducing than prison. "See what you can find out at work, and meet me in Blumenau on Thursday."

"Okay. Take the gun."

"Don't worry about that." He would've preferred to have Edilson next to him 24-7, but the guy still had a job. He called Thiago next.

"Will, *meu Deus*! Are you okay?"

"*Bom, obrigado.* A fine mess you've gotten me into."

A heavy sigh on the other end of the line. "I told you my cases were never easy. What next?"

"Have you talked to Sergio? I'm worried."

"Don't be. His only problem this morning is keeping his head from exploding and keeping his guts inside his body. Don't be offended, but there's a big difference between killing a well-known reporter and killing you."

"Oh, why should I be offended at that? Listen, have you found out anything that can help me?"

"Possibly. I have been doing research on permits Stumpf has applied for in his various projects. He usually uses the same people for everything. Especially for foundation work. Very important."

"Sure. Fuck up the foundation, and ..."

"Everything else is fucked." Thiago didn't usually swear much. Were the hard edges wearing on him?

"So?"

"So, he usually uses a company out of Campinas. Very reputable. There are only two exceptions listed on the permits I could find."

"Southern Cross and ...?"

"Yes, and a project south of Blumenau. Two kilometres from where they found Marco Hellmer yesterday."

"Looks like I am going to the right place. Who are these guys Stumpf used?"

"Nobody's ever heard of them. They appear in no other permit applications I could find, period. And you won't believe their name."

"Condor?"

"*Exactamente.* Condor Foundations LLC. Pretty bold, isn't he?"

That was one word for it. "Arrogant shit."

"Arrogant and dangerous. Be careful, Will."

"Why start now?" He heard Gabi stirring upstairs and knew why.

"You have protection, Will?"

"I do now. And the girls and Luke will be some-where safe."

"Good."

"And what about you?"

"Don't worry about me. A lawyer who doesn't know how to shoot is more dangerous than a crook who does."

Interesting theory. "Take care. Call every day. Let me know if you find out anything else. And watch Renner carefully."

"I will. *Tchau.*"

"*Tchau.*"

He hurried upstairs for Gabi, his mind racing. She was distraught. Rubbing her eyes, she called out, "*Papai!* I had a bad dream."

He climbed onto the bed and hugged her. She threw her arms around him. He coaxed out the details, which she related in low, confidential tones. She had fallen asleep with her ponytails in, blonde hair askew in different directions. Her lake water blue eyes were moist.

"There were bad guys, Daddy. And they were chasing you ..."

He faked a smile. "And did they catch me?"

"Yes, and they made you lie down in the ground, and they squished you." She sobbed.

Fucking Condor Foundations LLC has paved me over in my daughter's dreams. He held Gabi tight, whispering soothing words. *Enjoy the fantasy win, assholes,* Will mused as he followed his daughter back to sleep. *That's not the way it's going down in real life.*

15

Curitiba, Paraná State

Will had been dozing as Silvia drove, and he woke as they entered the outskirts of Curitiba.

They hadn't wasted any time in packing up and heading south. Six of them were packed into the Toyota, everyone except Roberto, who was staying home to watch over things, unwilling to leave his business on autopilot, doubtless afraid his relatives would rob him blind if he did. They did have a history of doing so. Roberto made things worse by being a pushover, turning a blind eye to every hand thrust into the till. Every hand, that is, but the PCC's. The man found some deeply hidden steel when they tried to shake him down. He'd simply ignored the not-so-subtle request a few years back, and nothing had happened. So the fear wasn't there for him. He'd simply wished Will *boa sorte* and handed him the keys. Will was going to feel a right shit heel if anything happened to Roberto.

He glanced over his shoulder to see his son and nephew sleeping head to head on his sister-in-law's shoulders. His daughter was slumped in her booster seat, and Tais was sleeping too, mouth agape.

"What time is it?" Silvia asked. She never wore a watch.

Will scanned his watch as he looked around. "Nine-thirty."

Curitiba. The start of the Brazil that worked. The one Oscar Stumpf wanted to expand. Even under cover of darkness, you could tell it was different. The streets were wider. Traffic moved. Fewer black faces, more blond hair. Less African, more European. Things clicked. It was still Brazil, but Brazil with a Swiss flavour. Public spaces, clean and relatively safe. Public transit, efficient and cheap. Everything wasn't built right to the curb, like in São Paulo; they'd actually left room for a lawn and a few trees. Hell, they even got snow once in a while. Will got it; he understood what Stumpf was talking about. He'd even bugged Silvia about living here.

"It's clean, and it's safe. I like it."

"It's boring, come on!"

"Boring is good."

"Says the cop."

Silvia was wedded to São Paulo, like those dyed-in-the-wool New Yorkers you read about who couldn't live without their Katz's pastrami and Barney's smoked sturgeon. Will found it ridiculous, but he hadn't grown up in a metropolis. Vancouver was a world city only in the sense of inflated real estate prices and a reasonable variety of ethnic restaurants. In every other sense that mattered, it was still provincial. That was just fine with Will. It wasn't with Silvia. Another one of the many tensions that made the relationship interesting. Will figured that as long they had something to disagree about, they wouldn't get bored. So far, the theory had held.

Curitiba was also the hometown of Oscar Stumpf. But Will had no time to snoop and precious little inclination to alert Stumpf to his presence here, for what he was sure were limited returns. Blumenau and its PCC honeypot was the objective.

The plan was to drop off the family in Jaragua do Sul, north of Blumenau, far enough away from the action that they ought to be safe until things blew over. That was the theory, anyway. Tio Fred in Jaragua was a good guy and handy with a double-barrelled shotgun, but was that really enough? Where your kids were concerned, you needed to be sure. Maybe he was just being paranoid. Surviving an assassination attempt would do that to you.

Will lowered the window and caught the cool air, the smell of ethanol, fried food, the smell of Brazil from one end to the other. A suicidally driven truck passing them on the right pulled him out of the mood straight away. *"Filha de puta!"* Silvia slammed on the brakes as the flatbed cut them off. A hand waved lazily from the driver's cab.

"Are we there yet?"

Jaragua do Sul, 21 hours later

Will crept into the kitchen as quietly as he could, hoping to grab a quick bite and be gone before the kids were up. He hated goodbyes. They seemed ... final. The weary family had rolled into Jaragua last night, after tarrying too long in Curitiba for his liking. Brazilians tended to insist you socialize before blowing out the door. He couldn't exactly explain to his wife's relatives what the hurry was, now could he?

In a similar vein, Tio Fred had insisted on feeding him cachaça shots as soon as he'd stepped in the door last night. His wife, Vilma (there was a *Flintstones* joke there, but he knew nobody would get it), had presented a starchy and meaty Germanic feast to go along with the booze. So he'd belched and farted his way to sleep last night and woken up thanking God he'd packed Tylenol. Hardly the early night he'd had planned.

But he'd always had the same problem in his football days, and he'd always powered through it. Will wasn't about to admit that age was making this harder. It was almost game day, after all. No room for negative thoughts.

Next to leaving his family, Will regretted leaving Jaragua. He had a soft spot for the orderly little city surrounded by rough hills and ranches. It was vibrant without being chaotic, well mannered without being stuffy. Full of tall, beautiful, model-calibre German girls. Fred and Vilma, as unremarkable-looking as they were, had produced their own leggy stunner, a 21-year-old currently in Milan on a contract.

Will reminded himself that these were exactly the kind of girls Oscar Stumpf was harvesting. It was the mission motivation he needed. Time to go.

He turned on the lights and saw Lucas standing in front of him.

"Jesus!"

"No, it's Lucas. Haha."

The boy hugged him tight. Oh God.

"Where are you going, *Papai*?"

"Who says I'm going anywhere?"

Lucas stared up at him, brown eyes boring in with a look inherited from his mother. *Don't bullshit me.* "You never get up this early, not since we came back to Brazil."

"Okay, I have something to do. Grown-up stuff."

"Like what?"

"A job with Edilson. A job you can't tell anybody about, except *Mamae*. *Entende?*"

"Okay, Daddy. I'm listening." He was ramrod straight and serious now. A crucifix looked down from the wall, Jesus saying, *Don't fuck this kid up.* No pressure.

Will sighed. "We have to go help some kids. Some kids who had bad things happen to them, buddy. It's a little bit dangerous."

"That's why we can't go with you?"

"That's right. You and Tio Fred have to stay here and take care of the girls."

"But what if you need help?" Lucas was biting his lip now, trying to be brave. Will knew he understood better than most kids that bad things could happen to people you loved. They already had.

"I have Edilson to help me. He is very brave."

"So you promise you will be safe, Daddy?"

The lie promise was out before he could second-guess it. "Of course."

He held his boy close for a lot longer than he'd planned. The boy fell asleep soon in his arms. He deposited Lucas on the couch and covered him with a blanket before setting out. He paused at the door. First light. Nobody but the roosters awake. He could see his exhalations. It was crisp and clear. It didn't feel final. But it felt momentous. He patted his jacket pocket and felt the Taurus, needing a reassurance touch like a rookie gangbanger packing heat for the first time. He hoped he wouldn't need it.

But he knew he would.

South to Blumenau

The hang-gliders were already sailing off the Morro das Antenas as he got to the outskirts of town. In other circumstances, Will would've joined them. Silvia thought he was crazy, but he'd been addicted since he'd first glided in Rio. In Rio, the ramp was on a mountainside high above a wealthy neighbourhood abutting the beach. You strapped yourself to the instructor, ran off the ramp like Wile E. Coyote, and sailed like an albatross for a good 10 minutes before landing on the beach.

Asa-delta was like a child's fever dream come to life. There was just something about seeing swimming pools and a highway under your feet that got him coming back for more. He never worried about the wing collapsing. There were so many less-pleasant things lined up to kill you.

Will passed rice paddies and small farms, horses running in the fields, roadside stands selling savoury corn and fresh cheese. It looked like Vietnam grafted onto Bavaria. The sun's rays began strobing out from over the hilltops, flooding the valley with light, which reflected off the still paddy waters, dazzling him. He pulled over for a moment to watch. The road was quiet. He had the view to himself. Will smiled at the secret pleasure.

A truck passing too close jolted him back to reality. This wasn't a vacation, he reminded himself.

The drive gave him time to plan. Blumenau was going to be tough. All they really knew from Luc Renner was the hotel where the investors had made their trysts. As good a starting point as any, he supposed, but he liked to have more. Maybe Edilson had gotten somewhere. Sergio had given Edilson a list of businesses associated to the Grupo Stumpf. One was a talent agency, a strange acquisition for a man whose profile was all real estate development, construction, and some manufacturing. That might be an even better starting point.

Will guessed Renner was still holding out. The old-school copper in him still wanted to bounce the little creep around a bit to find out more. He wondered how long the guy would last without Edilson to babysit him. It was idle speculation. He might have started out as the client, but this case wasn't about him anymore.

And what about the PCC? He'd never seen any overt signs of gang activity on prior trips to the area. It wasn't like São Paulo. But he knew they had a presence there, just like Stumpf did. He had a feeling enough snooping would draw them out of the shadows. Blumenau was small and clannish. People would talk quickly about the outsiders asking questions. They had very little time.

He drove through Pomerode without stopping. Things got seriously German here. Blond-haired kids stared at Will from the back seat of a VW bug as he drove under an arch festooned with German and Brazilian flags. It wasn't just an affectation here. The government of Brazil used to worry about assimilation so much they mandated Portuguese-only schooling. Will's mother-in-law had spoken only German until she was seven. It was just a bigger version of the ethno-bubbles so many immigrants to Canada now lived in, he reflected. You could get by in Vancouver these days speaking nothing but Mandarin, Korean, or Punjabi.

The attitudes could be pretty German too. One of his wife's aunts had freaked when she'd found her son teaching his kids the Hitler salute. The war and the widespread association of the area in foreign minds with *The Boys From Brazil* were touchy subjects.

Will hadn't exactly come intending to make the place look any better. The people here were usually pretty friendly, but he was going to be pulling off some Band-Aids here. He needed to watch his back.

He entered the city, promptly getting lost. He always did. After two stops at service stations to sort it out (for some reason, GPS was less than reliable in this country), he found himself crossing the bridge into Centro. Recent rains had made the brown and fast-flowing river high and angry. But the sun was out, and the city warmed as noon approached. People were out in numbers along the riverbank, strolling past the Bavarian-style city hall building with its Hanseatic banners. Will was beginning to think a Pilsner and some brats were a damned good idea as he turned onto the Sete de Setembro, looking for his *pousada*. He found it and pulled the Toyota into an impossibly tight spot on a side street. If there was anything besides his Portuguese he'd improved on here, it was parallel parking.

As he was checking in, his phone rang. It was Edilson. He bit his lip. This wasn't going to be good news.

"Renner's gone."

"That fucker!"

"I know. Sorry, but I couldn't watch him all the time."

"Any idea where he went?"

"Your guess is probably right. I bet he's drinking wine with some rich assholes right now."

"Or he has a set of electrodes attached to his balls, and he is riding the lightning, courtesy of Oscar Stumpf. Shit!" He realized the desk clerk was eavesdropping and stepped into the stairwell. Hotel desk clerks were notorious ears. He ought to know; he used them himself.

"That's probably what happens next." Edilson sighed and then continued, "I wish I could help, but if you want me down there ..."

He needed the help now. It was more important than the fate of an unsavoury client who wasn't helping much anyway. "No, stick to the plan. Leave tonight. Give Ken a few bucks. Maybe he can find him."

"Ken? *Meu Deus*, Will!"

"Yes, I know, I know. But the guy can be pretty resourceful. You'd be surprised."

"Hmm. Ken."

Will knew Edilson was visualizing the gotch-eyed, snaggle-toothed stickman walking into an upper-crust wine tasting and dragging Renner out by his hair. Maybe that was what was called for.

"Okay, I will talk to Ken. See you tomorrow. Don't talk to anybody till I get there, okay?"

"Except for barmaids, I promise."

"*Tchau*, Will. Careful, *entende*?"

"*Sim. E voce, amigo.*"

So Renner was gone. Will wasn't surprised. The only possible drawback was that he would of course tell Stumpf everything under duress, revealing the array of forces against him. But he knew very little about Will or Edilson. Thiago and Ken, on the other hand ... He was pretty sure Ken had dealt with worse. But Thiago was more vulnerable. He dialled.

"Thiago, your client is missing."

"I know." He sounded sleepy.

"Were you sleeping?"

"So what, my hours are not normal. Quit fussing."

"How did you know Renner was gone?"

"He just called me. He was drunk. He said he didn't give a shit what Stumpf did to him, he was going to live a little while he still had time. Can you blame him?"

"I can blame him for a lot. He didn't perhaps say where he was, did he?"

"I said he was drunk, not stupid." The little lawyer loved verbal jousting. Probably why he'd gotten into lawyering.

"Okay, so forget him. What about you?"

"What about me?"

"Lay low for awhile. Have you got somewhere you can go?"

Thiago sighed. "We've discussed this. I'm not hiding."

Will lost his temper. "Listen, buddy, you may not give a shit about your own life anymore, but you'd better start giving a shit about your friends. You know how you're gonna stand up to torture? No? Because Oscar Stumpf wants you to find out. You may think you're a hero, but I got news for you: everybody breaks. And when you break, they are gonna find me and Edilson and maybe our families too. So drop the fuckin' hero act, and hide your sorry ass now!"

Thiago's voice was small and hurt. "Okay, Will. I will do this for you and Silvia."

Silvia. That was what really mattered. He felt his friend's despair. "I'm sorry I yelled at you, buddy. I don't have so many friends in this country. I can't afford to lose one."

"That's okay, Will."

"Call me when you get settled, okay? And don't tell Renner where you are. Get a throwaway phone, understand?"

"I understand. I will call you tomorrow, my friend."

"Thank you."

When he walked back to the desk to collect his key, the clerk stared unsubtly.

Great. These walls have ears.

16

Rodoviária de Blumenau

Last night's beer and sausage sat uneasily in Will's gut as he waited for the 10:15 Cometa bus from São Paulo. Last night he'd wandered down to Centro in an inexplicably jaunty mood after passing out in his room for six hours of badly needed sleep. He'd hit the first *bierhaus* with enthusiasm, and after that, things got foggy. He was pretty sure he'd tried to kiss a bar girl with big tits. That was so like Draft Dude.

Draft Dude was a name he'd picked up at UCLA. It was a Jekyll-and-Hyde thing. Copious amounts of draft beer brought out his inner savage. Usually a priapic one. But whenever he'd tried to explain the latest outrage committed by Draft Dude to his father, the old man had always had the same reply: "A drunken man's deeds are a sober man's thoughts."

Was he just conforming to the stereotype of the booze-sodden PI? Whatever, he felt like shit. But when the Cometa disgorged a gap-toothed, wiry policeman, he felt better. He always warmed up to that naive grin.

"Oi, brother. This reminds me of that James Bond movie." Will smirked as Edilson tossed him a suspiciously heavy duffle bag.

"What James Bond movie?"

"The one where he shows up on a bus."

"I don't remember that one."

"Exactly."

"Fuck you, Will."

"Hahaha, it's actually good to see you. Without you, I could have wound up married to a barmaid last night."

"I thought something worse would have happened. Like marrying the bouncer."

"Not that there's anything wrong with that."

"So you gringos say."

"You don't have to sleep with him. Welcome to Blumenau, asshole."

"Thanks. Am I the only black guy?"

"Possibly. There may be some lawn jockeys you can hang out with."

"Fuck you, Will."

They walked out to the parking lot. It was drizzling again. Will hoped they wouldn't get caught in a flood. The river looked close to cresting. The last bad one had been in 2008, and everyone's house still smelled like mould. They arrived at the Toyota.

"Remember that James Bond movie where he drives a Toyota Fielder?" Edilson asked.

"No, I don't."

"Me neither."

"Fuck you, Edilson."

It was a short hop to the hotel. The rain had cleared the streets.

"What now?" Edilson had the duffle bag on his lap. It was bristling with weaponry. He sorted through it as they spoke.

"Well, how about we try not to get arrested for starters?"

Edilson shot him a wounded look. "Hey, I'm a cop."

"Not here you're not. Can we just keep a low profile?"

"Do you really think that's going to happen, Will?"

The Toyota's windshield wipers worked overtime as the rain picked up. A *dona de casa* with a newspaper over her head sprinted across the street, forcing Will to slow. Brazilians, perennial optimists, never brought umbrellas.

"You may have a point," Will said. "Should we alert the local police?"

"Do you really want to explain this?"

"You bring anything in there for me?"

"That's the spirit."

They shook themselves dry before entering the *pousada*, trudging past the potted palms and brunchgoers enjoying their café colonial. The desk clerk looked at Edilson as if he were an Ebola carrier. Edilson shot it right back. The room was intimate, the beds hard. The Germans and comfort were strange bedfellows. Will and Edilson stretched out on opposite sides of the room and talked strategy. Outside, the rain drummed on the windows.

"There's a talent agency in town I think is supplying 'talent' for Oscar Stumpf. We should start there," Will said.

"Estrelas do Mundo?"

Maybe Edilson was coming along as a detective. "How the hell did you know that?"

"Our intelligence watches all PCC members very carefully when they leave prison. Guess who is running that agency?"

"A PCC *ladrao*."

"Yes. His name is Mauricio Panelas. And his only qualification is being a pimp."

"Sounds about right. The other lead is the hotel."

"The Alpenhaus Blumenau."

"Yes. Did you find out anything as sensational about that one?"

"No. An old couple owns it. Maybe they just need the money."

"Lot of that going around. So, where do we start?"

"Why waste time?" Edilson had propped himself up on one arm and was scarfing Cebolitos and swilling Xingu beer. "You talk to the old people; I'll take the pimp."

"Your kind of people, huh?"

"I have a plan."

Agencia Estrela dos Mundos, later that afternoon

The rain had quit when Edilson found himself standing in front of the agency on a steep residential side street. A cat regarded him lazily from behind a row of windowsill plants. His "plan," such as it was, was reflected in his dress: Bermuda shorts, a T-shirt with holes, tennis shoes on his feet. Plus the fact that he was a skinny, half-black guy with facial scars and less than optimal teeth. Edilson knew from a lifetime of experience how people looked at him, especially when he wasn't wearing the uniform. For once, he was hoping to use that to his advantage. Will had taught him the importance of getting your enemies to underestimate you.

The "agency" had glamour shots of long-legged models lining the entrance hallway. At the end, a fussy-looking blonde sat at a small desk. She was reading a copy of *Ti Ti Ti*, catching up on the latest novela. Edilson dimly recalled from Deyse that it was something about a girl who got kidnapped and forced to work in a brothel in Turkey. How ironic. She looked up from her magazine to see a reedy-looking black man.

"Can I help you?" The look on her face was more *I'm calling the police*, Edilson thought.

"Yes. I am an investor in the Southern Cross project, and I was looking for a girl I met at a party Mr. Stumpf put on. She mentioned that she worked here. I was wondering if you could help me find her?" He gave his most sincere smile. "She was really nice."

The receptionist looked up at his gap-toothed grin in horror. "You're an investor in Southern Cross?"

He was pretty sure her invisible right hand was on an alarm bell right now. "Sure I am. I have lots of money to spend. I really like blondes." He leered.

She was saved by the sudden appearance of Mauricio Panelas. *"Oi, gente! Qual e problema?"*

Mauricio was fireplug short and obviously liked working his lats. He wore a shiny burgundy blazer, which he compulsively adjusted as he flexed his shoulders. Why did all Mafia types do this? Edilson wondered. He idly toyed with the idea of just beating the shit out of this baby pimp right now, to give the blondie a real show. He swallowed his pride instead.

"No problem, sir. Perhaps I had the wrong address?"

"Yeah, maybe you did." Mauricio stared at Edilson for a moment. The blonde chewed a fingernail. Edilson's practiced eye picked up a shoulder holster under Mauricio's cheap jacket. He backed up the hallway.

"Another time, then." Edilson held his hands up in supplication. All he could think about was shooting this muscular little shit in the kneecaps.

"Fuck off, *negao*."

Oh now, that really wasn't nice. Edilson felt the heat rise up his neck. But Will Bryant had taught him good detectives didn't mind looking the fool if it got them what they needed. It wasn't like dominating your beat as a PM. It took some getting used to. *"Desculpe. Muito desculpe."* He backed out the door and walked briskly to the Toyota. He was pretty sure they wouldn't do the deed on the street, but his hand was on his Glock anyway as he rounded the corner.

Fast, but not too fast. Have to let them see the car. Edilson knew PCC could be drawn out like sharks. Put some blood in the water; let them smell a victim. That was the whole point of today's exercise, why an unsubtle guy like him was doing it and not Will.

Blood in the water.

Edilson reached the Toyota just as two obvious *favelados* appeared down the block. They scanned left and right, obviously looking for something. Mauricio was nowhere to be seen, but Edilson was pretty sure these two had gone out to do his dirty work. They affected a Mexican-style narco look, with tight acid-wash jeans, big belt buckles, and lizard-skin boots. Subtlety wasn't a PCC strong suit either. Everybody had to know who they were in a town so white.

Edilson moved slowly and made sure he gave the two clowns on the corner time to get on the cellphone before he drove away. He did his best to look nervous.

Edilson Lopes hadn't been nervous in 20 years, since he'd asked Deyse to marry him. He was elated. Blood was in the water now. He reached over the seat and pulled the duffle bag upfront.

He'd been waiting for this since 2006. He'd never really been satisfied with the aftermath of Gustavo's death. Sure, the São Paulo cops had settled a lot of scores, but a lot of killers were still out there. Watching football, enjoying bum-bum, laughing their asses off. In 2012, they'd surfaced again. They liked to kill cops in front of their families. So his brakes were off.

Sorry, Will. He looked in his rear-view mirror and saw two motoboys gaining on him on Yamahas. *Sure, I wanted to be a Polícia Civil. I wanted to arrest Oscar Stumpf. But I want to kill these fuckers more.*

The inadvertent convoy crossed a river toward Will Bryant, who was at this moment trying a more subtle approach.

Alpenhaus Blumenau

In contrast to Edilson, who had known his plan for years, Will Bryant was winging it until he walked into the worn-carpet lobby of the Alpenhaus. Alpenhaus Blumenau was a low-slung faux-Bavarian pile with a slanted roof and a balcony that encircled the building. No doubt, witness to many atrocities. He was dressed as respectfully as his limited wardrobe on this trip would allow—tan Columbia lightweight pants and a baby blue snap front. Obvious tourist.

He still had zero fucking clue what he was going to ask, until he remembered something Luc Renner had mentioned. All the investors had had their dates in one of three rooms on the second floor. Bugs, most likely. Wouldn't want your blackmail targets performing statutory rape without a permanent witness. As a square-shouldered man with dark eyes strode toward him, Will pocketed his wedding band as deftly as he could.

"Bem vindo, senhor!" A swishy desk clerk looked a little too excited to have company.

"Do you have a room available?" Will asked with a dry mouth.

"We have many right now, *senhor*. It's a little slow, so there's a discount too!"

Will wished he'd ever enjoyed any job as much as this guy did. Or he was really good at faking. "Well, it's a bit strange, but I have to have a certain room."

"Oh, what is your preference?"

"Well, I was told to say I am a client of Grupo Stumpf."

The clerk tried not to show his reaction, but it was there. His smile was frozen. Behind the front desk, a wizened hand pulled the office door ajar ever so slightly. One of the owners was suddenly very interested in his new guest. The clerk recovered. "Yes, of course. Grupo Stumpf has a block of rooms on the second floor. We'll put you in one of those. Will you be expecting anyone else?"

You know damn well I will, asshole. "Yes, a lady friend."

"May I please have her name, so I can send her up when she arrives? We take security very seriously here."

I'll bet you do. "Gretchen."

Again a reaction. Again the frozen smile. Will figured he'd make a pretty good poker player if he could learn the game someday.

"*Excellente, senhor. Uno momento, por favor.*" The clerk hurried into the backroom. No doubt to confer with the owner of the wizened hand. Will strained to listen, but it was all too indistinct. He hoped he'd dropped the right name. The clerk came out of the backroom, beaming again. "Room 217 for you, *senhor.* An excellent view of the river."

"That will do nicely." One of the goodies in Edilson's little bag of tricks was a sanitized Visa card. The other was a fake license. Will didn't ask how Edilson had gotten this done, and he figured he was better off not knowing. He held his breath for a moment as the clerk took the phony card and license.

"*Obrigado*, Senhor Petrie," the clerk said. Will wiped the back of his hand against his forehead. The clerk smirked at him. Will figured he was used to seeing Stumpf's clients sweating with excitement.

The fact that he had no bags to check clearly surprised nobody. After breathing a sigh of relief when the Visa went through, he took his key card and walked up the wide stairwell. It was one of those old hotels where the once-thick rugs wrapped around the stairs with brass fixings were now worn smooth in the middle. Years of visitors. How many victims?

Room 217 was almost at the head of the stairs. He walked up to the door, hesitated. He stepped off to the side, putting his hand on the Taurus resting in the paddle holster on his belt. With his weak hand he inserted the key card. He swung the door open and saw a mirror. Nobody around the bed. He stepped in gingerly and cleared the room. Soft white curtains billowed from the open balcony. The room had a huge bed and little else. What else was needed?

Will walked into the bathroom. A tub big enough for two. He felt nauseated. He walked to the balcony for fresh air. The clerk was right; it was a good view. Cars convoyed across a nearby bridge as the brown river roiled underneath. He took it all in and breathed deeply.

Time to get to work.

One of the other goodies Edilson had brought was an RF-signal detector, for finding bugs. He took it out of his jacket pocket and switched it on. He got immediate indications. He walked around slowly to pinpoint the signals. *The room is wired, buddy. You're being watched.* He stopped in his tracks. Well, that was one question answered.

If a seasoned professional like him, knowing there was a hidden camera in here, had acted like nobody could see him, what chance did an amateur blinded by lust have? But what the hell was he supposed to do now? He figured he had minutes before they were here.

A woman's scream answered his question. He brought the Taurus out and held it low. He opened the door quickly, took a deep breath, and jumped into the hall. He listened for footsteps on the stairs. Nothing yet. More screams.

"Puta! Creatura!"

"Ai, nao, nao, nao! Ajuda!"

There was a crash of furniture, breaking glass. Will walked quickly down the hall. Room 213. He stepped back against the opposite wall, kicked his foot out, and splintered the door at the jamb. His shoulder got him in all the way.

A pantless man in his forties, still wearing a dress shirt and a tie, slicked black hair hanging over his face, was trying to pull a young, skinny blonde dressed only in a black bra and a thong off the floor by her long ponytail. She screamed again and tried to crawl away. The man dropped the ponytail and stared at Will. He opened his mouth to say something. Will stepped back and then gave him an almighty kick in the balls. The man dropped to his knees as the girl crawled out from under him. He grabbed at Will, his mouth open, face twisted. Will threw a knee into his jaw and brought the barrel of the Taurus down hard on his skull. The man toppled over on his side and lay still.

The girl rolled onto her back and stared at him wide-eyed, panting hard.

"It's okay; I'm here to help. But you need to get dressed." She stared blankly. He was painfully aware that her right breast was poking out of her bra and he was staring. She was gorgeous. She was also a child. He looked away. "Get dressed. Others are coming. We need to leave, now!"

She seemed to understand, reaching her arm out for the edge of the bed and pulling herself up. She wiped blood off her nose with the back of her hand and grabbed a dress off the bed. As she pulled on her dress, Will checked the action on the Taurus. Pistol whipping the sack of shit at his feet had put it out of battery. He slapped the mag, racked the action, and grabbed the round as it flew out of the ejector port. The girl watched him, bewildered.

"Are ... are you a policeman?"

She did speak after all. "Well ... it's complicated, but I'm here to help." He knelt down and checked the man's pulse. Shallow, but still there. Will's interest was strictly selfish. Dead bodies caused complications, and he already had one on his hands. He looked up and saw a wallet on the dresser. Instinctively, he grabbed it. Might be useful to know who this prick was. More blood than he thought possible was running down the man's face from the deep cut in his scalp. Time to move.

"Come on. Maybe we can slip down to the lobby through the fire exit." He held out his hand. She took it. Her hand was tiny, delicate. "What's your name, kid?"

"Gretchen."

His blood hammered in his ears. Shit. They had less time than he thought. They would've called as soon as he'd given that name. They would've ...

The smashed door behind Gretchen hung on two hinges. It swung open slowly as a razor-thin, mantis-like, mahogany black man with a face full of gold teeth stepped cautiously into the room. Will heard bounding feet coming up the stairwell.

He pulled Gretchen around behind him so hard she cried out. The black man stared at him, mouth agape, and brought a pistol up.

Will snapped the Taurus up to his hip and fired twice. One shot went wide; the other punched through the man's stomach. He staggered back into the doorway, shooting back wild. Will brought the Taurus up in a two-handed grip and got a proper aim, firing twice more. The black man's carotid artery opened. He stared astonished at the spray, fell backwards, died.

"*Fora! Merda!*" The dead man's friends in the hallway threw themselves against the wall. A pistol poked around the corner of the doorway, the owner firing blind. Will dropped to his knees and fired three more times at the doorway as Gretchen crawled for the balcony. Will dropped and rolled across the floor in her direction. More wild shots from the doorway. Gretchen was crawling over the balcony rail when the window above Will's head shattered with a wild shot, covering him in broken glass. He crawled forward, his arms reaching outside just as the man he'd knocked out came to life and grabbed his leg. He looked over his shoulder and kicked at the blood-drenched face, but the motherfucker wasn't letting go. He looked back toward the balcony as Gretchen disappeared over the rail, the blonde ponytail plummeting behind her.

Will was going nowhere fast. Gretchen's date was holding him down, pulling him back in. Panicked, he scrambled for a grip to pull himself away. Gasping and bloody, the man started to crawl up Will's leg like a zombie nightmare. *This fucker is strong.* More voices in the stairwell. Reinforcements.

"*Ajuda, ajuda! Polícia, ajuda!*" the man screamed.

Will looked into the man's one open eye. *Well, asshole, it's you or me.* He shot the man in the forehead, and the grip on his legs released. He kicked off the dead weight and fired two more shots at the doorway. He scrambled to the railing and went over the side without looking, just as another pane of glass exploded behind him.

He fell on his ass, rocking his tailbone. He felt sick to his stomach, dazed. *Up, up, get up.* He staggered to his feet. Where was the kid? Where was the gun?

On his feet now, standing in the open, he heard a crack. He looked up and saw a thick white guy in a leather jacket sniping at him from the balcony. *Where is my fucking gun?* He spun around, saw it under the rear wheel of a car. He ran for the car and scooped it up, more glass from the hatchback window exploding on his head. He wheeled, fired, pulled the trigger, ran empty. He scrambled around behind the car to get cover, dropped his mag, and fumbled the change. He leaned down to pick up the magazine as a round that would've gone through his eye socked into the car behind him. He slammed the mag into the pistol and fired back two-handed, forcing the sniper to retreat.

He looked around for the girl, heard screams. He zeroed in on the sound and saw a huge musclehead picking up a flailing Gretchen. He got to his feet and ran straight for them as auto glass exploded around him again. Gretchen wriggled out of the mesomorph's grasp as Will got to them. The muscleman looked after the sprinting girl and, exasperated, turned to face Will.

Will paused. Like a dog chasing a car, he didn't know what to do when he caught it. The muscleman had both his ears pierced, and he smiled a rotten smile that lifted his earrings high on his head. Will decided to just shoot him as the muscleman stepped forward—into the path of a rapidly accelerating Toyota Fielder. The muscleman bounced off the hood, flew into a signpost, twitched, stilled. Will stood unsteadily as Edilson screamed at him, "Get in, now, now! We're being followed!"

Will staggered across to the Toyota as two motoboys raced up behind the car. One took the corner too sharply, and the bike wobbled, riderless, as its master vaulted over an embankment. The now-out-of-control bike slid past Will as he dodged around the hood. The other rider kept his mount and powered up the driver's side.

"Edilson!"

But Edilson had already thrown himself across the shifter onto the floor. The motoboy fired a submachine gun the length of the car as he raced past. Will dived behind the right front wheel and brought up his pistol as the motoboy executed a tight turn and came back toward them. Will fired repeatedly, but his opponent was weaving, moving fast. The windscreen gave off glass vapour puffs as the motoboy's rounds hit home.

The motoboy raced past again. Edilson rolled out of the driver's seat, knelt on one knee, and brought up an SMG. A staccato burst to the back blew the motoboy out of his saddle. Arms spread wide, the motoboy seemed to stop in mid-air for a moment in a cloud of pink mist as his Yamaha raced away from him. Edilson stood up and tossed the SMG through the shattered back window. Will heard sirens.

"*Vamos agora,* Will! Move your big ass!"

Will pulled open the passenger door as Edilson jammed on the gas. One of his feet was still outside as the Fielder sideswiped a parked Clio. A sharp pain shot through his ankle as the door crashed back against him. Edilson reached over and pulled him in. Two Polícia Militar cars raced down a side street, crossing their path. Edilson cranked the wheel and pulled a U-turn, racing past the hotel entrance just as the surviving motoboy staggered into the road and fired at them. Edilson ducked, opened the driver's-side door, and knocked the man off his feet into the back of a delivery truck. More shots rang out from behind as the hotel goons raced into the street.

The hotel disappeared behind them. Will closed his eyes, gasping for air. He looked down, saw the brains of the man from Room 213 on his pant leg. He tasted vomit in his mouth, felt hot and faint.

"Will, are you okay?" Edilson threw the car hard right onto a narrow side street and then down an alley, killing a dog that was too slow to get out of the way. *Christ*, Will thought, *everybody's getting a taste today.* He nodded to his friend, swallowed his puke.

The girl. They had to find her before the PCC did.

"Gretchen. We have to find her!" He grabbed Edilson's shoulder. "Now!"

"Gretchen? What ...?" Edilson had never looked at the end of his rope before, but today was different.

"Renner's girl. She was there. We have to get her before they do. Turn around."

"Fuck!" But he turned around.

The two of them scanned, cruising slowly, listening for sirens and looking for a barefooted girl with a ponytail running for her life.

They were passing a corner *padaria* when she found them. Will saw the girl running behind the car and waving her arms. "Stop!" he shouted, and Edilson did a brake stand in front of an astonished old man holding a little blond boy by the hand. Will reached back and threw open the back door as Gretchen scrambled in, gasping. Will hadn't said "Go" when Edilson took off.

"Shit!" Will said as two *policials* on motorcycles passed them. The helmeted men nodded to each other and U-turned back toward the Toyota. Edilson raced toward a roundabout, narrowly missing a Honda pulling out of a filling station. He did a centrifuge-fast turn and headed straight back toward the motos, who only now were catching on. Too slow. Will realized too late what Edilson was going to do. "Hey, Edilson, hey!"

The motos veered to opposite sides of the road as Edilson drove between them, forcing the man on the left harmlessly into a low hedge. But the man on the right catapulted over the hood of a taxi and onto the sidewalk in front of a knot of people waiting for a bus. Edilson gripped the wheel tight.

"We have to lose this car!"

"Edilson, those cops back there ..."

"I know, I know!"

As they passed a *supermercado*, a Hail Mary play occurred to Will. "Edilson, turn right."

"Here?"

"Yes. Trust me. Head for the hills."

"Okay. You know this town better than I do."

"Well, this town sure as shit knows you."

"Guess I haven't improved their opinion of black guys."

"No, probably not. Turn left here."

Tante Ruth's little house was at the end of a steep road where the city gave way to country, and roads turned to red dirt. Will knew she had a tarp for storing a car and hoped she would be accommodating. Gretchen was a good selling point. Rescuing her was about the only socially acceptable explanation for hiding a car full of bullet holes. He hadn't wanted to drag family into this, but Ruth lived on her own and would probably appreciate the excitement.

"There!" They turned onto the red-dirt path. "Pull in behind the house; get us out of sight."

Ruth was inside, watching an old novela while she chatted on the phone with one of her sisters. She looked out through the window of the tiny house when he knocked. A short, round woman with ice blue eyes and non-stop mouth, she was an acquired taste.

"*Guten tag*, Tante. Where's Walter?" Walter was her nosy boyfriend. Best to make sure he wasn't there.

"*Guten tag*, Will!" She gave him an effusive full-body hug. "Walter? I got tired of him. He couldn't keep up!" She pulled back and looked at him. "But what has happened to you? Where is Silvia?"

He looked over his shoulder as Edilson and Gretchen came into view. Sheepishly, he said, "Well, about that ..."

"You are in trouble! Come in, come in!"

Later, sitting in Ruth's kitchen with a cold Skol, he began to come off the ceiling. The Fielder was covered with a tarp in the backyard. Ruth was bandaging Gretchen's sliced feet as Edilson sprawled on the couch, exhausted. Will hadn't really appreciated the value of his wife's family until he'd desperately needed them. They were like a hidden army, spread throughout the southern half of Brazil, as unquestioning and reliable as a network of KGB safe houses. Without them, he had no idea what they would've done.

As he slowly digested his new reality as a hunted killer, Ruth led Gretchen off to her bedroom. They did not return for a long while, so he wandered into the hall and peered through the doorway. Gretchen lay on the bed as Ruth stroked her hair and sang softly to her, closing her eyes. He was surprised by how moving he found it. Finally, this abused child felt a touch that wasn't associated with lust. Finally, she was someone's daughter again.

He walked back to the fridge for another beer and then fell asleep at the kitchen table.

17

Blumenau, morning

Will awoke to the sound of Ruth bustling around the kitchen. He wiped the drool off his face with the back of his hand as he blearily realized she was staring at him. God, his ass was sore. Next to his right arm, the Taurus lay in plain view. He dimly recalled awaking to investigate noises in the night, wondering if they'd been spotted. No intruders. But now, some explaining to do.

Ruth was still staring. "What kind of trouble did you bring this poor girl into? I should call Silvia!"

"She knows already." Not exactly. What happened yesterday would likely leave his wife a hell of a lot less understanding. "And the girl was already in a lot of trouble, Tante."

Ruth set a cup of coffee in front of him and sat down. "*Eu sei.* Lots of trouble. She told me some things, Will. Terrible things." She looked haunted.

"Done by terrible people. Who want us dead. Say the word, and we'll leave. This doesn't have to involve you."

"*Meu Deus*, you are already in my house, Will! Anyhow, I can't send this girl away. Let her stay with me." Ruth had had a daughter once, but she had died of cancer as a child. Will knew her motives were selfish but pure all the same.

"I think she would like that."

The door opened, and Edilson walked in with a newspaper under his arm and a bag of groceries. "*Oi muleke*," Edilson greeted him casually. He nodded at the Taurus. "Forget something?"

Will scooped the pistol off the table. "Isn't it a little hot to be roaming around?"

Edilson grinned. "No, it's very nice weather."

"That's not what I meant. Hot as in 'hot,' understand?" Guy could be so fucking obtuse sometimes; it was infuriating to Will. They'd upended the city yesterday, and 12 hours later he was out for a morning stroll.

"Oh, you mean this?" He tossed a copy of *Jornal de Santa Catarina* on the table. Will picked it up as Edilson settled on the couch and opened a Skol.

"Bit early to be drinking, isn't it?"

Edilson regarded him evenly. "After yesterday, who gives a shit? I'm lucky to have the lips to drink this beer. Want one?"

"Not just this minute." Will spread out the *Jornal* on the table. There it was, in full colour: the dead motoboy sprawled on the pavement. Ruth glanced at the photo and turned her head, suddenly finding somewhere else to be.

If it bleeds, it leads. But the story wasn't the way he remembered it. The official version was a robbery attempt gone wrong. Hotel security intervening. Policials injured in the pursuit. A prominent politician, dead. No mention of an underage hooker. Grupo Stumpf was in full damage-control mode.

Wait a second, what was that about a dead politician?

"Did you read the part about the dead politician?" Edilson asked around a mouthful of Cebolitos. "That could be trouble."

"Bit late for that. Who is this guy?"

"Don't ask me; they aren't saying yet. But didn't you take his wallet?"

Goddamn it, he'd completely forgotten. But where was it?

Edilson scarfed more salty onion rings and reached under the couch cushion. He tossed a thick brown leather billfold at Will. "You didn't know what the hell you were doing last night, so I thought I'd sleep on it."

Will opened it up and looked at the national ID card. Rigoberto Soares. A stern, moustachioed visage. Elsewhere in the billfold: platinum credit cards, VIP cards for strip joints and Vegas casinos, a Partido dos Trabalhadores ID card. PT, the Worker's Party. The ruling party. And he'd shot the guy in the head.

"Edilson, gimme a goddamn beer!"

His partner threw a Skol into the air in response. Will sucked it back and leaned back in the chair, closing his eyes. Who had he killed? Why had Soares been there? He hoped the answer was the obvious one. Obvious. As if anything about this fucked-up case was obvious.

Edilson strolled over and picked up the wallet. "Rigoberto Soares? He wasn't on the list, was he?"

The list. The six politicians they knew from Renner that Stumpf had rumbled as pedophiles. "No, he wasn't, was he?"

Edilson tipped the wallet, and a glassine envelope with three Viagra fell out onto the table. Will felt strangely embarrassed for a man he had killed at close range less than 24 hours ago.

"PT?" Edilson held up the ID. "Fucking Communist. Good thing you shot him."

"Easy now." Will had always had the uneasy feeling Edilson did some moonlighting taking out the trash. It wasn't uncommon for Brazilian cops to fix problem people on their days off.

Edilson sat down next to him. "There's only one way to find out what he was doing in that room, man."

"Yes, I know."

They had to wait a long while for Gretchen. She disappeared into the shower as soon as she woke up and stayed there for the length of a novela. Will didn't wonder why. She was a chrysalis now, shedding the skin of her old life, preparing for whatever came next.

And now he had to drag her back for a bit. He had no choice, if he wanted to know who he'd killed. The man in the doorway was a hired gun. Will knew why he'd been there. But he was stripped of assumptions with Soares. It could be anything from him just being another pervert Renner didn't know about to him being on the same hunt Will was on.

That last one he couldn't face. It was the kid in the Tim Hortons all over again.

Gretchen finally stepped out of the bathroom into the hallway, staring at him after a moment's inattention. She bit her lip. She wore a baby-doll dress of white linen. It was a child's dress, borrowed from a long-ago dead child, and it somehow fit perfectly.

He stepped forward carefully, suddenly conscious that he had beer on his breath. "Gretchen, can we talk for a moment?"

She looked around as if for an escape route. She seemed to do a mental calculation. "If I tell you what you want to know, will you let me stay here?"

Will exhaled. "Of course, *Filha*."

She walked down the hall to the back door. Looking over her shoulder, she asked, "Can I go outside?"

He stared for a moment. "You don't have to ask anymore, Gretchen." How the hell could you convince this child she wasn't a slave anymore?

He saw her smile for the first time. *"Muito bom."* She opened the door and stepped out into an orchard. A light breeze toyed with her dress. Will followed, feeling light-headed. A child's memories.

Gretchen turned to face him, beaming. "And I can stay here with Ruth, if I help you?"

He couldn't play leverage with this kid. "Even if you don't. I won't send you back to them. Never."

She stared at him and bit her lip. In a hushed tone, "Why?"

"In the normal world everyone understands why. Because you don't do that to kids."

"I'm not a kid."

"You should be. When did you stop being a kid?"

Her face dropped. She seemed to realize that Will was still going to press her. "I was 12. My mother sent me here to a modelling agent. She wanted me to make lots of money."

Will was quiet for a moment. He looked up, saw a hawk riding the thermals. Whatever family dynamic had brought Gretchen to a whorehouse was something he was too squeamish to imagine.

Gretchen broke the silence. "Mauricio showed me how things worked."

Panelas. That fucking asshole had broken her. Will had known enough pimps to understand standard procedure. "He showed you what to do?"

Her face was expressionless. "He taught me how to fuck."

Will looked up again. The hawk was gone. No doubt some field mouse was getting it right now. Predation. It was everywhere.

"Do you remember a Frenchman, Gretchen?"

Her face became animated. "Yes, Luc! He was very nice, not like some of the others. He brought me treats, jewellery, stuffed animals ... I liked him."

Will suppressed his disappointment. He wanted more reasons to hate Renner. As if raping a child wasn't enough. But in Gretchen's world, it was all relative. Compared to some sick puppies she'd probably encountered, Renner came off as Prince William.

"Did you always see clients in the Alpenhaus?"

"No, usually it was a fazenda outside of Pomerode or a hotel in Centro. But Mauricio told us these men were special."

"Did he say why?"

"He just said they were very rich and important, and we should ... well, we should do whatever they wanted." She was biting her lip again. Was that how she had learned not to cry?

Before he could respond, she continued, "But they weren't allowed to really hurt us. That was the rule. And it was kind of strange, because my friend Helga asked Mauricio what we should do if we were getting hurt, and he said 'just wave your arms.' So that's when I figured they had cameras in the rooms."

"Did you find out why?"

"Luc told me. One time he made me promise to meet him in town, and he took me for ice cream and then to the park. And he told me all about Southern Cross. I didn't really understand it all, but I guess this guy Oscar and Mauricio were using us to take all these guys' money."

"You understood right. Did you just see Luc, or were there other guys? I mean, how many others did you go to the Alpenhaus with?"

"Four others, not including that ... that man from yesterday."

"And do you know how many other girls work in your 'agency'?"

"About 30, I think. Some from Santa Catarina, like me and Helga. Some black girls from Bahia. A lot of Paraguayan girls ... Guys like the black hair and white teeth." She giggled.

Jesus. An average of four clients a girl meant 120 cash cows for Oscar Stumpf. Maybe more. How much would those tapes be worth, and how many movers and shakers were on them?

"Gretchen, did you recognize any of the men, even any of the other girls' clients?"

"No, I don't really watch the news ... Wait, Helga had a client who was a *jogador*. My big brother had his poster on the wall ..."

"Marco, from Santos FC?"

"*Sim, sim* ... that was him!"

"Did Helga tell you anything about him?"

"Not much. She didn't like him, though; he was brutal. And, oh, he said he would kill Oscar and Mauricio someday. She was scared of him."

Everybody was scared of Marco Hellmer. Everybody except Oscar Stumpf.

"Tell me about the man from yesterday?"

She shuddered. "It was a surprise date. Mauricio told me to be ready in one hour. Usually we had more time."

"Was anything else different?"

She thought for a moment. "Yes! He told me to dress older. That wasn't what they usually told us."

"When you got to the Alpenhaus, what happened?"

"I went up to the room and waited. There was always a security guy there to let me in. If we got there early, they wouldn't let us in, because everything wasn't ready."

"You mean the microphones and cameras, right?"

"Yes. I'm not stupid. I looked in once when they left the door open, and there was a guy in there making sure the others could see him and hear him."

"So what happened when your 'client' appeared?"

"He looked really nervous. I mean, usually the guys are nervous, but this guy was bad. He was sweaty, and he was shaking. I told him to relax and let me give him a massage. That's what Mauricio told us to do with the ones who are *muito nervosa*."

"Tell me what happened next." The breeze began to pick up, and Gretchen pulled her hair away from her face. Will thought the images and words were out of sync, like a badly dubbed Japanese movie.

"He relaxed a bit and started telling me I was beautiful. He kissed me, hard, like I don't like, but I went along with it. Then he unzipped my dress, so I made sure I had my condom in my hand ... Are you okay, *senhor*?"

His expression of discomfort must have been obvious. He willed it away. "I'm fine. Go on."

"He pushed me on the bed, and he looked excited, like they do when they want to fuck. But then, I think he noticed something, because he got really mad right away. He grabbed me by the throat. I couldn't breathe. He said, 'You are trying to trap me, *puta*? You are trying to make me Stumpf's bitch?' I couldn't say anything, and I thought I was going to pass out. But I used to be a gymnast, and I am really flexible, so I rolled my hips really hard and fast, and I threw him off of me. I was trying to get to the door when you showed up."

He must have noticed a camera or a mic. Maybe he'd had an RF detector too. But if the room was bugged, why hadn't the watchers gotten there sooner? "Did you think I was security?"

"Yes. They usually get there that fast when there's a problem, because they are watching everything."

"It's happened before?"

"Sometimes dates get rough. But Mauricio takes good care of us." She smiled. He stared at her a moment and let it pass. Stockholm syndrome was pretty common in cases like hers. His sudden arrival must have distracted the watchers. They weren't crewed up to keep an eye on two rooms at once without prior notice. The next question wasn't one he'd planned.

"Why'd you jump? Why come with me? You knew they'd protect you."

"I don't know. Instinct? *Eu nao sei.*" She walked over to him and took his hand. Will swallowed hard. *"Obrigada, senhor. Obrigada."* She stood on tiptoes and kissed his cheek. Holding hands, they walked back to the house.

Overhead, the hawk was back. Will tightened his grip on Gretchen's hand. He couldn't have this mouse.

18

Blumenau

They sat in a Peugeot borrowed from Tante Ruth, at the end of a red-earth trail. With no fucking idea which way to go.

Edilson had on wraparound shades. Will figured he thought it made him look like the Terminator. Actually, it made him look like a Eurodouche, but he didn't need the shades to make that rep anyway. He had the body count already.

Will turned to Edilson, who was loudly smacking gum in the driver's seat, trying to avoid a decision. "So, which cliff do you want to drive over, Thelma?"

"Huh?"

His attempts at humour so often failed here, but he never stopped trying. "Which way do we go?"

"South, I think." He didn't look sure.

"South? Why? Our business is in São Paulo." Will knew he had lost the thread of this case, if he'd ever had it. He had to admit that his much-patronized partner had a much better grasp of things now. Well, it was his fucking country, after all.

Edilson paused, exasperated, and turned to him, the midday light glinting off his ridiculous glasses. "What business? What do we go back to São Paulo with? 'Stumpf, we know you were running hookers and bugging the rooms.' And? We know more than before but not enough. Soares, the fucker you shot, was from Floripa. He wasn't here for the same reason the rest were. So we go to Floripa. Besides, they expect us to go north." He turned to face the road and grabbed the shifter, decision made.

Floripa. Florianópolis, the Jewel of the South, capital of Santa Catarina. Will had been there once, on his honeymoon, and had been dying to go back. At the time, he couldn't have imagined the circumstances of his return if he'd tried.

"Okay." What else could he say?

Edilson ripped the Peugeot out of Ruth's driveway in a cloud of red dust.

SC-108, South of Gaspar

They were chiding themselves for being paranoid when they came to the roadblock. Coming fast around a blind corner, they saw it too late. Nowhere to turn. Next to a deserted fruit stand, two *polícia* SUVs. Back at the corner, well hidden by overgrowth, two more cops on motos. More watchers 200 metres down the road at a *posto de servicio*. Some Transito traffic-control types on their bikes to make it all about "road safety," when it was all really about shaking down dopers and robbers.

In and of itself, it wasn't exceptional. Polícia Rodoviária roadblocks in Brazil were common. In Will's experience they were usually just looking for motoboys to hassle. That's all he'd ever seen them pull over. There was always a knot of them standing around and looking dejected as cops ripped apart their rides. He still didn't get it. The kids didn't look like Hells Angels, after all.

But it still made him nervous. One look at Edilson, and he could tell he wasn't alone. Edilson was slipping his Glock under the driver's seat, and Will took his lead. In Will's experience in this scenario (from the other side), the body search was usually more thorough than the vehicle toss. But Brazilian cops could do both, without a warrant. As they pulled abreast of the contact officer, he wondered what Silvia and the kids were doing.

The officer was wearing a white square ball cap and high boots with riding breeches, an affectation typical of the breed throughout Brazil. The mirrored Ray-Bans were an American touch that had somehow become universal. He was mid-size and angular, with a chiselled face. His name tag read "Gasparini." He got to the point right away. "Your documents."

Edilson held out his driver's license and vehicle registration, making sure his Policia Militar ID was visible in his lap. Gasparini caught it. "Hmm, São Paulo, eh? What are you doing here?"

"Blondes and beer, brother."

Gasparini's lip curled. He probably didn't like that very much. He handed the documents back anyway. *"Boa viagem."*

"Obrigado, gente."

Will smacked Edilson on the shoulder as they drove away. "'Blondes and beer'? You might as well have told him you were here to screw his sister ... Remember where you are!"

Edilson shrugged. "Maybe he didn't like it, but what the fuck is he going to do about it? Besides, all white guys think black guys are after their women."

"Because you are."

"Hah! So why bullshit the guy, right?"

"I guess." Will looked in the side-view mirror. Two motoboys were shooting around the curve they had just left, gaining fast. "Uh, Edilson ..."

Back at the roadblock, Gasparini had put the Paulistas out of his mind as he sized up the next car. Even if he'd been approached to keep an eye out for them, he would have said no, with his fists. Like a lot of Brazilian cops, contrary to the stereotype, he couldn't be bought.

The young man on the Transito motorcycle watching the roadblock was a little more flexible. He dialled his mobile phone as they pulled away.

Now, up ahead, Edilson was looking in his rear-view. Right behind the motos was a Jeep Cherokee. It hadn't been behind them at the roadblock either. To his right, Will had his pistol out and was looking over his shoulder. Edilson looked around. Up ahead on the right was Industrias Schneider, a massive factory, warehouse, and truck park. The main gate was 100 metres in front. Edilson was pretty sure there was a rear exit onto a back road. Pretty sure. Behind them, one of the motos was making his move, coming up on Will's side, his front wheel rearing. For the first time, Edilson noticed there were two men on board.

Standard Colombian *sicario* style: one guy shoots, another guy scoots. Time to decide.

Will was twisting his large body in the seat to shoot when Edilson shouted, "Hold on, Will!"

Will just had time to wrap the seatbelt around his left arm as Edilson threw the wheel over hard right. The moto making the move was on their bumper when it happened. Will hit the door hard and his neck wrenched over as his head hit the half-open window. "Fuck!" Will caught a glimpse of the moto rocketing into the plant fence along with its riders. The Peugeot smashed through the wooden barrier arm into the plant.

The Peugeot smashed through the gates into the plant just as a human body travelling 95 km/h catapulted off the back of the overturned moto and flew into the guard-house windows. The astonished guard inside lay on the floor, breathing hard, covered in glass and specked with the gunman's blood. The submachine gun the corpse had been carrying flew clean through two sets of windows and bounced off the trunk of a parked car.

Edilson leaned over in his seat as the Peugeot's tires screamed out. A hard right turn with a fishtail let him just clear a row of trucks on a long loading dock. Heading straight for a forklift, he swerved, smoking a pushcart and sending the remnants into the air.

Will was facing forward now, pressed into his seat. "Goddamn it, Edilson, this was your fucking bright idea?"

Edilson laughed out loud. "You wanna drive, Will?" Edilson turned hard left and drove past two admin buildings. More warehouses spread out ahead. Goddamn, this place was huge.

"Watch the rear, Will?"

"How could they make that turn?"

"Just watch it!"

Behind them on the road, the Cherokee cranked a U-turn and raced back for the entrance. Ahead of the Cherokee, the surviving moto was already shooting through the plant gates and going after the Peugeot.

At the other end of the plant, Edilson was frantically scanning for an exit when he saw three guards manhandling Jersey barricades into position. "There!" he shouted and steered for them. Will turned his head at the shout, and then out of the corner of his eye he saw the moto behind them. The man on the back of the moto raised his outstretched arm as the rider hunched down.

Will stuck the Taurus out the window and fired left-handed. The riders stayed up and sent a ripping burst in response just as the Peugeot clipped a barrier and nosed its way out of the plant, headed for an upslope.

The Peugeot coughed, lurched, stalled. Edilson looked in his rear-view and saw the moto sideslip and stop on a dime in front of the barricades. The passenger jumped off and ran toward them. A guard held out his hand in a futile attempt to do his job and was cut down with a quick burst. The rest scattered. Edilson made a decision. "Will, stop them here!"

"Okay!" Will was already on his knees beside the car. Edilson yanked the duffle bag into the front seat and pulled out the SMG. He rolled out of the driver's seat and onto the red dirt as the motoboys opened up. Glass sprayed on him. He crawled forward, cradling the SMG.

The passenger with the firepower sprinted for an abandoned guardhouse, dropping his mag. Will tried to lead the running target and started to fire as fast as he could. The man dived through the open door of the guardhouse just as his partner, already nestled in the doorway, started shooting at Will. Will dropped on his face and ate dirt, stunned by a round smacking into the bumper close by his head. "Edilson! We've got to get out of here!"

Will looked over just in time to see Edilson leap to his feet and sprint for the right of the guardhouse just as the white Jeep Cherokee came flying down the fence line toward them. Sucking air hard, he reloaded with trembling hands. He looked up cautiously again. Edilson had edged around the other side of the guardhouse.

Three seconds of silence. Then the guardhouse windows exploded outward. A body toppled out of the doorway and into the road. More shots as Edilson finished his work.

On the road, the Cherokee was pushing the barriers aside, the men in the back seats now sticking their heads out of the windows to bring their guns to bear. Will had recovered his composure and calmly fired with careful aim at the driver. Glass clouds rose with each hole. He knew he'd accomplished something when the Jeep reared left and slammed into the guardhouse door. A sprinting Edilson emerged from the guardhouse, keeping the Cherokee's occupants down with a long burst on full auto as he ran to the Peugeot.

Will tasted dirt and blood in his mouth as he staggered to his feet and threw himself into the Peugeot. Edilson had the car started and in gear before both of his feet were inside. The Peugeot lurched backwards and slammed into the Cherokee just as Mauricio Panelas was gathering the courage to poke his head above the dash. His neck snapped back, and he passed out next to the driver, who was breathing a death rattle through a hole in his trachea.

Mauricio missed the sight of the Peugeot scooting up the dirt road onto the embankment, following the river, headed south.

"We won't get far in this car." Will lay back and closed his eyes. Two days, two shootouts. Was he actually getting used to this? He felt decidedly less stunned than yesterday. Maybe he was like Edilson. You really could get used to anything.

"*Calma.* We're on a side road. Night is coming. Those fuckers couldn't shoot for shit; we only have a few holes. And this isn't São Paulo or even Blumenau. The cops out here take their time to get moving."

"We still have to ditch this car. Any idea how?" They passed farms, rice paddies. Though they heard sirens in the distance, none passed their way. "Well?" Edilson was clearly lost in thought, biting his lip, as if debating whether to disclose something.

Will leaned over. "Buddy, speak to me. Now is not the time."

Edilson turned to him. Finally he spoke. "My friend, we are going to stop somewhere quiet. Some men are going to come get our car and bring us another car. And then we are going to drive to Floripa."

Had he lost his mind? "I am glad you are so confident. You mean, this sort of thing happens to you so often you have an insurance policy?"

"I didn't say this happens often. But there is an insurance policy."

"We need to talk."

Edilson's expression was even and calm as he watched the road. "Agreed."

Will figured it was time to re-evaluate his friend. He really had no idea what the guy was capable of.

As night fell, they turned down a dirt road flanked by tall palms and dense bush. Edilson found a tributary road with a rotting farmhouse at the end. "Good enough!" he said aloud. He parked the Peugeot under a stand of trees. Both men lay back for a moment and closed their eyes. When Will opened his eyes, he looked down and saw blood on his shirt. He felt his face. It was coming from his lower lip. Gingerly, he probed a ragged cut.

"Looks like you caught a little piece. So we've both been shot twice now." Edilson was smiling at him.

"Yay," he said without enthusiasm. Will opened the car door and stepped out with rubbery legs as Edilson made a phone call. Out across paddy fields to the main road, cop cars raced the way he and Edilson had just come. The lights and sirens receded south. He hoped Edilson's mysterious "insurance" would show up soon. This car could be traced back to Ruth. Ruth meant Gretchen. Maybe she meant Silvia and the kids too. Could Edilson control that? Looking at the car, he realized for the first time that it now had São Paulo plates.

"Nice, huh?" Edilson was standing beside him. "I guess James Bond does ride a bus, hmm?"

"Edilson, who the fuck are you? I mean, I thought I knew, but now ..."

"I'm exactly who you thought I was, *amigo*: a cop. But you don't know enough about this country yet."

"Tell me about it. But forget about the country. What about you? Phony plates, fake ID, sanitized Visas, a bag full of firepower and spy gear ... What the fuck, Edilson? Who are you working for?"

Edilson looked away. The crickets were starting to chirp in the fields. "Thiago, same as you."

"Bullshit. And?"

"And some other cops."

He had suspected it all along. Maybe since the Mercado, but he had really known when Edilson had gotten off the bus in Blumenau. Maybe not Bond's entrance, but he'd had everything else but the martinis.

"Tell me, partner. I have a right to know."

"I know you do." He exhaled. "You know that a lot of police work in this country is done 'unofficially,' right?"

Ah shit. "You mean death squads?" The road was quiet. It had gotten dark and cool fast. The crickets built up to concert volume to fill the silence.

"No! Not like those assholes in Rio, killing street kids in their sleep. I'd never be a part of that. But look at our country versus yours, Will. What happens in Canada if a cop gets killed?"

"We flood the streets and shut everything down until we catch the killer or fry him."

"The way it should be. And the funerals are big there, right?"

Fat lot of good it does you, Will thought, *listening to bagpipes in a pine box.* "Yes. Huge."

"Also as it should be. And what happens if a gang targets police? I read about this, the bikers in Quebec ..."

"Yes, they get fucked up." The Hells Angels in Quebec had made the mistake of putting out hits on two prison guards, one of them a single mother. They'd been made to regret it.

"None of this happens in Brazil, Will. Cops get killed. Lots of us. One hundred in São Paulo this year alone. And what happens? Big manhunts? Big funerals? None of it. The politicians and the people just yawn and go back to their football and novelas. The PCC has gone after us twice, in 2006 and 2012, and we know it's going to happen again. So some of us are doing something about it."

"So you're a Star Chamber?"

"A what?"

"Judge, jury, and executioner?"

Edilson scoffed. "Don't be so Canadian! What did that guy who killed the three cops with the rifle get last year, that crazy guy?"

"Justin Bourque." Justin Bourque had dressed up like Rambo and gone Mountie hunting on a quiet street in Moncton, New Brunswick. He hadn't had the stones to fight to the finish, but his life had been over anyway. "Seventy-five years without parole."

"He'll die in jail. Nobody in Brazil can get more than 30 years for a single murder. And when they're in prison, they just carry on like they're outside! Phones to run their business and call in hits, sometimes on us. Dope, booze, whores. It's no solution. We need something more final."

"Death. A 'final solution'?"

"Some people need it. My organization targets only the very worst, not kids stealing cars ..."

"And if those kids stealing cars witness you doing a hit? What happens then?"

"It's never happened yet."

"Let's see when it does."

"What would you and your perfect colleagues do if you were in our position, Will? I know you. The same damned thing. Why else are you out here with me?"

Will was silent. He knew it was true. But he also knew Edilson was missing a point. "Be careful what you wish for, friend. If what happened to me in Vancouver happened here in São Paulo, I'd have been back on the street as soon as I healed up. Instead, I got fired. Apathy is a double-edged sword."

"You wanna talk philosophy now, Paulo Coelho?" Edilson smiled, gap-toothed and mocking. His friend the assassin.

"Fuck off, James Bond. So tell me about your Phantom Police Force, then?"

Edilson rested his head on his forearms on the car's roof and thought a moment. "What the hell, you are my partner. But never tell Thiago or anyone else, especially not that fucking reporter."

"Give me some credit. I was a cop once, after all."

"I don't know how many of us there are. Maybe a few hundred, maybe more. There are officers involved up to the rank of colonel, maybe higher. My orders come from a major."

"Is it just your guys?"

"At first, but now we have Polícia Civil, even some Federal. And politicians help us too. We have links all over Brazil. Including here."

"Your 'insurance'?"

"Yes. I have numbers to call in case we need help. From here to Paraguay."

"Paraguay?" Will's long hunch that this wasn't his case anymore was pretty much confirmed now.

"We'll get to that later. But here's the important thing, Will: we know the PCC is trying to expand, to go global, to be as big as the Colombian or Mexican cartels ever were. They have people all over Latin America now. And now they have a rich political friend."

"Oscar Stumpf."

"That's why I didn't hesitate when you asked me for help at the Mercado. We've wanted him for a while now. Southern Cross is a mess, sure, but it's too big an opportunity for us to miss."

"A little help would be nice. If you've got hundreds of guys, why is it just you and me all the fucking time?"

"My bosses insisted on secrecy. You had to think I was just a pirate like you."

"Thanks."

"But now you have to know, so you know. Are we still partners?" He held out his hand and gave Will that earnest look he was so good at.

Will shook his partner's hand. "As if I have a choice." The sun's last rays disappeared, and an astonishing array of stars came out above them. Edilson handed him a warm beer, and they toasted.

"To killing Oscar Stumpf." Edilson shot back his beer with gusto.

"Hmm." As if he hadn't promised Silvia exactly that.

They dropped the beers as headlights approached. Both men grabbed their pistols and disappeared into the bush. A four-by-four with a man standing in the pickup bed blinded them with high beams and fog lamps. Will could dimly make out another car behind. They weren't cop cars. Were they PCC? Will drew a bead on the man in the truck bed.

The four-by-four stopped, and the driver stepped out. *"Jacare, safados!"* he shouted with his hands cupped to his mouth.

Edilson shouted back, *"Jacare, muleke!"* and stepped into the light. The other car pulled up close and stopped. The driver walked up to join the others as the man in the bed leaped to the ground.

Will figured it was probably okay to step out and did so just as the driver of the four-by-four walked up to Edilson.

"Blondes and beer, eh?" said Gasparini.

19

The sign in front of the construction site read "Fundacaoes por Condor LLC." It was a holiday (Will couldn't remember which; this country had so many), and the construction equipment sat idle. Gasparini was distracting the lone security guard while Edilson and Will wandered the half-timbered foundation pads.

Condor Foundations LLC. The sole source contractor on both this project and Southern Cross and, according to Will's working theory, a PCC front more expert in disposing of bodies than building lasting foundations. Still, to his inexpert eye, the foundations looked fine. Smooth, even, no obvious cracks. He suddenly remembered that Thiago hadn't called. And he hadn't called Silvia. And what was going on with Ken?

Southern Cross had devoured his entire extended family. *Might as well pour concrete on them,* he thought glumly. He looked over at Edilson, who was kicking the edges of a foundation pad as if it would disgorge a dead body.

The building site was godforsaken, hacked out of a patch of thick rainforest, surrounded by misty gloom, and currently drowning in mud. Aside from covering Oscar Stumpf's sins, it was hard to see the attraction for a developer. But did Stumpf really need another reason to build here? Will wondered idly who was being blackmailed to float this project. It was hard to see how else it would get funded. Maybe there was a shady lawyer in Blumenau or Floripa looking for a PI to help some pathetic pedophile client, tricked into investing in this shithole. The idea made him snort out loud.

Edilson glared at him. The misty wind picked up again, forcing them all to burrow deeper into their clothes. For once, Will regretted his Canadian bravado and thin jacket.

He had so many questions now that Oscar Stumpf was almost the last thing on his mind. What was Edilson really in this for? Who was he associating with, and what were their real goals? Here he was, palling around with Gasparini on the basis of what, cop solidarity? He wasn't even a cop anymore, had never been, at least in this country. But here he was, neck-deep in someone else's fight.

Well, he had wanted to be Brazilian, hadn't he? And how had he explained it all to Lucas? Kids in trouble? He felt like a cynical prick. Well, at least he had saved one kid in trouble. For now.

Last night the rescue party had wrapped the hot car tight, and they'd all left the scene, winding up at Gasparini's parents' fazenda. Will had let Draft Dude out a bit. Homemade wine made for a brutal hangover. At least there had been no barmaids with big tits this time. So he remembered. The news had been all over the chaos at Industrias Schneider. But there had been no perp walk, so Panelas must have gotten his shit together and gotten out before the cops had gotten there. Gasparini had implied Panelas' days were numbered anyway. From what Will was learning now, that was no idle talk.

He looked over at his partner. "So, how does it all end?"

Edilson looked at him quizzically. "What?"

"You seem to know a hell of a lot more about this case than I do, so maybe it's time you told me. I get the feeling I'm being used, and I don't like it, brother. You know, I was getting shot at too yesterday." He let it hang in the air. Edilson looked down at the red earth. "Don't want to tell me, or your major ordered you not to?" He couldn't resist pushing it further. "You know, I thought the one good thing about getting fired was that I was finally free of bullshit police politics. But here we go again."

Edilson spat, "Shut up, goddamn it! You have really got your head in your ass when it comes to this country, Will." He got closer and was stabbing a finger at Will, who was amazed that his laconic friend had it in him. He noticed Gasparini looking over at them out of the corner of his eye. Edilson had the floor now and wasn't letting go. "Do you think you would still be alive if it wasn't for me? For us?" He swept Gasparini in with a hand gesture.

"Would I be here in the first place if it wasn't for you? I'm pretty fucking sure I wouldn't have had three near-death experiences this week if your little Star Chamber hadn't decided to set Oscar Stumpf up for a fall."

"So go back to teaching English, Will." He was really in Will's face now. Will had a different perspective now on how dangerous the guy really was. "Don't act like you don't want this. The quiet life, it's not for you."

Will sighed and sat on the foundation. "Okay. Whatever."

Edilson massaged his temples in frustration. "What does it mean when you gringos say this? 'Whatever'?"

Will rested his hands on his knees. "It means I am gonna trust you. Because I have no fucking choice. But I want you to answer one question. Just one."

"What?"

"There are hundreds of cops, all of whom know the crooks, not to mention the language, way better than me. Why am I even here?"

Edilson smiled. "Because Thiago asked you, not me. He knows nothing. Besides, you're a Canadian. Everybody thinks you're harmless."

"Thanks. So what now? And please don't leave anything out. Try and act like I'm Deyse, and you just got caught balling that hot PM with the super-tight pants. What's her name?"

"Adriana." Edilson smiled wider. "Adriana," he repeated needlessly.

"Um, yeah, I see the thought has crossed your mind. What I mean is, restoring trust is essential. Well, in this situation, I wanna know everything, no more surprises. I am out here acting like a cop, so you can treat me like one of your guys now, and you can tell your major that, okay? And my family fucking well better be looked after ..."

Edilson surprised him by grabbing his shoulders and looking intensely at him. "Don't ever worry about this, my friend. Gasparini has PMSC guys he trusts watching Silvia and the kids in Jaragua now. My guys from São Paulo are keeping an eye on your brother-in-law."

"And Thiago? Sergio?"

Edilson straightened up. "They are harder, Will."

"What do you mean, 'harder'?" He was getting suspicious again.

"Yamada is a reporter, and he's probably pretty good at spotting surveillance. He won't assume it's there to protect him, and then we have a problem if he starts asking, 'Why were there cops watching me?' etc. Thiago we just can't find."

"What? What does that mean?" He started to panic.

"*Calma se.* You told him to disappear, remember?"

Right. Guess he followed that advice. "What about Renner?"

"Don't tell me you care."

"He is the client, after all, in this fictional private investigation. We can't have him dying; it's bad form."

"You also got Ken to try and find him. Are you getting Alzheimer's?"

"No, but I'm a bit distracted by all the people trying to blow my fucking head off lately."

"Me too."

"I thought you'd be more used to it."

"You never get used to it."

Gasparini wandered over. He'd kept a safe distance while things were heated. Will had him figured for a survivor. "He doesn't know much," Gasparini said. "He says the project kind of stalled after the foundations were laid last autumn. He is just a security guard, though."

Will glared at Edilson. "A mushroom, huh? Kept in the dark and fed bullshit? I know the feeling."

"Shut up, Will. So, let's go, then. This is not the place for a hangover."

They clambered into Gasparini's four-by-four and started the drive to the main road just as the first drops of rain began to fall. A thought occurred to Will.

"Hey, Gasparini?"

The cop looked in his rear-view warily. "Yes?"

"Is the whole Gaspar-Gasparini thing just a coincidence, or—?"

Gasparini cut him off. "*Nao*, gringo. My family founded this town." He looked back at the road, slammed on the brakes, and skidded. "*Merda!*"

An old man was in their path, struggling to get a pull cart off the shoulder and back onto the road. He gaped for air as he struggled, revealing a nearly toothless mouth. The men in the car were waiting, whether they liked it or not. The old man slipped on a rut, regained his footing, and continued the struggle. He was barefoot.

Will blurted out, "All right, I'll do it," and stepped into the quagmire.

As he put a shoulder into the back of the cart, the leathery old man gave him a toothless smile. "Thanks for the stopping and the helping" was what he thought he heard. A second language from a toothless mouth was an uncertain proposition at best.

"*De nada*," said a begrimed Will as he levered the cart's rear wheels out of a vicious rut.

"There hasn't been this much excitement here since '71! Look at all these ruts!"

Will stood up. "Since '71? What happened in '71?"

The man pulled a bottle of Pitu out of the wagon and took a celebratory pull. "Lots of vans. Combis. Right where you were just now. They told me to go away, so I did." He handed Will the Pitu bottle. Will passed, his gorge rising. Pitu was strictly utility-grade cachaça, one step above what was in their gas tank.

"Did you know who was in the vans?"

"Nah, who knows in this crazy world. They could have been ETs for all I know. They probably were, come to think of it ... They called them Tupamaros ... but the next day, they were gone."

Stumpf was lucky a guy with this mental firepower was an eyewitness. But what had he witnessed? Will started coughing when it came to him. Tupamaros, the Marxist guerrillas of 1970s Uruguay. Stumpf's first posting. Will's Southern Cross theory was holding water. The leathery old man waved as he remounted the roadside. Will turned and looked back at the project field.

Gasparini laid on the horn. Edilson shouted out the window, "Did you get his number, *veado*? *Vai!*"

Will stalked over to the car. He said to Edilson, "Sunshine, I just found us another one of Oscar Stumpf's mass graves. But we can get a burger now, sure." Covered in mud, he flopped into the back seat, to Gasparini's horror.

Edilson looked at him. "Okay, how about you tell me where to go? It was always your case anyway."

"Floripa. The *deputado* I shot probably has an interesting backstory. If nothing else, we can rate bikinis and get some decent fish."

"South makes sense. They expect us to go the other way."

Will leaned against the headrest and closed his eyes. "Then they're idiots. Who the fuck ever does what you'd expect in this country?"

20

Bistro Isadora Duncan, Florianópolis

Out on the *lagoa*, shrimpers fished by lantern light, giving the illusion of a moving aquatic constellation. It was practically the only illumination in the dark little restaurant. He found it mesmerizing, even if this time he wasn't gazing across the table at Silvia in a low-cut dress. He watched Edilson puzzle over the wine list.

"A few more choices than just 'red' and 'white,' huh, buddy?"

Edilson lowered the list and grinned. "Fuck, man, I'm glad I'm not paying. We'd have to run for it."

"Star Chamber's picking up the tab, huh?"

"Visa Death Squad Platinum. Anyway, our contact picked the place; it's his favourite."

"Mine too."

Edilson squinted out at the *lagoa*. "Don't know why. It's dead down here."

"That's the idea. It's peaceful. Intimate. Romantic." He winked at Edilson, who squirmed in return.

"You'd better order the wine, *veado*. I'll have a beer."

"All class, Edilson, that's what you are." He looked around at his surroundings. Low-lit, natural wood, only six tables. Run by a family of Franco-Brazilians who prepared the best Brazilian seafood using French techniques. For a closet foodie like Will it was heaven. For a poor kid like Edilson raised on baile funk music and *por kilo* restaurants serving rice, beans, and leathery meat by weight, it must have been like going to Sunday service. Still, he was determined to enjoy himself here, even if the subject was going to be death squads and child prostitution. Hell, watching Edilson try to figure out what to do with the cutlery selection was going to be worth it on its own.

But there was business to be done. Gasparini and two of his cronies waited outside in case there was trouble. They weren't expecting any, but things had gotten pretty intense lately, and it seemed like the right precaution. Will suddenly remembered something he needed to do. "Give me a second, partner. Gotta call the Trouble and Strife."

"What the hell are you talking about?"

"Sorry. We aren't far enough into your English lessons yet to talk about the Cockneys ... Gotta call my wife. Also, order this, will ya?" He pointed out a Chablis on the wine list to his befuddled partner and stalked down the stairs to the lobby.

He trembled a little when he dialled the number, as he had when they were dating. A few days away from someone you had slept beside for a decade was a strange thing indeed.

She picked up on the third ring. She sounded sleepy. *"Oi, Will, tudo bem?"*

"Tudo, e voce, meu amor?"

"Where are you? What's happening?"

He hadn't thought this through. How much to tell her? The events of the past week had led him to conclude that he made better decisions in gunfights than he did in conversations with his wife.

"Floripa. Bistro Isadora Duncan."

"Ai, Will, without me?"

"Don't worry, baby; there's no woman involved." Will visualized her skeptically evaluating that statement on the other end of the phone. "We're meeting someone. Edilson is here too."

"Ruth called me. I was worried. She said you rescued a girl. And there were guns involved. What are you doing, Will? I hope you know. The kids are asking about you. Lucas is very worried. He can't sleep."

He closed his eyes and leaned against the wall. He'd felt this conflict—between doing the right thing and doing the right thing—many times but never so intense.

"Tell the kids I'll be okay. We're not alone now. We have lots of help. And you'll be safe."

The door opened, and a tanned man with wavy hair and a sweater wrapped around his shoulders strode in. Movie star handsome, like a mature Rodrigo Santoro. Will knew that was the guy. He looked well fed, fit ... polished. "Silvia, I have to go. Kiss the kids. Kiss yourself."

Silvia sighed. "I also was going to tell you to do something romantic to yourself, Husband."

He laughed. "I bet you were. I love you. I miss you. Don't worry."

"I love you too. And Will?"

"Yes?"

"Kill him."

"Yes. I promise."

He hung up, feeling drunk and spaced, like it was a play where everybody had changed roles at the last minute. But his peace-loving wife appeared to have figured out the only possible play on this down a hell of a lot quicker than he had. Will was constantly thankful for being surrounded by people smarter than he.

He wasn't sure what he brought to the party. Being a decent shot? A Canadian passport? Being able to throw people out of windows? He looked up the stairs and started up. What was more important was what the guy with the sweater around his shoulders had brought to the party. At least right now. Maybe he could fill in the blanks on Rigoberto Soares and tell them why he was in that hotel room with that underage hooker. Gretchen. He caught himself. She had a name. And maybe Will was going to be sitting across the table from the friend of a man he'd shot in the head. And he was going to have to keep that very cool.

Will plodded up the steps with the fervent wish that the wine had arrived.

His guess was right. The man with the sweater was already seated next to Edilson, making small talk. Will already knew this man to be Geraldo Buscetti. He walked up and introduced himself as William Cousins.

"Ah, Senhor Cousins. My friend Sergio told me about you. You write for *McLaren's*, yes?"

"*MacLean's*, yes."

He laughed openly. "My English sucks on the shit, forgive me."

"*Meu Portugues comer merda, desculpe.*"

"Excellent, mutual incomprehension."

"The secret to every good marriage."

"Sexually and politically."

"So it was with you and Rigoberto Soares."

Buscetti shook his head. "Right to the point. *Muito norteamericano.*"

"The legacy of the Scots, I'm afraid. I just have to wonder what a centrist like you and a socialist like Soares had in common. And how that got him in a bugged hotel room with a very young prostitute."

Buscetti's candlelit face showed the briefest glimpse of distaste. "Fear."

"Pardon me?"

"Come on, Senhor Cousins. I know enough from Yamada to understand that you know what Oscar Stumpf is capable of. I heard he almost made you part of the São Paulo Metro?"

Jesus. Will sometimes forgot that, for all their obvious similarities, cops and reporters were two different breeds. Cops had to have their mouths forced open. Reporters loved to talk, about everything but their sources. He'd remember that. Yamada had left Buscetti better prepared for this encounter than he would've liked. He probably knew "William Cousins" was a crock of shit too. But Buscetti was too smooth to let that slip.

"Possibly an accident. Possibly not. And how is our mutual friend?" Out of the corner of his eye, in flickering candlelight, Will saw Edilson watching them as if they were Sampras and Federer. The Chablis arrived, and Will did the honours.

Buscetti ignored the query and observed him. "You are an oenophile, *senhor*; it is obvious."

"I like wine. I know nothing."

"Let's drink to that." He raised his glass, and all three clinked. "To knowing nothing. We'd all be better off if we did." Buscetti took a long pull. It looked like he was nervous too.

Will gauged the man. Geraldo Buscetti. Up-and-comer in Brasília for the big-tent PMDB, Partido do Movimento Democrático Brasileiro. The party of all comers, taking in everyone from ex-guerrillas to former bankers. They were so keen on power-brokering that they hadn't even run a presidential candidate in the last election. They played it smart, knowing there was no way the conservative candidate Alckimin could unseat Dilma. The PT had perfected mobilizing the masses.

"What did you and Soares have in common?" Will asked.

"Knowing nothing. We arrived in Brasília at the same time. We sat on opposite sides of the aisle, but it's a small town, by Brazilian standards. We were both young, with lots of money and power."

Will hadn't been expecting the frankness. But then, sudden death of friends and family could shake things loose in people. He flashed back uncontrollably to that room. *Get off my leg.* The calm, deliberate decision to shoot. The inkwell black blood flowing out of Soares's mouth. He decided to order something stronger. He looked away, at the *lagoa*, the drifting phony stars. He was aware of both men watching him. PTSD reared its head more and more these days. *Pull it together.*

"Tell me about him." The simple, open-ended question that saved so many detectives, engaging the natural human instinct to tell a story.

"He was a crusader."

Edilson smiled slyly at Buscetti's unwitting comparison to them both.

"A labour lawyer from the sticks with big ideas. But also big appetites," Buscetti continued. "He liked the high life. There is a lot of that in Brasília."

That explained the cards in his wallet. "You went to Rio with him? To Vegas? Miami?"

Buscetti smiled openly. "Yes, and I'd do it again. We lived. And we did good work."

Edilson couldn't resist. "Who paid for those trips?"

"How the fuck do I know? Petrobras? Embraer? Coca-Cola? Who's paying for you?" The charmer was replaced by pure steel in an instant.

Edilson tightened his grip on his glass. Will knew he didn't like being talked down to, especially by rich white guys. He interceded. "We get it; we're all whores. And you're right. Tell me about the good you did?"

Buscetti took a deep breath and looked around. "What I'm about to talk about, not a lot of people in this country will, especially not politicians."

"Operation Condor, yes?" Will was less and less concerned with subtlety and more and more concerned with time.

Buscetti was taken aback. "What do you know about that?" He turned to Edilson accusatorially. "Your friend did not mention this. This is a dangerous subject to be discussing in a restaurant. Are you amateurs, or what?" he hissed.

Edilson sat back in his chair, stone-faced. "No, we're very good at killing people now. The rest is your fucking problem. Maybe everything doesn't end in pizza this time, *hein*?"

Will put his arm out to steady his partner. He sensed this was the wrong way to play Buscetti. Edilson was silent now. Buscetti glanced at the stairs and then back at Will. Even in the dim light, Will noticed he was red and perspiring.

"I can tell you're trying to decide 'Should I stay, or should I go?' Either way is trouble, but at least staying can tell you what you're up against. The danger doesn't go away if you leave."

Buscetti slumped back in his chair. It was clear to Will he was going nowhere.

"Condor. Why were you investigating it?" Will asked.

"That's quite an assumption." Buscetti's objection was half-hearted. Lawyers.

"But it's the right assumption, isn't it?"

Buscetti nodded. "Both of our fathers crossed paths with Oscar Stumpf in the seventies. Mine got away with a beating and a warning. Rigo's dad wasn't so lucky."

"He disappeared?"

"No, they found him, shot in the head in his car."

"Where?"

"Rio Grande do Sul. He was working with the Tupamaros. At that time, the army was trying to help the Uruguayans get at Tupamaros hiding in the state. Rigo's dad was helping the Marxists, doing logistics for expatriate guerrillas, nothing too hands-on. The army helped the

Uruguayans in a kidnapping attempt on a couple of Reds in the state, Senhor Soares's friends, but they botched it. Publicly. Very embarrassing. You see, press freedom was limited then, but it wasn't non-existent. So it was all over the papers, and someone had to pay. Guess the army blamed Senhor Soares. And when the army wanted you gone back then, they sent Oscar Stumpf after you." Buscetti took a long pull of Chablis.

"When was this?"

"The stuff with the Tupamaros was early seventies. But Rigo's dad wasn't killed until '78."

Edilson interjected, "Stumpf does hold a grudge."

"How did you implicate Stumpf?" Will asked.

"Well, my dad obviously knew him."

Will filed that away. Why "obviously"?

"And he was a liaison officer in Uruguay at the time. Plus, the Arquivos."

"The Arquivos do Terror from Paraguay?"

"Yes."

"How did you find information there?"

"Sergio Yamada. He heard rumours that we were sniffing around, and he came to Brasília."

"Sergio never mentioned that." Fucking reporters.

"We told him not to, in return for an exclusive. I guess the deal is off."

"How close were you to a story?"

"I don't know. The Operation Condor stuff was frustrating. Lots of clues, but no payoff. You could never put the guy at a specific crime. All of the witnesses were either dead, scared, or implicated themselves. We knew he was busy for about 10 years, working in Uruguay, Argentina,

Paraguay. Lots of cables back and forth around the time of 'actions,' unlikely to be coincidental. But that was it. Besides, there's not a hell of a lot of people in Brasília very excited about reopening the past. Some of them wouldn't come off looking too good."

"And Brazilians aren't exactly known for introspection."

Buscetti smiled and upended his glass. "Exactly." He signalled for another bottle. "We love to look ahead. Look at Brasília, a classic example. If this was a country that cared about history, the capital would still be in Salvador."

"So you were going to give up, then? Why was Soares in Blumenau, anyway?"

Buscetti rolled his eyes and recited slowly, "Because that is not all we found out about Oscar Stumpf."

"Humour me."

"Of course, my friend." This guy was why people hated politicians. The assumption of superiority. The airy familiarity. "We found out from contacts," he said, giving a subtle nod to Edilson, "that Stumpf had made an alliance with the PCC. He was using them to traffic girls from Paraguay. They were also acting as muscle for him. It was working for both of them quite well. Stumpf got the girls and the gunmen; the PCC got respectable cover for smuggling and money laundering."

"Did you find out why he needed the girls?"

"I assumed it was blackmail. But we couldn't prove it, until a guy we knew in the Polícia Federal told me there was something funny going on in telecommunications. They were investigating a guy at one of the Internet service providers for data mining. He was called in for an interview, but he 'accidentally' fell off his 10th-storey balcony the night before and never made it. I got a list of clients whose data went out the back door." Buscetti put the list in front of Will. He recognized a number of names immediately. The investors in Southern Cross.

Buscetti was studying him closely. "You know who these people are, don't you?"

It was Will's turn to drain his glass. "Yes, I do. Have you ever heard of a real estate development called Southern Cross?"

"That's a planned community Stumpf is building in the Litoral Norte in São Paulo. It's supposed to have been open only to select investors. Very secretive, like much of what Stumpf does."

"I have a list of the investors." Will held up Buscetti's list for him. "Right here."

"Jesus. So that's why some of these men were showing up in Blumenau."

"I know that too. But why was Soares there?"

"When the source on the Polícia Federal investigation into the ISP was killed, the investigation ran out of steam. They had the dead guy's bank records, but of course all the transactions were in cash. Some calls from throwaway mobiles, stuff like that. They suspected Stumpf, but they didn't know enough without the witness. They knew a lot of the stolen data was child porn, so they figured it was either blackmail or vigilantism. They weren't willing to proceed without more. The whole thing was kept quiet, in case something came up later that they could use. And Rigo got frustrated. He said he was going up to Blumenau. He asked me to come."

"Why didn't you?"

Buscetti looked around. "Look, I don't mean to speak ill of the dead, but ..."

"But Rigo liked the ladies, is that it?"

"Yes. And going with him up there, well, my marriage couldn't take it."

Will felt at least a little relieved. Soares's motives in that hotel room probably hadn't been that pure. But he would've still been worth a lot more alive.

Buscetti hesitated and then asked, "What happened up there?"

"He was your friend," Edilson said with surprising gentleness. "You don't want to know. But it was no robbery."

"I knew that. Maybe it's better I don't know. But I do want to know this." He looked at Edilson. "Why are your people so interested in Stumpf all of a sudden? Certainly you have no interest in his past wrongs. A lot of your people have dirty hands too."

It was a direct challenge, usually a bad play with Edilson. But he accepted it with equanimity. "We don't care about what he did in the seventies. But he signed his own death warrant when he started working with the PCC. Now let's eat."

Buscetti looked at Will. "You're not a very convincing reporter."

Out on the *lagoa*, the torches flickered out one by one as the shrimpers caught their fill.

21

Hercilio Luz Bridge, Florianópolis

Will had dozed off, his head slumped against the window, his knees up to his stomach in the too-small rental car. He came awake on the bridge to an impressive vista. The bridge vaulted above the inland waterway separating the island from the less picturesque mainland. It might have been a conscious imitation of the Golden Gate, but it was striking nonetheless. He sat up in his seat as best he could and regretted he was leaving so soon. The morning sun reflected off the mild swells below, on which he could he see boats weaving and bobbing. Will reflected on the value of the life he'd lately been risking without much consideration. Beside him, his partner stared straight ahead. Edilson wasn't much for introspection.

"*Bom dia*. Sorry we didn't have time for the beach." Edilson grinned. "Too bad, *mane*."

"Next time. Maybe you can tell me something about our next destination?"

They'd come back late from the restaurant last night and had both sacked out fast. The pace of the last few days was beginning to tell. There had been no time to debrief on their interview with Buscetti, who had been picked up by a woman who didn't look like his wife and disappeared without a "*boa noite*." Will figured the unofficial Chamber of Deputies investigation into Oscar Stumpf had died with Rigoberto Soares. Which meant that Will Bryant had killed it. Not a fact he wanted to dwell on. This morning, Edilson had been unceremonious in waking him.

Will had felt the bed shudder with a vicious kick. He had opened his bleary eyes to see a naked Edilson. "*Vai, principe!* We've got a flight at nine. No time for bikinis."

"Aw, fuck, Edilson, not the first thing I want to see in the morning!"

So here they were, working their way back to São Paulo, to whatever culmination was in store. He felt only marginally wiser than he had two weeks before. Each answer seemed to come with a new set of questions. His latest was "Where the hell are we going?"

"We're flying to Campo Grande, then driving to Pedro Juan Caballero."

"Where the fuck is Pedro Juan Caballero?"

"On the Paraguayan border."

"Great. And what are we doing there?"

"We're going to talk to a man named Wilson Guimares. He's a PCC pimp and human trafficker. He's wanted by the Polícia Federal."

"I am guessing this won't be a sit-down over coffee and *pao de quejo*."

"No, we're going to kidnap him." Edilson delivered the craziest shit as a matter of fact.

"Mind telling me why?" Will was stunned enough by the subject and the early hour to be distracted by a sailboat below them letting out shimmering white blankets to catch a rising breeze. How much better to be down there, holding a caipirinha, surrounded by thonged asses? *Happy place.*

"If you want to make a link between Stumpf and the PCC, the obvious man to grab is Panelas. But he's pretty hard to get to, right? The next best guy is Guimares. He's too hot to operate in Brazil, but we can't touch him in Paraguay. There he runs guns, dope, and whores for Panelas. He knows a lot, and since he's looking at 30 years, he might be motivated to talk."

"And he is the easier guy to get to, being that he's in another country and may have cops on his payroll? Explain that to me."

"I have a plan."

"That's what you said in Blumenau."

Edilson grinned at him. "Yeah, and we made it, didn't we?"

"Edilson, at this time I only consider myself temporarily alive."

"Everybody's only temporarily alive."

"Some more than others."

Traffic was clearing, and they were about to exit the bridge when Will suddenly remembered something. He rolled down the window and launched Soares's wallet over the bridge deck.

Edilson stared daggers at him. "Don't get me a ticket, will you?"

"Would you rather explain that at airport security?"

"Good point."

Avenida Getúlio Vargas, Ponta Porã, Brazil

They waited in the gradually cooling sun outside Polícia Federal headquarters. Will's legs were rubbery from the four-hour drive from Campo Grande. He contemplated the risk of what they were about to do. Ponta Porã and its Paraguayan neighbour Pedro Juan Caballero were bandit country, plain and simple. The PCC ran the show, and any reporters or judges foolhardy enough to go against them lived in armoured compounds. He'd looked up Pedro Juan Caballero in his Lonely Planet guide, which he still carried with him whenever he left São Paulo. According to the author, "If you spend more than one night here, make sure it's for hospitalization."

So for him and Edilson to be here seemed only natural. It didn't help that the border between the two countries was a wide avenue with no border control. Guns and dope, human beings too, it was all easy to come by in Paraguay. No wonder the PCC had grown roots here. For most people coming from Brazil, the cheap electronics and clothing were the main draws. For the PCC it was quite another thing. So why Edilson thought he could walk across the border and grab a made guy, no doubt surrounded by lots of help, and then drag him illegally across the border again, that he had to hear. It wasn't the hearing it that made him nervous; it was the doing of it.

Edilson squinted into the sun as they waited. "I see the problem here, my friend."

"And what is that, partner?" His friend enjoyed Sphinx-like utterances.

"Look at the size of this fucking building! This wouldn't even be a post office in São Paulo!"

It was true. The baby blue two-story building looked like somewhere you'd drop off your kids for piano lessons. Will had been expecting something a little more imposing for a town with this kind of problems.

Edilson continued, "I've never been here before. Partner, I've never even left Brazil. But I know all that coke and all those guns I've seen in my career were coming from somewhere else. If the people in power were really interested in stopping it, this building would be five times larger."

"True story." As a former border cop, the whole idea of this town drove Will nuts. He couldn't imagine how frustrating it was to try to police it. You could walk across the Avenida National into Paraguay and back without talking to a single cop. No gun control on the other side. Cocaine flown straight into the municipal airport from Bolivia. And the results of all that easy smuggling were displayed in every favela in Brazil, every night.

Lately, there had been some efforts, as the Brazilians were putting pressure on their more laid-back neighbours to take action. But there was pushback, unrest. Things had been easy for so long that narcos wanted in Brazil were standing for office in Pedro Juan Caballero and winning. So walking across the street and grabbing one of these assholes must be pretty damn tempting to Edilson.

But Will had made it clear to Edilson that he wanted to see a plan first. He was reserving judgment. When the subject was survival, it seemed the logical course of action.

He looked up at the sun as a rivulet of sweat ran into his open mouth. Seasons didn't mean shit here. Hot and dry or hot and wet, those were your choices in the Sertão.

Just then a compact man with thick black hair and a gunfighter's moustache, wearing a Polícia Federal vest and a drop-leg holster, stalked out of the front entrance and went straight for them. He didn't look happy.

He marched up to Edilson and stood on his toes. "What the fuck?" he hissed. "I know you gave me a break, but whatever it is you are doing in this town, I am not interested! It's too late to blackmail me anyway!"

Edilson held up his hands in supplication. "*Calma*, brother. Nobody came here to blackmail you. I came to make you a proposal."

The man looked back at the building and then back at Will. "Who is the gringo?"

Edilson hesitated. "He's a cop. He's working with us."

The man grimaced. He moved closer to Will. "He'd better not be DEA. I hate those cocksuckers."

Will spoke up. "I'm not DEA. I'm Canadian."

"What's the difference?" This always made Will want to punch people, but he figured now was not the time.

"Fewer Mexicans," Will replied.

The man cracked a smile. "Okay, let's walk and talk a little. I owe you an audience, Lopes."

"You owe me a lot more than that." Edilson had that over-relaxed smile on his face that warned Will from experience that someone was about to get fucked up.

They walked a couple of blocks and turned into a red-dirt alleyway. The cop turned to face them. "Okay, what do you need? I am Waldemar Galtieri, by the way, gringo."

"I am Will Bryant, Galtieri." They shook hands. Galtieri was one of those guys who tried to assume dominance with a bone-crushing grip. Will gave it back until it got stupid for both of them.

Galtieri turned to Edilson. "Well, what bullshit do you want to involve me in now?" He smirked. Edilson laughed out loud and punched Galtieri in the face. Galtieri staggered back against the wall, clutching at his face. He opened his mouth as blood dripped from his nose. "Lopes, what the fuck is wrong with you? *Puta merda!*"

Will was just as surprised. "Edilson, what the fuck, man?"

Edilson was calm. He held his hands in front of him and looked both ways down the alley. "Did you forget why you owed me one? Because it really seemed like you did back there. Do you remember hitting that cyclist in São Paulo when you were so drunk you pissed yourself? Do you remember how you begged me, fucking begged me, man, not to turn you in? Because I wouldn't forget the man who saved my career and my life. Well?"

Galtieri looked up at the sun. He wiped his nose with his hand. "No, I didn't forget. I'm sorry if it seemed like I did. What can I do for you?"

Will was embarrassed for the man. But he wondered what had happened to the cyclist. Still, in the predatory narrative of this case, Waldemar Galtieri was an opportunity to be exploited.

Edilson said, "It's more of a question of what I can do for you. Do you want Wilson Guimares?"

"You know damn well I do." Galtieri wiped his nose again.

"And I bet you even came up with a plan, no?"

"Yes, a pretty good one. But nobody would approve it."

"Consider it approved." Edilson, a lowly beat cop, was approving cross-border raids now. Will shook his head.

"What's the catch?" Galtieri wiped his nose again and looked around.

"He talks, he gets a break. We're after bigger prey."

Galtieri shuffled his feet. "You know that's not a decision I can make."

"Yes it is. If it's all informal."

"I don't like that word, 'informal.'"

"What choice do you have? This way, at least you get a chance to talk to him. Right now you have nothing."

Galtieri found his spine again. "Edilson, fuck you! You know why I don't have a choice! Because you can ruin my career and send me to prison! That's why. So it doesn't matter what I say. Okay, let's do it!" He blew a length of bloody snot out of his nose at Edilson's feet as an exclamation.

Edilson reached a hand out and put it on Galtieri's shoulder. "I told you I didn't come here to blackmail you. I meant it. You have to go along with this. I am asking you to work with us. There is something much bigger at stake."

Will suddenly felt like he shouldn't be there. This was family business.

Galtieri stood up straight and wiped his face again. He took a deep breath. "Lopes, you are a blackmailing asshole." Galtieri sighed and reached a decision. "But let me tell you how we're going to get Wilson Guimares."

Avenida National, Pedro Juan
Caballero, Paraguay

There it was. A wide avenue separating two countries. Not a cop in sight. Edilson was right; the powers that be really couldn't give a shit if they let this go on. The two men walked across the road into Paraguay. On the other side, it was pretty much a mirror image: stray dogs, almost as much Portuguese on the signs, people pushing you to buy things. It made Will think about what borders meant, anyway. The sight of a shambolic, dirt-caked taxi dodging monstrous potholes made him think of an old Clash song. "They've got the weed. They've got the taxis ... in the dirt."

He was sure there were worse places in South America. But probably not by much. Even Edilson looked uncomfortable. "I wish we'd had a chance to test these guns. I think those pricks in Campo stiffed us," he hissed in Will's ear. True, the guns their contact in Campo Grande had given them as replacements for the ones they'd had to leave in Floripa looked a little rough. His was a weather-beaten Taurus knock-off of a Beretta 92. He wouldn't trust the sights worth a damn, but it was a rugged gun and would probably be fine. Was "probably" good enough? He was suddenly very aware that he had just crossed a border with an illegal gun and a fake passport.

Just then, a Hyundai four-door screeched to a halt on the curb beside them. The cadaverous man in mirrored shades in the front passenger seat turned to face them. "Get in, please." His English was schoolboy perfect.

Will and Edilson looked at each other and shrugged. They got in the back seat. The car peeled out and sped off. The driver was a heavy, bald man who reminded Will of

Shrek. He drove hunched over and obsessed, muttering to himself at every near miss.

The driver began performing death-defying antics in the approved Latin manner, first dodging a heavily crowded municipal bus, then nearly sideswiping a taxi. Will had long since learned to tune this out, and he focused on the man in the passenger seat.

"Our friend called you?" Edilson probed cautiously.

"You'd better hope he did, or you're about to die!" the cadaver replied. Will was reaching for his gun when the man laughed raucously. "Relax, gringo; Galtieri called me." He turned to face them and held out his hand. "Capitan Benevides, SENAD. But you can call me Felipe." He jabbed a finger at the driver. "This is Reyes. He's an idiot."

"Gracias, Capitan," the man mumbled. He put two wheels on the curb to avoid a stalled subcompact.

SENAD, the Paraguayan anti-drug police. Will had heard mixed reviews. But they did seem to be the only game in town.

"So, we're finally going after that fucking asshole Omar, no?" Benevides stubbed a cigarette into the car lighter and suck-started it with gusto.

Will asked, "Omar?"

"That's what that fucker calls himself here. We all know who he is, but he's got a full set of papers saying he's a Paraguayan, so all his buddies in the government won't let us deport him, which we'd like only slightly less than filling him full of holes."

"He's that bad, huh?" Will knew he sounded naive, but the brutality of Latin American crime and punishment required adjustment.

Edilson interjected, "Worse than you can imagine. They say he set a lawyer on fire in the *microondas* once."

"That's a crime?" shot back Benevides with a poker face. Edilson laughed.

Will felt queasy. Even in a country as violent as Brazil, that couldn't have happened very often. And Edilson's jollity couldn't conceal the fact that he knew it too. Had this guy killed Usman al Khattib? Had he killed Thiago's best friend? And they were just gonna let him go if he talked? How would Will explain that to Thiago? He started feeling sick, something the godawful *churrascaria* meal in Campo Grande and Reyes's swerving were not helping. He rolled down his window, and the handle came off in his hand. He guessed the Paraguayan anti-drug police weren't nearly as well equipped as their opponents.

Benevides noticed his chagrin. "Sorry. Believe it or not, this piece of shit is our best car. We were trying to impress the big shot from Canada! Ha!"

Will smiled back. He figured Benevides had probably gone a little bit insane out here. But if you were a clean drug cop in this town, and Edilson assured him Benevides was, that was part of the job description.

Thiago, Usman, what were they going to do? And Edilson had to have known. Clearly he was withholding again.

But how much did a lawyer he'd never known mean to Will? More than getting Stumpf? More than ending the implied threat to his family and friends and the explicit one to himself? He wouldn't know what he was gonna do until they got face to face with Guimares. The improvised last-ditch play was his strong suit.

They pulled into a dirt lot behind a supermarket. A woman with her face wrapped in a shawl ran to the back door and hopped in on Edilson's side. Reyes peeled out crazily.

Will leaned over in the crowded back seat and watched as the woman revealed her face. She was fortyish but still strikingly beautiful. Jet black hair fell over her face in bangs over deep chocolate eyes. She wore a tight black dress with plunging cleavage. He stared a moment. *"Como esta, senhora?"*

She took his hand and smiled beguilingly. Benevides spoke up. "She doesn't speak any English or Portuguese, so save your pickup lines, stud!" Will glared at him as Edilson snickered. "She's not from around here."

"Who is she then?"

"Senhora Beatriz Rojas Benitez. She's from Asunción. She's here because Wilson Guimares pimped out her daughter and the girl disappeared. So she's going to help us if we agree to find out about her daughter." The woman gripped Will's hand and stared at him intensely. He wondered if she knew they were gonna let the pimp son of a bitch walk.

Edilson spoke up as Will disengaged from Senhora Benitez's grasp. Her eyes stayed fixed on him. "Let's go over it again. We know Guimares likes to drink on his own in the bar Lo de Pepe. He thinks his hangers-on are too scummy to drink there, right?"

Benevides snorted. "As if he isn't! That's a classy place! It's good for this job because it's only a block away from the border. If he's unescorted, should be easy to get him out. If he's unescorted."

Will couldn't fathom the arrogance. "Why would a man wanted a block away in a town with no border controls go drinking in public on his own?"

Edilson replied, "You don't understand our criminals, Will. They have to be seen not giving a shit. It's important for their 'street cred,' as you call it."

"Yeah," Benevides interjected, "it's why so many of them wind up in the morgue. Still not enough, if you ask me."

"Amen," replied Edilson. "So we know Guimares makes a living pimping out young girls, but what he really likes are the classy older broads like Beatriz here." She looked up at the mention of her name. "That's why she is the bait. She strikes up a chat with him at the bar, slips him a roofie, and you and I come in on a signal as his Brazilian buddies coming to scoop him up."

Outside the windows, hordes of Brazilian *muanberas*, roving junk merchandise peddlers, went from store to store with huge expandable bags, stocking up on cheap goods for the long bus ride home. It was the town's only real legal industry.

Benevides called to Reyes, "Turn right on Lopez. It's on the corner."

"I know where it is," the hunched-over Reyes replied with the voice of the oppressed. "You don't have to show off." At least Will thought that was what he heard.

They passed a tranquil-looking park surrounding a lagoon. Families clustered on blankets laid on the grass. Will was surprised by the concession to anything other than commerce. Benevides noticed. "Every city, even this one, has a heart. And decent people trying to make a living. That's why I am still here. Until they kill me." He looked ahead again. Will noticed a jagged bullet scar on the back of the *capitan's* neck. They turned onto Marshal Lopez.

Marshal Lopez. It would be like Berlin having a Hitler Street. The maniac had started a war in the 1860s that had killed more than half the population. And recent history hadn't been much kinder to Paraguay. Now the PCC and the Red Command had set up shop here to make a bad situation even worse.

Benevides turned to Beatriz and spoke to her briefly in Spanish. She nodded as they pulled to the curb. She got out with a final look at Will and strode down the street. He watched her swaying walk just a moment too long.

"Now we wait. I already have a man in the bar who will call me when Guimares shows up. It's usually around six." Benevides lit another smoke on the embers of his last and exhaled through his nose. "For guys who everybody wants to kill, narcos are so fucking predictable."

The last light was dying as Pedro Juan Caballero switched from sort-of to very dangerous. Will voiced a thought. "What if there is an escort?"

Benevides was confident. "There never is. If there's any sign of trouble, SENAD shuts down the street. It happens a lot; people barely notice. And it won't be us picking you up. Galtieri has that covered. If all goes well, you won't see my face again!" He grinned.

"And if we do?" Will noticed Reyes studying him through lidded eyes in the shadows.

"Well, then I'll have to shoot you. You know, as foreign invaders, etc. No offence." He smiled maniacally.

"None taken." This was a crazy town. Why shouldn't it have crazy cops? The sun disappeared as they all fell silent, waiting for the call.

22

Halfway across the continent, Ken Scribbins was sitting in the front seat of his old Ford truck, which was parked across from one of the fanciest wine bars in São Paulo. He knew he stuck out like a sore thumb. He figured he was better at the crook stuff than the cop stuff, so he just went along for the money. Besides, it was fun. He'd always wanted to be one of the good guys. He'd watched *Adam-12* and *Dragnet* growing up. He'd always secretly wanted to be a cop, even when he was being arrested by them.

But what chance did he have with a mother who always reminded him, "Boy, your father and your uncle are both rottin' in jail, and that's where you're headed too." Gotta hand it to her, the bitch was right.

Not like his job was very glamorous. His job was to try to find Luc Renner, that simpering little short eyes who had started the whole fucking mess he was now ass-deep in. This was Ken's third night of trying. It was surprisingly

215

hard to find someone who didn't want to be found. Kind of made him wonder if he'd needed to knock up all those chicks just to stay in Brazil. Maybe nobody would've ever found him. Maybe they weren't even looking?

But he figured he finally had the gist of it. Renner liked wine, right? And rich assholes who liked wine liked to congregate in places where they could talk a lot of bullshit about "noses" and "subtle hints" and so on. And gatherings like these were where Luc Renner could find some people who didn't despise him for being a fucking baby raper.

This was the most important thing, Ken figured. He remembered this from being on the run himself. When you are a hunted man, you feel the whole world is against you. One reminder that it isn't, even for a few hours, is worth the risk. That was why Ken had stopped going over the wall. He knew he'd always fuck up like that and get himself caught. When he'd seen the ad in the paper for a wine event here, he'd figured this was the kind of lure that would draw in a smug little prick like Renner who needed people to like him more than anything else.

He saw a skinny man with an umbrella crossing the street a block over as the first thick drops of a rainstorm started pelting the windshield. Ken glanced ruefully at the right-side window. A stream of water began to pour out of the sill and down the armrest. He looked back at the man. *He ain't Brazilian. He carries an umbrella. And he stops at the light.* The man looked up at the wine bar entrance as Ken slumped in his seat. He saw the face. Luc Renner.

Now that he had him, Ken wasn't sure what happened next. Will hadn't been too definite on that. Grab him? Talk to him? Punch him out? That last one was his choice, but honestly he had no idea.

Ken was still working this out in his mind when a well-suited blond man stepped outside the entrance, made a phone call, and then went back in. He didn't know why, but he registered it.

He looked up into the lit windows. The better class of people were enjoying themselves tonight. Valets were running through the rain to park BMWs, Jaguars, Range Rovers. No Ford pickups there. Ken was surprised no rented goon had knocked on his window yet.

The rain made him want to piss badly. He groped underneath for an empty bottle and heaved a sigh of relief when he found one. As he unzipped and hooked up, he wondered why they never showed this on cop shows. Maybe they were better at holding it? He was still thinking this through when a black Mercedes SUV pulled up in front and stopped in the valet zone. The valet's objections were quickly met with flashed IDs and abasement. Two minutes later, an ashen-faced Luc Renner was escorted outside by two sharply dressed goons, one wide and black, the other a greasy-haired shithead, who deposited him in the back and sped off, leaving the valet with a handful of cash.

Ken figured he'd done his job for today. He also figured that was the last anybody would be seeing of Luc Renner. At least he got a plate number. Ken popped out the dashboard lighter and stubbed a Marlboro against it. He inhaled deeply, put the truck in drive, and coasted away from the good life.

Bar Canada, later that evening

As soon as he got back to the bar (he hated mobile phones and never carried one), Ken called Will, Edilson, and Thiago. Nobody was answering. He shrugged and went back to his business. He'd done his bit. Luciana had looked after things by herself while he was out, which wasn't too hard tonight. A couple of regulars, a few *turistas* from the States (why come to a fake Canadian bar in real Brazil?). Jesus, he felt like blazing a joint. He wondered if Jefferson was holding. It was almost time to close up when the two men in grey uniforms showed up.

They walked in the door abreast, rain dripping off their overcoats and Polícia Militar square ball caps. They scanned the room, not acknowledging him. Ken felt that very bad vibe he had learned never to ignore in the joint. Then he placed the faces. One wide and black. The other a greasy-haired shithead.

"Luciana, sai de aqui! Agora!" Ken dropped and rolled just as the two phony cops dropped their rain slickers and riddled the bar with submachine gun fire.

In all his years of crime, the only time he'd heard gunfire close-up like that was when a drunken Jamaican had started shooting a MAC-10 in the air at a beach party in Aruba. This was 10 times worse, a ripping and smashing that pulled out your fucking eardrums. Ken forced himself to move for the rear. He scuttled through the kitchen swing door as it splintered behind him, to find his cook Jefferson lying on the floor, choking in his own blood, which was running down his ample stomach in rivulets. Ken took the stupid chef hat off his head, not wanting the man to die looking ridiculous.

"Sorry." He knelt in the blood for a moment. It was stupid but it was all he could think of to say. He heard clicks and slams on the other side of the perforated door to the bar. The killers whispered to each other. Where was Luciana?

"This one's almost dead," one of the men said. A shot followed.

"No 'almost' now. Heitor, be alert; I think the other one is coming out back. Take him," the other one said.

Luciana. You fucking cocksuckers. Ken stood up and bolted to the cupboard where he kept his only insurance. He scrabbled in the back for a furious couple of seconds and opened the inner door behind a row of pots and pans. A sawed-off double-barrelled shotgun came out in his hand. He broke the action open, saw two shells, reached back in, and grabbed two more. He tried to still his breathing. He thought they called it "combat breathing." It was something he'd always had to do in the joint when it was time to fight. As he pondered his next move, he heard glass scrunching underfoot on the other side of the door. They had to be behind the bar now. The kitchen lights went out.

Ken would've really liked killing both of those assholes, but he guessed Heitor was alone. He hoped Heitor wouldn't have much firepower. He sucked in a deep breath and hit the panic bar hard. He launched himself headfirst into the alley.

Heitor was behind a Dumpster. He had the firepower Ken Scribbins was afraid of. But he didn't know how to lead a man moving as fast as Ken Scribbins. His burst of SMG fire lit up the doorway and shot out the light. Heitor stood up, trying to see the man he thought he had killed, pushing back his borrowed Polícia Militar hat. He looked to his left in time to see the muzzle flash from both barrels of Ken Scribbins' shotgun. The phony cop with baby blue eyes was pushed into the wall. He had time to look down at the gaping hole where his lungs had been before he toppled onto his face.

Ken popped open the action, and two spent shells flew out. He reloaded as fast as his trembling hands would allow, keeping his gun to bear on the doorway he'd just dived out of.

The men inside were not coming in after him. Instead, they backed out of the bar hurriedly and fish-hooked around both sides.

Ken scrambled for the Chevrolet Heitor had left with its engine running and threw it into gear just as the black killer charged into his path and ripped the windshield with a burst of rapid fire. The windshield exploded, and Ken felt his shoulder punched open with poker-hot pain. He forced his screaming right arm onto the shifter and steered with his left, right at the black man.

I want a hood ornament, and you're it, asshole. Ken hit the killer square in his shins with the front bumper, reefed the wheel over hard, and drove 50 metres with the gasping big man on his hood before doing a brake stand and throwing him into the street. He seriously thought about running him over again. Would Forrest Gump do that?

Luciana. Jefferson. *Fuck you, Forrest, and your mama too.* He was throwing it in reverse for a good rev-up when his rear windshield exploded. Behind him, a big man with greasy hair screamed in rage, firing on full auto at the Chevy as it rolled backwards toward Heitor's body, now half submerged in a massive puddle.

For Ken, revenge would have to wait. Cursing, he shifted the Chevy into first on the third try and peeled out into the street.

Guarulhos, later that night

Press release from Polícia Militar Corpo de Bomberos:

> Molotov cocktails were thrown into the residence of a well-known criminal defence lawyer. The structure was consumed by flames and was a total loss. Nobody is believed to have been home at the time, and no one is believed to have been injured. The incident is under investigation at this time.

23

Bar Lo de Pepe, Pedro Juan Caballero,
Paraguay

Will looked at his watch: eight-thirty. Beside him, Edilson's head was back, mouth agape, as he snored mightily. Poor Deyse, on top of everything else she had to put up with from this guy. In the front seat, Benevides and Reyes were playing cards. Will asked, "Aren't you worried they're going to make us as cops? I mean, a car with four dudes with short hair on the same street for three hours?"

Benevides yawned. "Nah, who cares? They get followed all the time. Some of these assholes are so protected, they wouldn't be worried if they found us in their bathrooms! They're gonna get a surprise tonight, though!" He elbowed Reyes, who dropped his hand. "Oh, tough shit, Reyes, that looked like a good hand. You'll have to draw again."

Reyes muttered bitterly as he picked up his cards with one hand.

The smells of the street drifted in: roasted peanuts, spilled booze, grilled meat, dogshit, exhaust. The shoppers were still there but mixed in with a harder crowd, night people. Young gauchos off the ranches, flush with cash and looking for trouble. Hookers wrapped tight in black dresses, looking to take that money. Dope dealers looking for a piece too. Obvious Brasileiros *criminosos*, gold chains and Adidas, permanent sunglasses and threat.

Guimares, "Omar" as the Paraguayans mockingly called him, had shown up just a little after six-thirty. Will had only seen a blurry faxed picture of the man, but he had no doubt. Edilson had turned in his seat as the man had come up from behind the car, walking straight past without looking. He was tall and muscular with a short-cropped afro over thick brows and a lower lip jutting out in insolent defiance of it all. He'd walked with the confidence mandatory in the pimp business the world over; essential gear for getting the innocent to become anything but. He wore a red Brazilian national team jersey over black jeans, a single understated gold chain around his neck.

As he'd entered the restaurant, Benevides's phone had rung. *"Si, lo se. Llamame cuando paso algo."* He'd turned to Will. "I told him to call us back if Beatriz starts getting somewhere."

Edilson had smiled. "I am going to enjoy this." He had closed his eyes.

That had been two hours ago. Will had figured something would've happened by now. Maybe Guimares was smarter than they thought and had smelled a honeypot. Still, apparently the two were deep in conversation and seemed to be hitting it off. At last report, Guimares was getting touchy-feely.

Ten minutes later, the phone rang. Benevides hung up, fast. "She did it! Let's go." Edilson was already awake and clambering out the door into traffic as Will stepped out.

"*Boa sorte!*" Benevides called out as they sped away.

The two men entered the bar to find a slobbering Wilson Guimares clawing at the bar trying to pull himself up. "*Puta*, you poisoned me!" Guimares burbled through dripping lips. Will felt a wonderful warm sense of schadenfreude. How many girls had he done this to? Beatriz smiled warmly as she walked past them on her way out. No doubt she felt the same thing.

"Oi, brother, remember us?" Edilson approached the staggering pimp like a long-lost brother. "Let's get you home!" He wrapped a friendly arm around the sagging pimp.

Will could tell that the bartender didn't buy it for a second as he scowled at them both. But there was no way he was getting involved. "Take it outside!" he said in Portuguese.

"Sure, boss, no problem." Will was consciously aware that he wasn't a very good gangster. He leaned down to scoop up the big man under the arms.

Edilson smirked into Guimares's face. "We've been told to take you outside," he whispered in the pimp's ear. "This should be no problem. I used to be a garbage man ... before I became a cop."

Guimares's eyes went wild, and he started to struggle, but the Rohypnol's effect was too strong, and he soon went limp. Will backed onto the street as Edilson carried the man's legs. They got outside and propped him up, *Weekend at Bernie's* style, as they walked toward the border. They quickly realized the flaws in their plan as they staggered through the jammed sidewalks beside the Centre do Mundo outlets, with their heavy and now-vomiting charge. But Galtieri wouldn't cross the border, and Benevides couldn't be seen helping them too much.

"Fuck this!" Edilson exclaimed and stepped into the street to hail a taxi, leaving Will sagging under Guimares's slumping weight. Edilson stepped in front of a taxi already with a fare. He waved a handful of cash at the driver, who turned to his passenger. They began a vociferous three-way argument.

Shit, Will thought as he scanned the streets, looking for cops. *This is getting ugly.* Edilson yanked open the back door, pulled a startled old man in a white suit to his feet, jammed a handful of cash in his jacket pocket, and said, *"Muchos gracias."*

Great, Will thought, *even in this town some cops are coming.* Together they dragged Guimares into the cab. The pimp wound up on top of Edilson and proceeded to empty his stomach again.

"Gaaah, fuck, *que sujo!*" Edilson was dry-heaving.

Will had no sympathy. "This was your bright idea. Hope we didn't kill him."

"At this point, I don't give a shit. Ponta Porã, *senhor, rapido!*"

The driver never looked back as he deposited them on the Brazilian side of the Avenida International. Apparently, whatever money he'd been given was enough to dissuade complaints. The fact that they were carrying an obvious gangster probably helped stifle curiosity too.

Galtieri was waiting with three other PF under a stand of trees. Two black Pajeros idled on the curb. Galtieri walked up to Guimares, leaned over, and pulled him up by the scruff of the neck.

"Oh my, *muleke*, you don't look well. We can't have you stinking up our nice cars, well can we?" At that, one of the other cops stepped forward with a bucket of water and drenched Guimares.

"Bem vindo a Brasil, minha filho." Galtieri smiled.

Northwest of Ponta Porã, Brazil

They took Guimares to a little fazenda on a dirt road north of town. Will figured the drive itself was torture enough, but Edilson and Galtieri had other ideas. When they pulled into the little farm at the end of the long road, Will got an inkling of what was about to happen.

Edilson stopped him with a hand on his chest. "This isn't the Canadian way, Will."

"We're not in Canada. I'm coming."

"Fine. But remember what this guy did."

"You remember too. Before you let him walk."

Edilson looked at him for a moment before responding, "It's not what I want to be done. It's what has to be done. If we kill him, you know what happens?"

"Maybe a full-scale war with the PCC. Maybe nothing. But it sends a message."

"They send messages too. In the form of dead cops. You don't have to walk around in uniform in public in this country. I do." Edilson stabbed at his chest. "I'm really touched by how willing you are to fight to my death."

Edilson began to turn away. Will grabbed his arm. "Don't talk to me about being a fucking target, brother. I've been nothing but for the last week. And don't tell me this isn't my fight. Would my family be under police protection now if it wasn't? But I just don't get you. In Blumenau, you went out of your way to poke the hornet's nest. Now that it's poked, you think you can control the swarm. Do you? Make this make sense to me, buddy! You and I are partners, right? Make it make sense!"

Edilson paused, shook off the arm. The crickets were going nuts chirping in the fields. "The whole aim of this operation is to cut off one of the PCC's arms: Grupo Stumpf. And to avoid a wholesale war while we're doing it. We'd rather fight them five years from now when we've weakened them than now. I've lost a lot of friends, Will. Think about it."

Will thought about it. He saw the other side for the first time since he'd spoken to Thiago about a blackmail case just a few weeks before.

"Edilson, I just want to know one more thing."

Wearily, Edilson asked, "What's that?"

"Why the hell are you still a *soldado*? With a mind like that you should've been a major by now."

"Way to put the margarine on me."

"Do you mean 'butter you up'?"

"Fuck off. Just don't tell the reporter. Come on."

But Guimares was out cold, and there wasn't much to see as the Federal cops administered oxygen and fed him Bennies. After three hours watching the PF try to rouse a corpse-like Guimares from the brink, so they could torture him, Will walked back to the car and fell asleep.

When he woke up six hours later, his back, neck, and trick knee screaming, he hit the luminescent dial on his watch: six-fifteen. Will stepped out of the car and landed in ankle-deep wet grass. The fire-fringed dawn framed the low hills in the east in a tumescent light. Will breathed deeply and smelled sweet grass and dying fire smoke. Holding his back, he looked around and savoured the little moment.

Then he remembered his sordid present. He walked back to the barn, half-expecting to see Guimares being stretched on the rack. Instead, when he walked in, Guimares was sitting with one hand cuffed to a school chair, sipping from a coffee cup with the other. Galtieri was talking to him in low tones. There wasn't a mark on their prisoner.

Galtieri acknowledged him. "Gringo, *bom dia*. You seem astonished to see Senhor Guimares in one piece." He nodded to the still-sleepy prisoner. "He's pretty surprised too."

Guimares took a long drag of his cigarette and blew out through his teeth. He still looked pretty defiant to Will.

Galtieri held up a digital recorder. "One of the interesting side effects of Rohypnol is a vulnerability to suggestion. Wilson here is very, very suggestible. Aren't you, Touro?"

Guimares nodded sleepily. Will was curious. "How'd he get the nickname Touro?"

"He gave it to himself. He saw *Cidade de Deus* a hundred times."

"I don't think he understood it. Isn't Touro an honest cop?"

Galtieri sighed. "If we could see ourselves as others see us ..."

The banality of evil. Hannah Ehrendt would recognize this sleepy, lounging creep. A guy whose head was full of movie fantasy, wrestling, and pornography. A guy who burned a man alive in a pyramid of tires.

Galtieri said, "He did a dozen things that will get him into hell. He tortured and mutilated a couple of cops in Rio. It's all I can do to keep from shooting him in the face. Right, fuckface?" He reached out and slapped the man.

Guimares's head rolled, but he kept smiling. "Hey, gringo," he mumbled.

"What?"

"Your mother sucks great cock." Guimares laughed.

"You're wrong. My mother wasn't a man, so how would you know?"

That got him awake. The handcuff chain rattled against the desk. "Fuck you, Policial! I am gonna catch you someday, give you to some *veados* who are gonna make you do everything they like. Then I am gonna put you in the *microondas!*" He sat back and smiled at Galtieri as if he had a friend.

Will sighed and stood up. He walked over to Guimares. "I see one thing wrong here."

Guimares laughed. "What's that?"

"I haven't done this to you yet." He lined up and drove a fist into Guimares's teeth.

Guimares reeled, sat up, spit out blood. Galtieri stood up and yanked the pimp's head back. Clearly Galtieri didn't object. The Fed looked at Will. "Have some fun," he said in English. "I know what I want to know already."

But Will only bent down and whispered in his ear, "All your assumptions require you to have a future. But you don't." He smelled the iron tang of blood, the man's sweat and fear. He felt very far from home.

Now the smirk was off Guimares's face. Will had seen it a hundred times, the street-tough veneer peeling off like cheap paint at the first hint of the suffering they freely dispensed to others. "*Pelo morte Deus* ... You can't kill me; I helped you! Tell this gringo to back off!" he beseeched Galtieri.

"Sorry, Omar, my English isn't very good." Galtieri drove a fist into his guts. He leaned down as Guimares was bent over holding his guts. "It's fuckers like you who hold Brazil back, who make everyone afraid to come here ... You are the past; I am the future." He backhanded the man to drive home the point.

Guimares found his voice again. "Fuck your future! It's a white future, for you, with us as slaves! Just like the past, the *pelourinho*! Well, you can bulldoze our favelas, build your stadiums and your condominiums, but we'll still be there with what you want: dope, ass, guns! You fucking hypocrites!"

Will was wondering what was going to happen next when he heard a faint clapping sound coming from the entrance to the barn.

Edilson walked up slowly. "Bravo, *heroi negao*, bravo. Tell me how you are going to deliver me from racist evil by getting 12-year-olds to sell crack and 14-year-olds to sell their asses for Oscar Stumpf." He pulled up a chair and sat on it backwards, facing Guimares. Edilson stared into his eyes so intently that Guimares looked away. "You don't have an answer for me, do you? Because what you're doing is really just for you, isn't it?" He searched out Guimares's eyes, a technique Will had learned long ago to utilize for its disconcerting effect. He wondered if Edilson had learned it from him.

Guimares looked up at the ceiling of the barn. His bloodshot eyes searched for the light.

Galtieri interjected, "The answer isn't up there, Omar. You know where it is."

Guimares spat out in frustration, "What answer! I told you everything!"

Will pulled a chair up in front of Guimares. In his hand, he held two pictures. Guimares shook his head from side to side. Will had seen a lot of people do that in his time. Like they believed it could miracle them out of whatever hopeless shit they were in.

He held up a picture of 14-year-old girl. "Who is this?"

Guimares laughed. "A good fuck."

Will smiled, reached over, and grabbed Guimares by the scrotum. "Who is this?"

"Ahhh ... fuck ... let me think ... fuck!"

Edilson leaned down. "Think all you like. Think about how strong my friend is. Think about how a pimp gets by with no balls."

Will upped the pressure. "My word, Edilson, the scrotum is a tender instrument."

"*Verdade, senhor!*"

"God, okay, okay ... I think it's a kid named Iris ... No, no, Lucia, that's it! I'm sure."

Will relaxed the pressure. "Lucia what?"

"Lucia the whore, hahaha."

Will punched him in the mouth before he could say anything else. "Inappropriate."

"What the fuck do you want from me? These girls are only numbers to me; they're not people. I don't know their stories or even their last names! Come on!"

Edilson reached over with gentleness and wiped Guimares's mouth with a napkin. "Just remember this one girl. She was from Asunción. Where did you send her?"

"Let me think!" He was panicked now. The thought of losing one's balls was a wonderful focus.

Galtieri stood in front of Guimares and lit a cigar with a butane torch. The symbolism was crude but effective.

Message received. The lights went on in Guimares's head. "Lucia Rojas Ruiz! That's it! We sent her to Blumenau. I remember now." He looked up expectantly.

"Why there? Demand for that type?"

Guimares looked almost offended. "No, she was the most beautiful. That's why she was sent there. Only the most beautiful ones went there. That was the order, since last year."

"Do you know what happened to her?" Will was thinking of Gabi now, of how it must feel to not know where your child was, with vermin like Guimares in the world.

"Does a toy factory keep track of its toys after they're sold? Who gives a shit?"

All three men wanted to hit him then, but they were all tired. He was an unrepentant shit, and that wasn't going to change until somebody put a bullet into his brain. And nobody had the green light. A drop of water landed on Will's face. He looked up and realized the ceiling was leaking. The chairs they sat on were old and rusted. He was so damned tired.

He was grateful when Edilson took the lead. He sat right in front of Guimares, chewing gum. "Hi, fucker."

"Same to you."

"How many people have you killed?"

"None of your fucking business. How about you, cop?"

Edilson chuckled conspiratorially. "Hmm, that is a bit personal. Okay, how many people have you burned in the *microondas*?"

Will noticed the exact moment Guimares's face changed colour. "Fuck that."

"So you never murdered a lawyer named Usman al-Khattib? No? Never? No reason why your DNA would be there? No reason why the DNA we pulled from you in a 2002 rape investigation would wind up there?"

Guimares stared with a slack face. He had no reply.

"DNA, you know what that is, right, you fucking dumb shit? Only you give it off; it's unique. So it could only be you, right?" Edilson was twisting the knife now, enjoying the moment.

Guimares put his head in his hands, and Will took over. "Tell me now. It's your only chance."

Events paused. Guimares finally lifted his head, seemed to regain his strength. Will knew the moment was gone.

"I don't know what you're talking about. Now, take me back, or kill me. I know you fucking *os homi* wanna turn me into a snitch, but I know you can't put me in jail with the fucked-up shit you did." He paused to spit out a tooth. "And I bet you can't kill me. So take me back to Paraguay."

Edilson stood up. He turned away from Guimares and said in a hushed voice, "You guys take a walk. I need 10 minutes."

Will took Edilson's arm. "Think about this."

"I have a plan." He smiled. "I always do." Will walked out reluctantly with Galtieri, who seemed much less reluctant. Galtieri pushed open one of the double doors, and they walked along a rutted path to the tree-lined road. Daylight was taking hold. The air was fresh and cool. Will looked down at his knuckles and saw they were torn. He hoped Guimares didn't have AIDS.

Galtieri handed him a sterile wipe. "Better clean up. Occupational hazard." He smiled. "What's he doing in there, I wonder?"

"Something smart. That's usually what he does. Something you wouldn't expect."

"Like punching me in the face?" Galtieri smiled ruefully.

"Yeah, like that. Some history there, huh?" He liked the guy. So he ran over a cyclist? They were so goddamned uppity anyway.

Galtieri puffed on his cigar and nodded. "Yeah. He should be a lieutenant by now. But he's impulsive. Makes me worry."

"You're not the only one."

Minutes passed in silence. Will was looking toward the road when he noticed another car, a blue Fiat parked on the road just past the boundary fence. It hadn't been there before. He drew his pistol. "There's someone else here. That car ..."

"Wasn't there before," Galtieri finished, drawing his pistol and following Will. After bounding toward the treeline, they stopped briefly to catch their breath. Galtieri scanned the road, signalled for Will to cover him, and walked cautiously around the Fiat. He brought down his pistol but kept it at his side. "Nothing but an old briefcase. Where could they be?"

Will walked up to the car. He looked inside and saw a beaten and frayed old leather bag on the passenger seat. He knew that bag. Thiago's father had given him that bag when he'd graduated law school. "Shit!"

Galtieri struggled to keep up as Will raced back to the barn. He hit the barn doors in 60 seconds but stopped short when he viewed the tableau. A sobbing Guimares held his head in his hands as Thiago spoke to him, seated and close. Edilson stood in the background looking at Will, a finger to his lips. Will held out a hand and stopped Galtieri as he reached the doors, panting and red.

Will turned to Galtieri. "No need to panic. Told you he'd be doing something smart. Let's get some more air."

Northwest of Ponta Porã, later that morning

Will had fallen asleep in the car. He woke with a start. Another dream about Soares. The kid from the Tim Hortons had been there too. His conscience, surfacing. He felt a serious need to take a piss. And get drunk. This last one almost as urgent. He climbed out of the little rental and walked into the field. Opening his fly, he felt blessed relief. Why did men enjoy pissing outdoors so much? he wondered. Was it some last sad link to a primordial past? He zipped up and wandered back to the barn. Galtieri was out cold in his Pajero, but his men were loitering outside and smoking. They gave him a half-hearted wave.

He figured he knew what they were thinking. *Are we gonna arrest this cocksucker or shoot him?* Will was beginning to wonder the same thing himself. He felt a weight in his breast pocket and suddenly remembered his phone. He'd had it off since they'd crossed into Paraguay. A man with this many loose ends couldn't leave his phone off. He turned it on with trepidation as hawks circled in the thermals ahead.

He looked around, seeing the place in proper daylight for the first time. A gentle set of rolling hummocks dressed in low grass. A thin creek bisecting it all. No noise besides the occasional squawking bird and far-off truck. The wide open spaces of Brazil had a million places like this. It seemed to Will to be a much-bigger country than his, if only because none of it was encased in ice.

The messages began to stack up. Thiago telling him he was coming. Silvia asking if he was okay. Sergio wanting an update. And Ken ...

He listened to Ken's message and ran for the barn. He stopped short when he saw a weary Edilson leading an exhausted Guimares, his hands cuffed in front, out of the barn. Thiago trailed behind.

The men loitering by the Pajero walked up to meet Edilson, who said, "Take him to Avenida International and kick his ass back to Paraguay. He understands that's where he lives now, doesn't he?"

A stoop-shouldered Guimares nodded. Will noticed he was fingering a rosary. Thiago came up behind the killer and whisper in his ear. Guimares nodded and clasped his hands. He walked away with the PF.

Now the three of them stood in the field. There was a moment of silence. The breeze began to pick up.

"I thought you were here to kill him," Will said to Thiago.

"So did I, Will. But it's not in me. I'm not like you."

That stung him. "Why not?"

Thiago sighed. "Cops think they know it all because they see things the rest of us avoid. There's some truth there, I admit it. You guys may look at a 5-year-old and say, 'That kid's going to be a criminal; I've arrested his dad 50 times.' A kindergarten teacher may look at the same kid and say, 'He's got potential.' Does she know any less? I know these guys like you don't. I've listened to their life stories, all their excuses and lies, yes, but also their childhoods, their dreams. I've met their families. I've defended them. Did you know that Wilson wanted to be a policeman when he grew up?"

Edilson smoked with heavy-lidded eyes. "A policeman who burns people to death. Your friends. I would've killed him by now if I were you."

Thiago held court like a professor, wearing a half-knotted tie over a rumpled shirt, even here. "But we can't kill him. You said so yourself. And if we had killed him, we wouldn't know this."

"What?" Will asked, his interest piqued.

"The PCC didn't have Usman killed. Well, they did it, but it had nothing to do with the narco he defended. The orders came from Oscar Stumpf."

"Why?"

"Usman was representing an Argentine woman whose sister disappeared in 1978. She figured her sister was dead, but she had a niece, a niece she had reason to believe was living with the family of an army officer in São Paulo, one of Stumpf's officers. Apparently Stumpf got scared the whole thing would tie him conclusively to Condor, so he had Usman killed. The PCC was willing to do it no questions asked because they saw him as a liability anyway."

"What happened to the woman?" Thiago had Will interested now. Edilson watched impassively. He had set the train in motion and was now letting it run.

"No idea. Wilson says they never touched her. Against the rules. But if I know mothers of the Disappeared, I bet she's still in São Paulo."

Will paused and then said to Thiago quietly, "He admitted that he torched your friend."

Thiago looked into the trees. "Yes. Guimares said he died bravely. As bravely as anyone can, in that situation." He shook his head.

Edilson touched his arm. "It's not too late to change your mind, you know."

Thiago rubbed his beard. "The quality of mercy is not strained. It droppeth as the gentle rain from the heavens above."

Will hesitated a moment. "You're a better man than any of us, you know that?"

Thiago looked up at the sun, now at its zenith. "No, just more deliberate. How many die if he dies now? His life will end in violence anyway. Why do I have to contaminate my soul by administering it? Edilson told me the plan, and the plan was right."

Will looked at Edilson. "I thought you said, 'Don't tell the lawyer.' What changed?"

Edilson looked after the Pajero's red dust as it drove away. "I had to bring him here; that's what changed. It was one of those 'flashes of inspiration' you are always talking about. Personally, I thought it was some bullshit, but, hey, it worked." He smiled.

"Galtieri said he had all he needed. What more did we accomplish by getting him to admit to Usman's murder?"

Edilson rolled his eyes. "How many concussions have you had, *jogador*?"

"Two ... I think. What am I missing?"

"Even without him as a witness, that gives us our first link to a killing ordered by Stumpf and carried out by the PCC on his behalf. Plus, it gives us a link to the child abductions we know occurred in the Condor years. Now we just need witnesses we can actually bring to court. All Galtieri has is evidence implicating Grupo Stumpf in smuggling and human trafficking. That will hurt him, but I bet he was smart enough to keep things 'compartmentalized,' as you gringos say."

"So we go back to São Paulo now?"

"Yes, for, I hope, the final chapter."

"Well, let's do it fast, because our client is missing and our bartender got shot."

"Merda!" Edilson had lost his self-satisfied look. Thiago ran back to the barn.

"Why the fuck didn't you tell me?" Edilson asked.

"Now you're mad at me for withholding?" Will was on the defensive. "I found out five minutes ago. It will take us four hours at least to get back to São Paulo. Anyway, we knew Renner was gonna fuck himself, and Ken said he already found an underground doctor to stitch him up. He said it was a through and through, nothing serious. They killed Luciana and Jefferson though. God knows what they did to the bar."

Edilson shoved him, hard. "The bar? Who the fuck cares about the bar? Are you hearing yourself? *Meu Deus*, ever since Blumenau it's been like your head's underwater. Can I count on you?"

Will looked down. "Sorry, *amigo*. It just ... it's a lot to get used to. I feel like I've gotten into something I don't understand and can't handle."

"Do you want out?"

Will knew he had passed that point back in São Paulo. "No. I've got your back. So what now?"

"Galtieri's agreed to wait on hitting Grupo Stumpf until we've had a chance to get back to São Paulo and generate something there. So we go back and talk to the fine people at Condor Foundations LLC. Plus we try and find that Argentine woman. Thiago thinks she may still be around. And we make sure your *prisoneiro* friend is okay."

"No heroic rescue for Renner?" Will smiled at him.

"Fuck him. He's dead already. For sure they hit Bar Canada on his information. Now what more do they need from him? He's a corpse."

"Ruthless, buddy, but right."

"Are you willing to take a bullet for a *pedofilo*?"

"No argument here."

"Let's get Thiago and go. Galtieri can help us get back."

Thiago walked out of the barn, dumbfounded. "They burned down my house. My house. With all my papers."

Will felt a rising tide of panic and rushed away to dial Jaragua do Sul.

Edilson asked, "Anybody hurt?"

Thiago looked confused. "No, my wife is in Jundiai. I think it's safe. But my kids could've been in there. My kids."

"Any regrets about letting that cocksucker Guimares go now? Think he wouldn't have burned your kids too, if somebody had paid him? You said us cops think we know it all. Personally I think we do know it all when it comes to pieces of shit like him."

"You didn't want me to kill him."

"I would've liked to have had to hold you back. That's why I brought you out here. But your way worked, I've gotta admit." Edilson leaned against the crash bar of a Pajero and lit up another smoke.

Thiago looked at him. "At what point in this case are you going to stop using Will and me? Are we friends and partners? Or just your tools?"

Edilson sighed. "In the end, we will get what we all want. You have to trust me."

Thiago scoffed. "Trust, but verify."

Will ran up to them. "What the fuck are we waiting for? Let's go!"

"Easy. You said Ken was okay. And we can't do anything for Renner, that fucking creep, or Luciana and Jefferson, Nossa Senhora." Edilson paused to genuflect. "Better to rest tonight and go back tomorrow with a solid plan. Did you talk to Silvia? Is she okay?"

"Yes, she's fine. She's a little pissed at Gasparini, who won't let her out of his sight."

"A lot of men don't want to let Silvia out of their sight." Edilson leered at Thiago, who turned and walked away. "Hehehe. That gets under his skin."

"Give the guy a break. I do, even though I know he'd replace me if he had the chance."

Edilson thought that he was no different; many men would have been glad to share a bed with Silvia Bryant. But this was one thing a Brasileiro would not tell his friend, ever. Canadians were more relaxed. He would've beaten the shit out of Thiago long ago if it were his wife.

"Silvia isn't the point, Will. We're at war. Does he have the stomach for it?"

"Don't ask me. You're the one who brought him out here."

Edilson formed a worrying thought. "Did Ken give you the name of his doctor?" Many back-alley doctors had ties to the big gangs.

Will thought a moment. "I think he said ... Mike?"

Edilson grabbed his arm. "We're going back now!"

Will stood his ground. "Why, goddamn it! All these fucking course changes, I—"

Edilson put a firm hand on his chest "The only doctor I know who calls himself Mike is Mohamed Abbas—a PCC doctor. We can write off Renner, but Ken knows where you live. He knows your family. He knows—"

"Well, fuck it. Let's move!"

24

São Bernardo do Campo, São Paulo

Ken awoke with a start. He was surprised to find himself in a dim room with damp concrete floors and cinder block walls. The only light came from a tiny window at the apex of a peaked ceiling. As he stared up at it, he became aware that he could not move.

He was handcuffed to something metal. Shit. He looked up and saw a thick metal bar running all the way to the ceiling. His shoulder throbbed. He looked down and saw what his 1,000 reais had bought him: a wadded-up dressing and a probable upcoming torture/beating session. Likely end: a bullet in the brain or something worse.

As his eyes focused on the other side of the room, he saw something worse. Luc Renner sat handcuffed as Ken was. He was naked from the waist down, his crotch the centre of a congealing pool of blood. His throat was slit. His cock and balls were stuffed into his wide open mouth.

Ken closed his eyes and breathed in. Jesus. He'd seen a lot of bad stuff in his life. But not for a long time. The worst thing about his life was that this wasn't even the first time he'd seen that done to a man.

Now, how to keep that from happening to me?

Ken was adaptable, and part of that strength was not panicking. Most people would, but he didn't. He'd read somewhere once that was a trait of psychopaths. If so, it was a gift from God, who had given Ken precious little else.

Another strength of Ken's was preparation. Part of the reason he was only alarmed and not panicked was he had a handcuff key shoved up his ass. Back in the day when Ken used to get handcuffed regularly (now he had to pay that saucy little Japaneira Monica in Tatuape for the privilege), he'd always kept a spare key keestered just in case. He had long since stopped doing it. Why would he need to? But he always kept a key on his key chain, just in case. And last night, following the emergency directions Marcello had written out for him, fighting through a haze of pain and nausea, it had come to him: *I'd better shove that key up my ass, just in case.* He had been about to go under the knife, with a doctor who by definition was operating as a criminal. He didn't know the man, and God knew where he would wind up. It had seemed the prudent thing to do.

His decision had seemed more prudent as the night wore on. "Mike," as the doctor called himself, only opened his spyholed metal door on the twelfth knock, even though Ken had called ahead. The bearded, balding Arab, whose name was very definitely not Mike, had said nothing but had admitted Ken through the door and motioned for him to follow. Ken had staggered down a narrow hallway with a flickering fluorescent light, aware he was leaving a steady trail of the blood he could feel running down his right arm. It had been an office of some kind, not medical. He'd had no idea where he was in the massive sea of a city. He had simply followed the turns. He had been at Mike's mercy.

The Arab had motioned him to sit on an exam table. At least it had been clean.

"*Tira blusa.*"

Christ, his Portuguese is worse than mine, Ken had thought. With difficulty he'd pulled off his T-shirt. The Arab had helped, none too gently. A lifetime of pain in scars and tattoos on display.

"Hmm." Mike had poked about in the wound, seemingly caring not about the pain he caused Ken. Ken had begun to understand why he had lost his medical license.

"Okay, one bullet, is easy. You want go to sleep?"

"No fucking way. Just gimme a local and get it out."

"Afraid I take your wallet, hah?"

Ken had thought, *No, more like you mistake me for a sheep and ass-rape me you fucking slapper head.*

"Okay, just a needle."

Ken remembered thinking, *Wow, that local is pretty fucking strong.* He'd seen Mike having a good laugh at his expense before he'd passed out. He hoped he could find that map. He was gonna put old Mike out of circulation for good, if he ever got out of here.

But now getting out of here seemed about as likely to Ken as being on the cover of *GQ*. Light flooded the room. A short, broad silhouette filled the doorway. Two men stood behind him. Oscar Stumpf stepped into the light. "*Bem vindo,* Senhor Stubbins. I believe you have met your cell mate?" Ken could make out the piercing blue eyes, the slick black hair. Who did he look like? He couldn't place it. But he knew the guy was a ruthless bastard. He was showing off Renner as if he was proud.

Ken had thought animals like Stumpf were in his past. Now, here he was again. He looked straight ahead and said nothing. Stumpf walked between him and Renner's corpse. He was wearing little leather lift shoes. Ken stored that up. He always liked to catalogue an enemy's weaknesses. Made him feel stronger.

Stumpf looked down at him. "The quiet type, hmm? Well, we will see. Nobody stays quiet for long, here." He knelt down beside Ken. "I know you are a tough guy, Ken. Much tougher than this fucking queer." He regarded Renner with an overhand wave. "He was pissing his pants before we even touched him. Haha." He reached over and pinched Ken's cheeks. Ken stared back defiantly. Stumpf studied his eyes. "You will take much more work, yes."

Avenida International, Ponta Porã/Pedro Juan Caballero

A tall, muscular black man in a bloodstained T-shirt limped across the boulevard, casting nervous glimpses left and right. Traffic surged around him. He kicked at a curious stray who got too close. Wilson Guimares was free, and alive.

For now.

Aeroporto International, Ponta Porã

Three men stood on the tarmac waiting to board a Cessna taxiing toward them.

"International? This place?" Will looked around. The border was at the other end of the runway.

"Sorry. British Airways first class was all booked. And there's no inflight meal." Edilson was clearly getting tired of babysitting the gringo.

"Edilson, looking at this plane, I don't think any of us will be inputting. There will probably be a lot of outputting, though."

"Do you have any idea what ropes I had to make to get this plane?"

"'Strings to pull,' Edilson."

"Okay, but do you?"

"I imagine it was hard. But I bet things are a lot harder for Ken. So I hope this pilot is willing to break all the rules. And I hope we're going to have help in São Paulo, yes?"

"My major has been briefed. He called Galtieri's commandant. When we land at Campo de Marte, we'll have GATE and COT at our disposal."

GATE was São Paulo's own Special Forces, and COT was the Polícia Federal equivalent. "This is getting pretty fucking official, buddy. I'm impressed."

"I told you, the powers that be want Oscar Stumpf to go down. He crossed the line when he got in bed with the PCC."

"So the Condor shit doesn't bother them so much?"

"Oh, it bothers them. It bothers them that he might live to get on the witness stand and make them look like shit."

Will looked closely at Thiago, wondering what he was thinking. He was impassive.

Edilson was buoyant. "Anyway, it's all coming together, *amigos*! Let's get that fucker in a body bag and move on to better things!"

The plane was getting closer. The last thing Will heard over the engine noise was Thiago saying to Edilson, "Don't celebrate yet. He still has a lot of tricks he hasn't shown us yet. Kill him, and we can dance on his grave later."

"Doesn't sound much like a lawyer to me."

"He burned down my fucking house. Fuck him."

The plane did a brake stand, and the pilot motioned frantically. They piled on.

They laboured into the sky with an endless vista of green and red beneath them.

São Bernardo do Campo

Ken had fought to stay awake until the next opportunity to use his key, which he had forced to the edge of his rectum with the carefully controlled impulses of a seasoned convict. But the moment had not come in time, and now he awoke in the last place he wanted to be.

Strapped to a torture table.

He looked up to a surgical flood lamp that drowned his retinas in nuclear luminance. His wrists were pinioned with psych-hospital straps, as were his legs. He was naked now. But he could still feel the key.

He closed his eyes. He thought back to the first and only time he had been raped in prison. He had not given his tormentors the satisfaction of seeing him cry or hearing him beg then, and they had mocked him for it.

"You just enjoyin' it then? That's why you so quiet!" Big Roy had crowed then. Ken had stayed silent and stoic, his face in the shower drain, willing himself far away as each man had taken his turn, memorizing each face.

Big Roy had died two months later in the same shower, a shiv buried in his bowels, and Ken had asked him then, as he'd writhed wordlessly, "You just enjoyin' it then? That's why you so quiet!"

One down, two to go.

A riot six months later had disposed of Pierre. Pierre had been in seg with a snitch jacket. Ken had spread the rumour, knowing the riot was coming and the snitches and skinners were going to get it first. Ken had watched as they'd cut his head off with a hacksaw. Revenge. You just needed to wait.

Marshall had gotten paroled two weeks before the riot. But Ken would see him again, someday.

Ken knew how to wait. And he knew how to suffer in silence.

And he would need that knowledge now. Beside him, two identical blonde men with angelic faces arranged their tools neatly on a surgical tray. They had thoughtfully propped Ken's head up so he could see their preparations. Some tools looked innocuous. Pitchers of water. Towels. Others caused Ken to suck in breath sharply through his filthy gag. Tongs. Torches. Scalpels. Electrodes. All the things of medieval nightmares. Ken began to doubt his earlier confidence in his stoic abilities. He was afraid now. He tried to focus on the light coming from the filthy windows lining the ceiling. The room stank of alcohol and mildew.

Ken supposed a lot of other men in this situation would find comfort in thoughts of their mother. Fuck that. Being her son was torture enough. In spite of everything, he laughed to himself.

Klaus seemed to notice, acknowledging Ken for the first time with a curious cock of the head. Ken let himself go limp. He was that feather. They were the breeze.

"Klaus, eine wasser."

It was beginning.

The table tilted with a thump. His head was inclined slightly toward the floor. A muslin sheet was draped over his mouth and nose. Cold water, at first a splash, then a torrent.

Drowning. Choking. Spasming. Vomit surging up in his throat.

Klaus or Erich, he had no idea which was which, said, "Tell us about Will Bryant and his policeman friend please, and we will stop."

He choked; he gagged; he threw up. He panicked, breathing in his vomit. Burning sensations in his throat and chest.

The table thunked upward. The cloth was pulled off his face. He sucked in air between coughs.

"Yes? We are waiting?"

Waiting, sure. For me to talk so you can kill me. I saw his face, you fucking idiots. Ken raised his head with great difficulty. "I am a tourist. Which way to Rio?"

Klaus or Erich sneered. "That was the easiest one. The rest are more fun. I am glad you have decided not to talk, gringo!"

Ken tensed his jaw and looked at the ceiling. *I bet you're glad.* Beside him, one of the brothers began to unravel a spool of electrical wire.

Aeroporto Campo de Marte, São Paulo

São Paulo was now ablaze in the lights of early evening as the Cessna cleared the tower blocks of Santana and headed for the glide path. Will gazed out the little window, mesmerized as he always was by the sight of this ocean of a city from the air. The feeder roads and great marginals with their slowly surging lines of red and white. The little empires of clustered tower blocks. The little dark spots that were all that was left of the once-great Mata Atlantica coastal rainforest. And off to their left, the fabulous chasm of light and sound that was Avenida Paulista. He could make out the Itau Tower, the Art Deco Banespa, the weird upended shoebox of the MASP museum. Will was surprised to realize that he had missed it. Was it home now?

The plane jolted on an updraft, and the pilot cursed. Edilson turned to Will. "We're here." Next to him, Thiago, his face an ashen grey, hovered over an airsick bag. *Yes, we're here.*

The Cessna hit the runway with two thumps and a bang. The props revved fearfully and then began to still as the plane began a fast taxi to the terminal. The pilot jammed on his brakes in front of the Polícia Militar hangar. In front of them, a bug-faced PM chopper lifted off into the night. Two more followed in quick succession. Unusual activity for this time of night.

The pilot announced, "Hitchhikers, out! Thanks for flying Polícia Federal!"

Will steadied Thiago as he stepped onto the tarmac. Will was painfully aware that he smelled like a dead fish and had no idea what to do next. There was no obvious reception, save a few harried technicians in the PM hangar.

Edilson looked around. *"Puta merda!"*

"No reception committee?" Will asked. "I thought we were going to have an army at our disposal? Or did somebody get cold feet?"

Edilson could only shrug. It was a common Brazilian response to life's disappointments.

"Can't we at least get a ride?"

"I'll make it happen." Edilson walked into the hangar. Surrounded by curious and challenging figures, he soon disappeared. Will walked a still-queasy Thiago to a concrete barrier and sat them down to watch the takeoffs and landings. Will looked to the south and could make out three distinct pillars of smoke, underlit by flames. Garbage fires? Or the explanation for their lack of reception?

Thiago was uneasy. "Something is wrong, Willao. Those fires on the horizon."

Will nodded. This might be his only chance to take stock before events accelerated again.

Scorecard:

Us:

Concrete evidence against Stumpf, linking him with the PCC

Possible live witness with evidence of child abductions linked to Operation Condor

No fucking idea where she is

No fucking idea where Ken is—possibly in PCC hands?

No fucking idea where Renner is—dead?

A more or less open war with the PCC and Grupo Stumpf

Support of police ... maybe?

Families safe—for now

Them:

Ken and maybe Renner too—torture for info?

Lots of PCC hitters ready to act

Friends in government?

Time

He would've underlined that last one if the list weren't only in his mind. Time. It was on their enemies' side. Witnesses and their memories were perishable commodities. The more time went on, the more hidden locations would be revealed, by accident or design.

What he needed now was information. He had little to offer. But he was betting Edilson could find Ken and maybe

Renner too. They knew the Arab doctor's name. It was a start. The Argentine woman was a blank.

Between blasts of jet noise and prop wash, Thiago said, "Sergio. We need to see Sergio."

Sergio. "Yes, Thiago, we do."

Edilson bounded over to them. He looked shocked. "It's started. The PCC hit us while we were in the air."

That explained the lack of reception. Every cop in the city had likely been recalled to duty. Special operators like GATE were going to be very busy in the next week.

"Bad?" Will asked.

Edilson seemed to notice the fires to the south for the first time. "*Puta merda.* They're burning buses as roadblocks again. Well, this time we were better prepared, but they hit with more force. Six stations in the Zona Sul and Zona Leste hit, a Base Communitaria in República burned. Some off-duty officers hit."

"How many?"

"We've lost 30 in the last two hours. Six missing. Two stations still under attack. That's where GATE went."

Jesus. Cops in North America had no idea. And he wondered why Edilson was such a ruthless motherfucker. "Where does that leave us?"

"Nothing has changed."

Will was incredulous. "Nothing?"

"Well, except we're on our own again."

"You were right; nothing has changed."

"At least we have a ride."

Sargento Andreatta walked up to Will, looking unfamiliar in a modish leather jacket and black jeans. "*Boa noite*, gringo."

Knowing Andreatta would never get it, he took his shot in English. "Does Justin Timberlake know you've been raiding his closet, Sarge?"

Avenida Reboucas, São Paulo

The streets were deserted by São Paulo standards as they headed southwest to Sergio Yamada's apartment. The usual traffic of a middle evening in São Paulo had died off as commuters hurried home and partiers found a reason to stay at home. Everyone knew it was cops versus gangsters. They also knew bullets couldn't tell the difference.

The car was silent as they passed a burning city bus. A cluster of cops dressed in riot gear approached, weapons levelled at them, moving on as Andreatta badged them. Will breathed in as the cops turned around. If it was him, he would have been itchy too. When you knew you were the target, it was hard not to take it personally. He'd learned a lot about that in the past week. Their eyes watered. The air reeked of fuel fires and cordite.

"I thought it was just in the south and east? This is a pretty decent area, isn't it?"

Edilson stared out the window. "Fuckers. Looks like my information is a little behind, brother. This is bad." Will leaned over the seat and noticed Edilson and Andreatta both had their pistols on their laps. He took his Taurus out.

Andreatta badged another checkpoint. The men were tense, nerves still trumping exhaustion. The Sargento was bleeding from the scalp. "Can we go further, brother?" Andreatta asked him.

"Do you have to? Take a look at me!"

Edilson leaned over. "Brother, we've got a score to settle, understand?"

The Sargento smiled. "I think I can spare an escort, if you're not going too far."

"Vila Olímpia."

"Getting some rich fuckers, hmm? *Sem problema.*"

"Hey," Andreatta asked, "get any?"

The Sargento motioned to a track-suited corpse splayed in front of a police car, next to an overturned moto. "What's it look like?"

Andreatta smiled. "Nice shooting."

The Sargento waved them on as a PM Blazer with three men, shotguns poking out the windows, arrived. They followed the red lights through the streets as the scene began to normalize. A few blocks on, and it was as if nothing was happening. Vila Olímpia was alien territory for the PCC, too many well-secured tower blocks, too many guns for hire.

The men in their escort car seemed to realize this too. They U-turned and drove past with a lazy wave, back to the battle. A few people remained on the streets as they passed. No burned buses here.

Thiago had been silent up till now. "What started it this time?"

Andreatta said, "We tried to move a couple of leaders to a prison in the interior. They didn't want to move."

"All this, for that."

Andreatta was philosophical. "Good chance to kill a few of your clients, *advogado.* Nobody's going to give a shit if they're burning the whole city."

"They kill you back."

"That's why they call it a war."

Thiago turned to Will. "It's not like this in Canada, is it, Will?"

Will smiled. "More lawyers. Fewer bullets."

Apartment of Sergio Yamada, Vila Olímpia

The four men stood in the cavernous upper-floor apartment and shook their heads. It was another planet removed from burned-out buses and dead bodies. Will was conscious again of his own smell. This time it was a heavy smoke-and-fuel aroma.

"I had no idea reporters made so much money." Andreatta looked around the modernist entryway, scrutinizing, but touching nothing. "I should have paid more attention in Portuguese class."

"Yeah, *Folha* is definitely an 'employer of choice,'" Will said. But Will was pretty sure *Folha de São Paulo* wasn't paying for the immaculate, white-walled, exquisitely decorated, and fantastically located aerie in São Paulo's newest fashionable neighbourhood.

Thiago voiced what they were all thinking. "The financial news beat really pays off."

Yeah, Will thought, *it sure does.*

Yamada came out of the kitchen and beckoned to them. "Whiskies on the patio? Come see the view!"

Will was guiltily aware that somewhere, something bad was being done to Ken Scribbins. But he went anyway. He needed a drink. And he needed to pretend that this was his life for a few minutes more. The men picked up their single malts and walked out onto the broad balcony. Andreatta took a long pull and shook his head. Will stared at the Ponte

Octavio Frias, a cable-stayed marvel crossing the Tiete, the towers lit by fluctuating colours. Yamada turned toward them, smiling expectantly.

"You fucking whore," Edilson spat. "If I had an apartment like this, you fucking reporters would be up my ass!"

"Hey!" Yamada held his hands up. "I'm good with money. All of us Japanese are ..."

"Bullshit!" Will turned in surprise to see Thiago pointing at his friend. "You made your compromises, like all of us. Me, with drug dealers and robbers. You, with criminals of a higher class. That's what paid for this. Admit it!"

Sergio was angry now, set upon suddenly. "I just wanted to help you, to give you somewhere to sleep! Now this is how you thank me? Well, fuck you, Thiago! And fuck you cops! You think I don't know you are part of the Scuderie Le Coq? Maybe that would make a good story?"

Andreatta was across the balcony and had Yamada by the throat before his whisky glass had hit the floor. "Awfully brave talk for a man living 16 stories up. In the middle of a riot. A lot of bodies. Very little investigation." Andreatta looked down theatrically, and Yamada's eyes followed.

Edilson stepped forward. "Sergio, Le Coq is old news. It's a social club now. Update your sources. And yes, I think you've made some deals to get all of this. Lots of us have made compromises, as Thiago said. But we're not compromising with Stumpf. With us, or against us. And we don't care about the rest. Okay?" He glanced at Andreatta, who released his hold. It was fascinating to Will to see how the structure of this secret police organization transcended rank.

Yamada shrank against the wall, eyeing them. "What do you want?"

"A safe place for Thiago while the rest of us attend to … police business. And we want the Argentine woman." Edilson smiled, expecting a denial.

"What Argentine woman?"

Andreatta scoffed openly before Yamada could finish his denial.

"Come on, Sergio! You hate Stumpf; that's why you helped us in the first place!" Thiago was pleading now. "She was Usman's client. Stumpf had him burned because of her! If he will kill a lawyer, he'll kill a reporter too!"

"That's what I'm afraid of!"

Will stepped in front of him. "Sergio, why did you become a reporter in the first place?"

Sergio sat down on a deck chair. "Truth." His voice was hushed. The noise of the city was a background susurrus.

"And where's the truth here?"

"Natalia Rodriguez. She can tell you the truth."

Will knelt in front of him. "Tell me where to find her, and we can give you one hell of a scoop."

Sergio was even. "Don't patronize me, gringo. You're all muscle, no brain."

Will smiled. "You've got your scoop, right there. Give me the Argentine, and I think we have it all. And you have a front-row seat."

Under the balcony, the buses burned in the distance to the sound of scattered gunfire.

25

São Bernardo do Campo

Ken Scribbins was riding the lightning, his back arched and his mind filled with pain. Nothing but a white-hot presence of pain. He had no air to scream as his diaphragm folded in on itself. He was nothing, thought nothing.

They weren't even asking him any questions anymore. The worst part was that his clever little handcuff-key-up-the-ass trick was multiplying the problem as the presence of an electrical conductor kept the pain radiating long after the shock had stopped. His body went slack, and he blacked out again.

Across the table, Erich sighed. "This isn't very helpful."

Klaus gave him a prim look. "Be patient. He is defiant. We are breaking him down. Tio Oscar says it is a strategy to make disciplined people like him give in. Their personality has to break. Cowards are easy, like the Frenchman. Pain is all it takes. The strong man has to be made to question who he is."

"Tio learned this from the French general?"

"Yes, with the Algerians. And from the English."

"They used these methods also? That is surprising. I thought they were more ... civilized."

Klaus laughed. "So are we Germans, and look at Auschwitz! No, the English were just as brutal with the Irish, simply more ... subtle. You will see."

Erich was silently resentful. His uncle was his hero, but Klaus was Tio Oscar's obvious favourite, his star pupil in this business Erich felt every bit as capable of mastering. He thought he'd proven that when he'd killed Marco Hellmer. But perhaps Klaus was right. Perhaps he needed to master something more "subtle" than killing. He was intrigued.

Klaus read his brother's look in the dim light, something he'd always been able to do on his fraternal twin. "You want to learn; I can tell."

"Yes."

"Then let this ugly specimen be your teacher! Come, let's move him."

"Back to his room?"

"No. We have something different for the next phase. Anyway, Renner is starting to stink. Makes me sick to look at that."

"That's a relief. I thought I was going soft."

"*Nein*, you may think I am Tio's favourite. Yes, I see that look on your face. But some of the things he does ... they scare me. Doing that with the man's thing in his mouth ... it's not ... appropriate. Not rational."

Erich was surprised. He saw a worried look on his brother's face, for the first time since Klaus had broken

Dona Genschler's window with a *futebol* when they were 10. Hesitantly, he said, "I agree. Do you have second thoughts?"

Klaus was silent, pensive. Finally he said, "No!" He raised his arm in a cutting motion. "I can question the means but not the goal. The *Führerprinzip* applies here, don't you think?"

Erich wasn't convinced. "Look where that kind of thinking got Germany."

"I know, I know! But we aren't talking about a country here, Erich. We're talking about our family. We're talking about us."

"Yes, I see." Marco Hellmer, his stupid little discount gun jammed on the first shot, that look of panic on his face as he tried to clear it in a pathetic comedy. Erich calmly shooting him in the face, watching the whole thing from the outside. "Like Hitler's generals, we're going all the way."

"All the way. Or we eat ashes. All of us. Greta and Mutti too."

Erich breathed in slowly and calmed himself. "Okay. Show me where to move this ugly bastard."

Vila Olímpia

In the driveway in front of Sergio's apartment, Will sat in the back seat of Andreatta's car. He held the Argentine woman's dossier in his lap.

Why had Sergio Yamada sat on this all this time? Too cozy with Stumpf? Too afraid? Will's money was on the last one. Granted, the address implied some compromises had been made in Sergio's 20 years of financial reporting. But Stumpf let his fearful reputation speak for him.

One thing was for certain. Sergio Yamada had known Oscar Stumpf had had Usman al-Khattib murdered in the *microondas*. And the dossier showed exactly why. He had to meet this Natalia. But there was something much more urgent to attend to.

Edilson turned around in the front seat. "Ken doesn't have long."

"He's tough. He's done time. Looking at his tattoos, I'd say serious time."

"Oscar Stumpf studied torture from the masters. It'll only take him a little longer with Ken."

"What's your idea? You know where to find the Arab?"

"No, but Sargento Andreatta knows who knows where to find him."

Andreatta grinned tightly in the rear-view mirror. At least Will thought it was a grin under the moustache. "His nephew is my bitch, ever since I caught him with a kilo of basuco and threatened to send him up for it. You see, Aftab is a fruit, and his kind don't do very well in our prisons. Also, nobody knows that's what he is. I have a lot of ammunition with this guy, gringo."

Ah, this case just got filthier by the second. If he survived it, Will figured he'd need six months at the beach just to wipe the psychic slime off of him. He'd never be able to explain any of this to Silvia. But what was gay blackmail next to shooting people? What the fuck.

"Let's go flush out the *veado*." Edilson pointed at the road. *"Vamos la!"*

They drove away from the clean fantasy of Vila Olímpia, back to where buses were burning and people were afraid.

Rua Frei Caneca, Consolação

Will forced his eyes open as they slowly trawled the streets looking for Andreatta's snitch, although Will really had no idea who he was looking for. A short, muscular brown dude with a unibrow who liked acid-wash jeans and gold chains. That didn't exactly narrow it down in this neighbourhood. Except that there wasn't much to choose from. This part of the city was quiet. No signs of trouble. The college crowd down here wasn't exactly a PCC stronghold, any more than Vila Olímpia. But the news was enough to keep the normally energetic university students off the street tonight.

The dashboard clock read 0123. Will thought about the last time he'd slept in a bed. He thought of Silvia.

"Aren't we wasting time? There's nobody out here," Will said.

Andreatta looked in his rear-view. "All the better for us. No big crowds. The college kids may stay at home, but the gays don't stop partying. Trust me, gringo. Aftab will be here."

"This is a gay neighbourhood? My wife used to live here."

"Probably so nobody would hit on her."

"Probably."

Andreatta pulled in behind a taxi. Two men were arguing with the driver. Thumping techno drew Will's attention to a facade of reflective metal, under which muscled young men in tight T-shirts and a scattering of *travestis* congregated.

"O Gato Loco," Andreatta announced. "He's here every week, same time."

Will nodded. Knowing your snitch was a creature of habit meant never having to look far. "Are we going in?"

Andreatta laughed. "Not unless you want your ass used as a pincushion. Besides, we'll stick out too much. And he never stays inside for long. He smokes."

"And he'll take us to Mike?"

"If he knows what's good for him."

Edilson yawned and stretched out in the front seat. "Mike will be pretty busy tonight. A lot of holes being made in his customers."

Andreatta smiled. "All the more reason to visit Mike tonight. We might catch a few more fish."

Will slumped in his seat. He'd wanted to stay out of this war, and now, here he was, right in the middle of it. But since Metro Clinicas there had been no way out. Will Bryant—English teacher, death squad associate member. A thin leather folio dropped in his lap.

Edilson smiled at him. "Welcome to the Polícia Militar de São Paulo, Soldado Ferguson!"

"Ferguson?"

"Maybe it will explain your shitty Portuguese. Anyway, we can't have you running around the city with a gun in the middle of this any other way. You'll get shot."

"I'll probably get shot anyway."

"Yes, but not by us!"

"Great." Andreatta did not look impressed.

Will felt an annoying urge. "I've gotta piss."

"Use the alley. I wouldn't whip my cock out in that bar, if I were you." Edilson sniggered.

Will stepped out of the car and stretched. A few partiers gave him a moment's glance and turned back to their conversations. Andreatta and Edilson seemed to believe the only way to keep their virginity was to stay out of the bar. In

Will's experience, most gay people were interested only in being left alone by straights. But he'd go in the alley anyway.

He felt the blessed relief that can only come with releasing a long-suppressed piss. Two leather boys making out in a doorway ignored him. He zipped up in a hurry when he heard *"Oi, Aftab, espere muleke!"* Andreatta's voice. Then, "Stop, Aftab, now!"

Will crouched behind the Dumpster until a stocky man in acid-wash jeans ran past. Then he jumped up and shouldered the runner into the wall next to the leather boys. Aftab, breathless, squirmed and clawed at the wall as Will stood over him.

Will held out his phony badge. *"Polícia."*

Andreatta and Edilson ran around the corner. Edilson leaned over and handcuffed the still-winded Aftab. Andreatta looked at 'Ferguson's' still-outstretched badge. "Just couldn't wait to use that, could you?"

Cingapura Zaki Narchi, Carandiru

Andreatta sat in the back with a handcuffed Aftab. Edilson pulled to the curb and stopped. Polícia Civil headquarters was just two blocks away, but tonight there would be no backup. The air was humid and close, with a soundtrack of TVs cranked too loud and ghetto blasters shooting out funk. Will looked up nervously through the light-polluted haze at the "Singapore" project towers.

Cingapuras were an attempt to relocate the illegal and haphazard favelas into orderly tower blocks, with security provided by the state, not the gangs. While nobody was ready to declare it a total failure just yet, it didn't look like anywhere he'd want to live. The towers were dark and gloomy, despite the festive paint jobs. Many of the occupants had no jobs, and those that did knew there would be no buses to get them to work tomorrow. So nobody felt any particular need to turn in early. Which guaranteed lots of witnesses to whatever fucked-up death squad shit was about to happen, Will reflected grimly.

According to Aftab, who was now cuffed in front wolfing down a Quarterao from McDonald's, his uncle's underground hospital was behind the tower blocks. Entry was in the back of a *borracharia*, a catch-all auto repair/salvage yard. Tactically it sucked. Narrow alleys. Enemy high ground. No backup.

Will reminded himself that things were sucking a lot worse for Ken right now. Edilson slammed the trunk shut and jumped in the driver's seat. "Put this on." He handed Will a ballistic vest. He tossed one over the seat to Andreatta.

Will cinched the Velcro ties as tight as they could go. It was still too damn small. He shot Edilson a look of exasperation.

"What can I say? We don't have a lot of cops your size." Edilson shrugged.

"Tell me you at least have a plan?"

Edilson held out his arms in supplication. "Me? I always have a plan. We get Aftab to knock on Mike's door. When Mike answers it, Sargento Andreatta and I grab him. We let Aftab go." He smiled at the man, the remnants of whose hamburger were dribbling down his chin. "Unless he fucks us. In which case, you, sitting in the car, will kill him. *Entende*, Aftab?"

Aftab nodded quickly. Andreatta cuffed him on the ear half-heartedly when he saw the mess made on his seats. "Fucking hamburgers. This never happens in a *quilo*."

Will watched as Andreatta and Edilson began to pull on latex gloves.

Eletropaulo Substation, Vila Olímpia

The two men in the pot-smoke-filled Renault sat outside the station fence. Beyond the bank, the Tiete chugged along slowly and fragrantly. The passenger, a young redhead in an Abercrombie & Fitch knock-off shirt, stared at the stolen Omega on his wrist while he hefted a metal ingot with the other hand. He nodded to the driver, who took out his cellphone and dialled the man waiting a few blocks away.

The passenger stepped out of the car, quickly judged his distance, and hurled the metal brick over the fence at the relays. A shower of sparks went up as metal impacted high-voltage leads. They knew which ones to hit. The safety systems quickly tripped to prevent a system-wide overload.

The relays arced as the Renault raced off. In Vila Olímpia, the lights started to go out.

Condominio of Sergio Yamada, Vila Olímpia

Ademir Cruz bit his nails nervously as he smoked on the loading dock. He looked at his watch for the tenth time in a minute as he waited for the phone call. *God forgive me for what I am about to do,* he thought. He had been a cop once, after all. But the security guard with the greying temples and ample gut needed the money. He had five kids to feed.

The call he had been dreading came exactly on time. It was terse. "Now," said the throaty voice on the other end.

"Yes," he replied. Ademir lit his flashlight as the lights went out and opened the stairwell door to the generator room.

São Bernardo do Campo

Ken Scribbins came to slowly. At first he thought his eyes weren't working properly. Then he realized he was in a coffin.

He tried to breathe deeply to control his panic. He lay on his back, his hands cuffed in front. When he tried to raise his head, he didn't get far, striking the lid about two inches above his head. His knees got no farther.

He remembered tricks from his time in solitary. Calm down. Listen. Think.

Calm down. Hard. But those twin Kraut dickheads knew nothing yet. Too early to kill him. They were fucking with his head, trying to break him down. He felt his breath stilling. He had enough air. This told him something.

Listen. He heard nothing. Ken guessed sensory deprivation was part of the mind-fuck.

Think. He was cuffed in front now. Opportunity. He began to squirm and shift his weight. He reached his fingers between his legs. After five minutes, he held a handcuff key in his hand. Ken felt a brief surge of triumph. In this situation, any little victory counted for a lot. At least it wasn't gonna be up his ass the next time he got shocked.

Only slowly did he realize that his coffin was getting hotter.

Cingapura Zaki Narchi, Carandiru

Will drove slowly past the tower blocks into the alley. Edilson sat beside him, scanning the street, an SMG at low ready in his lap. Will could hear Aftab breathing heavily just behind him.

"*Calma.*" Andreatta addressed this to all of them.

Will could feel a thousand eyes on him, but the only person he saw on the street was an ancient leather-skinned man pulling a cart loaded high with cans and bottles. He struggled past them in the opposite direction without a second look.

They reached a tall tree in the mouth of the alley. "Stop here," Andreatta commanded. Will looked in the rear-view and saw him screwing a silencer onto his pistol. Andreatta's eyes met his. "Lookouts."

Will scanned the shadows. He saw nothing.

"Get out, Aftab. You know what to do." As Aftab opened the door, swallowing hard, Andreatta grabbed his arm. "Don't fuck us, boy." Aftab nodded and stepped into the alley.

Edilson watched the street as he said to Will, "We're going in and coming out the same way. If we're not out in three minutes, we're not coming out." He looked at Will. "Understand, brother?"

Will looked at his partner. "Sure. But you're coming back."

Edilson punched his shoulder. "Sure. Mike goes in the trunk, okay?"

As Aftab cautiously edged around the corner out of sight, the two cops slipped into the alleyway and followed. Andreatta and Edilson rounded the corner, weapons raised. Ten seconds went by. Then Will heard a muffled pop. Aftab came running around the corner, past the car, and disappeared.

Will tightened his grip on his pistol. The alley seemed to get darker. Dogs were barking their heads off in excitement now. So much for stealth. Worse, a PM helicopter now began to flood the alley with its spotlight.

Andreatta and Edilson had rounded the corner just as Aftab had pounded on the metal door. Edilson had grabbed Andreatta's vest, and the two had moved sharply to the right to avoid the lookout's view through the spyhole. There was no cover. They both took a knee as Aftab did a nervous dance in front of the door.

Edilson felt the shadows shift as a PM helicopter passed overhead, its Nitesun briefly paralyzing them in their exposed position. *Not now boys, not now ...* The light passed them by as Aftab turned and shrugged at them. *Don't look at us, idiot!*

A muffled voice came from behind the door. *"Aftab? E que isso?"*

"I'm hurt! Help!" Aftab squealed shamelessly.

The door unbolted. A large bearded man in blood-smeared scrubs stepped out and looked straight at them. His mouth began to open. Andreatta put a hole in his cheek. The man toppled to the ground, his body holding the door open for them as they rushed in. Aftab, his job finished, ran in the opposite direction.

The hallway led straight forward, branching off to the left eight metres down. Another branch two metres after that. Andreatta held position by the entrance as Edilson moved down the hall to the first junction, heart racing.

He hated building clearing. All a child's bogeyman fears brought to life, armed. Edilson steadied his breathing as he reached the junction and waited for his sergeant. On the opposite wall was a picture of the Kaaba in Mecca. Criminals always carried the trappings of the devout—Catholics, Muslims, it didn't matter.

Nobody was doing God's work here tonight. Andreatta came up on his shoulder. "Clear," he whispered. Edilson nodded and walked slowly down the hall to the second turnoff. An office. File cabinets. A makeshift exam table. Blood-spattered sheets and a tray of instruments. A couch along the wall. Two men under bloody sheets, both black and tall. Brothers?

One man's eyes opened and met his. The man's yellowed eyes went wide, and he reached up to the top of the couch with his right arm.

"Gun!" Edilson shouted and riddled both men with a full magazine.

"Fuck!" Andreatta rushed down the hall to the front entrance as Edilson slapped in a fresh magazine, pocketing his used one. He heard a muffled pop, and then the front door opened. Edilson rushed forward and saw Andreatta running full speed after a short man in a surgical apron, ducking and weaving around junked cars. The two men disappeared onto the street.

This is what happens when you don't cover all the exits. Edilson cursed his plan, reversed course, and ran back toward Will in the alley.

Back in the alley, Will had heard Edilson's shots and had started the engine. He drove forward and slammed to a stop in front of the back door just as Edilson came out.

Will saw the body lying in the doorway. He looked over at Cingapura. Groups of people were huddled on the balconies, watching. Edilson jumped into the back, breathless.

"Andreatta ... in pursuit ... Back up and go to Zaki Narchi!"

Will threw it in reverse as he pulled the emergency brake and came out of the alley in a J-turn in time to see a moto rip around the corner on the boulevard, headed the way they'd come. He was startled when Andreatta jumped in beside him.

Gasping, all Andreatta could say was "I hope you know São Paulo!"

Will stepped on the gas and tore onto Zaki Narchi. The moto shot through a red light and headed for the Polícia Civil building. That was a mistake. Tonight there was a roadblock there.

The rider realized this too and turned sharp left, going against the traffic, headed for the Marginal. Will had no choice but to follow. As they passed Shopping Centre Norte, the moto dodged sparse oncoming traffic as Will followed. Horns screeched, and a startled truck driver went over an embankment into a deep ditch. Ahead, the rider's surgical apron flapped in the wind as he hunkered down and accelerated, entering the Marginal. The wide road was practically deserted tonight, the PCC having made what would have otherwise been suicidal merely unwise.

The rider weaved and surged across the lanes, seemingly uncertain of where to go. Will accelerated, the rider having wasted momentum and allowing him to catch up. "See if you can get in front of him, slow him down," Edilson suggested.

"I don't think he's armed," added Andreatta.

Will was about to cut him off when the rider throttled back and then accelerated and shot off the roadway up an embankment. Will, cursing, executed a sharp turn and drove up an off ramp. He reached the top just in time to see the rider surging across the bridge, in the oncoming lane again. Will followed with the traffic, trying to stay parallel to his target.

He realized he was actually having fun and smiled to himself. Andreatta noticed. "It's nice being a cop sometimes, huh?"

"Yes, it is!"

The rider easily negotiated the sparse oncoming traffic, even taking the time to look over at Will and extend a middle finger. Will was getting frustrated with this asshole when he realized two things: (1) They were on Avenida Cruzeiro do Sul. Southern Cross. (2) They were headed straight for a police station.

The rider looked over his shoulder, missing his last chance to turn. When he looked ahead again, he saw blinking red lights and the shadows of men in the roadway.

"Stop," Andreatta told Will. "He's dead meat now."

"Shit," Edilson said quietly.

They heard a fusillade of shots from down the road. "Go up now. Let's see if he can still talk." Andreatta motioned ahead. Will cruised forward slowly. A cluster of PM were around an inert form on the median. His moto lay on its side 10 metres away, slowly leaking fuel from a perforated tank. Andreatta signalled for him to stop. Will unbuckled his seat belt. Andreatta put a hand on his shoulder. "You should stay here. I don't want to have to explain 'Soldado Ferguson' on top of everything else."

Will seethed but said nothing. He watched the scene as Andreatta approached the group of PM, his ID held out, and was admitted to the circle.

"What happened back there?" Will quizzed Edilson as he watched Andreatta. "Lots of shooting for a stealth operation, partner."

"We encountered resistance."

"Is that how you write it up?"

"Brazil is the way it is, Will. You can't change it. If that's why you're going after Stumpf, you're wasting your time."

"I have my reasons. As do you."

"Yes I do."

"If Mike is dead …"

"I don't think there's any 'if' about it."

"Then how do we find Ken?"

"How the fuck do I know? I thought you were supposed to be giving me detective lessons!"

"Easy, Edilson. We need to—"

Edilson's phone rang, and he held up his hand. He stepped out of the car to take the call. Watching the body language, Will could tell it was Deyse. Every cop's wife in the city was freaking out right now. She would be freaking even more if she knew half the shit they'd pulled in the past week.

Will tried to collect his thoughts. A lot of threads had to come together to wrap this case up. It was close, he could feel it, but what to do now was the question. If Ken had broken, they wouldn't have much time. And how they'd ever get to him without a source on the ground was …

The ground. That was something. But what? Will struggled to pin down the thought while he still could. He'd never felt himself an especially smart person, but he knew he had moments, glimpses ... They could probably be chalked up more to instinct than intelligence, but whatever they were, they served a purpose. He felt a glimpse coming on now.

The ground.

Overhead, the PM helicopter had followed them and floodlit the scene as the knot of men surrounded their unfortunate quarry. Andreatta walked back to the car, shaking his head. "Dead. Oh well."

"Oh well? Oh well?" His irritation with Andreatta was suddenly subsumed with a realization.

Well. Ground. Digging. Condor Foundations LLC. They were going there anyway. It did Stumpf's dirty work where he had the biggest secrets to hide. It was staffed by rough men. It was as good a place to look for Ken as any.

Edilson was still negotiating with Deyse when Will shouted over at him, "Edilson, we're going, now!"

Edilson gave him a helpless look.

"Agora!" Will pushed hard. "I know where we're going next!"

Edilson extricated himself from the call with difficulty and walked over. "What?"

"You wanted a fucking detective lesson? Well come on."

Vila Olímpia

Ademir had been taking 5,000 a month for the last year. In return, he'd had to promise to do two things when the time came. One was to make sure the emergency generator didn't go on. He'd done that part already. The other part was to let a team into the stairwell. He was pretty sure they weren't here to set up a surprise birthday party, but other than that, he knew nothing. He didn't even know who they were after. He hoped it was someone else bad. He wedged open the now-unalarmed stairwell door.

Ademir was supposed to walk away at this point. But his curiosity got the better of him. He went down two floors and got the best vantage point he could. He watched as three men wearing masks walked in, looking around, and then started up the stairs.

He didn't know what he'd expected to see. He felt sick and sat on the stairs for a long while.

He was still there when the men in masks left the same way they had come in, 20 minutes later. But he wasn't looking anymore.

26

Condor Foundations LLC, São Bernardo do Campo

Ken woke up, soaked in sweat, his mouth the only part of him that was dry.

He had passed out from the heat. As the heat had risen, so had the panic in his little box, and he'd begun flailing his limbs, as much as he could, and screaming at the top of his lungs.

Anyone out there was ignoring him. If there was anyone out there. It was worse than the longest stint he'd ever done in the hole. The most profound despair he'd ever felt sank over Ken Scribbins, and he began to sob uncontrollably. They were breaking him.

Erich and Klaus watched and listened to it all from the next room. They had a webcam with a night-vision lens at his feet, pointing at his face.

"Do you think he's ready?" Erich was eager to get on with it.

"Not quite." Klaus was more cautious. "Let's try cooling. Now is the time, while he's soaked in sweat. He'll freeze nicely."

Erich felt uneasy, but he turned a dial on the control panel anyway. When he'd been in university, he had read about an American psychologist's experiment to see how many people would give lethal electric shocks when ordered. Erich had always thought he wouldn't act like one of Stanley Milgram's subjects. But now he knew he was full of shit.

Avenida Martin Luther King, São Bernardo do Campo

Will came awake in the back seat. His eyes adjusted to the pre-dawn light. "Where are we?" São Paulo could be a shapeless mass, away from Avenida Paulista and Ibirapuera Park.

Edilson looked back. "Almost there. I hope you're right."

"Me too. Or I'm all out of ideas."

Edilson yawned. "No offence, but I would kill you for eight hours of sleep right now."

"Right back at you."

"Shut up, you jackasses." Andreatta assumed command. "Soldado Ferguson!" He said it with the slightest trace of irony. "You know where we are going?"

"Yes." He held up his phone and looked at the screen. "Next right. First lot on the left past the big parking lot. A single building at the entranceway. Looks like a tall fence on Google Earth, but we have the tools. We get through the fence and take the guardhouse. We find out where we are going from there."

"It's a big lot?"

"Yes. Lots of room for material. No idea how much is there right now."

"Other buildings?"

"About 300 metres from the fence line, against the far perimeter. A big sand shelter and what look like four workshops or offices. Single-story."

Andreatta seemed reasonably satisfied with Will's reconnaissance, for once. "Okay. I take care of the dogs. You two cut the fence and head for the guardhouse, agreed?"

Both men nodded. The vests came on again. This time, Will put on latex gloves too. Each man re-checked his weapon. Andreatta turned onto the target street and drove slowly. Will could see the target ahead. A tall fence with solid walls, topped with razor wire. Not easy.

Andreatta pulled in behind a cube van parked on the street. Edilson was out first, clearing the cab of the van and checking on a subcompact parked in front of the target. He gave them the signal to move. If there were cameras, the clock was ticking.

Andreatta popped the trunk and headed over to meet Edilson. Will retrieved a bundle from the trunk. He hustled over to the other two men and broke it open.

Edilson called it his "search warrant." The contents were simple. Two bridging mats made of old Kevlar vests sewn together by Deyse and a pair of grounded bolt cutters. Necessary for any covert entry to the most humble São Paulo residence or business. They were all little fortresses. Will tossed the first bridging mat over the wire and boosted Andreatta up. Andreatta climbed over Will's back and cut the electrified razor wire on both sides of the bridging point. Will tossed the other mat over. Andreatta took a deep breath and bellyflopped onto the mat. It held. He twisted his body with surprising agility and landed on his feet at the base of the wall. Andreatta raced for the guardhouse wall as Edilson scrambled over Will, landed on his belly on the bridging mat, and twisted himself over to drop down.

Edilson was in mid-drop when he saw a Rottweiler charging full tilt at him. Two muffled pops, and the dog was twitching in the gravel. Andreatta was a man of his word. The sergeant waved lazily at Will and then went back to watching his corner. Edilson waited for Will with some impatience as the big Canadian struggled to get his ass over the wall.

Finally, Will dropped, landing heavily on one knee. "Shit!" He looked down at a steadily leaking rip in his calf. The razor wire had cut deep.

"It's a good thing you got out of law enforcement alive while you still could," Edilson goaded him.

"Why am I wishing that Rottweiler had ripped your nuts off?" The two men hustled for the guardhouse wall and stacked behind Andreatta. Edilson patted him on the shoulder. "Go!"

Andreatta reached around and tried the door handle. The Sergeant turned to Edilson in astonishment, mouthing "Unlocked" to him. Will ran across the doorway and got a position on the right side. Andreatta opened the door and walked in.

A heavyset man in his fifties, his face wrinkled like a Shar Pei's, looked straight at the door as if alert. He wore an ill-fitting guard's uniform and sat behind a heavy wooden desk. A TV on the other side of the room hissed static. Will could tell the man was very much asleep.

Andreatta sighed and took aim at the man. Will caught the motion out of the corner of his eye and brought his arm down on Andreatta's.

"What the hell, gringo, you aren't in charge here!" Andreatta hissed.

Will was firm. "Go ahead and kill all the gangsters you want. I won't interfere. But don't fuck up my case."

Andreatta looked at him but said nothing. Will hoped he wasn't storing up a grudge. But Will wasn't comfortable enough with killing to engage in it for no reason. He hoped he never would be.

The *guarda* woke up just in time to see Edilson levelling a submachine gun at him from the doorway. He fell out of his chair. Will stepped around the desk and saw the man looking back at a panic button under the desktop. He pointed his pistol at the man's head. "*Espere, senhor.* We didn't come here for you. Don't make trouble. We're cops."

The man put up his hands, slowly. Andreatta walked around the other side of the desk and ripped the man's gun belt off, tossing it to Edilson. Will felt a sense of disappointment. This couldn't be the place. Not guarded by this guy.

The *guarda* watched with the passive eyes of a beaten man. His hands were folded in his lap. Andreatta cleared the rest of the guardhouse, and Will sat on the desk to keep their prisoner away from the alarm. Edilson scanned the yard as he pulled the *guarda's* revolver out of its holster. He examined the weapon and whistled. "Brother, you ever clean this thing?"

"Officer, I don't even know how to use it."

Will thought, *I can believe that.* The guy looked like he couldn't harm a can of tuna.

"Maybe you can help us. We're looking for a friend." Will smiled at him. "We think he might be here."

"The second workshop on the left. That's where it happens."

Will leaned over and looked at the man, who looked back in discomfort. He smelled body odour. The water shortage was hitting some neighbourhoods bad. Not everybody got to shower every day.

"Where what happens?"

"Where the twins take people. And they come out in boxes. I don't know anything else." He held up his hands. "I'm not allowed to go in there."

Will could feel his excitement mounting again. Maybe he was right.

"Are they there now?"

"I think so. But I was asleep for a while. Is there a blue BMW out there?"

"Edilson? Is there a blue BMW in the lot? Maybe by those workshops?"

"I'll check."

Andreatta moved over to the door as Edilson slipped into the yard. He came back quickly.

"Yes, Will, yes, there is." He smiled. "We'd better get some help."

200 metres away

Ken had gotten his shit together as the temperature in the box started to drop. He even got a little philosophical. He wondered how he could even be thinking about getting accustomed to this.

He no longer knew how long he had been in there. He didn't know if it was night or day. He had come very close to losing himself, closer than he'd ever come in solitary.

But Ken Scribbins was still very much in there. And he had that handcuff key in the right cuff, just so. They were going to have to open that box sometime. And when they did, he was going to play them. He had it all worked out.

But then the sweat started to chill him. He could see his breath. And he started to shiver.

The guardhouse

Andreatta watched the workshop out the back window while Edilson paced on the phone. Will watched his partner's emphatic conversation out of the corner of his eye while he chatted amicably with their guest, whom he now knew to be Anderson Alves. From Edilson's gestures, it didn't seem like getting help was going to be very easy in a city where every cop suddenly needed to be in three places at once.

Anderson Alves, on the other hand, was not stressed at all. He actually seemed relieved, more so when Edilson had promised him he wasn't going to jail if he cooperated.

"I was in Carandiru. Bad place. I'm never going back."

Will understood. Before it was a park and a community centre, Carandiru had been the scene of an overcrowded and violent prison. In 1992, the Polícia Militar had ended a riot there with gunfire, killing dozens of prisoners.

It had been the birth of the PCC.

Talking to Anderson painted things in a different perspective for Will. He was an ex-cop, so he tended to take the cop's perspective on things like the police-versus-PCC war. But the violence in Brazil was hardly one-sided. A cycle of atrocity and counter-atrocity had hardened hearts all over. Cops like Edilson were quick to distance themselves from the worst excesses, but Will couldn't stop wondering if even Edilson knew where the line was anymore.

Did Will? There was a lot of blood on his hands too. He thought of Soares. He pushed it away. But it never really left, one of two faces now staring at him in the night. The rest didn't bother him. Heat of battle.

Anderson Alves had been a car thief who had been paroled after the Carandiru massacre and wound up doing odd jobs until his brother had gotten him a job doing foundations here. It was hard, physical work. Anderson had never gotten the knack of working the machines, so he was stuck with manual labour.

He had been injured last year and given a consolation job here. It was a considerate move, by Brazilian standards. Stumpf's companies actually tended to have a pretty good reputation. It didn't really surprise Will. Guys like Stumpf were usually real princes until you told them they couldn't have something they really wanted. Then they showed their true colours.

But what really interested Will was when Anderson talked about the last job he'd worked foundations on. It was Southern Cross.

"You worked the Southern Cross job?"

"Yes, that's the one on the Carvalho Pinto, by Caçapava, right, the big one?"

"Yes. Do you remember anything special about that job?"

"Hmm. There was a lot of security. Not just at the gate, but inside too."

"Like what?"

"Like there were always these guards, not like me, *muito seriousa*, you know? They only guarded some parts of the job. And they were very specific about where we couldn't dig. I thought it was because of power cables or something. But then I found something strange one day."

He looked down at the floor and wrung his hands.

"What was strange, Anderson?"

"A bunch of rotten old shoes. Men's and women's. Out there in the countryside. It was very odd. I told my supervisor. He looked angry, and he asked me where I'd been digging. I showed him, and he got very nervous. That wasn't one of the places we weren't supposed to dig. Then I saw a bunch of them arguing."

Will could feel his excitement building. His theory was looking sound. Why so much commotion over a bunch of shoes? "Who was arguing?"

"My supervisor. Senhor Grasselman, the chief, and Senhor Stumpf himself."

"Stumpf was there?"

"He was always there. That was another thing that was strange. He has a lot of companies I think. Lots of places to be. But he was at this job a lot."

"Did you ever see him do that before?"

"Only once."

Will knew the answer before he asked the question. "Where?"

"The Santa Catarina job, south of Blumenau."

The mass grave of the Tupamaros. But who was in this one?

"What did they do about the shoes?"

"Well, Senhor Stumpf got very angry with my supervisor, and he said something like 'Fine, I'll do it myself!' He came to see me with Grasselman later. They gave me 5,000 reais, and Senhor Stumpf told me to bury the shoes at night. My supervisor and Grasselman would help. Grasselman looked very worried, but Senhor Stumpf was calm again. He said, 'I might ask you to do something again for me. Can I rely on you?' I said, 'Of course,' and since then he has been very good to me."

That explained the soft landing. This simple man had something on Stumpf. But Stumpf was judicious in his killing, and he couldn't simply eliminate the problem. So he met the problem's simple needs and kept him happy.

"Where did you bury them?" Will had a crude map of the project and unfolded it on the table beside Anderson. "Show me."

Anderson bit his lip and then stabbed a finger at the lower left side of the project. "There, I think. By where the fence is now. We paved it over at night. I remember, just me, my supervisor, and Grasselman. It was a bit strange."

"How many shoes?"

"Oh, at least 80 pairs."

Will felt a chill. "At least? Men's and women's? No kids'?"

"No. At least I don't think so. Hard to tell, though, they were so rotten."

"Did he ask you to do anything else?"

"Yes, one other time. He came to me when we were finishing up one evening. He asked if I wanted to make another 5,000 easy. I said sure. He asked me to meet him three hours later."

"You went?"

"Of course! It's Senhor Stumpf!" He smiled.

"And 5,000 in cash?"

"That helps!" He winked. Will had to like the guy, even if he was covering up an atrocity.

"What happened next?"

"I hung around with nothing to do. I had some pinga with the watchmen, but I stopped because you don't want to be drunk around Senhor Stumpf. He doesn't like drunks. I met him in the centre, where the foundations were already poured and we weren't allowed to go. There was a big shaft, like a well, already dug there."

"What did he have you do?"

"It was him and two of his guards, a big *negao* and a guy with long, greasy hair. They pulled off a tarp and showed me all these waterproof bags. They looked like they had files or something inside. He told us to toss them all down the shaft. Then he had me cover it in cement."

"Did you see what was on the files?"

"No. I am *analfabeto*."

Analfabeto. Illiterate. A good choice to conceal incriminating files. Stumpf hadn't gotten where he was without choosing people wisely. He just couldn't have guessed that this guileless man would be sitting in a room with Will.

So. The shoes definitely indicated the presence of a mass grave at Southern Cross. The files were a curious addition. Why not just burn them? But Germans were inexplicably addicted to record keeping. Maybe it was genetically impossible for Stumpf to destroy them. It was the same instinct that had gotten Eichmann's neck stretched on a Tel Aviv gallows. Or maybe he wanted to use them as leverage? Maybe there were a lot of other people mentioned in those files. A lot of people who might be able to get Oscar Stumpf out of a jam if they thought they were going down with him.

Seen in this light, Southern Cross was the ultimate insurance policy for a war criminal turned oligarch growing old and feeling vulnerable. The blackmail scheme became a necessary addition when oil prices made the project a possible DOA. Now, with oil prices tanking, it was redundant.

But the damage had been done. Stumpf had pushed Luc Renner, who couldn't give any more, and Marco Hellmer, who wouldn't. And that would be his undoing.

That and his unholy alliance with the PCC, an ally very much occupied with other things right now. The timing would never be better. But Edilson's police friends were also very occupied. And in that respect, the timing sucked.

"Finally!" Edilson threw up his hands. "I finally convinced a colonel in Choque to give me a ROTA team coming back from Zona Sul. They're pretty beat up, but they're better than nothing."

"How beat up?" Will was skeptical. If they'd had the kind of night he'd had, they were one espresso away from a total collapse.

ROTA was a tactical unit in the Polícia Militar that inspired every feeling except neutrality. To cops and many citizens, they were heroes, with a reputation for fearlessness in pursuit of violent crime. But they had a lot of blood on their hands too, something Will had learned was unavoidable in Brazilian policing. Some people viewed them as assassins, a reputation they were probably happy to use.

They would be at the top of the PCC's hit list this week. They had been, ever since Carandiru.

Edilson slumped into a chair. "They've been at it since midnight. The fuckers hit the Batalhao in Diadema with a front-end loader full of explosives! Can you believe that shit? It's like something out of Iraq ... Anyway, they finished a half hour ago, and they're on their way over. They're pretty tired, though."

"No shit."

"Okay, Will, go grab our frame charges and night vision, then."

Will was silent. Andreatta walked in. "ROTA, hah? You don't want anyone coming out of there alive, Edilson?"

ROTA had a shoot-first type reputation. Edilson was pissed. He tossed the phone across the room. "Call the fucking Navy SEALS then!"

Will tried to calm him. Everyone's nerves were past breaking. "Okay, okay, ROTA is good. We can do this. Why don't we scout things out first?"

Edilson sat on his chair, his head in his hands. He rocked back and forth. Will sensed victory around the corner but knew it was a race against collapse. Collapse seemed to be winning right now. Finally Edilson lifted his head. "Scouting. I'm good at that. Give me a minute." He stood up, walked into the little bathroom, and puked his guts out.

Andreatta shook his head and a lit a cigarillo.

Anderson looked up at Will and said, "You boys work too hard."

200 metres away

The sun was beginning to peek over the horizon as Edilson sprinted across the clearing to the workshop. The rush of air felt good on his face, and the threat invigorated him. He felt his way around the featureless slab of a building. The only windows he could see were set into the base of the peaked roof.

Edging his way around the back, pistol in hand, he could see there was only one entrance. He breathed out through his teeth. Bad situation, if the twins expected trouble. But if they expected trouble, why did they have a burnout like Anderson Alves on point? He stilled himself and listened. Nothing. Everyone in there could be dead, for all he knew.

Edilson braced himself and sprinted for the guardhouse. He was out in the open when two grey Toyota Hiluxes pulled out front of the fence line. He slowed to a jog and waved.

A dark-camouflaged figure bailed out of the passenger seat of the lead vehicle and brought an assault carbine to bear on him. He realized he was about to be shot.

"Polícia, polícia!" Edilson shouted.

The passenger lowered his rifle. The driver stepped out. "*Merda*, Lopes. Black man running at cops with a gun in his hand, tonight? You really do need our help!" He was tall and fit, black hair on top of white skin blackened by soot from a night of battle. "Let's get this over with. I need Johnny Walker and bed, in that order."

Edilson smiled. "Thanks for coming." He pushed open the Unicam door on the gate and wedged it ajar for the new arrivals.

"Nilton Pereira. These are my guys." Six men laden with equipment and weapons stood on the pavement around their leader. Edilson took it all in. "We used to be eight. Don't know if Daniel is going to make it," Pereira added.

"So let's do this quick. Only one entrance. Right ahead of you, that windowless building on the left. See where the BMW is?"

"Yes. How many?"

"Two suspects, one hostage. Two blond-haired, blue-eyed twins and a very ugly gringo."

"Sounds like my last trip to the circus. Just when I thought this night couldn't get any more fucked."

"Welcome to Operation Cruzeiro do Sul. Let me get my colleagues ready."

"Sure. We move in two."

"Meet you at the guardhouse."

Pereira was already scanning the target building for weaknesses. He noticed right away that it wasn't quite windowless. "Fine," he said.

As Edilson ran for the guardhouse, Pereira assembled his resources. "Wagner, grab the frame charge. No, the smaller one. Silvio, three flashbangs please. That will do. No gas. Make sure you are topped up on ammo. Wagner, Silvio, Josue, and me, the assaulters. Renato, Emerson, Abdul, you are the support team. Renato, grab a Polecam. I want you to ram it in through one of those windows as soon as the frame charge blows the door. No surprises for the entry team! If I fall, you take over, okay?"

Renato smiled. "Sure. You never get shot."

"Never say never. Tonight could be the night." Nilton Pereira was a tall and tautly muscled man with a lean, hungry look. His father had been on the original ROTA of the much-feared Capitano Conte Lopes. In those days, just a glimpse of the dark grey Chevys of the unit was enough to send the *ladraos* running. Today it was different. Phone cams and crusading journalists. But tonight, tonight was like the old days. Tonight they had already gotten some good work done. Four dead gangsters. And now a hostage rescue to top it off. His dad would have been proud.

But his dad had died on a mission just like this, 30 years ago. Nilton checked his Impas carbine again. His dad could've used a weapon like this. Deadly accurate, laser-sighted, and made in Brazil, the best part. For all its undeniable problems, his country was moving forward. That was why he was out here.

That and he liked to fight. He raised his arm. "Ready, men? *Vamos la!*"

200 metres away

In the coffin turned refrigerator, Ken Scribbins was shaking head to toe now, his teeth chattering uncontrollably.

But he was still in there. Him. Ken. Waiting for them to open the lid. The heat had beaten him. Nobody wants to burn, like a poor hostage in a cage. But the cold, he could handle that. He was Canadian. *Go ahead, give me a chance.* His chatter was a rapid-fire smile.

In the next room, Erich was curious. "How much can he take?"

Klaus was sleepy. "Hmm?"

"I said, how much can he take? It's almost at zero in there. We do want him to talk, don't we?"

Erich was beginning to wonder if Klaus's sadism had overwhelmed his mission orientation. He wondered the same thing about Tio Oscar.

"Okay, Erich. Since you're so friendly, why don't you go in there and open him up? See if he wants to talk. And as for me ..." At this, he opened a desk drawer and produced a pistol. "I will be ready in case he doesn't. I don't know much about Canadians, brother. But from what I've read, they don't know when to stop fighting."

Erich was unimpressed. A "scientific" torture device, seemingly perfected over the course of 40 years, defeated by what? A passport? His twin was beginning to seem as unfamiliar to him as a telemarketer from Mumbai. But he kept that to himself.

"Okay. I'll go in." He picked the keys up off of the table and walked into the next room.

The guardhouse

Edilson was breathless when he rushed in the door. "They're here. They're going now!"

Will grabbed Anderson Alves and walked him into the backroom. Alves followed meekly. "Get down." He had the man kneel on the floor as the three of them got their front-row seat. Behind the guardhouse, they had a clear view across the lot.

The workshop where Ken Scribbins lay in a coffin with no idea of time or place sat placidly, no outside clue given to its sinister nature. The sky was a deep purple, slowly shifting to orange as the sun came up with Latin laziness. It was going to be a hot one.

Will exhaled slowly. He had once watched the Vancouver City Police Emergency Response Team carry out one of his high-risk warrants and had been painfully aware of his amateurishness then. Then, as now, he'd been a spectator, hiding behind the engine compartment of a police car while men braver and more fit than he had done his job. He felt that same way now.

After three shootouts, he still had something to prove?

As he watched the men from ROTA stack up and move in two chains, swiftly and stealthily across the pitiless uncovered ground, he realized he still very much did have something to prove.

He reacted, out of fear and circumstance. He might react well, but he still reacted. Men like these initiated action, sought it out with aggression and purpose. They, and their kind, from Paris to Rio, Baghdad to Los Angeles, were of a different breed.

"Out of every 100 men, 10 shouldn't even be there, 80 are just targets, 9 are the real fighters, and we are lucky to have them, for they make the battle. Ah, but the one, one is a warrior, and he will bring the others back." One of the few things he remembered from his classics in university was that Heraclitus quote. He was proud to consider himself one of the nine in a hundred. He'd proven himself a real fighter, especially in the last week, and he knew the man he had faced those dangers with was definitely in that company.

Will looked over at his friend and watched him shake his head. As the ROTA men crept up to the building and enveloped it, two of them emerged and secured a frame charge to the doorway. The two men worked methodically, unhurriedly. Doing a job.

"Beautiful," Edilson whispered. "That's what I want to be when I grow up."

Will smiled. That was Heraclitus's 1 percent. He looked at Anderson Alves, who had a haunted look but couldn't pull himself away. He reminded himself that ROTA had shot its way into Carandiru. This wasn't Anderson's first ringside seat. Will then looked over at his shoulder at Andreatta, who sat in the next room, back turned to the action, cleaning his nails as he puffed one of his endless cigarillos.

As if sensing the attention, Andreatta said, "Body snatchers. You've seen one raid, you've seen them all. Once they get here, there's usually not much left for us."

Will hoped his ugly ex-con friend made it out alive. He'd put him in there, after all.

Out in the yard, the pre-dawn darkness blazed into whiteout for a split second as the frame charge blew. The noise was assaultive. How it sounded inside the little building was another thing entirely, Will guessed. After the three men in the guardhouse recovered from the shock, they opened their eyes to peer across the courtyard and see seven laser sights come on and cut the swirling smoke.

Four black-and-grey-camouflaged men entered the blasted doorway with carbines at the high ready.

200 metres away

Erich opened the coffin and stared at the inert form of Ken Scribbins, bathed in chilled sweat, a congealed grimace on his face. A sweat-sock smell of a person wrung dry assaulted Erich's nostrils. *Christ, we've killed him.* Erich cursed quietly at his bloody-minded brother as he leaned over to look at their victim.

Then, the world exploded.

A sonic wave of overpressure assaulted Erich's ears and skull as he toppled forward onto Ken Scribbins. Erich opened his eyes and stared back into Ken's fish-eyed visage just as the former occupant of the coffin worked one hand-cuff open.

There were shouts and shots in the other room, causing Erich to look away for a fatal moment. Fatal because that was the moment that Ken Scribbins hooked the ratchet of a handcuff through Erich's cheek and began pulling on his head like a great white chews on a seal.

Ken was, to put it mildly, a bit put out.

Workshop entranceway

Two seconds after the frame charge blew, Nilton Pereira was the first in through the doorway, sweeping the swirling smoke, third-eyeing with his laser sight, feeling his men behind him, feeling that same funny mix of elation and terror he always did. That crack-like jolt.

He always went first. His dad had warned him against that, but he felt it was what was expected. And besides ... he loved it. He was almost touching the table Klaus had been sitting at when he realized he was looking down the barrel of a pistol.

He moved his laser sight up four centimetres to his best guess for centre mass and fired three rounds. Another sight painted the target, and flashes popped from Wagner's carbine.

Klaus's torso sustained four .223 high-velocity hits inside of one second, causing him to rag doll and drop to the floor, the pistol he was holding firing only once.

That single round from Klaus's pistol went up Nilton Pereira's neck, under his jaw, and out his brainstem, severing all autonomic nervous system functions and killing him instantly. A family tradition.

As their leader's body slumped to the ground, Silvio and Josue broke left and headed for a closed door. A single red dot painted the doorway, Silvio sighting while Josue shot his boot into the jamb.

The door flew open to reveal two men locked in struggle. Silvio and Josue had a split second to decide who to shoot.

27

Erich was dead already, but Ken Scribbins couldn't stop beating him.

An ever-widening pool of blood framed the man's deceptively angelic face as the gotch-eyed ex-convict bounced his head off the concrete floor. Again and again. Ken, now freed from his coffin, screamed with the rage he hadn't felt since he'd held his stillborn second daughter in his hands in a hospital in Recife, so long ago. The lifeless torturer absorbed every blow without complaint, now a therapy tool for a man in need of so much.

Silvio and Josue stared, questioning if they had shot the right man. They were uncertain of what to do until they heard Wagner scream from the next room, "The chief is hit! *Socorro!* Renato, *vai!*"

They backed out of the torture room fast to find Wagner cradling Nilton in his arms. On the other side of a wooden table, the sprawled form of Klaus demonstrated that Nilton had died as he'd lived.

Renato and the support team clustered in the doorway. Renato yanked off his helmet and threw it at Klaus's body. "You fucking shit! *Assassino!*"

Across the courtyard, Will watched and heard the screams. He rose to his feet. "Will, stay down!" Edilson hissed at him. "They haven't cleared us!"

Will headed for the door. "I'm going to get my friend. I owe him."

Edilson cursed through his teeth. "Fucking Canadians." He looked over at Andreatta. Will was already out the door and halfway across the courtyard. "*Sargento*, look after our guest. The gringo needs minding."

Andreatta rolled his eyes as Edilson raced out the door after his partner. He turned to Anderson Alves. "Do you have a *bandera nacional*?"

"*Sim.*"

"Find it. I think we're going to need it." Andreatta looked out at the workshop as Alves moved off in search of a flag. Strong, distraught men wandered out of the workshop on uncertain feet, holding each other in search of brotherly reassurance. Andreatta shook his head sadly.

Across the courtyard, Will Bryant shouldered past the stunned ROTA troopers into the workshop. The iron tang of blood mingled with cordite and smoke assaulted his nostrils. A dead ROTA man sprawled at his feet, a helpless comrade by his side. Another dead man, an enemy no doubt, on the other side of the room.

Gabi, running through the waves at Ubatuba. An image, unwelcome, surfacing through the horror. He ached for his family. Ken, where was Ken?

He heard panted breathing from the other room. He started there with leaden feet, afraid of his discovery.

Edilson almost ran into him.

"Will, stop! We go together, okay?"

Will nodded. He put an arm on Edilson's shoulder, and the two walked into the narrow doorway.

Inside, an open coffin. A dank, sweaty smell. More iron and cordite. Another dead man, shot and pummelled. And in the corner, a hollow-eyed Ken Scribbins squatted and stared at him. A single handcuff dangled from his right wrist.

"Ken! Are you okay?"

Ken Scribbins laughed ironically. He put his prison mask back on and smiled darkly through stained teeth. "Buddy," he replied, "I'm fucking tip-top."

Will offered his hand. Ken waved it away and painfully rose on stiff legs. He walked out of the room slowly, not looking back.

Just then, Will heard men singing the *hino nacional*. Curious, he stepped into the next room, in time to see the ROTA men carrying Nilton Pereira to his hero's grave in a wrapped-up Brazilian flag. As the men stepped into the courtyard, they were met by an impromptu honour guard: an embittered old street cop and an illiterate ex-con. Andreatta and Alves came to attention and saluted Nilton Pereira as if they had rehearsed it. Will Bryant watched, feeling envious of this strange nationhood that seemingly transcended class, crime, race. So very Brazilian. A pure hero for a mongrel country. He felt himself tearing up as an honour guard of warriors bore their leader into the sun.

Revenge. He'd promised Silvia. Now he promised Nilton Pereira.

Vila Olímpia

Will came to as Andreatta drove too fast over a massive speed bump, his head bouncing off the window.

Andreatta looked at him in the mirror, another cigarillo dangling from his lip. "Good, I needed company."

Beside him, Edilson slumped forward, drooling on the driver's seat. Anderson Alves snored loudly beside Andreatta. Outside, a deserted city woke up with a hangover. Cops prowled, only a few curious or foolhardy citizens daring to be out. A steady grey wall of cloud was moving in from the east. Will got the sense everything was winding down. Rain would seal the deal.

"I hope it rains." Andreatta was thinking the same thing. "Hard to have a good riot in the rain."

"You think it's over?"

"Maybe for now. Now we kill them. We don't mind the rain." He grinned.

It was so different here, cops and crooks. So much more ... primal. Courts were unreliable, and prisons were sieves. So the gun solved all problems.

The worst thing for Will was he was getting used to it. "Soldado Ferguson" fit right in. He looked into the gaunt, thousand-yard stare of a young *policial* as they slowly passed a checkpoint.

Mirror, mirror.

Alves snorted loudly and shifted his bulk. He let out a horrendous fart.

"Jesus Christo, what does this fucker eat?" Andreatta frantically lowered the window.

Will laughed. "Looks like you need to housebreak your new pet, Sargento." They passed the burned-out bus from last night. A skinny man in tight jeans and high-tops snapped shots on his iPhone. Already the battle was becoming social media chatter. Will tried to process that and Nilton Pereira heading into the sunrise. Two different worlds.

Andreatta watched him in the mirror. "You're trying to understand it. Don't. It will make you crazy. Try to survive instead."

"What's your secret?"

"When I started, I thought a lot, like you. Every dead body, every beaten kid, every raped woman ... it got to me." He paused, looking warily at the gringo for a moment before going on. "Then one night, my partner and I went to a fire in the favela. Three kids burned up with their mother. Caught behind iron bars. It happens a lot here in Brazil." He paused again, lighting another cigarillo with the last. Andreatta sucked in the smoke and seethed it out through his teeth. "I couldn't stop seeing the little charcoal bodies. Their mother's arms, wrapped around them. I started to cry, and I couldn't stop. For days. My partner thought I was finished. But my wife saved me."

"My wife saves me too." Will realized it as Andreatta smiled.

"I don't know how yours does it. But mine kicked me out of bed one day and told me, 'You signed up to be a cop.

What did you think it was going to be, parades and pizza? You have a family here to feed; stop crying over someone else's. Find a way to stop thinking about it!' I said, 'Easy for you to say! Stop thinking about it?' But then I thought, *She's right.* Graciana might be a *vaca* sometimes, but she's what a man like me needs. I stopped thinking about it. Well, mostly. And I don't worry so much now."

"How?" The kid at Tim Hortons. The politician with a bullet in his brain.

"I whistle."

"What?"

"I just whistle. If you whistle, nothing seems so bad. Try it sometime." He began to tunelessly whistle a Tim Maia song.

"For you, maybe. For me, it's torture," Edilson said. Andreatta laughed as Edilson sat up slowly. "Stop it, Sarge. I love that song."

They pulled onto the wide avenue running parallel to the sluggish, stinking Tiete. The street in front of Yamada's *condominio* was cordoned off. Cordoned-off streets were the norm today. But Will had a terrible feeling nonetheless.

Edilson grabbed his arm. "Isn't that Yamada's ...?"

"Yes. Fuck it!"

Andreatta glanced over his shoulder. "*Calma.* You know nothing yet. Let me find out." He pulled to the curb and stepped out. Will started to whistle "O Calambeque" by Roberto Carlos, completely unaware he was doing so.

"What the fuck are you doing, brother?" Edilson hated whistling.

"Sorry."

Edilson shook his head. "Fuck this, let's go. I'm sick of waiting in the car like Andreatta's wife all the time."

Will followed him into the street. "Alves, Edilson. Shouldn't we watch him?"

Edilson looked back at the fat man curled up in the front seat. "He's not going anywhere. Come on, I have a bad feeling."

"Me too."

They walked toward the light show, noticing two TV trucks parked on the other side of the tape. TV trucks were a bad sign, Will figured. There was no shortage of news in São Paulo this weekend. Whatever had happened involved somebody of note. Like a prominent reporter. Or a lawyer. He began to breathe deeply.

"Easy, Will."

Calambeque

Cara businar o calambeque

Bee-bo-deep-oh-bee-deep-bee-doo

Andreatta was right about the whistling. Will walked into the crime scene, calmed by the nonsense song. Andreatta was standing in a knot of cops surrounding a car with a smashed-in roof. A roof smashed in by a battered body. A body surrounded by deformed metal and solidifying viscous blood. He had no idea who it was. He looked up and saw heads peering over a balcony high up. Kind of about how high up Sergio Yamada lived. He whistled louder, and people started staring.

Edilson came over to him. "Not so loud, for God's sake. Are you losing it again?"

"Sorry. But it's Yamada, isn't it?"

"Hard to tell. But he's about the right height and weight. And the clothing looks right."

Will pointed across the scene to a shiny object on the sidewalk. "Is that his watch?"

"Jesus."

Andreatta left the mob and came over. "I thought I said, 'Wait in the car'?"

"I'm not good at following orders. Is that Yamada?"

"Most likely, yes. Positive ID will have to wait."

Edilson looked up. "Jumped, or pushed?"

"Looks like jumped under duress. Looks like. And Will ..." Andreatta hesitated. Will had never heard him use his first name before, and he knew Thiago was dead.

"I want to see him."

"No. Absolutely not."

Before he could reply, Edilson said, "It's our case, boss."

"Not now. Now it's the Delegacia's."

"Come on, Arturo! After all we've been doing, you're going to get official on me now? Do I have to call the Major?"

Andreatta stepped forward. "Don't forget your place, Soldado."

Edilson stayed put. "My place and yours will be the same: hell, unless we end this soon. And that means not waiting for the Delegacia to fuck it up. Sargento."

"Maybe you should call the Major. I don't think I could get us in there if I wanted to. And I don't want to, understand?"

Edilson was exasperated. "Then why are you a part of all this anyway?"

"I told you, Lopes; maybe you didn't listen. I like killing these guys. They deserve it. They've killed enough of my friends. My partner, my brother. That's why I do it. I don't want to play detective, like you!"

"If by 'playing detective' you mean proving Oscar Stumpf killed these guys while he was helping the PCC, then that is what I'm doing. Thinking ahead. Would you rather kill the stupid foot soldier or the general who gives the orders? Stumpf is the man you should really want. Stop thinking like a foot soldier and start thinking like a detective! I know you, Arturo; you're smart enough."

"If you feel that strongly about Stumpf, why haven't you killed him already?" Andreatta had to know the answer; he just wanted a reminder that he wasn't going out on a limb, that someone higher up was backing them, Edilson figured. He looked around for Will and saw him across the street, staring into the Tiete. At least he'd stopped whistling.

"Sarge, you know how well protected this fucker is. And you know we won't get the green light until we have the facts. We have to have a dossier our bosses can drop on a desk in Brasília, so everybody can feel good about it before it all gets burned. This isn't like erasing some *favelado*."

"That makes me nervous."

"It should. I didn't say it was going to be easy."

Andreatta motioned to Yamada's battered body. "Obviously."

Will walked up to them. "Are we going up there, or what?"

Edilson dialled the Major while Andreatta walked away muttering.

"Yes, Willao. But I need an invitation first."

Will looked up. "I can't do this much longer, buddy. By this time next week, he's dead."

"Or we are."

"Looks that way."

Around them, crime scene technicians raced to put up a folding tent over the car that was Sergio Yamada's last resting place, before the rain wiped everything away.

28

Condominio of Sergio Yamada (deceased),
Vila Olímpia

After a long, pleading, cajoling call to the Major, Edilson
had gotten Will on his way to the last place he wanted to
be. Now Will needed to make the last phone call he wanted
to make.

He cradled the phone between face and shoulder, hoping
his wife wouldn't answer. "Love?" Goddamn it. "Honey?
Honey?" He didn't know what to say.

"He's dead."

"Who? Honey? *Fala*, Will, *por favor!*" He looked up as
the elevator ticked off the ascending floors, en route to one
more nightmare for his collection. Edilson stared at the
floor. Andreatta whistled soundlessly. He'd always done
it; only now did Will realize.

"Thiago, my love. Thiago."

"*Meu Deus*, Will. My God." She began to sob.

The elevator arrived at an awkward moment, and the
three men stepped into a lobby humming with busy cops.

Will hurried into the quietest corner he could find, a finger in one ear.

"Please, Silvia, I need you to be strong. Please." He would need even more than that.

"I have to call Jacquie. Does she know?"

He hated himself for what he was about to ask. "No, she doesn't. She needs to hear, from a friend."

He imagined his wife, how she must look now in the morning light, feeling her strength. Needing it to add to his own failing resources. He paused to listen as his wife breathed deeply. Finally, resolute: "Yes. I will do it. But Will ..."

"Yes?"

She emphasized each word now, as she always did when she figured his concussed brain couldn't get it otherwise. "Do ... your ... job. Understand?" In other words, kill him.

"I'll enjoy it."

She was silent for a minute. He could hear Gabi enter, singing. "Don't enjoy it, Husband. Just do it."

"I have to go. I love you."

"We all love you. Come back, Husband." She was going to make him make a promise he couldn't guarantee.

"I promise."

"Beijos, meu amor."

"Beijos pra voce." He hung up. He was going to walk into that apartment and see his dead friend. And then he was going back to war. No family. No sweetness. Nothing but the end.

Edilson sought him out. "Ready?"

When was someone ever ready for something like this? But he had insisted, hadn't he? "Yes."

"We need to hurry. PM controls the scene, but not for much longer." His eyes searched out Will's. "You don't have to, you know."

"I need to. I need the hate. Do you understand?"

"You really have to ask me?"

Will wrapped his forearm around his friend's neck, and the two touched foreheads. Edilson exhaled.

"Edilson, no more dead friends, okay? Only dead enemies."

"And lots of those. *Chin chin.* Let's go."

Will followed as Edilson led the way into Yamada's apartment. Will's eye was unpractised to be sure, but he noticed no signs of forced entry on the way in. Inside job? Or supposed friend?

Andreatta was inside already. He peered over the balcony. Last night they'd been having drinks on that balcony. The thought occurred to Will that their prints were all over the place. Andreatta turned around to face him. "Yes, prints. Don't worry. These guys know the score."

For the would-be poker player he fancied himself, Will was giving away a lot these days. But maybe Andreatta was just scary good at reading tells.

"Such a long way down. So close to your comfortable life. But always there." Andreatta had an ironic smile as he leaned on the sliding glass. "Cops understand this every shift. But not everyone does."

Will stared for a moment. He couldn't digest Andreatta, at least not all the way. Maybe he'd gone too far down the river, past the Do Lung Bridge.

"Will!"

Will followed Edilson's voice to an open bedroom door. A pair of shoe soles lay pointed at him. Edilson stood in the doorway, genuflecting. Thiago's shoes. Thiago.

Will sucked in a breath. Andreatta was there. "*Calma se.* There's only one thing you can do for him now." Andreatta touched his shoulder. He pulled away.

Will was conscious enough to straddle the blood trail, at the end of which his friend had come to rest. Edilson watched him closely. "Will, we can't touch anything. I'm sorry ..."

"I know. I'm here." He reached out for his partner. "I'm on the job."

Looking down at Thiago, he was surprised at how detached he could be. His friend was dead. He smelled the iron tang of blood and cordite. He knew how much danger he and everybody he cared for were in, right now.

But he was looking for something. He was working the case. Thiago lay at the centre of a large pool of congealed blood. If he'd had to guess, the scene was at least three hours old. Most of the blood appeared to have come from a close-contact wound under the left eye. The stippling and powder burns were evident at the entrance. The blood had poured out of the exit. Head wounds always bled. But he guessed that was the final touch. The chest wound that had stained Thiago's shirt had led to the blood trail.

In Thiago's hand was the .357. Usman's gun. A very unlucky gun. Will stepped over the corpse. Edilson shifted. "Will, be careful!"

"I know what I'm doing."

Andreatta scoffed. "Famous last words."

Will could see the cylinder of the revolver better from this angle. He could see what looked like the front view of one spent shell. *So he got one off. At least he didn't he go down without a fight.* He looked up and saw the black speck made by Usman's gun in the wall five meters away. Will was uncertain of where to go next. He needed to be certain, or he'd start thinking about where he was. He looked down again and noticed Thiago's left arm was stretched out, reaching.

Reaching for what? Will saw a low cupboard at the end of the pointed arm. There was blood on the cupboard handle. A TV played *Mais Você* on top of the cupboard. A grown woman and a stuffed parrot entertained the citizens of São Paulo this morning while the bus fires burned out and the bodies were collected. Will touched the cupboard open with his shoe.

Edilson was nervous again. "Will, don't disturb—"

Will turned and coldly snapped, "Why don't you get some air? I have a job to do."

Edilson said nothing, watching as Will slowly pulled open the cupboard door. On the inside, a stack of DVDs and CD cases. On the other side of the door, in browning blood: Nata R. Barbaro.

That was what Thiago had been doing while he'd waited to die. Telling them where to go next.

"We're going. Now."

"Where? Why now?" Edilson's arms were outstretched.

"I told you. This ends, now. Thiago just reminded me of something."

"You want a Ouija board? You have lost it. What the hell are you talking about?"

"Natalia Rodriguez. Works at Barbaro, an Argentine restaurant by Ibirapuera Park. He just reminded us."

Will held the door open with his toe as Andreatta whistled. "Yes, he did. *Merda*."

After the others had left, Will waited a moment with his friend. "Thanks. I won't forget."

He was stepping out of the death house in a fog when his phone rang. It was his brother-in-law.

"I just talked to Silvia. Come home. You need a rest." Roberto. There when you needed him.

"Who was it?" Edilson asked after Will hung up. Edilson leaned against a wall, shattered.

"Eight hours of sleep. Come on, dinner service won't start till late anyway. My brother-in-law will put us up."

"Will, what about Thiago?"

"Thiago is dead, Edilson."

"That's it, then?"

"Would you be happier if I wrote your valediction now?" Will knew he sounded callous, but what could he do for Thiago now? There was no time to mourn. Revenge would have to do.

"It can wait. Sleep sounds good, I guess." Edilson stood in the hallway, looking lost.

Will walked over to him. "Now I have to give the speeches? One more round. That's it. We talk to the Argentine woman. Then we figure how to fuck Stumpf. Andreatta, are you coming?"

The moustachioed cop shrugged. "Why not. I can't samba."

Tremembé

Will awoke to rain drumming steadily on the slate roof. He opened his eyes and realized where he was. Home. In a bed. Guarded. All the things he had taken for granted before he'd made an enemy of Oscar Stumpf. He reached for his watch and realized he'd slept the day away.

He looked at the pillow next to him and saw a long copper hair. Will thought of Silvia. Thought of her calling Jacquie. He lay in bed for a while, not wanting to go back into the mess he'd made.

He gave me the job. And what did I give him?

The case was like a headless chicken now, insensitive to its masters' fates or anyone else, propelled by impulses to its doom. He stared up at the ceiling.

Oscar Stumpf was not going to wait patiently to be arrested. Maybe whatever the Argentine woman told them would be good enough for a warrant, maybe not. And they had Anderson Alves. But they needed to come face to face with the man. They had to let his ego and his fear prompt an overreaction. They had to wait for him to attack again but this time make sure he was there.

It was a waiting game Will was usually good at playing. But not now. Ordinary life for his family had ground to a halt. But how to force the pace? Stumpf was careful but also reckless. He was rich, and he had close to limitless resources. But Will had the State on his side ...

Stumpf was rich. Rich people tended to think everything could be bought. Maybe that was it. Maybe the only way out was to convince him they could be bought too. Make a meet. Show him what they had. Give him a price. The moment he paid, he'd be making an admission. And once he did that, that was enough for Brasília. Once he did that, he was a dead man.

Will was pretty sure Stumpf would deal. He was pretty sure the ROTA operation in São Bernardo was off the radar, given the chaos of the last 48 hours. And he was pretty sure also that their snatch and grab in Paraguay wasn't common knowledge either. So maybe Stumpf would conclude he was still dealing with a couple of renegades who could be bought. But his nephews were dead. They couldn't hide that. So whether Stumpf agreed to deal or not, he'd never let them walk away alive. But that was okay. They had no intention of letting him walk away either.

Just then, Will realized they hadn't accounted for Thiago's phone. Will figured there was no point calling the Delegacia to see if they had it. He knew who had it.

Torre Grupo Stumpf, Avenida Paulista

The man who had Thiago's phone sat behind a massive mahogany desk and stared out the picture window at the downpour. Thirty stories up, the rain was an atomized mist, its progress disrupted by the massive tower and the others like it forcing their way into the clouds.

Oscar Stumpf drained his Scotch and stared at the framed photo of his nephews. They had been 12 then. He had taken them to the Pantanal to fish and bird-spot. It was a bright memory. He set the picture on his desk. He reached for the bottle and poured another. For once he didn't care about overdoing it.

Control. It was always so important. But somehow his enemies had reached out and taken the most precious things he possessed. And he couldn't control that. So why bother? He looked around the penthouse office. A bookcase lay toppled over, a file cabinet kicked into the wall. He remembered there was now a pistol on the desk.

All of this had erupted when that useless shit Grasselman had called in a panic and told him the police had Condor Foundations sealed off. The security guard was missing, and there were two dead bodies.

He knew then. He flew into a black fit. Anger, long repressed, long ... controlled, had risen and found expression.

Forty-five years of serving Brazil. Of patriotism, industry, family. And it was all ending. Stumpf stared into his Scotch and swirled it. He looked down at spotted and lined hands. Hands that had done many things. Built, signalled, destroyed. Tortured.

But he'd never doubted. Not once. It was for Brazil and, later, for him, a hero of Brazil.

But today he doubted. He'd brought them into it. And now they were gone. Klaus was hard, like him. He would've found a way into this sort of life, eventually, on his own. He was strong, and he was proud. And Klaus was going to run Grupo Stumpf one day, Stumpf had already decided.

But Erich. Little Erich. He was a thinker and a dreamer. Stumpf despaired as he recalled the moment he'd relented and let the curious young man into his dark business. Erich had so badly wanted to prove himself. But he hadn't needed to. He had always been his *tio's* favourite.

As a phone call had destroyed Oscar Stumpf's world, he now destroyed his sister-in-law's. She had spit venom at him over the phone for dragging the boys into this. She had even hinted she might talk. The two had been lovers for a long time, and she did know a lot. He was too numb to care.

That was why the gun was on the desk. He remembered now.

But Oscar Stumpf was not, by nature, an emotional person. He began to think as the rage and sorrow subsided. The Scotch helped.

Oscar Stumpf had never admitted defeat. That was why he was on the 30th floor of a building he owned, drinking $500-bottle Scotch. But he had to admit, it seemed like he was very close to defeat now. What was he facing?

A Canadian ex-footballer and ex-cop. His partner, a PM of some reputation but no real importance. A lawyer and a reporter, but he had taken care of them. That much he knew.

But there had to be more. Bryant and Lopes were formidable. He knew that from his first attempts to remove them from the picture. But he knew they had help. They had tracked down Ken Scribbins in the middle of the largest city in the Americas in record time and then freed him by assaulting a very hard target with absolute ruthlessness.

And he couldn't very well have Grasselman ask, "Pardon me, have you seen our hostage?" could he? Idiot probably would too. So his hope to eliminate them at the source by getting Scribbins to take them right to him was gone.

And his theory about Bryant and Lopes having help had been confirmed by Grasselman a half hour ago. He had reported that a *mendingo* had seen at least 10 cops, some in black tactical uniforms, assembling on the property early that morning, followed by explosions and shooting. Right after that, a report from "Ze," one of his PCC contacts, had informed him that "Mike," the PCC "doctor" who had turned over Scribbins, had been killed at a police roadblock in Zaki Narchi in the early morning, following a raid and chase. Three other PCC gunmen had been found dead at his clinic.

So, he was up against the police. Maybe not all of them, but some of them.

He gulped his Scotch as he stared at the gun. He had always been on the side of law and order, even when operating covertly. Yes, he had done some hard things, but it was always pro patria. Now he was the threat to the State. Now he had to be eliminated.

And he knew all about that.

He also knew exactly why. He would never have gotten in bed with those degenerates in the PCC if rising oil prices hadn't threatened his bottom line. But he'd made a deal with the devil to use his transportation networks to help move PCC product across the Andes to the greedy coke bazaars of Rio, São Paulo, Belo Horizonte, and Salvador. And he'd laundered a supertanker full of drug money for the bastards too. So guilt by association was part of the deal. The PCC was most definitely a threat to the State. And so, by extension, was he.

Now, he cursed his clever blackmail scheme. Too clever by half. Drugs and prostitution created victims nobody cared about. But rich men felt entitled. Rich men had rights. They complained, regardless of how disgusting they truly were. And, eventually, they brought men like Will Bryant to your door.

This wasn't about some blackmailed *pedofilos* anymore. If it ever had been. And it wasn't about some long-dead

Marxists rotting in the red earth out by Caçapava. It was about an existential threat to the State. And the State didn't go away. He knew that very well too.

Goddamn the *favelados*. He used to shoot people like them; now he was their partner. They had to stage another kamikaze attack on the cops now, when he was up to his ass in it? Hadn't Klaus warned him about this? Even that big idiot Grasselman had, come to think of it.

So, how to get out? The same question he'd always asked himself, since his first firefight in Uruguay, all those years ago. Trapped in a dead-end alleyway in Montevideo. The Marxists closing in. His partner dying loudly. Down to two shots in his useless little revolver.

He felt like that now. Only now there was so much more to lose than a young man's life. How to get out? Maybe there was no way. Targeting families? Not his way. Turning himself in and talking? Also not his style, although the thought of making some of those sanctimonious fat shits in Brasília sweat did put a smile on his face.

How to get out? Maybe the question ought to be *what* to get out. Maybe the answer was revenge.

He thought for a moment. Then Oscar Stumpf pulled out Thiago's cellphone.

Tremembé

Will was walking downstairs when the phone rang. He gripped the railing hard when he saw the call display.

Thiago. A dead man's phone. Would it be Stumpf, or a flunky?

He was surprised when he heard Oscar Stumpf's voice. Will sat down on the steps to steady himself.

"Is this Will Bryant? Or should I ask for William Cousins?" The deep voice sounded slurred. Was the master of control actually drunk? Will noticed Edilson at the foot of the stairs, regarding him quizzically. He held a finger to his lips and then mouthed, "Stumpf." His partner disappeared quickly.

"Yes it is. Is this Oscar Stumpf?"

"You know it is."

"What do you want to discuss?"

"Ending this. We have both lost a lot already. Ask yourself, is it worth it?"

"Are you negotiating?"

"Life is negotiation."

"Or in your case, negotiation plus murder and torture." Will couldn't resist. Stumpf was so fucking arrogant, lecturing like a college professor while killing like a gangster. He could hear what he thought was the clink of ice against glass.

"You prefer to score points? Do you think this is a game?"

Edilson creeped slowly up to Will and then held a micro-recorder up to the phone.

"If it's a game, it's your move."

"And so I am making it."

Will couldn't have envisioned this before yesterday. Maybe the death of his torturing little surrogate sons had rattled the old bastard. He was vulnerable now. Edilson stared at him with that don't-fuck-up look he knew so well.

"What do you propose?"

"An immediate end to violence, investigation, and surveillance on both sides. I will end my relationship with the PCC. And I will pay a substantial fine, to be collected informally, in return for being allowed to continue my business activities and remain a free man."

Edilson's eyes went wide. Jesus. Stumpf was throwing in the towel.

"You think we'll just let you walk away from the damage you've done? Just because you've got a big wallet?" Will's theory was proving bang-on.

Stumpf laughed and took another drink. "Mmm, Bryant, time to accept reality. You are an outsider; allow me to educate you." That fucking arrogance again. "Maybe you won't let me walk away. Maybe your policeman friend won't either. There have been casualties, after all."

Casualties. A clinical way for him to put it.

Stumpf warmed to his theme as the Scotch warmed him. "But you don't seriously expect me to believe that all of the havoc over the past two weeks has been caused by two renegades? I know I have angered the State. An error I intend to rectify. They cannot accept an alliance with the PCC. So I will fix this problem. The State will be satisfied. They do not really want to go any further, even if you do. If you proceed on a mission of revenge, you will do so on your own. Accept peace now, and you have still accomplished a victory. You walk away alive, with a substantial informally collected fine in your pocket. How much do you think I should pay?"

Will looked closely at Edilson. They did say every man had his price. Edilson thought for a moment and then mouthed, "He'll kill us."

Of course he would. But the part about the PCC worried Will. Maybe they would be on their own. But a thought occurred suddenly, and he knew his dance card wouldn't be empty, whatever strings Stumpf could pull.

Will smiled. "Twenty million dollars for the widows' and orphans' fund, Stumpf. You've left a few behind."

Stumpf laughed again. "Audacious, but fair. I won't try and bargain. Agreed."

Too easy. "We need to meet."

"How about we meet where it all started? Southern Cross. I'll show you around."

To my very own unmarked grave, no doubt. "Sure, out in the countryside, no witnesses, what's the worst that could happen?"

Stumpf chuckled. "The worst can happen anywhere. You ought to know that by now."

"Or anytime, like six months from now when I'm sitting beside the pool."

"Twenty million buys a lot of security. And I want to go back to making money. This has been an expensive distraction. Two days from now, noon, at Southern Cross. Agreed?"

"Noon. How dramatic."

"Not the best time to commit a murder, don't you agree?"

"I'll take an expert's word for it. I'll be there. But if I sense an ambush, the deal's off."

"I intend to deal."

"Sure you do. You're a son of a bitch, Stumpf; don't forget that."

"Same to you. See you in two days, Detective." The last word, dripping with sarcasm, before the line went dead.

Edilson switched off the recorder. "I have to tell my superiors, Will. They'll want to hear this."

"And they're idiots if they buy it. But if they do, it changes nothing."

"What do you mean, 'nothing'? If my bosses think Stumpf is going to cut out the PCC, they might make a deal. That's the only reason we've had help! They don't give a shit about Operation Condor! Some of them probably want to shake Stumpf's hand for it, if you ask me. If we go out on our own, we're dead."

"It changes nothing because I know one group of men who are about as interested in seeing Oscar Stumpf dead as we are. A certain ROTA team in need of a new leader. We won't be alone."

Edilson smiled. "I'll make the call."

Will stood up and stretched. "First, coffee. Then, how about a nice big Argentine steak? I know a place."

29

Rua Doutor Sodre, Vila Olímpia

Will knew he was going to Restaurante Barbaro to speak to Natalia Rodriguez, but his stomach had other ideas. He squirmed with discomfort in the back seat of Roberto's Honda Fit as his stomach acids roiled. Thirty-six hours at least since he'd had a decent meal. He was ready to rip someone's liver out just for the nutrients. Not for nothing did the Jamaicans say, "Hungry mon is an angry mon." As they turned the corner, he picked up his first whiff of broiling meat.

Will felt vaguely ashamed. His friend was dead, and he was thinking of meat. But people were machines, and this machine needed fuel. Who knew when his next chance would come? Maybe it would be his last meal.

As his brother-in-law, a Corinthiano, passionately debated Corinthians versus Santos with Edilson, a Peixoto, Will's thoughts wandered away from intrastate sports rivalry. People were returning to the streets. Traffic was picking up. As Andreatta had predicted, the rain had killed the riots. Hard to set an *onibus* on fire in a downpour.

Now the cops were killing gangsters in their living rooms, instead of the other way round. He wondered what Andreatta was doing.

"Andreatta said he'd rather eat his wife's pussy tonight than an Argentine steak." Edilson again showed his creepy skill for poaching Will's thoughts. Roberto snorted. A few shots of cachaça had loosened up the usually straitlaced businessman. The guy was fun sometimes, you just had to unwind him. "He hates Argies," Edilson said. "You did call ahead, right?"

"Yes, Edilson, I did."

His first conversation with Natalia Rodriguez had been to the point.

He'd called the restaurant, and a hostess had answered. *"Oi, Restaurante Barbaro."*

"Natalia ta aqui?"

"Una momento."

A brief pause and then: "Natalia. Who is this?"

"My name is Will Bryant. I am going to destroy Oscar Stumpf. Will you help me?"

Natalia had gasped. "Who are you?"

"I'm a policeman."

"The police have never cared before. Never."

"They care now. I know you have been alone for a long time, Natalia. No more."

"How do I know this isn't some trick?" Her accent had been slight but still noticeable.

"Sergio sent me. And Usman too."

She had taken a deep breath. "Okay. Come here tonight. I will serve you."

"I was hungry anyway."

"If you do what you promise, you'll never pay for steak again, gringo."

Fuck, was it still that obvious? "See you soon."

Now, as they pulled up in front of the valet, Will had the feeling, definitive and final, of culmination. It was liberating. Whatever, wherever, whenever. The end was coming. When he walked out of this restaurant, he would have more than a full belly. He'd have the last piece in the puzzle of Southern Cross.

Maybe Operation Condor and the fate of the Disappeared and their children didn't matter to Edilson and his shadow police, but it mattered to Will. As far as he was concerned, Oscar Stumpf could personally kill every last PCC member in São Paulo, and Will would still hunt him down and put him in the ground.

All those shoes without people. All those children without parents. And Thiago too.

Restaurante Barbaro

The restaurant was Argentine yet typically Brazilian. They walked through the deserted patio under low ceilings and took a table by the terracotta wall at the back. Snapshots of customers. Photos of meat porn. Awards from *Guia* and *Veja*. Hustling waitresses with platters of obscenely large steaks. Raucous noise and clinking glasses. Close, cozy, red-tinted, and booze-fuelled. Will's kind of place. He realized he had no idea what Natalia Rodriguez looked like.

"I'm starving," Roberto declared. "I've been feeding myself too long."

Edilson nodded in agreement. "When this is over, Deyse isn't allowed to leave the kitchen ... unless she's in the bedroom." He smiled broadly and leaned back from the table.

"More kids, Edilson? Papa Francisco is going to send you a gift basket."

"If God wants it, Will, why argue?"

Will thought, *Because with the shit you're into, you're just going to leave more orphans behind.* But he said nothing. That answer wouldn't make sense to a Brazilian. Brazilians never let the threat of death deflect them from the promise of life. He didn't get it, but he still admired it. He felt a soft hand on his shoulder and looked up.

She was stately, tall, and curvaceous, long dyed-blonde hair falling over her breasts. Her nails were long and immaculate. A beauty mark on her cheek drew his gaze to deep green eyes. She smiled.

"You have to be Will Bryant."

"How did you know?"

"A gringo like you stands out tonight. This place is too quiet, thanks to the narcos."

"Quiet? This is quiet?" He had to raise his voice to surmount a singing drunk.

She smiled warmly. "Will, for this place, only last night was quieter, and we were closed. How about we get your friends some meat, and we can talk somewhere quieter, yes?"

A *bife lomo* was carried past the table, trailing a salty aroma. Edilson looked as if he were going to have a seizure.

"Yes, Natalia, that sounds fine. But first this gringo needs some Malbec."

She smiled. "I thought so. I don't trust men who don't drink wine." She turned on her heel for the bar. Will looked after her. She didn't look so bad from behind, either.

Edilson scooped up tapenade with a crust of bread. "This woman went after Oscar Stumpf? She looks like a—how do you say it?—'soccer mom.'"

"The most dangerous person in the world if you're after a child. I'm dying to hear what she has to say." His hunger had subsided, at least for the moment. A tall old woman in a red dress began singing an Argentine folk song, to the accompaniment of guitar and accordion.

"I'm dying to eat the ass out of a cow." Will looked at Roberto, who never usually talked like that. "Hey, my wife's a vegetarian. And she's out of town."

"*Sem problema*, brother." Will watched the Amazonian Natalia return with their wine as he said, "You can eat the whole goddamn cow. Dilma's buying."

Natalia opened a bottle with practised flourish as the singer warmed to her song and the rowdy crowd began to clap along. Will took his glass and swirled it. He inhaled a tart, raisiny aroma.

Edilson laughed around a mouthful of bread. "You gringos. I think you look like an old French fruit."

Natalia scolded him. "A man who loves wine loves life. A man who appreciates a glass like that, imagine him with a woman." She smiled at Will and held out her hand. "Come with me."

Will cocked an eyebrow at Edilson, who silently chuckled.

They walked through the back of the restaurant, past the flaming grills and crashing pans, and out the back door into a surprising little oasis enclosed with a gate leading to the street. Safe and quiet. He needed safe and quiet now. He looked at his new friend.

In the harsh light of the bulb over the exit, he could see the lines and wrinkles previously hidden by the restaurant's soft lights and a layer of thoughtfully applied makeup. She was getting old but not that much older than him by the calendar. Events were most likely responsible.

She studied him. "A gringo policeman. In Brazil. What a strange meeting. You are trying to decide how old I am, no?"

He smiled sheepishly. "I won't touch that one."

Bugs fought or mated or merely danced in the overhead light. "I was 13 when my sister, Ana Rosa, went missing in 1978. There ended my childhood." The green eyes looked away.

Not so much older than him, then. The strain of an empty space in your life was telling. Or in this case, two empty spaces. Where the people you loved should have been.

"Tell me about her."

She looked up at the murky sky. "Ana was impulsive. Always. I was the good girl." She smiled ironically. "Now look at me."

He smiled back. She was a charmer. "Where did you grow up?"

"Bariloche. My father was a wine merchant."

"That explains a lot."

She laughed. "Yes, Will, a family obsession. My father did very good business, good enough to send his girls to university. Of course, Ana was eight years older than me, so she left when I was 10. Off to Buenos Aires. That's where the trouble started."

"She fell in with leftists?"

"When she was 19, she came home on a break. I could tell quickly that she had met someone. And she was in love. More than that, she had been … influenced. We never talked politics in our house. It was the way of the times. Politics were a dangerous subject. But now, she started telling me about the Montoneros."

Will had read the dossier Sergio and Usman had compiled and knew enough to understand that, in 1976, Ana Rosa Rodriguez was believed to have joined a Montonero cell at the Architecture School in Nunez, part of the massive University of Buenos Aires. According to the Arquivos do Terror, she was recruited by Jose Amales, a bomb maker for the Montoneros guerrillas and occasional student at the school. The two were able to lay low for some time, despite an ever-escalating series of arrests and disappearances targeting the urban left.

But in 1978, Argentina would be hosting the World Cup. Both the Junta and the Montoneros stepped up their efforts. Bombs were in demand. And so the hunt for the people behind them intensified as well.

"She drifted away. She came home less often. My parents were so worried. They didn't know what to do. The last time I saw her was just before Christmas 1977."

She sat on the edge of a railing and held her hands in her lap, very still. A long habit of being composed when staring into the abyss. He tried to imagine someone he loved disappearing completely and failed absolutely. Just as well.

Will reminded himself that Ana Rosa had probably been making bombs that had maimed and killed completely innocent people. Still, justice had to have a face. You couldn't just make people vanish, could you?

Natalia was looking at the leaden sky again. São Paulo was quiet for once while he waited.

"It took us a while to realize she was missing. We reported it to the police, but of course they lied to us. 'We're investigating; be patient,' they said. One time, we saw some cops laughing in the back of the office. I was 14 then. I said, 'Hey, what are you assholes laughing at?' My parents got me out of there, quickly. You didn't do that in Argentina, 1980."

"How did you wind up in São Paulo?"

"I am ashamed to say that I gave up very early searching for Ana Rosa. Life goes on, and in the dictatorship years you couldn't get any answers anyway. I went to university myself, got married, started a life. My parents both died never knowing what had happened." She paused to wipe her eyes. "My mother got very religious. She would travel to Buenos Aires, join the other mothers of the Disappeared. One day there she got pneumonia and never recovered. My father never went with her to the plaza. My father just drank. I suppose I was angry at Ana for killing them. I tried to forget about her."

"What changed?" Smoke swirled around her face. A voice in his head was telling Will, *Be careful.*

"In 1996, my husband left me. I was at a loss and all alone. It was for very selfish reasons that I started caring again. My sister was all I had left, even if she was probably dead. I started asking questions. I found out about the Arquivos in Paraguay. I learned about Condor. I hired a lawyer with the money from my divorce settlement. One day, he brought me a picture." She looked up at the sky again, breathed in deeply. "It was an identification picture, taken by SIDE in August 1978. Ana Rosa was pregnant."

Will breathed in. Pregnant in hell. Bomb maker or not, it was an awful fate.

"Sorry if I am rushing you, but how did this put you in São Paulo?"

She laughed, unexpectedly. Will couldn't help but notice how pleasing that was.

"You Canadians! It's true what I've heard ... so polite!" A manicured hand touched his. He let it linger, guiltily. "Let me tell you. In my research, with my lawyer, I found that my sister and her boyfriend were taken to a processing centre in an old auto factory called 'Orletti.' This had been turned into an interrogation factory. Agents from all of the Condor nations could interrogate the subjects they were interested in. It seems Brazilian agents were interested in my sister and her boyfriend, in particular." She took a long drag.

He was a cheater in his heart, if not his body. He savoured new women and the experiences that came with them, even if he really loved only one. He watched Natalia's lips as she exhaled. Will forced himself back on mission.

"Why were the Brazilians interested, Natalia?"

"Jose was making bombs for the Tupamaros. He had been for a long time. He was involved with a guy named Soares, who was a liaison between the Montoneros and the Tupamaros. They were all trying to work together, like their opposition. The Cubans were helping. Brazilian military intelligence wanted to know about the links between all three. So the liaison officers came to Orletti. It was like a *supermercado* of torture." She exhaled again in that beguiling way. For the first time in years, Will felt like a smoke.

Soares. Goddamn it. That meeting in Floripa. He had missed something while he'd been savouring the *peixe* and the *lagoa*.

"Natalia, do you know how Soares died?"

"How do you know about Soares?"

He sighed. This woman was baring it all. Why should he keep his shorts? "I crossed paths with his son, briefly. He was after Stumpf, and we tripped over each other." Will was too much of an open book for this work. The lie felt dirty, but was he supposed to admit to an assassination? It felt like he was covering up a crime. Was it a crime? He felt that touch again. The green eyes, intense.

"Soares was a Communist," she said. "He was turned, made a double agent. He lured Jose and Ana into a meeting. The meeting that led to their capture. Then the Brazilians started working on them." She shuddered. The night wasn't that cold. Against his better judgment, he put his arm against her. She didn't resist.

She moved ever so subtly. His hands moved too. Will needed Edilson to straighten his head, but he wasn't there.

"Will." She turned to him, inches away. "Do this for me, please?"

Without warning, she pulled him into her orbit and held him very close. He felt that uncertainty that came with mingled breath and very personal smells. He wanted to run but knew he needed to stay close.

"Yes, I will."

She spoke slowly through glossy lips. His hands were brushing against her breasts now. He didn't know how they got there, but neither of them moved.

"Find her."

"Her? How do you know?" Will probed for information even as he continued to grope her. He came away, ashamed, only to have her step forward again and put him right back where he'd been.

"I spoke to a woman who was there for the birth. It was a girl. She was taken away immediately."

"By whom?" It was surreal. He enveloped her with his hands as he played detective. Trancelike, he imagined that he watched from above.

"An army officer working with Stumpf. He was known for looking for pregnant girls. The rumour was that he and his wife couldn't have kids, so he wanted one from the prisoners."

At this, she could hold back no longer and pushed forward to kiss him. He pulled her hair as he moved aggressively against her. They stayed still for a long time. Gunfire sounded in the distance. He thought of Silvia and began to pull away. Natalia pulled him back.

"Mais, por favor. Una momento."

He kissed her again, long and hard. She came up for air, panting, her eyes shining. His head was swimming. Now, Natalia pulled away, steadying his head in her hands.

"I found out his name, Will. Buscetti. The father of a *senador.*"

He pushed her away gently. Buscetti. Soares. He'd assumed too much in Floripa, had taken the very polished

Geraldo Buscetti at face value, and had failed to ask the right questions.

Rigoberto Soares had been on a revenge mission when Will had shot him in Blumenau. Stumpf had probably had his father killed. That was no revelation. But why was Buscetti working with him, investigating his father's old boss? Were the two working at cross purposes? And did Buscetti have a sister? Will cursed himself for not doing a background check. Kind of hard to do on the run from assassins, to be fair.

But surely Soares knew about his partner's background? So why were they working together? Maybe Buscetti could still be useful. Maybe the sister was the key.

He walked into the courtyard to clear his head. The air swam with meat smells, but he had lost his interest in food again.

"Will, what is it?"

He had to show some cards. "I met Geraldo Buscetti last week. In Floripa. He was working with Soares's son to investigate Stumpf."

She sighed. "They couldn't have been investigating very hard. I heard from Sergio what they were doing and tried to contact them, after Usman died. I had nothing else to go on. They never returned my calls or emails. Always 'out of the office.' I even went to Brasília, but they wouldn't see me. I can't afford another trip."

Strange. If you were investigating Oscar Stumpf, you wanted to talk to this woman. Maybe the connection was too close to home for Buscetti. A family secret.

"You said you met Buscetti? Was Soares there?" She asked the right questions.

His mouth felt dry. He was on dangerous territory. Nothing new here. "No. 'Out of the office.'" He covered the lie with a smile. Clearly she wasn't keeping up with the news. If it came up, he'd feign the same ignorance. "Have you ever met Buscetti Senior?"

"Ottavio Buscetti died in a car accident in 2001. I saw the pictures. An idiot could see there were three sets of skid marks."

"Some accident." So, Buscetti was on a revenge mission too. The reason the son of a Communist and the son of an army officer were working together. But Will couldn't afford a total disclosure. Too much was at stake.

Natalia hugged herself tight. The night was getting cold. "All I need is to meet her. Fuck revenge, everything else. Please, Will, help me meet her." Her eyes were moist.

He was afraid of another embrace, but he gave one anyway, this one as chaste as he could manage. He was already hating himself. She hadn't stopped feeling good and smelling better, though.

This time, she pulled away. She lit a Dunhill and savoured it. Her bangs fell over her right eye, and she blew them away with a puff of smoke.

Overhead, a bug got too close to the light and exploded audibly. He thought of Usman.

"What happened with Usman?" he asked.

She took another, deep, drag. "You asked how I got to São Paulo, remember?"

He smiled. "I forgot. So much has happened since."

She shook her head. "*Usted es un churro.* Very charming. Well. Usman I met through Sergio, who I knew from the Arquivos. By 2011 I couldn't do anything anymore in

Argentina. My money was gone, and I knew my niece was here in Brazil. I knew about Buscetti. But I had, as you say, 'hit the wall.' I needed a job, and Sergio got me one, here. I worked in the kitchen until my Portuguese got better. I always knew English." She smiled. "And I needed a lawyer. Brazil's bureaucracy is impossible to navigate without help. And when you are pissing off someone with as much money and power as Oscar Stumpf, you need protection."

Too bad Usman had gotten rid of the kind of protection he'd really needed. At least his friend had gotten some use out of it. He grimaced. "What did he accomplish?"

"He couldn't tell me much more about Stumpf in the Dirty War. He did confirm from witnesses that he visited Orletti while Ana Rosa was there. But mostly he found out, with Sergio, a lot about what Stumpf was doing now."

"The PCC."

"*Sí.* Usman showed me a diagram one night, just before he died. It was like a flow chart, showing what Grupo Stumpf and the Comando did for each other. Stumpf gave them his transportation routes; they gave him muscle and prostitutes for entertainment and blackmail. But he said he couldn't understand yet why Stumpf was blackmailing businessmen. He was working on that when he died."

Will raised an eyebrow. Southern Cross was the missing piece, the one Usman had been about to uncover. The one that had put him in that funeral pyre.

"Did he tell anyone else?"

"No. Only me. Because he knew, that even though Stumpf was ruthless, he probably wouldn't hurt a woman."

"But he killed or had your sister killed. Why not you?"

"He was ordered to. Now he gives the orders."

He shook his head. "Germans."

"Exactly. Telling Sergio or his friend Thiago, that could get them hurt too. He was a noble man, Usman."

But he couldn't protect his friends, in the end. Neither could Will. He swallowed hard. "Do you have this diagram?"

"No, Will, I'm sorry. I looked through his papers, but I think he had it with him, the night he …" The sentence ended in a shudder. A sob stifled with practiced control. Another dangerous embrace.

He let the silence linger until she composed herself. He had to ask. "You went through his papers?"

She lit another Dunhill. "By the end, he was more than just my lawyer, Will. I told you, he was a noble man. I have my sister to thank for something, at least." She wiped her eyes and smiled. "At least I met a nice man once in my life. Well, maybe twice."

Oh God. He was putting his line out too far, as his dad used to say. He needed to get back on target. "Why haven't you found your niece?"

"Because the trail goes cold after 1997. Buscetti and his wife divorced then, and a Brazilian passport issued to a Carla Buscetti is, I think, the last record of her or her so-called 'mother' that we could find in Brazil. They could be anywhere."

"Why do you stay here, then?"

"Because Stumpf is here." She looked up as the first drops in a renewed deluge began to fall. "And I knew one day somebody like you would come after him. I just had to wait."

"You are very patient, Natalia."

"Love waits forever." She pulled him in and gave him a last kiss. He savoured it with eyes closed. She pulled away slowly, putting the Dunhill to her lips. "And so does hate," she whispered through cigarette smoke. She pivoted on a stiletto heel and walked away.

30

Restaurante Barbaro

Will came back to the table feeling strange. The band was well into a raucous tango by now, and the obligatory dancers performed in a tiny space. It was a cliché no one seemed to tire of. Right down to the rose between the woman's teeth.

"Will. Will!"

Will realized he was staring into space as Edilson shouted at him over the din. There was no sign of Natalia. "Sorry. Lost in thought."

"Yes, I'm used to it. Your steak is getting cold." In front of Edilson were the remnants of what appeared to have been a ridiculously large steak. He was so skinny. Where had he put it all?

"Where's Roberto?"

"*Banheiro.* What did you do to Natalia?" Edilson had to shout to be heard over the music.

Will looked at him suspiciously. "What do you mean?"

Edilson sighed. "I mean, she walked right out the door and didn't look twice. You didn't tell her anything, did you? I don't trust them."

"You mean Argentines? If I could find a Brasileira who could tell us what she could, we'd be at a Habib's right now."

"Ha!"

"Ha, what?"

Edilson leaned over and grabbed his arm. "I know you. You're a sucker for a big pair of tits. Don't start thinking with your dick now, buddy. We're too close."

Will pulled his arm away. He was steaming. The fact that Edilson was right made it worse. "Fuck you, super-cop! You're not the only pro at this table. Do you wanna know what I found out, or do you want to keep lecturing?" He stabbed at his steak and savagely sliced off a piece as emphasis.

Edilson held his hands up. "Don't get hot, brother. Just watching out for you. Sorry. But you didn't fuck her, did you?"

Will chewed the salty beef and snarled, "Did I have time to fuck her? Seriously?"

"Sure, if you didn't bother with introductions."

Will laughed so hard he almost choked. Edilson handed him a glass of wine.

"Thanks."

Roberto came back to the table. "Oh, you're back. What happened to the girl?"

Edilson smirked. "We're still trying to find that out, Roberto."

Roberto's face was red. He'd obviously had more wine than he was used to. He shouted over the music, just as it ended, "You didn't fuck her, did you?"

The eyes of the restaurant settled on them for a long minute before the music started again.

Edilson held up his hand. *"A conta, por favor."*

Marginal Tiete

Edilson drove with the assurance of a man who knew he would never get a DUI, no matter how much he'd had to drink.

Will couldn't relax. Assurance didn't mean skill. Edilson was as relaxed as Dean Martin at a roulette wheel, but that didn't mean they'd get home alive. Will gripped the armrest as Edilson made a swerving lane change in front of a truck.

"Goddamn it, Edilson! It would be a real pain in the ass if we got killed by you instead of Oscar Stumpf!"

"Don't worry, brother. I can do this with my eyes closed!" They shot down the Santana exit, past Shopping Centre Norte. Will had taken the kids there last year to see Papai Noel.

"I'll take your word for it. Just get me home so I can call Buscetti."

"Why?"

"To say he left a few things out when we talked to him is an understatement."

They were interrupted by a resurgent Roberto from the back seat. "Hey, hey, you know what?"

"What, Roberto?" Edilson liked toying with Roberto. Come to think of it, he did that with everyone.

"I am officially drunk. How did that happen? I mean, really." He slumped down again and mumbled to himself. Will turned in his seat.

"Well, Roberto, you drink a lot of alcohol. That's usually the best way. Come on, Tais is out of town. Live a little."

Edilson said, sotto voce, "The last time that guy lived a little was 1986." It was probably true. Roberto was notoriously straitlaced.

Will looked out the window as they passed some Polícia Civil. The roadblock where Mike had narrowly avoided meeting his end slowed them momentarily, and they flipped out their IDs.

A young *soldado* eyed them approvingly and then noticed Roberto, now snoring in the back seat. "Who's this guy? A casualty?"

"Of the Guerra da Cachaça, brother. How is it tonight?"

"Mostly quiet. A few problems in Cingapura earlier. But they're solved now." The young, pale-faced cop smiled grimly. "Permanently."

"Amen to that. Good luck, brother."

"Same to you."

Will looked over his shoulder at the locked-down towers of Cingapura, surrounded by cops. He was glad he didn't have to drive toward them tonight. But in 36 hours he had a more menacing appointment.

He lowered the window as they came onto Cruzeiro do Sul, checking out the Os Gemeos and Vitche murals under the Metro tracks. Wide-eyed creatures with too-small heads cavorted in brightly coloured, magical realist worlds, surrounded by the dinginess of the real thing. The rain had let up again, and the air was wet and warm now.

"I'm gonna miss this." Will stared out the window wistfully.

"What, brother?"

"Life."

Edilson gave him a concerned look as they drove past the site of the old Carandiru Prison. Vanished now but still a place of ghosts. "Come on, Will, it's not that bad. You think I would let us walk into an execution? I have a plan."

Will smiled. "You always have a plan."

"That's right; I do. ROTA will be there. So will Andreatta, maybe more. Stumpf is fucked."

"Maybe he knows it and doesn't care, Edilson. Maybe he wants to go down shooting."

"Does that bother you?" Edilson kept a poker face.

Will smiled. "Nah. Getting used to it, actually."

"Welcome to the Polícia Militar, Soldado Ferguson!"

Under the bravado, Will couldn't stop worrying. One more time, and it was all over. He thought of Gabi, sitting on Papai Noel's lap in stunned awe, her list of demands forgotten. He stared silently out the window the rest of the way home.

Tremembé

When they got back to Roberto's house, Anderson Alves was cleaning the kitchen.

"Anderson, it's past midnight. What are you doing?"

The big man shrugged as he wiped down the stovetop. "Helping out. Roberto gives me a place to stay, for now, and he needs a hand. Anyway, I can only sleep in the day."

"Why is that?" Will asked, but he had already guessed the answer.

"Carandiru." He shrugged again. "You never slept at night there, if you wanted to live."

"*Claro.*"

He was putting off making the call. He was still tired, and now his head was roiling after his encounter with Natalia. But there was no time to lose. He needed to know whose team Buscetti was on. It was his only unanswered question.

That and who would be alive in 36 hours. That one would have to wait for Caçapava.

Buscetti picked up on the sixth ring. The voice sounded groggy. Good. Groggy meant vulnerable.

"How did you get this number?"

"You gave it to me. In Floripa. You said 'call anytime.' Well, I took that literally. Us gringos are like that, Gerry."

There was a pause on the other end and a woman's voice, indistinct. "Give me a moment, Bryant." Rustling noises, movement, a slamming door.

"Okay, Bryant, we can talk. What do you want, my friend?"

Friend. That was open to debate. "I guess you figured out I'm not 'William Cousins.' My, but you are resourceful. I wanted to tell you something, friend. Tonight I met Natalia Rodriguez."

Another pause. "Who?"

"Really? We're going to play that game? If we're going to play games, why don't we play them at Isadora Duncan? At least I get a nice meal to go with my bullshit."

"Now listen, I—"

"No, you listen. In a day and a half I am going toe to toe with Oscar Stumpf. Something you haven't shown much willingness to do. I may be doing you some very big favours. The least you can do is tell me the whole truth. I don't think that's too much to ask, do you?"

Quietly: "No."

"Okay. Question one: Carla Buscetti is really Ana Rosa Rodriguez's daughter, isn't she?"

"Yes."

"And question two: Your father, Ottavio, took her from her mother just before her murder, sometime in late 1978, am I right?"

"Yes. My mother couldn't have any more kids after me. My father loved her very much, and she wanted a girl. All of the Argentine officers my father was working with were doing it."

"Abducting kids, whose parents they then murdered?"

Hushed again. "Yes, that's true."

"Question three: Your father worked under Stumpf in Argentina, yes?"

"And for many years after. He went to work for Grupo Stumpf."

"Question four: If it was such a close partnership, why did Stumpf have your father murdered and make it look like a car accident?"

"You know a lot."

"Natalia Rodriguez would've made quite a cop, Senhor Buscetti. Why did Stumpf turn on your father?"

"My father had started keeping a journal. He was worried that what was happening in Argentina—inquests, trials, public revelations—would happen in Brazil. He wanted to be useful if that ever happened, to testify against Stumpf. But he knew our family was vulnerable because of Carla."

"Question five: Where is Carla?"

"My mother took her to Uruguay in 1996. My father wanted to tell her the truth. My mother was terrified."

"Do you talk to them?"

"All the time. I never returned Natalia's calls because I began to think my mother was right, that she should never know. But I watched from a distance what Natalia was doing. When Usman Al-Khattib was killed, I knew Stumpf had done it. That's when I convinced Soares we had to do more than just go through old files."

His numbered question system forgotten, Will pressed ahead. "Did Soares know who your father was?"

"Yes. And he didn't care. All he wanted was to get Stumpf."

"How did Stumpf kill your father?"

"His car was hit by two different trucks, one on each side, on the Rodovia Ayrton Senna. The trucks were never found. My father and his bodyguard were both killed. My father's briefcase was missing. The police at first seemed very interested, then suddenly, not. Suddenly it was a hit-and-run accident, not a murder. I decided to quit wasting my fortune and getting high. I decided to get revenge."

"How did you find out about the journals?"

"My father's girlfriend gave them to me after he died. When I read them, I knew two things."

"Which were?"

"One, my father was a monster. And two, Oscar Stumpf was far worse, and he killed my father to hide that fact."

"If your father was a monster, why risk everything to go after Stumpf?"

"He was my father, after all." Buscetti said it as a self-evident fact. Which in a way, it was.

"Has it been just you and Soares working together?" Another question he already knew the answer to.

He hesitated. "We had ... friends. Let's just say that, for now."

"Do you want him dead, Buscetti?"

"There is nothing I want more."

He considered. Should he reveal? Why not? "Then meet me at Southern Cross, noon, the day after tomorrow. You may get your wish. Bring your friends. I am."

"Thank you, Will. I am sorry I didn't tell you sooner, but my family has a lot to lose."

"Everyone has a lot to lose."

"Anything I should bring?"

"Firepower. See you then."

As Will hung up, Alves walked around the corner into the living room with two glasses of cachaça. "Here, boss."

Will took it gratefully. "Anderson?" He sipped at the fiery liquid. "We are going to Southern Cross the day after tomorrow. Can I count on you?"

Alves was thoughtful, his wrinkled face more furrowed than usual. "I am not a gunfighter. But I will help anyway I can."

"Why?"

"I'd like to be on the right side, for a change."

The two men drank in silence as the rain started up again.

31

Rua Fuad Mussa Cheide, São Bernardo do Campo

Will had gotten the call far too early after a night of drinking. His head pounded as he cruised the street slowly in the bright sunlight, looking for a short, wiry, ugly gringo in an assless hospital gown. Shouldn't be too hard.

"You gotta come get me. I broke out, dude." Will had been punchy and had taken a while to place the voice. Ken?

"Mmmpf ... broke out? Ken? Broke out of where?"

"Hospital, dude. It sucked. I ain't got no money."

"Hospital is not prison, Ken."

"It is if the nurses are ugly, dude."

He'd had a point. But goddamn it, the cops were supposed to be guarding him! "How'd you slip your guard?"

"You kiddin'? Dude was a drunk. Waited till he fell asleep. Now come and get me. My ass is hangin' in the wind, and people are startin' to stare. You owe me, bro."

Will had looked at his watch: 7:20. Shit. He did owe the man. "Okay, I'm coming. Where you at?"

So now he cruised the rundown street by the hospital. Of course, Ken wasn't where he'd said he would be. Cons never seemed to develop the habits of reliability everybody else did. Of course, not too many people in Brazil did either. Maybe that was why Ken felt at home here. Will's head throbbed. He took a swig of water and looked across the street to see Ken sitting in his hospital gown at a corner bar.

Jesus Christ. Guy brought the party with him. He smiled to himself.

He pulled the car to the curb and got out. As he walked up, he could see Ken was buying the *bebooms* a round. Or, more accurately, Will Bryant was buying the rounds.

"Hey, Will! *Oi, amigos,* this is my buddy Will! He's a gunfighter!"

"Shit, Ken, drunk already? You know they don't understand English, right?" A bar full of early-morning drinkers eyed him and Ken vacantly.

"They don't have to! I'm buying, dude!"

"You mean I'm buying? You forget all your Portuguese?"

Ken frowned for a moment. "I forgot a lot of things in that fucking box. I think I've earned a little drink." He embraced Will, who tried not to look down at the open-assed gown.

"Okay, you did." Hair of the dog? "What are we having?"

"Yee-haw!"

Only an hour later, after picking up what seemed like an extreme bar tab and extricating his friend from the clinging drunks, was Will headed back to Tremembé. Strangely, he felt better.

Ken snoozed in the back seat. Guy was indestructible. Outside, the sun was strong, the clouds were gone, and daily life was returning. The headlines in *Folha* this morning had proclaimed a police victory over the PCC. "Only" 49 cops dead, with the toll of gangsters "killed resisting arrest" at 80 and climbing. Will considered the irony of working with a death squad to bring down a guy for running a death squad. One man's terrorist was another man's freedom fighter?

Bullshit. Now was not the time for moral relativism. That was a luxury for the café set, not for men with guns and a target on their backs.

The retaken city stirred to life as they headed home.

Tremembé

As the garage door opened, Edilson was running out. "Will, Ken has gone missing. I just got a call—"

Will put a finger to his lips and motioned to the back seat. "Shhh. Don't wake the baby."

"Filha da puta." Edilson shook his head.

They left the snoring Ken where he was and headed upstairs. Andreatta and Renato Barbieri, the new head of the ROTA squad, were waiting, drinking coffee.

Andreatta greeted him. *"Oi, Soldado.* Let's talk tactics. Or do you want a cigarette and a blindfold?"

The four men gathered around the table to plan the end of Southern Cross. Later, when Will would look back on this meeting, he would never be able to get over the feeling of unreality. How had his life put him here, made his path cross those of these remarkable men? There was still so much he would never understand. He would try harder, if he got the time.

Understanding could wait. This time tomorrow, he'd settle for respiration.

Torre Grupo Stumpf, Avenida Paulista

Nunes, Stumpf's security chief, spoke in front of a large Landsat map of Southern Cross. "The area is not exactly remote, but the people tend to mind their own business. We should have freedom of action against the criminals."

Oscar Stumpf rocked slowly in his leather chair as he paid minimal attention to the briefing. Poor Nunes. So straitlaced and trusting. The army Nunes had come from still believed in those qualities as virtues.

Oscar Stumpf had come from a very different army. He viewed men like Nunes as necessary yet naive. Naive enough to believe a man like Oscar Stumpf was beset by common criminals.

Oscar Stumpf smiled to himself. *No,* he thought, *I am a man beset by his own country for associating with common criminals.*

A veteran of the more shadowy army he had come from wouldn't believe any of it for a second. That was why he had Nunes involved and not Crespo, whom he had dispatched to Piaui on some useless errand. Crespo wasn't useful here. Too suspicious, too questioning. Probably wondering right now why the hell he was in Piaui. Crespo was too like him for this situation, Stumpf had concluded.

Oscar Stumpf had come to believe that success always came down to picking the right team. In this respect, he had to admit that lately he hadn't followed his own advice. Why in God's name had he dispatched his sister's idiot son,

Angelo, on not one but two errands that couldn't be fucked up? And they had both been fucked up. Yet somehow, the greasy little shit had come away without a scratch. But two of his best men hadn't been so lucky. Duda hadn't been picked up so much as scooped off the Metro Clinicas tracks, and Roberto wasn't going to walk again without help. Two of his best.

And yet still, that smug little wop survived. After the last fuckup, he'd thought seriously about killing the halfwit. But he'd changed his mind after the twins had died. He couldn't afford any more dead relatives. So he'd come up with something even better.

Grupo Stumpf was building a uranium mine in Roraima State. So far from the rest of Brazilian civilization that it was actually in the Northern Hemisphere. Angelo was so ignorant of geography he seriously thought head of security for Roraima was a promotion.

Stumpf chuckled to himself. Angelo would really have to cut down on his hair products. The bugs up there loved them.

"Sir?"

Stumpf realized he was ignoring Nunes completely now. "Sorry, Edu, continue."

"And in conclusion, sir, escape for the criminals should be impossible, if we control these choke points." He indicated with his laser pointer. Nossa Senhora, did he love that laser pointer.

"Thank you, Edu. I have complete confidence in your arrangements."

"Very good, sir. With your permission, I will fly to Southern Cross tonight to wait with the advance team."

A group of Seguranca Stumpf commandos were already in place, camouflaged and watching for infiltrators. It had been the first thing he'd arranged after getting off the phone with Bryant.

"Any movement?" he quizzed Nunes, aware that had probably already been covered.

"Nothing."

Stumpf thought that was unlikely but kept his tongue in place. "Excellent. Have a safe flight. I will see you tomorrow."

"Sir." Nunes came to attention and then turned 180 degrees and marched out the door. Stumpf wondered how long he could count on any of these men once they realized they were fighting men like themselves, not *favelados* or narcos.

He wouldn't have had that problem if he had used PCC. All he had to do was pick up the phone. But the whole supposed subject of this meeting was him ditching the PCC. And he couldn't very well have PCC men hearing that, now could he?

And they'd fucked up badly too, both in Blumenau and in their pointless attack on the police in São Paulo. Even the Viet Cong had launched only one Tet Offensive. These crazy *trafficantes* seemed to believe they could wade into a bloodbath every few years and avoid serious consequences.

He was well rid of them. He hated everything they represented, the Estado Novo he feared. Too violent (yes, even for him), too sexual, and too ... black. But he had manoeuvred himself into a position where he couldn't do without them.

He looked at his phone for a minute before dialling.

Tremembé

The phone seemed to ring forever. Eventually the familiar voice responded. "Love? *Tudo bem?* I am worried. I had a dream last night ..."

Damn it. Silvia believed in a spirit world Will viewed skeptically, at best. It was going to be hard to convince her things were going to be okay. It was going to be hard to convince himself.

"You can't worry about dreams. And you can't tell me, baby. Negative thoughts, you know?" He could visualize what she was doing in the silence on the other end. "Stop chewing your nails."

"*Aiaiaiai, desculpe!* I can't drink, man, so what do you want?"

He laughed. "You."

"And only me?"

He had a guilty remembrance of Natalia. But he didn't lie. "Only you."

"Love, tell me, are you ready? You have made your plans very well?"

Silvia understood precious little of his former, and now current, world. It wasn't that she couldn't, for she was, if anything, more intelligent and insightful than he. No, she simply didn't want to. Dead bodies and blood were a poor fit with astral projection and afterlives.

"As well as I can be. Napoleon said the plans won't survive anyway."

"What?"

"Don't worry. I'm taking the right guys."

"Edilson will be there?"

"Always. He's a very brave man, Silvia."

Southern Cross

"So are you, my love. I am proud of you."

He felt himself tearing up. He was going to cut this short. "No, not brave. Just too stupid to know when to stop."

"You don't know yourself, Will. When this is over, I will take you to the *centro espirito*, and you will see."

"Sounds like fun."

"Liar. The kids are sleeping now. Do you want me to ...?"

God, no. He would really lose his shit then. "No, my love. Let them sleep. Kiss them for me. Is Lucas brushing his teeth?"

"Yes, but ... he didn't want me to tell you ..."

"He's wetting the bed again?" Jesus. He had put that kid through hell once, and now, the encore.

"Yes. He's so worried. He knows more than you think. He saw the news, about the PCC. He asked me if the bad men were shooting at you and Edilson too."

"This isn't helping, honey."

"Sorry, but you asked, Husband. Gabi is better, though. She is too young still, I think."

"Thank God. Kiss them both. I need to sleep now. We start early tomorrow."

She sighed, and he imagined the long copper hair falling over her shoulders ...

"Be strong. Be fast. Come home. *Te amo, meu marido.*"

"I love you too. *Boa noite.*"

He meant to sleep, but it was long in coming. Outside, the rain started with a snare drum and built up to a Neil Peart solo. Sleep came, finally.

32

Rodovia Presidente Dutra, Litoral Norte, São Paulo

Will had nodded off in the back seat and came to as they passed through another mid-size city, blurring out the windows. Anderson Alves snored beside him. In the front seat, Andreatta was arguing Corinthianos versus Os Peixes with Edilson. Even on their deathbeds, Brazilians couldn't stop talking football. Will rubbed his eyes. "Guys, where are we?"

Andreatta looked over his shoulder. "São Jose dos Campos. Still a half hour, at least. Go back to sleep, if you want."

"I've slept enough."

"Suit yourself." Andreatta shrugged and went back to the battle of the superfans.

As if he could sleep, now. He had read once about an astronaut who was so cool and collected that he'd fallen asleep on top of a Saturn V moon rocket. That wasn't Will Bryant. Last night's rain had passed, and the land was now bathed in brilliant sunshine. As the little city faded away, the vista shifted to red rolling hills dotted with termite cities, forlorn bus stops surrounded by people who lived God knew where, clutching everything in little plastic bags, all dressed in Bermudas and Chinelos, tan soles worn hard on black feet.

Brazil. Vast and unknowable. You could take a whole lifetime and be no wiser than when you started. He loved that. Maybe if he died here ...

Will snapped his head back. Negative thoughts. Negative training for the mind. They were not lambs going to the slaughter, after all. His feet shifted against a heavy duffle bag between them. His insurance against the abattoir.

He'd picked his gun out last night. Renato had brought a selection from the Choque armoury. The Impas carbines the ROTA men favoured looked to him like something Arnold Schwarzenegger ought to be chasing Michael Biehn around Los Angeles with. Besides, he had very little experience with long guns. A pistol was all he'd ever carried. Finally, he'd settled on a Heckler & Koch MP5. He'd actually fired one in Vegas once, and it was pretty easy. Plus, it had an idiotproof laser sight. He knew he wasn't much of a marksman. He needed all the help he could get.

He sweated under the thick vest. They'd put them on at a *posto* 10 klicks back. Level three, maximum protection. Also, maximum sweat. He wished he'd brought one of those little fans.

Renato's intricate prep work had boosted Will's confidence, but he still had serious doubts. They were meeting on ground Stumpf had chosen. Far from the highway. Probably lots of construction equipment to drown out the gunfire.

They had no idea how many bodies Stumpf was bringing, although advance reports from the men Renato already had watching the site suggested at least a dozen already there. Already the odds were even.

Will was a firm believer in not fighting fair. Ever.

But what did he expect? Oscar Stumpf was not going to just obediently slip his head into the noose. There had to be a hitch.

But Will Bryant could make his own hitches. Like Gilberto. Gilberto was a PMSP helicopter pilot Will had befriended five years ago and had kept in touch with. He'd even had him as a house guest in Canada two years ago. Now he called in the favour.

Gilberto was on his way back from a medevac job in Ilhabela, on the coast. Southern Cross wouldn't be far enough out of the way to arouse too much suspicion.

Will craned his head out the window, looking toward Southern Cross. Nothing but stark blue sky and unrelenting heat. Too far away to see anyway.

His phone was ringing as he pulled his head back in. He answered it.

"Gilberto? *Fala!*"

"I just had time for a quick pass." The voice was scratchy and faint under rotor noise. "And I couldn't get too low because of the patient ..."

"And?"

"The site is surrounded, Will. I can see fighting holes, at least five. Six vehicles under netting. Two with heat under the hoods on the FLIR. They just got there. It's an ambush. Don't go."

"They have the road covered?"

"Yes, one position by the road. From the heat, probably three men, but it's hard to tell. It's late in the morning, and the ground is hot." He said more, but it was lost in squelch and static.

"How many in total?"

"I say 30."

"Jesus!"

"Don't go. I have to go now ... Will ... be ..."

He lost the signal. "Guys, my buddy Gilberto just did a flyover. He thinks 30 guys, in foxholes. They have the road covered."

Andreatta yawned. "What did you think, Ferguson, he would show up naked with a slingshot?"

"Fuck you, Sergeant."

Andreatta smirked and shrugged.

Edilson snapped his phone shut. "Yes, I just got the update. Two vans just showed up with lots of guys. One of them looks like Stumpf."

So, he had decided to dance after all.

"I don't like the numbers either, Will." Edilson's face was serious. "They need to bring at least 20 more for a fair fight." His face broke into a wry grin. He pointed at the bag between Will's feet. "You sure you know how to use that?"

"You're about to find out."

Projeto Cruzeiro do Sul

Stumpf stood under camouflage netting in a small copse. He studied the men around him. Aside from Grasselman and Nunes, the faces were unfamiliar. It made him uneasy.

He wished the twins were here. God, the heat. He mopped at his brow with a handkerchief.

But he wouldn't be here if the twins were still alive. He would still be dancing and feinting with his enemies, until one of the many hungry and motivated PCC assassins made the problem go away. But the twins had changed everything.

Still, if the basic mission was revenge (that was probably all he could hope for; survival against the state was unlikely), there was still no room for rashness.

"Men!"

The ex-army troops who now formed his army stood to attention. He scanned the camo-painted faces. Young, so young.

Himself, in the mirror, Montevideo, 1971. Honour and duty. Before he'd ever tortured a man or killed a woman. When he'd believed.

"The renegades we face today think I came here to bribe them. We must let them believe this until the last possible moment. Then, they will find out I came here to destroy them. Discipline is key. Wait for orders, understand?"

In unison, they shouted, *"Sim, Senhor Stumpf!"*

He suppressed a cynical smirk. These boys still believed. He could use that belief to his own ends.

Nunes dismissed the troops to their positions. Stumpf lit a cigar and stared at the sky. A helicopter passed overhead, its features indistinct. Stumpf watched closely, but it did not come back.

Perhaps these renegades had less help than he thought.

Posto de servicio, Rodovia Dutra

"Almost here." Edilson turned. "Are you ready?"

Will nodded tightly. Edilson looked at him for a long moment, as if he wasn't sure.

"I'm ready, partner." He elbowed Alves, who squirmed and came to life slowly. "We're here. It's not too late to change your mind, friend."

Alves rubbed his eyes. "I am going, Officer. But thanks." He smiled bashfully. Will had a bad feeling but didn't feel he could voice it now. The man had a right to risk his life.

"You remember what to do, Anderson?" Andreatta asked, glancing in the rear-view.

"*Sim, Sargento.*"

"He listens better than you, Ferguson." Andreatta needled Will. It seemed to be his hobby.

"*Sim, Sargento.*" Will figured this might be his last chance to ask Andreatta something that had been bothering him for a few days. "Why are you here?"

Andreatta sat up bolt straight and announced, "To serve the people of the State of São Paulo!" They took the exit for the *posto*. "But seriously, it's like Shakespeare ..."

"How so?"

"'Gentlemen in England now abed will think themselves accursed they were not here ...' I forget the rest."

"'... and hold their manhoods cheap whiles any speaks, who fought with us upon St. Crispin's Day,'" Will finished. He looked at Andreatta.

"Hmm, you are surprising, Ferguson. Here I thought all you did at university was throw a football and chase women."

Edilson laughed. "Better than you, Sarge. All you know how to read is a beer label."

Andreatta negotiated his way past a line of trucks into the *posto* lot. They were ubiquitous in the huge country, a necessity on the long roads linking Brazil. Overgrown gas stations with self-serve restaurants and gift shops, pit stops that turned into hour-long ordeals on family road trips.

Will caught himself. He might miss those ordeals.

"There!" Edilson signalled for Andreatta to pull in next to an ambulance. Two suspiciously fit paramedics loitered behind it. Will stretched as he stepped out. One of the "paramedics" gave him a hard look.

Andreatta walked up and shook their hands. "Ready, *mulekes*?"

The taller of the two, who Will seemed to recall was called Silvio, replied, "Yes, we're ready. Where's our patient?" He seemed impatient. Maybe he was afraid he was going to miss it all. Guys like him couldn't stand that.

"Right here," Andreatta said. "This is Anderson. Anderson, this is Silvio and Josue."

"Great." Josue spit on the pavement. "Let's go over it."

Will noticed that Edilson was absent and then saw him walking the lot in a broad circle, scanning for threats.

Andreatta said, "We make contact with the principal. You wait at the entrance to the road with Anderson, to watch our backs. You intercept any reinforcements. We report when the job is done, and you bring him up. Agreed?"

"*Claro, Sargento.* Does this guy know how to shoot?" Josue jabbed a thumb at Anderson, who stared at the pavement, clearly ill at ease.

"No, but if your 'ambulance' breaks down, he can always hot-wire something new." Andreatta wasn't about to take shit from the "Tropa de Elite."

"Great." Josue spit again.

Silvio strode up to Will. *"Boa sorte, Policial."* Will took the outstretched hand. The grip was firm.

"Good luck to you, but I don't think you need it as much."

"We all need it. Thanks, gringo." Shit. He still couldn't pass for a native. "Be careful over there." Silvio pointed at the red-earth slope bisected by a dusty road opposite them. "Anything can happen."

"Yes, it can."

Southern Cross

Will was alone in the back seat as Andreatta negotiated the rutted gravel road. A cloud of red dust came up behind them, announcing their arrival to anyone in the vicinity.

He looked at his watch: 11:45. They were expected anyway.

The sun was now almost directly overhead, and it was clearly going to be dangerously hot. Will hoped he'd brought enough water. They passed a sign, "Projeto Cruzeiro do Sul, Fabrica Industrias Stumpf." A fitting place for the finale, almost cute in a way.

Will closed his eyes and opened them. He tried to imagine the same road, 1978. Unmarked snatch vans with prisoners, beginning to sense the end. Another Industria Stumpf in the making.

Ana Rosa Rodriguez. What had she been thinking? Had she had a window to look out of and ponder last thoughts, like him?

He was veering toward the morbid again. He needed to recover the quarterback he'd once been. Today was game day.

Ahead, the road forked. A low cluster of buildings surrounded the intersection. A good place for an ambush. Edilson looked back at him.

"I know what you are thinking. And they're probably there. But they won't. Not yet."

"How can you be so confident?" Edilson was always confident.

"Stumpf wants to know what you know. Then he can kill us."

"But he doesn't know about Renato."

Andreatta interjected, "We hope. They're good, ROTA, but they're not perfect. Even BOPE fucks up." BOPE were the legendary commandos of Rio, feared and avoided by the worst criminals. Will figured they'd be mad when they realized they'd missed this one.

"Not very often!" Edilson hero-worshipped BOPE as he did Santos FC.

"But they do," Andreatta continued. "What if they're trussed up in the trees like butchered hogs, *hein*? Be ready to fight your way out on your own, *entende, Soldados*?"

Will nodded.

Ahead, an ornate faux gate announced the perimeter of Southern Cross. A billboard flanked the entrance. A happy, smiling white family frolicked in a swimming pool. If they only knew.

"All right, you idiots, we're here," Andreatta announced.

They proceeded slowly past apparently abandoned construction huts. Earthmovers and dump trucks sat awaiting their next job. Will could feel eyes on him and shuddered.

Ahead was a clearing. Perhaps a future park. It was backed by a copse of trees. A likely meeting spot.

"He wants us there. Lots of cover for him, none for us." Andreatta spoke what they were all thinking. "I'm going to park over by that last row of foundations and make him come out a little."

They passed a long, curving row of future homes. Judging from the foundations, they were going to be big, by Brazilian standards. Will looked up the surrounding gentle hillside, caught a glint of light.

Edilson caught it too. "Sniper, three o'clock."

Andreatta was laconic. "I guess Barbieri made it after all."

"How do you know it's ours?"

"If you're Stumpf and you put a sniper there, you are an idiot. Does he seem that stupid?"

It was a good point. Will was guessing all the guns Stumpf had were pointing out from the copse. They were surrounded for sure, but they'd probably already passed the men detailed with cutting them off. He took a calming breath.

One last thought. Silvia running through the waves on Ilhabela. His first trip to Brazil. Why was every golden memory on the beach?

Andreatta pulled up next to a big foundation pad. "Our Alamo, men. When it explodes, we get back here, fast. Now get your bags. We get out and talk to this piece of shit before we kill him."

Will stepped onto red dirt. The sun burned, his Oakley's barely shutting it out. He squinted and looked around. Four slow breaths, as he was taught, combat breathing ... how to breathe after you'd just shot somebody and didn't want to make a total ass of yourself on the radio. He put the strap for his bag across his shoulders, keeping it on his strong side for quick access. He took a careful look around him.

Will began to understand why Andreatta had picked this place. It was isolated from the other units and wider than the other foundation pads ... a recreation centre, perhaps? Recessed stairwells, ideal for fighting positions. Flat ground behind and to the sides. No cover for the enemy. Recognition hit him.

"This is where the shaft is."

"What, Will?" Edilson was scanning the treeline with binoculars. "What shaft?"

"Where Anderson buried the documents."

"If we're still alive in an hour, remind me to look."

"Shut up, idiots." Andreatta gazed at the treeline. "Movement."

Will suddenly remembered his earbud and put it in, in time to hear, "Movement ahead of you." Renato's voice.

Andreatta responded, "I see it. We are going to try to get them closer."

"Okay, you are covered."

Edilson chuckled and handed the glasses to Will. "That fucking prick."

Will raised the glasses to his eyes and watched as Oscar Stumpf confidently strode into the clearing. He wore combat fatigues and carried an M4 carbine casually slung over his shoulder. Two men dressed in the same manner flanked him on each side. One was in his fifties and getting fat. A red sheen of sunburn and sweat covered his bare bald head. He was very tall.

"That's Grasselman," Edilson said. "He's not been hitting the gym much, I see."

Will nodded. Grasselman looked very out of place. A paving contractor playing soldier. On the other side was a man who was not playing. Average height, squared shoulders. Young, maybe 35. Fatigue sleeves rolled up to reveal knotted muscle. Striding with purpose. He carried his M4 at Belfast arms.

"Nunes, his security chief. Just got out of the army last year. Had some problems in Rio on a Pacification job."

"Problems" in a Rio pacification mission probably meant unaccounted for dead bodies. Will would have to watch that one.

The other men had their faces painted in camouflage. They stopped in the middle of the clearing.

"Well?" Andreatta looked back at them. "Shall we?"

"Not too far." Edilson was cautious. "We have to be ready."

"Yes." Andreatta lit a cigarillo. "We also have to trust our snipers."

Edilson made the sign of the cross as he stepped forward.

"Are you that worried, buddy?" Will asked.

"Not for me. Remember, Will, this is a giant grave we are standing on."

"Let's hope it's not ours."

"*Amem.*"

The three men walked slowly away from the Alamo, crossing the road, watching their reception.

North of Mogi das Cruzes, São Paulo State

The pilot of the big Augusta had no idea why he'd been diverted from his normal routine to a fazenda in the middle of nowhere. He had no idea why he was taking on extra fuel from a tanker on an obviously makeshift landing pad. And he certainly had no idea why, while he was sitting hot on the pad, awaiting a quick takeoff, he and his co-pilot had been handed body armour and ceramic floor plates. But when you flew for Aero Stumpf, you learned not to ask questions.

His co-pilot went to intercom. "Extra fuel? Armour? There had better be a bonus in this for us ... What the hell, Joao?"

The pilot turned and patiently regarded his younger colleague. "If you don't like it, I am sure Senhor Stumpf won't mind if you get out. He wouldn't want you to do anything you aren't comfortable with, Marcello." The pilot smiled icily.

Marcello stared ahead. "You don't need to be an asshole about it, *Captain*."

"Relax, son. When you work for Aero Stumpf, you accept that anything can happen. And not all of it's legal!"

The pilots' headsets hissed. "Take off and head south-southeast now. Coordinates to follow inflight."

"Roger, understood." Joao turned to Marcello. "Coming?"

"Asshole."

The Augusta slowly lifted off, heavily weighted, and headed toward Southern Cross.

Aeroporto Campo de Marte, São Paulo

A line of disciplined men boarded another helicopter. The pilot of this machine did not need to be told where he was going. The settings in its navigational computer were almost exactly the same as the one taking off from the fazenda at the exact same time. Its journey was also a short one.

One man on the helicopter was not so disciplined. He looked out the window at the towers of São Paulo, lost in thought.

Southern Cross

Cautiously, both groups of men edged forward, until they were 10 metres apart. Grasselman craned his head around nervously. He looked like he wanted to run. Curiously, this made Will calmer. *I might look scared, but not that scared.*

Oscar Stumpf did not look scared. He smiled at Will. "Oh, I wonder what is in those bags, Mr. Bryant? At least we declare our intentions honestly." From the look on Nunes's face, the intention was clear.

"We brought some snacks. Thought you might like a picnic."

"Not to my tastes, I'm afraid."

"Too bad."

"I see you brought the police."

"Always a good idea when meeting a criminal."

"But it seems you didn't bring enough. Unfortunate."

"Yes, it seems that way." Will was now sure Stumpf had no intention of dealing. He visualized making the quick grab for the MP5. He hoped he wouldn't fuck it up this time. Behind his opponents, a heat shimmer rose from the ground. He began to pace his breathing.

"You should know that the government is aware I am no longer in business with my old partners. Therefore, the help you were counting on will not be forthcoming."

"I wonder how your old partners will feel about that. They aren't known to be very forgiving."

"I retain friends who make my old partners seem quite tame by comparison."

"I assume you are talking about Nunes? Wonder how he feels about shooting cops?"

Just the slightest irritation registered on Stumpf's face. For the first time, Nunes shifted his gaze to his boss.

Stumpf laughed. "You are good, Mr. Bryant. You should've come to work for me."

"No thanks. But I'll still take your money." Nunes was studying Will very closely now.

"Of course. But I need some assurances, first."

Two of the security men took off large backpacks and placed them on the ground. Stumpf signalled, and they unzipped them to reveal thick wads of US bills stacked inside. Edilson's eyes widened. He drove a 10-year-old car.

"I assure you it is all there. We won't demean each other by counting, will we?"

"That is the least of my worries, *senhor.*"

"I brought the guns because, as a soldier, I believe in precautions. Frankly I am more worried by the fact you have chosen to conceal yours." Stumpf looked like a disappointed father. Will would've laughed if he wasn't in combat mode.

"Why worry? As you've pointed out, we didn't bring enough cops."

Stumpf laughed and shook his head. "So, no *High Noon*, then?" He lit a cigar. "I was so looking forward to it."

"You chose the time, remember? You said you wanted assurances? You have them." Through his earbud Will heard a man exhaling. Out of the corner of his eye, he saw a dump truck, parked within running distance. Another behind it. He started to plan.

"Very well. But I was wondering if you would answer one question?"

A bead of sweat dripped into Will's eye. "What's that?"

"How many people are buried here?"

"Eighty."

Stumpf gave an icy smile. "Incorrect. Eighty-three."

Will's feet started him moving for the dump truck before Stumpf could finish. His hand reached into the false-bottomed bag and found the pistol grip of the MP5.

The treeline, 300 metres away

Statue-still, exhaling slowly, Wagner squinted through the power scope at his opponent at the other side of the clearing. He had been watching him for three hours now. He had long since lost the battle against nature, and his fatigues were soaked with his own urine. He lay in seemingly impenetrable brush. He was aware of termites, but as long as they were not fire ants, he could resist.

He held the Imbel AGLC sniper rifle with practiced lightness. Beside him, his carbine lay ready. His earbud hissed. *"Luz verde!"* Renato announced.

The man opposite him drew up his shoulder and moved his finger. His face was painted black and green. His finger had just brushed the trigger when Wagner blew his head open.

His opponent's body hadn't hit the ground yet when Wagner had picked out his second target. The bolt flicked open and shut, slamming the round home in time for another trigger pull.

In the clearing, automatic weapons started to rip.

The clearing

Will sprinted for the dump truck and prayed his friends were following. Their opponents seemed flat-footed for the briefest second. The wrong people had been sniped.

Stumpf brought his M4 down to the hip and fired at Will, leading him wrong, just behind the surprisingly fast big man. Realizing he had no cover, Stumpf ran, cursing, in the same direction, headed for the other dump truck.

The second Oscar Stumpf had uttered his death sentence, Andreatta had already been bringing up a pistol on the big security man opposite him. The man was a poor poker player and had already started bringing a little machine pistol out from under the stacked cash in the backpack. He died looking disappointed that he wasn't faster, falling heavily across the backpack and pouring black blood into the red dirt.

Andreatta felt a jackhammer kick in his stomach and chest as Grasselman fired a Sig pistol at him from can't-miss range. Andreatta dropped to his knees and fired three shots back. One found its mark in the builder's throat, and the man staggered wildly backwards. A bullet from a hidden sniper opened his head. Andreatta, whole thanks to his vest, pulled himself up and ran for the Alamo. A glancing rifle round skidded across his back and went out his left tricep, slamming him down again. Panting, screaming silently, he crawled the rest of the way.

When Will finally made it to the dump truck, he was surprised to find Edilson already there.

"Fuck, you are slow." Edilson was sheltered behind a massive truck tire.

"Where's Andreatta?"

"Don't know. Get your gun out, idiot!"

Will looked down stupidly, realizing his MP5 was still in its bag. So much for the quick draw. He yanked it out just as Nunes started to find his range. A round shattered a headlamp next to Will's face. Two more gonged the metal around him and rang in his ears. He dropped to his belly and fired underneath the truck at moving legs.

Oscar Stumpf reached the dump truck, feeling every second of his age, just as Nunes screamed and dropped. Stumpf pulled him behind the thick tires. There was a hole in Nunes's boot. Blood leaked onto the ground.

"Can you fight?"

Nunes winced as he cleared a stoppage and slammed in a new magazine. "Is there a choice?" He spun around the tire and fired at Will. Stumpf got on the radio.

Edilson bided his time and watched the shadows creeping up the right side of the huge vehicle. Noon was a bad time for an attacker. Nice long shadows. He smiled to himself as he edged around the corner.

The security man who had been silently edging up on him had time only to register surprise before a full auto burst opened his throat and face. He dropped to his knees and toppled over, face down. Edilson grabbed the man's web gear and dragged him forward.

"What the fuck are you doing?" Will was fighting to clear a jam on his unfamiliar weapon.

"Did you bring endless ammo? He's got some! No, move the bolt like that. That's it."

A round from the other truck puffed the dirt between them.

"Fuck!" Will panted. "This truck's too fucking small!"

"Idiots, are you there?" Andreatta's voice on the radio.

Edilson was relieved. "Where the hell are you?"

"Alamo, where you are supposed to be. Where are the rest of them?"

Renato chimed in. "I don't see any movement in the trees. We got their snipers. We are going to clear the treeline now."

"Okay, we're going to—"

Just then, heavy machinery roared to life from the direction of the roadway.

"Guys!" It was Silvio. "Three bulldozers just started. They are moving! At least 10 men! Coming for you now."

Andreatta was decisive. "Don't you reveal yourself!" He sounded pained, wounded. "Stay hidden. More are coming."

"But ..." Silvio started.

"No buts!" Renato said. "Wagner, you and Abdul will clear the treeline. Emerson and I are coming to you, Andreatta. Stay where you are!"

Another burst ripped the dirt between Edilson and Will. Will stared up at the sky for a moment.

"What the hell are you looking for?"

"A way out."

"You're holding it. Now start shooting." Edilson slipped around the other side and fired at Nunes's gun barrel.

Behind the barrel, Nunes winced at another close call. He was in it now; might as well ask.

"*Senhor?* What happened to our snipers? Three renegades didn't do that. You owe us the truth!"

Stumpf seethed, but Nunes was all he had right now, until the bulldozers showed up. "I don't know, son. But we have to fight now. Answers can come later." A bullet knocked dust into his eyes, and he squinted. "Now is not the place for debate, Major! Now find the rest of your men!"

Nunes looked at Stumpf and wondered. Those men opposite them. There was something about them ... and they had called Stumpf the criminal, not the other way round. Still, he got on his mic. To his surprise, he got a response.

The treeline

Wagner and Abdul had left their sniper's nests and now edged together, just keeping sight of each other, into the enemy positions. Wagner heard bulldozers, getting closer, behind them. He wanted to be there. But discipline, a job to do, kept him here. To his right, he heard a three-round burst as Abdul finished off a man. They kept moving forward.

The Alamo

Andreatta was calmly building a nest as the bulldozers churned up the road toward him. He had staunched the blood from his wound with a dressing and arranged all his spare magazines for quick access. He had a niche in a half-finished stairwell, which gave him perfect cover from all sides except one, and he knew the guys on that side would be his. Andreatta whistled as he waited for the bulldozers to come into range.

The clearing, dump truck park

Four men occupied corners on two parked dump trucks. They did not shoot. Nobody was stupid enough to leave cover. Nobody had an advantage. They waited for the odds to shift.

The treeline

Wagner was staring down at the body of the first sniper he had killed. That sniper had made himself a little nest too. He leaned over and picked up the man's radio. As he stood up, he noticed a little gilt-framed Nossa Senhora the man must have set in his nest. It was specked with blood. He picked that up too.

His earbud cracked. It was Abdul. "Movement! Five, no, six, headed for the clearing! Wagner, get here now! *Agora!*"

Wagner pushed his way through the tangled brush as Abdul opened fire.

The Alamo

"Covering!" Renato announced his presence as 100 kilos of man and equipment slammed into the side of the foundation. A few desultory shots from the men riding the bulldozers followed Emerson as he reached safety. The dark-skinned leader with a square jaw and livid neck scar breathed hard. The younger Emerson, tall and trim, with strange red hair Andreatta thought too long for a cop, was calm.

"Welcome, friends."

"You're hit." Renato reached for Andreatta's wounded arm while Emerson trained his carbine on the enemy.

Andreatta pulled away. "Fuck off. I'm fine. Anyway, we'll soon have more holes in us."

The men looked toward the growing red cloud. The bulldozers were rounding the corner.

The treeline

"Filha da puta!" Abdul screamed in frustration as the running men closed the gap with their comrades at the dump truck. One of the enemy lay sprawled and still from his efforts.

"Shit! We have to get to them!" The two men pelted down the slope toward the dump trucks. "Ferguson, five enemy coming for you!" Wagner panted into the mic. "Watch your right flank!"

They sprinted toward a fold in the ground.

One of their enemies lay very still in a hole he had dug yesterday. Listening to pounding feet and jangling equipment.

"Ferguson, did you copy, did you ...?"

The man in the hole rose up when they were three metres away and opened up on full auto. Abdul, hit five times, staggered forward with momentum and then toppled over. Wagner dropped to his knees, clutching his neck, blood filling his undershirt from an unseen wound.

The man in the hole met his eyes. He paused and then his bolt shot forward on an empty chamber. His camo-rimmed eyes were wide with surprise as Wagner pulled out his Taurus and shot him twice.

Wagner stared at the sky and then fell over Abdul's legs.

33

The Alamo, Southern Cross

Andreatta peered through a notch in the foundation at the advancing bulldozers, staying as low as possible. Emerson had crawled around the other side of the wide concrete slab. Renato was somewhere to his left and front. The dust was choking now. He pulled his scarf up to his nose.

Just then, he heard the grinding of gears and halting brakes. The dust dissipated as the source of it halted. This was the best chance, now. He peered through the notch again. The three dozers, blades held high, had stopped in a staggered line about 30 metres from the Alamo. Behind him, Andreatta heard rapid fire. He wondered about his comrades.

As he hefted the grenade in his hand, he thought, *You are on your own, friends. This is the best I can do.*

The first men were jumping off the back of the dozers as he pulled the pin. Standing tall, he tossed the metal egg like a softball at the cab of the first dozer. As he dropped down, grenades arced into the air from Renato and Emerson.

That should make them think. The grenades exploded as he picked up his carbine and took aim.

The clearing

Edilson squinted in the bright sunlight. *Damn it, my glasses. Those were expensive.* He was tight to the massive wheel of the dump truck, knowing that his opponent was doing the same thing just 15 metres away. Occasionally, he would force himself to peek out quickly to check his opponent's position. The last time he'd done that, they'd locked eyes and exchanged a brief, pointless salvo.

This was what made him afraid. Fear, in Edilson's experience, only arose when you had time to think. Now, he had time.

Behind him, the noise of bulldozers stopped. Then, three explosions.

Across from him, Will held his corner, shifting briefly to look at him. *I don't know either, buddy,* Will telegraphed wordlessly. Edilson knew his partner was feeling the same edgy frustration as he.

Behind that next dump truck was Oscar Stumpf. So close. But he might as well be on the dark side of the moon.

The tornado of gunfire from the Alamo obscured the sound of running men to Edilson's right.

The Alamo

The grenades produced shock and awe but not much else. Only one enemy lay still in front of the first dozer. The rest had managed to get behind the blades or had reached the far end of the foundation. Andreatta began firing three-round bursts anytime he saw a head pop up. Fire from his flanks came in measured doses from Renato and Emerson. But the targets were fast and experienced; they knew not to show themselves. Andreatta shot dry, dropped his mag, reloaded, and looked for an opportunity. He hoped they'd brought enough ammo.

The clearing

Out of the corner of his eye, Edilson saw a movement. Suddenly there were two men running parallel to him, shooting from the hip. He shifted his weapon and fired on the slower man, who dropped to his knees but raised his carbine again. Edilson put his last three rounds into the man, who toppled to his side.

"Will!" Edilson just had time to scream as the man who had run past him opened up on full auto.

Edilson had been shot before, but this time he felt as if he were on fire. He dropped the carbine and sagged against the tire.

Will Bryant left his corner, the MP5 to his shoulder. The laser sight found the face of Edilson's assailant, who was struggling to change his magazine, and Will squeezed the trigger. A cloud of pink mist sprayed into the air as the gunman pirouetted and dropped. Will grabbed Edilson's harness, bent at the knees, and threw his friend over his shoulder.

Edilson drooled blood and mumbled, "No, no ..."

"We are leaving!"

Will ran without thought or hesitation, headed across the road for the Alamo. From the other dump truck, the surviving new arrivals joined Nunes, pouring fire in the direction of the runner and his cargo.

Will would never remember how he got across the road. But he did, and he slammed Edilson into the ground at the feet of Andreatta, who was firing repeatedly in the other direction.

"You made it." Andreatta seemed almost nonchalant. He glanced down at Edilson. *"Merda."*

Will sat down for a second. He was stunned and panting hard, still not believing he was alive. A bullet smacked into the wall opposite him.

"Dressing, idiot!" Andreatta yelled at him.

"What?"

"Put a dressing on your friend before he bleeds to death!"

Andreatta tossed him a trauma kit with his left hand while continuing to fight with his right. Will ripped open a pressure bandage and put it on the most worrying-looking hole he could find. Edilson was going pale.

"Will?" Edilson whispered. "I'm dying, right?"

"Shut the fuck up!"

"Okay."

An enemy in front of Andreatta raised his carbine above the lip of the foundation and blindly sprayed suppressing fire. Andreatta shot the enemy's weapon into the air with a burst that shattered the man's forearms.

"Oh, Ferguson?" Andreatta said as he reloaded.

"What?"

"Watch the rear, will you?"

Will looked up and saw a dump truck roaring to life and moving. He reloaded hurriedly.

At his side, Edilson lay still.

The clearing

The survivors of the massacre inflicted by the ROTA men in the treeline had arrived at the dump trucks. Nunes gathered the four men and gave a hurried briefing.

"You four will take that truck down there and help Paulo and his group in the bulldozers. Help is coming, soon. I am getting Senhor Stumpf to safety now. Go!"

"You presume too much, Nunes." Stumpf stood with hands on hips, looking to Nunes like a petulant Napoleon.

"Sir, your presence is no longer required. The helicopter will be here soon. I intend to get you out on it."

Stumpf looked across at what would have been the centrepiece of his triumph. Smoke puffed every time a round hit the concrete. Muzzle flashes lit up, behind each one of them, a desperate man. Part of him wanted to be down there. The other part knew Nunes was right. The job was getting done. And his friends had offered him an exit strategy.

"All right, Nunes, let's go. But finish the job."

Nunes stiffened. *"Sim, Senhor!"*

Just then, Nunes's radio crackled. "We are two minutes out."

The chopper was coming.

Fighting hole, northeast of the clearing

Wagner held the little gilt-framed Nossa Senhora in his left hand. He could barely move, so he contented himself by gazing at the Virgin while he waited to die. It was obscene, he knew, lying across Abdul like that, but he lacked the strength to move his body. He knew the Virgin, and his friend, would forgive him.

All through his boyhood, he had looked to her for help in times of need, and she had consoled him. Later, as a man, he had drifted apart from her, his experiences as a policeman causing him to doubt such love really existed.

But his enemy had brought her here for a reason. So he gazed at her and held on. She was telling him not to give up.

Just then, the radio he had taken from his pious enemy crackled to life. Wagner strained to hear, and he understood why the Virgin was keeping him.

Road entrance to Southern Cross

Beside the ambulance, parked under a stand of trees out of sight from the road, Silvio paced.

"Will you stop it? We have orders!" Josue was that type.

"We have to adapt with the situation! Do you see anybody coming up that road? Do you? The battle will be won or lost down there!" Silvio motioned to the moving dust cloud churned up by the dump truck, now moving slowly toward the Alamo. "That's where we should be!"

"And if someone does come up that road? Who's going to stop them, him?" Josue gestured at Anderson Alves, who sat impassively under a tree trunk, chewing on a blade of grass.

"You do what you like; I'm going!" Silvio had just stooped to pick up his web gear when the radio came to life.

They strained to hear the weak voice. "Renato, Renato, helicopter ... helicopter coming. One ... minute now."

Josue's face fell. "That was Wagner. *Meu Deus.*"

Silvio put on his web gear. "Looks like the battle's coming to us."

The sound of rotors grew in intensity as they prepared.

Aero Stumpf Augusta, southwest of Southern Cross

"*Puta merda.* What have you gotten me into?" Marcello stared at Joao accusatorially before looking out the window again. "There's a fucking battle going on down there!"

Joao shook his head as he stared down at the clearing ahead. That was supposed to be their landing site. Obviously out of the question now. Muzzle flashes and grenade explosions, apparent dead bodies strewn about, all bad signs. "What can I say? We're on overtime."

Their headsets crackled. It was Nunes. "Beware ground fire. The original LZ is too hot."

"No shit," scoffed Marcello.

Joao began to gain altitude. But not fast enough.

The Alamo

"Jesus Cristo, that is a helicopter. And it's one of Stumpf's!"

Will didn't hear Andreatta cursing the latest shitty turn in their fortunes. He was engrossed in a one-man battle with a dump truck.

The truck edged across the road slowly, haltingly, clearly at the hands of an inexperienced driver. Will concentrated on taking the driver out. His MP5 was accurate, but at this range it lacked penetration. Puffs of glass dust came from repeated hits on the windshield, but still the behemoth moved forward. The gunmen in the bucket of the truck would pop up from time to time to fire harassing shots. Will ignored them. The driver stalled, grinding the gears.

Will looked over at Edilson. He still breathed, if only shallowly. And there was an M4 carbine slung across his back. Will lifted his friend's head gingerly as he pulled the carbine over his head. Edilson moaned.

"You still haven't stopped that truck yet, gringo?" Somehow, engaged in his own gun battle, Andreatta still found time to piss Will off.

"You got a fucking rocket launcher?"

"I wish!" Across from Andreatta, an enemy made a wild, firing rush from the second dozer to the shelter of the foundation wall. Distracted, Andreatta fired and missed. *"Filha da puta!"*

Will brought the M4 to bear on the driver as the man fought the gears. The truck lurched forward. The enemy yelled in triumph.

Will unloaded a full magazine on automatic at the driver's cab. The windshield shattered. The driver fell, or jumped, out the door as the truck veered crazily to the right. The left rear wheel of the truck pulverized the driver as it rolled over him.

"Got that truck, Sarge."

"You're a hero now, Ferguson."

The entrance

Silvio and Josue sprinted forward as the big Augusta, weighted down with fuel and armour, slowly gained altitude. It was now directly over their position as they sheltered against the low stone wall framing the entrance gate.

Behind them, Anderson Alves watched silently, dreading for the men in the helicopter.

Renato's voice was in their earbuds, against a background of battle noise. "Stumpf's ride is here. Silvio, cancel his taxi."

"Now." Silvio raised and aimed his carbine as Josue followed suit.

Aero Stumpf Augusta

"Fuck!" The fuselage metal gonged repeatedly as Silvio's and Josue's rounds punched into the chopper. Joao cursed as he tried to steady the bird.

"Put it down!" Marcello was looking up as he shouted. Joao followed his gaze and understood why.

Thick black smoke poured out of the engine housing above and behind them. The panel in front of Joao was a sea of fire and warning lights. "Autorotate!"

"Ah shit." Marcello braced as they began to spin down to the ground.

Rodovia Dutra

The people at the *posto* and those waiting for buses along the busy highway had heard a lot of noises coming from Southern Cross. It was easy to write it off as construction noise. But a fiery explosion and a black pillar of smoke started people dialling the *bomberos* on their mobile phones.

The Alamo

Will had stopped the dump truck, but it was close now, and the survivors onboard kept up an irritating and persistent fire from their impervious position in the bucket. Every so often a gun barrel would sparkle from the lip of the bucket and then disappear. To Will it had an air of unreality, like some video game he was too old and slow to master. He fired back every so often, just to deter any attempt to get closer. He knew he wasn't hitting anything. The sounds around him, constant gunfire, screams, shouts, ricochets … all merging into a silence. He couldn't hear a damn thing. For the first time he had a moment to think of his family. Were they still having lunch? Was Gabi eating? Was Lucas being mean to her?

A bullet close to his face brought him back quickly.

"Wake up, idiot!" Andreatta changed magazines. Will saw a lot of empty ones at his feet and wondered how much was left. "They're advancing! We need to move soon!"

Move? To where? Looking past Andreatta, he saw that the enemy behind him was now hugging the other side of the foundation, in places as close as 10 metres. The ROTA men holding the flanks were in serious danger now.

He looked at Edilson, felt his pulse. His friend held on but only just. Will dreaded having to move him again.

"Fuck!" Andreatta shouted as a concrete chip ripped into his cheek. He retreated from his firing post, squinting. As if sensing the opportunity, one of their enemies pulled himself over the foundation and reached his arm back in a familiar motion.

"Grenade!" Will shouted as he fired at the thrower a moment too late. He threw himself over Edilson, who moaned in pain.

He heard a ping as the metal egg bounced off the far wall and then a roar. Hot needles in his legs. He pulled himself off Edilson, his eardrums pounding.

The thrower was almost on top of Will when Renato shot him in the back. The big enemy toppled across Andreatta's firing pit, inadvertently saving the Sergeant's life as the enemy's colleagues, emboldened, unleashed a barrage that riddled their comrade instead.

"Friendly!" Renato shouted as he rounded the corner. He was grimy and bloody, his fatigues ripped in 10 different places. *Holy shit*, thought Will, *do I look that bad?*

"You look rough, friend." Guess he did.

"Thanks. You look *GQ*. What's your secret?"

Renato ignored the joke. "We need to get Emerson, now. I see him shooting, but he doesn't answer. They're going to outflank him."

Before Will could respond, Andreatta had pulled himself up. "I'll go, idiots. But do one thing for me."

"What?"

Andreatta put a grenade in his hand. "It's the last one. Throw it when I say. And remember to pull the pin first, idiot." Andreatta smiled.

Will nodded. *"Sim, Sargento."*

"We'll make a *policial* out of you yet, Ferguson."

Renato looked at them both quizzically but said nothing.

"Ready, boys?" Andreatta asked.

The entrance

Silvio and Josue were still staring at the gash the Augusta had made in the trees and the pillar of thick black smoke that had resulted when they heard the sirens. They turned in time to see the ambulance they had arrived in, being driven full speed toward their position.

They realized that only Anderson Alves could be driving. When the ambulance exploded in gunfire, followed by a grenade thrown in a shattered window, they understood why.

Oxygen bottles and medicinal alcohol, set off by the grenade, turned the ambulance into a blowtorch. Alves staggered out of the driver's-side door, his clothes aflame, doing a horrible zombie walk toward them. The once-stealthy attackers he had disrupted were now running past him, headed for the wall.

Josue launched himself over the wall and then reached over to help his less agile companion. Silvio landed headfirst on the other side of the wall with a grunt.

Josue was peering through a cornice. "Looks like our patient found the rearguard."

Six men in fatigues leapfrogged each other cautiously, working their way toward the wall.

Silvio and Josue stared at each other helplessly. Alves became fully engulfed in flames as he staggered into a patch of high grass.

"Mother of Christ." Silvio raised his carbine. "We can't let him ..."

A three-round burst from Josue stopped Alves's agony. "I know."

The first grenades came sailing over the wall.

The treeline

Nunes had watched his boss as the helicopter had dropped from the sky. He'd never seen Oscar Stumpf like that. As the chopper had fallen, astonishment, rage, then ... despair.

Stumpf threw his arms up and looked at Nunes. As if looking for the answer.

Nunes had his answer now.

The Alamo

Andreatta paused for a moment to consider his run. He realized with some amazement that he might actually be scared. It was one hell of a lot of open ground to cross to get to Emerson. And maybe his radio was just fucked?

There was really no option but speed, Andreatta thought. The men in the dump truck had cut off the only other way. Over the top, then.

"Tchau, amigos!"

Will threw the grenade with a quarterback's aim into the enemy position. Blasted men screamed as Andreatta scrambled up and over to Emerson, unscathed.

"Idiot! Don't you listen to your radio?"

Emerson gestured weakly at his chest. His radio was shattered. His left arm hung limp. His usually pale face was paler still.

Meu Deus, filho. "Come on, son, we're going. Keep shooting."

"Okay." Emerson smiled faintly. "I'm getting married next week, you know?"

"Yes, you are."

The entrance

"Reloading!" Josue knelt down to replace a magazine as Silvio took his place, rising to the lip of the wall and unleashing three-round bursts at their attackers.

Their Seguranca Stumpf adversaries were good. They had used classic infantry tactics, securing themselves behind a low hummock as a base of fire, just within grenade range of the wall. Josue and Silvio could see no bodies. Their attack disrupted, they had adapted and overcome.

But they still had to close the distance to the wall. For now, nobody was going anywhere.

The Alamo

"Ahhhh … *Deus meu livre* …" Andreatta winced as Emerson cried out. Their chances of getting across were diminishing with each second. *Should've saved that grenade*, Andreatta thought ruefully.

"Kid, don't be so dramatic. We're all shot. Ready?"

Emerson nodded painfully.

"Okay, Will, now!"

The radio message resulted in a barrage from both sides of the fighting pit, Renato and Will burning through precious ammo rapid-fire to cover the two men, now rolling across the naked foundation. Puffs of dust rising from the concrete showed the enemy was finding the range as they poured fire at the vulnerable, struggling men.

"Keep going!" Andreatta pushed and dragged the big redhead. "You're not going to be on that cake!" Now he was just dragging his comrade, who seemed to have lost consciousness. Either that or he was dead.

Andreatta was a boy again, watching his brother Claudio drown in the surf at Santos. He wasn't going to just watch again. *Come on, kid, come on!*

He could see Will getting up out of the pit, shooting one-handed, reaching out to them, screaming.

In the dump truck, a man stood and aimed at a perfect opportunity. Three struggling men in the open.

Andreatta rolled over Emerson and pushed him toward Will. He felt his burden being taken. He had saved Claudio. A bullet went through his neck as he felt the surf roll over him.

34

The treeline, Southern Cross

Oscar Stumpf was not given easily to panic. But he couldn't ignore the rising black smoke coming from where his helicopter was supposed to be. His exit strategy was burning up.

And to top things off, his bodyguard was clearly having second thoughts. Nunes had dropped any pretence of servility and begun to act more like a prosecuting attorney. He leaned insolently against a tree trunk, his carbine cradled in his arms.

"Those are some very capable renegades, sir, aren't they?"

Stumpf was irritated. "Yes, so it seems. Perhaps they are terrorists also."

"And perhaps they are in the Justice League and have Superman helping them?"

"Don't be an idiot! Nunes, I need you to keep your head." Stumpf pulled out a satellite phone. "Bear with me, one moment."

"Sir, have you ever heard of Occam's razor? They taught us about this in the academy."

Stumpf wondered if he could beat this young, fit warrior to a gun. He was feeling his age again. "Yes, I believe I may have. Sherlock Holmes, I think? But what does this have to do with—"

Nunes cut him off, a sure sign he was off the team. "When you eliminate the impossible, whatever remains, however improbable, is the truth."

"Yes?" Stumpf wiped away the sweat. *Deus*, it was hot. Almost as hot as …

1978. A field full of bodies. Uncertain-looking young men, like this one. Only back then, they hadn't dared ask questions aloud. Back then, they had obeyed. Stumpf had taken care of them—Grasselman, Buscetti, and the others. Until they'd asked questions.

Nunes warmed to his subject. Stumpf noticed the barrel of Nunes's carbine was starting to drift in his direction.

"You see, sir, if I apply Occam's razor here, I have to conclude that it is impossible that three renegades killed half my men and shot down your helicopter. Given that these renegades are admittedly policemen, I also have to conclude that, however improbable, the truth is, I am fighting against my own country. Brazil, sir. And I took an oath more important than my duty to you, *senhor*."

The barrel was pointing right at Oscar Stumpf now.

The entrance

Josue and Silvio could only cover so much ground. On the unwatched right flank, three of Stumpf's men crawled around the hummock and over the wall.

The Alamo

Will looked around at the shitty little pit that had become his home. The fire was more or less constant now, and he and Renato conserved their ammo, only firing when someone got too close. On the plus side, the enemy seemed to have run out of grenades. But they still had lots of ammo.

On the foundation, Andreatta's body twitched every time a bullet hit it. It angered Will, but Renato forbade him to try to retrieve the corpse. Anger was more powerful than fear now. Maybe Will had just accepted the fact that he was going to die.

Beside him, Emerson lay still, dead or dying it seemed. He dared not think of Edilson, so he couldn't even look.

Andreatta would have approved of the fact that he was whistling.

Renato seemed to like it too. "What's that tune, gringo?"

"'Men of Harlech'!" For some reason he felt like Michael Caine in *Zulu*. God knows why.

"Why that one?"

"Because it's what you sing when you're up shit creek without a paddle!"

Across the foundation slab, a bulldozer roared to life.

Renato was grim. "Final chapter, brother."

Will was resigned. "Good, I'm sick of this shit!" He nestled his carbine to his shoulder and slapped in his last full magazine.

The entrance

Josue peered around the right side of the hummock. He saw the grass moving 20 metres away, but no clean shots. He fired a quick burst to discourage movement. He rolled over to check his right flank. Pressed up against a work shack, on his side of the wall, were three men, less than 10 metres away. Their leader, face crazy-camo-painted, raised his rifle.

"Silvio!" Josue cut down the leader before two grenades lifted his body off the ground on a bed of fire.

The treeline

Oscar Stumpf thought about going for the pistol in the small of his back. Yes, Nunes was fast, and he was good. But he might hesitate to shoot his boss, even if he had figured out that his boss was a son of a bitch.

A bird of prey circled overhead. Stumpf savoured the moment as he looked up. A metaphor for the more poetically minded. He smiled. Forget about the gun. He had created this graveyard. It was only fitting he should be the last occupant. He'd never wanted to get old, anyway. He was surprised he'd made it this far, as it was.

Nunes had the carbine levelled at him casually. "You aren't denying a thing, *senhor.*"

"Get it over with, Major. Men are dying." He straightened his back. "I don't pay you to talk."

Nunes nodded. "You betrayed Brazil. You betrayed your men. For that, I sentence you to die."

"I loved Brazil." He closed his eyes, saw the Marxists slowly edging down toward rough pits to their ends. He smiled, a lover of irony. *Soon, it will be me.* His executioner was not interested in confessions.

"Then say goodbye to her." He raised the carbine.

Her. That one girl. "Where is my baby? Tell me! Before you do it, tell me!" Her mouth had been open when he'd fired. He fixed his eyes on Nunes. *Say goodbye to her.*

"Do it."

The bird overhead took off, startled by the shots.

Eduardo Nunes stared for a moment at his old boss. Twitching. Expelling as the dead do. Even the rich. Then he keyed his radio.

The Alamo

Renato was shooting at the dozer, which was now about to drive right over them. Will frantically worked to keep the men in the dump truck down. He dreaded the click he was about to hear. Rounds complete. Game over.

Last thoughts? He was too fucking busy.

"Is that a helicopter?" Renato shouted. The bulldozer was mounting the far end of the foundation, its treads grinding at concrete.

Yes. Yes it was.

The entrance

The three Seguranca Stumpf men behind the low hummock were so focused on the battle raging behind the wall that they didn't notice the sound of rotors until it was much too late.

Startled faces looked up as the Huey emerged from the trees behind them, low and slow.

Behind the wall, Silvio had gone to ground as grenades exploded close to him. He rolled into a stand of tall grass and waited.

The approach of rotors startled his attackers. One man rose and stared at the chopper. Silvio stood and fired from seven metres with devastating effect. His partner ran forward, yelling, emptying his magazine.

Silvio, hit three times, swung his carbine, meeting skull. The two men went hand to hand as the chopper descended.

Above Southern Cross

The pilot told the VIP passenger, "Enemy sighted, behind the mound in front of the gate. When we come out from the trees, it's going to get hot."

"Understood." The passenger looked out his window at a convoy of police cars, fire trucks, and ambulances heading up the road. So much for a quiet clean-up.

"Gunner, ready to engage, target nine o'clock!"

"Ready!" The crewman swivelled his minigun as the men on the port side of the Huey took aim. The pilot cautiously edged out from behind the trees.

The air exploded. A noise like ripping metal assaulted the passenger's ears. He heard the thwack of a few impacting rounds in response.

But the issue had been decided.

The Alamo

The bulldozer had stopped. So had the shooting.

Renato and Will exchanged a wordless look. What now?

The two men nearly jumped up with fright when an object flew over the lip of their pit. It took a moment to realize that it wasn't a grenade.

It was a radio.

Will tentatively picked it up. "Who is this?"

"Eduardo Nunes. Formerly head of operations for Seguranca Stumpf. Now unemployed."

Renato raised an eyebrow. Will probed tentatively, "And what do you want to discuss, Senhor Nunes?"

"The terms of our surrender, Mr. Bryant."

"Your surrender?" He was shell-shocked. Now the "unemployed" bit caught on. "What happened to Stumpf?"

"Oscar Stumpf is dead." Will stared at the radio, mouth agape.

Renato put his hand over the mic. "It's a trick."

"And if it is? What are our options?" The two men looked around.

"You have a point. But I want to know why, before I step out there."

"The chopper?"

"Maybe. And how do we know Stumpf is really dead?"

"Only one way to find out, Renato." He keyed the mic. "Nunes, why are you surrendering?"

"We are loyal Brazilians. So are your men. Stumpf was a traitor. We surrender and ask for fair treatment."

Will shrugged at Renato. "Show yourselves!"

"Men! Throw down your weapons," Nunes commanded. "Show yourselves."

Ten men dropped weapons and stood up. Will and Renato stood up and looked around.

"Jesus Christ." Will couldn't believe it.

Renato was incredulous. "Time to buy a lottery ticket, gringo."

The entrance

Four Polícia Federal COT troopers rappelled out of the Huey and hit the ground in front of the astonished local cops just now arriving on the scene. The chopper went into a low orbit around the site to cover them.

The COT troopers cautiously probed the area around the mound. Where Stumpf's men had sheltered behind the hummock was now an abattoir. Even the hardened troopers were sickened. Their leader sent the rest of his men forward to explore the crash scene. He walked back to the road to deal with the Polícia Militar.

A fat major stood with his hands on his hips in the middle of the road. The COT leader sighed. He knew the type. He walked up to the Major, who appeared to be about to launch into a speech.

"Polícia Federal. We have jurisdiction. Stay here. If we need you, we'll send for you."

The Major opened his mouth and then closed it again.

The team leader was walking past the burned-out ambulance when he saw a hand grasping the edge of the wall ahead.

Silvio pulled himself up and waved at the COT leader weakly. *"Socorro, amigo."*

The leader ran back to the road. "Send up an ambulance, now! Officer down!"

The Major began hurriedly clearing vehicles off the road as the team leader ran back to Silvio.

Above the Alamo

As the Huey orbited, the passenger looked down at a knot of men milling about a foundation pad. It looked as if there had been a battle. Bodies and weapons were dotted around the epicentre.

The passenger noticed a man waving his arms. He took out his field glasses.

"Pilot, I want you to land in that clearing."

The pilot cursed under his breath. *Goddamn politicians come along for the ride and try to take everything over ...* "But, sir, we have to provide top cover!"

"No buts, damn you. That man waving his arms is the reason we're here. Now land!"

The Alamo

Will looked up as the Polícia Federal helicopter flared for landing. He grabbed two of his "prisoners."

"Get all the wounded ready to go." He indicated Edilson and Emerson. "These two first." A Seguranca Stumpf man lay propped up against a dozer blade with a gruesome stomach wound. "Him too."

The "prisoners" organized themselves as the chopper landed. A squad of black-clad men Will took to be COT operators jumped out first, followed by two men in plain-clothes. The operators formed a circle around the chopper, their weapons aimed at everyone outside. Will walked toward the two plainclothesmen.

Geraldo Buscetti held out his hand. "Mr. Bryant. Glad to see you are in one piece." He smiled as if he were on a campaign stop. Will noticed he was wearing ridiculous safari duds. Will was in no mood.

"Buscetti, a lot of these men aren't in one piece. So how about putting them on your nice helicopter and getting them to a hospital?"

"Of course."

The other man Will recognized as Galtieri. "Is the scene secure?" Galtieri asked.

"I think so. We just took their surrender. Their leader is on his way down from the woods over there." Will pointed up the slope. "He says Stumpf is dead, though it's not confirmed."

Buscetti was thoughtful. "He's really dead?"

Will thought that was an odd way to ask. "Let's go find out."

Galtieri pointed out a figure approaching. He seemed to be holding something. "Is that him?"

"Goddamn!" Will ran toward Nunes, who carried Wagner in his arms.

"I found your man down. The other was dead. He needs to get out, now."

The blood-covered man was mumbling. In his right hand he clasped a gilt icon.

"Take him to the chopper!"

Wounded men were hoisted aboard the helicopter in a hurried and messy operation. A lone medic on board did what he could. Will broke away from Buscetti when he saw Edilson. He grabbed his friend's hand.

"Boa sorte, Policial!"

Edilson could only nod weakly. The medic shooed Will away. "Get away! We're going!"

Will stepped off the skid as the Huey launched like an express elevator. His hand was covered in blood. He sat down in the dirt for a long minute.

The others watched him. Finally, Nunes limped up to him. "Senhor Bryant. Do you want to see Stumpf's body, before they take me away?"

He looked up. "Yes, I want to see that. I need to know it's over."

Buscetti said, "Me too."

Will glared at him. *As if you took the kind of risks we did. You were just along for the ride.*

"Sure, Buscetti. Let's go," Will said.

As the COT troopers organized the prisoners and collected their weapons, the three men plus Galtieri trudged up the hill. Will stumbled from fatigue, and Nunes caught him. "Thanks."

Thanks? How strange, this man was trying to kill me 30 minutes ago. Now we're being polite. Still, he sensed a kindred spirit, and the two walked on ahead of Galtieri and Buscetti.

"How did Stumpf die?"

"I killed him."

"Why?"

"He told us we were fighting blackmailers, corrupt cops. When I realized what was really happening, I decided to end it."

"Just like that."

"Yes, Mr. Bryant. I don't know who you really are. But I sense you know enough about soldiers to understand that we aren't robots. A good soldier knows when to stop following orders."

"When did you decide to stop following orders?"

"I started to suspect his story when you asked how I felt about killing cops. And you seemed to imply he was the criminal, not the other way round. Then my snipers were killed. Then ..."

They both paused at Abdul's body.

"Meu Deus."

"Come on, let's get going!" Buscetti was impatient to claim his kill.

Galtieri said softly, *"Senador, por favor. Respeite."* He genuflected.

"Okay," Will said after a moment. "Thanks, brother." They carried on.

"Nunes?" Will said.

"Yes?"

"Thank you. I don't know what else to say." Will felt awkward as Nunes limped beside him.

"You shot my fucking toes off, you know."

"I'm not apologizing."

Nunes laughed. "When I get out of prison, I'm coming to work for you."

"Okay then. I'll try and see that you don't have to."

"Don't make promises you can't keep."

"That's not my style, Nunes."

Suddenly, there he was. In a little clearing, Oscar Stumpf lay on his back. Three holes in his chest. A thin trickle of blood coming from his mouth. Too peaceful. More than the 80 who lay under his foundations had ever gotten. Will felt robbed for a moment.

No dramatic confrontation. No confession.

Idiotic. Nunes had done him a favour. No execution. The kid in the Tim Hortons and Soares. Enough psychic pollution.

Nunes was matter-of-fact. "He had already taken his body armour off." There it lay, beside him. "I figured you wouldn't believe it was him if I shot him in the face."

Buscetti looked at Stumpf silently for a moment. "Excuse me, I need to make a phone call." He walked back into the clearing.

Galtieri exhaled. "Let's all go back to São Paulo. We control the scene. We can call it however we like. Medals all around. Nobody goes to jail." He winked at Nunes, who remained impassive.

"Who is Buscetti calling, Galtieri?" Will had a hunch, but that was all.

"I have no idea."

"You are so full of shit."

"In a moment, you won't care. Trust me." Galtieri winked again.

There was that feeling again, Will thought. That puppet-on-a-string feeling. "But what about Condor?"

"Condor?" Nunes was baffled. "Condor Foundations?"

"No, Nunes. Operation Condor." Galtieri sighed. "A touchy subject, in some quarters." He looked out at Buscetti.

Pedro Juan Caballero, Paraguay

Wilson Guimares was sitting on his couch, getting a blowjob, when the call came in. He looked at the call display. The blonde head between his knees started to come up. He pushed her down again. "I didn't tell you to stop, did I?" He snapped his phone open. *"Fala."*

"He's not coming. It's taken care of."

"Too bad. I was looking forward to it. We still have a deal?"

"Yes," Geraldo Buscetti said. "We still have a deal."

Southern Cross

Buscetti wandered back to them. He looked down at Stumpf for another long moment. "Bryant, let's go for a walk."

Will whispered in Nunes's ear, "I know you don't like him. If I don't come back, promise me you'll rip his head off?"

"Sem problema." Nunes stared at Buscetti. "Enjoy your walk."

Will walked into the clearing with Buscetti. They stayed silent for a long time.

Finally, Buscetti said, "Forget Condor. It's over."

Will was stunned. "What do you mean, 'over'? We are standing on it!" He spread his arms wide. "This is Operation Condor, right here!"

Buscetti nodded patiently. "I know it is. But it is also a real estate development."

"Who fucking cares!" he sputtered, now thinking of all the dead people Oscar Stumpf had left behind, wondering if one more would matter. "Keep talking!"

Buscetti stepped back. "You must be Irish."

"Maybe!" He knew that vein in his forehead was bulging, the one Silvia always talked about, the one that always got confessions.

Buscetti waited a moment, like a patient teacher with a bratty child. "Brazil is not ready to face its past."

"Bullshit! This is personal for you. You don't want Daddy exposed for what he really was."

Buscetti sighed. "I was hoping not to have to do this."

"Do what?"

"Soares." He let it hang.

"What about him?"

"You killed him. Will, I have the evidence. But I choose to do nothing with it, you see?"

The face, screaming, livid. His decision. The black blood, pouring out. He knew it would come back to haunt him. "Yes, I see."

"Will, this is your country. You've convinced me of this." He was in full politician mode now. "You know that this country looks forward, never back! One day, I will be president. And I promise, I will make a better country for your children. Help me now, and I promise you will always be looked after. You have Stumpf. I have Stumpf. What else do you need?"

So, he had run straight into presidential ambition. Perfect ending for a fucked-up case. He decided on two demands from the heart, not the head. The people under this earth cried out for justice; it was true.

But Lucas and Gabi needed a father. The living versus the dead. Kin versus strangers. He made his choice, the only one possible.

"Two things."

"Name them."

"One, a Paraguayan girl in a PCC brothel. She is going home."

"Okay ... and?"

"Your sister. She needs to meet her aunt."

Buscetti turned away. "I promised ... I ..."

Will walked up behind him. His hand was large, and its pressure on Buscetti's shoulder was calculated. "I made a lot of promises too. But this one's non-negotiable."

Buscetti's shoulders slumped. "Okay. It is the right thing to do." He pointed to the knapsack full of cash, pinned under a dead man. "And what about that?"

Will raised an eyebrow. "What about that?"

Buscetti casually rolled the dead man off the bag with his toe. "That looks like a lot." He looked at Will. "I'd say twice as much as the Polícia Federal will recover, officially."

Will looked around. Buscetti had him over a barrel with Soares. Now he would implicate him in corruption too?

Buscetti studied him. "I know your type."

"Do you now?"

"The honest cop. But you took this on as a private investigation, didn't you? Did you ever get paid your fees? I know how you were making money before this! Teaching English, *pelo morte Deus*! A man like you? And what about all these cops you dragged into this? Most of them can barely make their car payments on the shit they get paid. And what about the families? How are Thiago's kids going to eat now? Be noble all you want, Will; just make sure you're the one paying the price!"

"It's too fucking easy."

Buscetti shook his head. "Take it from a politician: sometimes the easy thing and the right thing are the same thing."

"How convenient." But his resistance was weakening. Hadn't they all earned it? And whose money was it, anyway?

"All you'll be doing is taking the fees you would have been paid anyway. Plus a bonus, for you and the others, from a grateful nation. It's not officially approved, of course, but I have been assured there will be no questions asked."

"You seem confident. How come?" Will was beginning to realize the presidential talk was not mere ambition. Buscetti was not junior varsity but operating at a higher level.

"I understand you thought Galtieri was in your pocket. You thought some long-ago indiscretion had put him there. But I put him there. He wasn't exaggerating when he said we can call this any way we want. Twenty million becomes ten. Renegades become heroes. The heroes walk away with money extorted from wealthy pedophiles. People who never deserved it anyway."

"You and Galtieri." Now it made sense. The right hook from Edilson in Ponta Pora was all street theatre for his benefit. "Your investigation into Stumpf never ended, did it?"

"Never. I just needed a new tactic. The data-mining investigation I told you about in Floripa gave me my opportunity."

"You fed Stumpf information on the pedos ... You acted like you were so damned surprised when I said Stumpf's list was your list too. For all I know, that 10th-floor 'suicide' was really your work. Why? Why do it that way?"

Buscetti raised a knowing eyebrow. "You want an initiation into Brazilian politics? Well, for starters, I had a list of what I knew about Oscar Stumpf. Weaknesses. Something he had taught my father to do. So, I catalogued what I knew ..."

Will slowly digested the fact that Buscetti hadn't disavowed the jumper. Add that to his own list on Geraldo Buscetti. Oscar Stumpf was such a good teacher. Buscetti became election-campaign expansive as he continued.

"Knowing his recent investments had left him cashpoor. Knowing from my father's diaries why he had to complete this development, whether it made economic sense or not. Knowing that wealthy men, with so much to lose from blackmail, would eventually fight back and hire someone like you."

"Seems like a roundabout way to do it."

"You know why I couldn't do it any other way. What's under here is as dangerous to me, and to a great many others still in government, as it was to Stumpf. Stumpf was dangerous to Brazil. My personal desire for revenge just happened to merge with an opportunity to serve my country."

"Brasília wanted him dead, obviously. And you get the credit. A nice way to make serving your country serve yourself."

"No regrets. And you? Any regrets?"

He looked around and considered his answer. He knew what it should be. But that wasn't what it was.

"No regrets."

35

Will sat beside Edilson's hospital bed and read him the headlines from the day's *Folha*. His own wounds were superficial, shrapnel picked out of legs and a few sutures in the *pronto socorro*. Edilson was going to be staying awhile longer.

"Millionaire industrialist killed in gun battle with police." The shot-by-his-own-bodyguard part was not discussed. Who gave a shit, anyway?

"PCC gangsters found dead at the scene." Bullshit. But easier than explaining why ex-army mercenaries were carrying illegal weapons on behalf of Stumpf. That might make people ask how they'd gotten there in the first place. Inconvenient. So why not make them the convenient enemy everyone hated for shutting down the city? Galtieri was stage-managing the aftermath as promised.

"Cops die as heroes." He wasn't going into details there. He and Edilson hadn't talked about Andreatta yet.

415

Hmmm, this one was interesting. "Polícia Federal raids Internet pedophile ring." Apparently the PF, free of Stumpf and the political heat that came with him, was moving on Stumpf's "victims." Thirty arrests in one day. Some lawyers were about to get very wealthy indeed.

Lawyers. He thought of Thiago. Will's family was coming home today. It seemed like a guilty pleasure when he thought of his friend. Maybe that was his one regret.

"Will, you look sad, brother."

Will looked over at his friend, tubed and transfused, five dressings covering seven holes, but still the same guy. Had to be some kind of record for absorbing lead, even on this force.

"And you look like shit."

"Hey, I'm a hero. The paper said so."

"Yeah, you are."

"Tell me who made it, Will. Nobody will tell me anything. Be straight with me, brother." This last plea, in English, caused him to look at his friend again. Tears ran down Edilson's face. "Tell me."

"Andreatta didn't make it."

"Fuck. Arturo. Fuck." He slammed the side of the bed with his one mobile leg.

"Of the ROTA guys, only Renato, Silvio, and Wagner made it. Wagner is still ... well ... holding on."

"Not the kid ... the redhead ..."

"Emerson."

"Yeah, him. Do me a favour, Will ... Get my valuables for me, okay? He gave me a ring, on the helicopter. He made me promise ..." His friend broke down again.

Will walked to the nurses' station thinking of more regrets.

Pedro Juan Caballero, Paraguay, two weeks later

The girl walking through the crowds on the Avenida Internacional was tall, thin, pretty. She was quiet, and each time she did speak, Galtieri, walking next to her, had to ask her to repeat herself.

He was hesitant to ask anything of her. So many people had taken so much from her, without bothering to ask. She had come off the bus from São Paulo, and he had met her at the *rodoviária* by prior arrangement with Will Bryant. A special delivery. The raids against Stumpf's *pedofilos* and the dismantling of Grupo Stumpf, now decreed a "criminal enterprise" by the Brazilian government, had demanded his attention back in São Paulo.

But Galtieri had some loose ends to tie up in Ponta Porã. Once a special unit operating against sex traffickers in São Paulo had located her, he made sure he was back here. It was the sort of personal victory cops got so rarely. Will Bryant understood, and so did the man waiting for Galtieri.

In the median, a cadaverous man in mirrored shades waited next to an SUV.

"Benevides. *Como esta?* Thanks for coming." The men shook hands.

"Happy to, brother. *Parabens*, I hear you are having some success against our mutual friends."

"With a little help, yes. Here is one success. Allow me to introduce Lucia Rojas Ruiz."

The girl with jet black hair and chocolate eyes shyly took his hand.

"Welcome home, Lucia. I have someone who wants to meet you."

Rambla, Playa de los Pocitos, Montevideo, Uruguay

Natalia Rodriguez tried to relax. She crossed and uncrossed her legs repeatedly. It was a nervous habit she'd shared with her sister. She smiled to herself. *I have brought you along, after all.* She sat with her back to the sea, watching the strolling crowds intently for any sign.

It was the third attempt at a meet. Each time, Carla Buscetti had gotten cold feet. But she kept answering her phone. That was a good sign. And Natalia got to hear that voice. Such a different accent but still so ... familiar? Perhaps she was just being dramatic. Will had warned her about that.

But how could this not be dramatic?

She turned her head and saw a woman with Ana Rosa's eyes staring at her. She was tall, taller than expected. On her face ... suspicion? Fear? Had Natalia expected gushing warmth? Will's voice, warning her. The same tight curls that she always fought to tame, this woman had let run free, like her mother had. Natalia stood up. She opened her mouth, but Carla spoke first.

"Tell me about my mother."

"There's a lot to tell."

The crowds pushed past them, oblivious to all but sun and sea.

Boa Vista, Roraima

Angelo sat at the bar, nursing his third Brahma and cursing his shitty luck.

Tio Oscar had made Roraima sound like a great opportunity. Like a big adventure. He really should've looked up the place before he'd agreed. What a fucking dump. The literal middle of nowhere.

But you never disagreed with Tio. That was always a mistake.

But now, Tio was dead, and Angelo was a fugitive. The day it had all blown up in Caçapava, he'd gotten a call from HQ. "We're being raided. Get out now. We'll call soon."

So now, two weeks later, he cooled his heels in Boa Vista. Boa Vista ... beautiful view? Fuck that! He'd already fucked the only good-looking hookers in town three times over. And why couldn't you score good coke this close to Colombia? Somebody had better call soon, or he was gonna get even ...

"You Angelo?"

He turned to sneer at a *beboom* in a dirty old Atletico shirt. "Who the fuck wants to know, old man?"

The man looked down at the floor with rheumy eyes. The rest of the usual drunks had something to watch besides *Faustao* now. "The man outside in the alley. He said he is from the company. He needs to talk."

Angelo looked around the bar and sucked his teeth. He ran his fingers through his hair. Not fucking good. This felt wrong. But he was running out of money. And he still had his gun. He stepped off the barstool and walked outside.

The night was humid and sticky. The dirt road congealed around his shoes. *Fucking Africa. Can't even own a decent pair of shoes. Fuck you, Tio.* He walked around the corner into the alley. He saw nobody. He turned slowly.

When he turned back, the man was there. There was something familiar ...

The skinny man with fish eyes and bad teeth stabbed Angelo rapidly in his abdomen, breaking the little blade off inside him on the last thrust.

Angelo, breathless, wordless, dropped to his knees. He felt hot and wet. He looked down and knew why. A hand grabbed a knot of his hair and pulled his head up. The familiar ugly face was close.

"Luciana and Jefferson. Those were their names."

Ken Scribbins left Angelo to die and walked off into the night.

Praia Felix, Ubatuba

Will sat against a palm trunk and sipped his caipirinha. The *quejo* man was on the beach today, grilling sticks of cheese over a tiny hibachi, and Will was getting hungry again. Maybe a couple of sticks of that salty wonder food would go nicely. Or maybe some more corn. Or a *pastel*. Why not all of it?

"Did you come here just to eat, man?" Silvia blocked his view and his sun. But he didn't mind. She wore a slightly too-small bikini she'd borrowed from her sister. Slightly too small was just right.

"No, my dear, I also came here to look at girls."

"What girls, man?"

"This one!" He spilled his drink as he pulled her down to him. He kissed her aggressively. His hand reached down her back.

"Will! *Que scandalo!* The kids!"

Lucas and Enzo chased a shrieking Gabi through the surf while Roberto and Tais watched. "The kids are fine. Let's go to the *lagoa!*"

"*Meu Deus*, Husband, if you aren't hungry, you are horny ... Eat some *quejo*, then come for a swim. Move your body, man!" She snapped her fingers and ran back to the waves.

Will watched her run. For the first time all day, he thought about Southern Cross. It came to him that this case, which had begun as an investigation of men blackmailed by other men, had in the end been about women. It certainly was for him at least. This woman running into the waves. The little woman being chased by her cousin and her brother. The Paraguayan pimped out by Panelas (he would remember that asshole), the Argentines and their murdered kin, Gretchen ... all of them. What little justice had come out of Southern Cross was their justice. For them and largely because of them.

And it was about money. Buscetti had talked him into taking his "fair share," but he'd made sure the others got theirs too. Of course, it all had to be done discreetly, but he was the only one who seemed to feel vaguely dirty about it. *Cacheias* his wife always called him, uptight, guilty. Brazilians were more practical. In their minds, they'd taken extraordinary risks, so they were entitled to extraordinary rewards. It still didn't sit right in his Canadian mind, though.

But it had paid for this vacation. No more English lessons. Except for Edilson. With his enhanced reputation, promotion or reassignment was a certainty. If he could get through rehab. And Thiago's family was taken care of, if still bereft. For some reason, Jacquie didn't seem to blame Will. She would if she knew more.

As for the victims of Condor, they had been only partially avenged. Will had done his best in a system that wasn't yet ready to face the awful past. That's what he kept telling himself, anyway. And the PCC ... it would take a lot more than Will Bryant and a few friends to knock them off. They were an institution now. A criminal volcano alternating between dormancy and spasm. But always there.

Which explained the pistol in his backpack. "Soldado Ferguson" couldn't be retired just yet. Besides, Buscetti had hinted he might call on him again. A very useful man he was now, to a future president of the republic.

But for now, he was just another gringo on the beach.

Will jumped to his feet and ran into the Atlantic Ocean.

CPSIA information can be obtained
at www.ICGtesting.com
Printed in the USA
LVHW01s1952131117
556111LV00003B/585/P